# Hang All The Mistletoe

John Gary Dewberry

FIREBRAND
PUBLISHING

*This is a work of fiction. Names, characters, places, and incidents either are the product of the author's imagination or are used fictitiously. Any resemblance to actual persons, living or dead, events, or locales is entirely coincidental.*

Scripture quotations taken from the KING JAMES VERSION (KJV): KING JAMES VERSION, public domain.

Cover designed by MiblArt.

*Firebrand Publishing publishes in a variety of print and electronic formats and by print-on-demand. For more information about Firebrand Publishing products, visit https://firebrandpublishing.com*

*ISBN* 978-1-941907-49-8 (*paperback*) *ISBN* 978-1-941907-50-4 (*eBook*)

Published by Firebrand Publishing

Printed in the United States of America

# Contents

# Foreword

## BY NAKIA DEWBERRY, M. ED.

I had the privilege of growing up around some of the best storytellers. I know you are probably thinking, "How does she know they're the best storytellers?" So, let me tell you.

I come from a family where stories are how we communicate and pass down our family's history, culture, and love. I learned the most about my grandfather, John Gary Dewberry Sr., from stories as he passed away well before I was born.

I learned he was a hardworking man who loved my grandmother and loved his children. Not only that, but I also learned he was not one to mess with. Many of the life lessons I've learned as a Dewberry woman were the same lessons he taught my father and my uncle, John Gary Dewberry II.

One life lesson that I carry with me everywhere I go is to *Never trust a person with wandering eyes,* and to also drink from a clear glass when I am not in my own home. I like to consider myself a legacy and carry the torch by telling stories and passing down our family's traditions.

Along with carrying on the tradition of storytelling, I am an educator and an entrepreneur. I currently work in my local public school district as a special education coordinator and special education teacher. As an educator, I am fortunate to carry on family traditions around the holidays, especially at Christmas, as I have the week off! I always loved Christmas growing up, and surprisingly, it was never just all about the gifts.

I loved being around all my family. My father, Gregory Dewberry, to this day, says I enjoy Christmas just like my uncle, and I'd like to think that is a special bond that we share. We both love music (to set the record straight, the best version of "Silent Night" of course, is by the Temptations.) We love the food, but most importantly, we love the magic. The decorations and the overall joy of Christmas are priceless.

My father has shared stories with me about how my uncle, along with my grandmother, Irene Dewberry, made Christmas special. It was my uncle who would bring out the ornaments and want the tree to go up right away. He helped create that Christmas magic. The same magic I love to create for my daughter Maleeya.

If there was anyone I could think of to write a book not only about Christmas, but with a black voice and flavor, it would be my uncle. From his iconic days as a DJ to his infamous fashion shows and all the creative endeavors he has down in our hometown (that I still hear about to this day), he has always had what we call the juice to grasp our attention as a reader and bring in a familiarity we can all relate to.

"Hang All the Mistletoe" is ours. It is for us and was carefully crafted by the Christmas Connoisseur himself, Mr. John Gary Dewberry II. My wish for all you wonderful readers is to feel the magic I was so blessed to grow up with on each page as the story takes life.

Ase!

Peace and Blessings.

# Preface

In the beginning, God moved the Spirit and said, "Let There Be Light." Before I colorize Christmas, I implore you to see that the Spirit of the holiday is colorless.

B.C. stands for Before Christ. I write within a time bubble that pops when baby Jesus is born, a miracle that represents the true spirit of the holiday.

In authoring this story, it struck me that my introduction to Christmas wasn't the skin color of the myth of Santa Claus come to life, but the paradigm spirit shift in the air that becomes the most wonderful time of the year. The Creator of all things imperceivable invokes the spirit, and the praise of all living creatures. Here below, Heaven comes forth in all the myriad of ways under the sun. The shifts are not based on race or color. Each Christmas has it's own wonder.

My Christmas story can be your first Christmas, or any other that you have experienced. I want to achieve a timeless quality that remains relative to the time you read, be it any season in the year.

Music is the key. There is a thread of music and musical inference throughout the chapters, which begins with a scripture that ties into the story along the way.

I fell in love with the story of "A Christmas Carol" by Charles Dickens at a young age. I played various parts in youth stage plays of the book, never missing an opportunity to audition for a role in my favorite story.

Now I've written my own, and I hope it becomes your own favorite story. Charles Dickens led me into his world of Christmas, and even though the original story was written in 1843, the human element reveals something new each time it's read.

I started to write my own take on 'A Christmas Carol' with my own modern view. My characters began to flourish within the chapters. Each one signed my heart with a unique signature. I invite you to let them come alive in your own hearts: speak with them, enjoy their company, and learn what they reveal. Please enjoy the sleigh ride.

# Acknowledgments

Thank God for the gift of Jesus Christ. I celebrate Christmas Day as His birthday on earth. Thank you to my wife, Karen Sylvia (Ware) Dewberry, for your great support and inspiration. Let us continue to hang all the mistletoe.

Thank you to my parents, who rest in eternal peace with the Lord. My mother Irene and father John Gary Dewberry Sr., who provided wonderful Christmas memories, full of love in the giving and receiving of gifts in the name of Jesus Christ.

Thank you to the teachers in my hometown of Springfield, Massachusetts, which carried me through from 1966 to 1978, beginning at Homer Street Elementary School. Next was Memorial Elementary, now Mary A. Dryden Veteran's Memorial School. From there, I went to Junior High at M. Marcus Kiley Junior High School. Rest In Peace, my English teacher Mr. Alvin B. Brown. I graduated from The High School of Commerce in 1978. Rest In Peace, my English teacher Mrs. Helene V. (Hill) Griffin.

Rest In Peace, black Historian/Teacher Ruth Ethel Dennis, (my wife's grandmother). Thank you for your book, *The Black People in America* and your records that teach Black History. Thank you to your daughter (my mother-in-law, Rest in Peace) Renee Francine Dennis (Ware), a renowned teacher in Springfield, Massachusetts, respected in Decatur Georgia, who encouraged me into ministry.

Thank you, Rodman K. Ware, (Rest in Peace, father-in-law) for blessing my marriage to your daughter and blessing my ministry to bring men out of Godly spirituality and into the truth of Jesus Christ.

Thank you, Joyce H. (Harvey) Ware (Stepmother), for your books *Common-Law wife* and *Love Soup For The Heart: All The Loves There Are,* encouraging me to become an author and a Minister Of God (Rest In Peace).

Thank you, Anita (Ware) Johnson, (Sister-in-law) Accountant/ Business Concierge, for teaching me math is truth and introducing me to social media.

Thank you, Jeff Ware, Cheryl (Ninky7) Cook, Jerome Frederick, Jr., (Morehouse 08), Grace Dyson, Mark C. Holmes, and Beulah Singleton.

Thank you, Sid, and Betty Burston, for molding my ambitions into becoming an author who embraces spirituality and thank you Pastor Eric L. Taylor Sr. and wife Franquetta, Minister Duane D. Nelson and wife Glenda for spiritual inspiration.

Thank you, Lloyd and Jennifer Key, Pastor and Co-Pastor of Riverside Community Baptist Church, Decatur Georgia. I praise the Lord for you.

Thank you, Evangelist LeRonia Clay (Roni) for helping me develop the Gospel song, *Jesus Don't Stop,* (*Ever Loving Me*).

# Introduction

## MEET N. O. CHANCE – THE BLACK EBENEZER

Welcome to North Star Village U.S.A., a picturesque city that has grown out of the Valley, formed by the surrounding Mountains. North Star Village is a 4-Season multicultural place, an example of many cities across America. North Star Village is a melting pot of good and bad things, good and bad people living their best lives. As the city motto goes, follow the North Star.

Meet N.O. Chance Jr, a lifelong resident of North Star Village, a successful Accountant and Award-winning business Owner of N. O. Chance Financial Agency.

N. O. Chance is also known as a mean-spirited man that hates all things Christmas. He is a melting pot of the best and worst qualities of Man and Mankind. When he's good he's really good, but his bad side has gotten the better of him this Christmas.

There's a battle going on in N.O. Chance′s soul. The truth can present itself as a wispy cloud, a confounding coincidence or a Celestial event such as a shooting Star. Will N.O. Chance Jr see past the first interpretation of the superficial kiss that hang all the mistletoe implies, and recognize the well wishes of friends and family?

What is the profit for a man to gain the world and lose his own soul? Find yourself in the people of North Star Village and the Spirit of this Christmas story of a Black Man that finds he is akin to others through time. A Black man that has lost his way in the world, only to find himself when he, Hangs All The Mistletoe.

# Prologue

Nickolas Kingsly is a man with a plan, happy to start a new holiday work schedule, even though it means the workday begins earlier. It's a cool perk of working on the eve of Christmas Eve; the cold winter air makes feet move at a quick pace. Mr. and Mrs. Kingsly set out to conquer the last full day for all things needing to be done before Christmas Day. Mary is the driver today, but she finds the time to make her husband a sausage breakfast sandwich before taking him to work.

The mid-morning break will be tasty for Nickolas and his co-workers, who look forward to sharing the three bags of fresh bagels he's brought with him. Mary steers the van merrily on down the stream, as Nickolas enjoys hot coffee from his travel cup.

Driving to work meets with the break of dawn's early light. It all comes together like pieces of a dream. The sight causes Nickolas to say, "I love that smile on your face, Honey. Thanks for the bagels and my sandwich. I feel sorry the weekend went by so fast, but I did get to take you out on the town."

Mary blushes and her dimples pop right on out of her cheeks when she says, "Mr. Kingsly, I love the way you love me. The parties ain't over yet. We've got New Year's Eve, plus my job is having our first after-Christmas and Christmas party in January. I've only got until MLK weekend to get ready."

Nickolas takes in a deep breath and says, "So, this is how the early birds look. It's different than my normal morning rush, and I could get used to this light traffic. It's not heavy like it will be in an hour."

Looking at his wife, he says with admiration, "Mary, I just got a flashback of you at the Community Center Christmas party wearing your red dress..."

# Chapter 1

## *Bingo!*

### Ruben

*A good name is rather to be chosen than great riches, and loving favour rather than silver and gold. 2 The rich and poor meet together: the LORD is the maker of them all.*

— *Proverbs 22: 1*

The Sun also shines in careful observation of the lost sheep. One who has favor and doesn't know it, is found by a Ray of this sunlight, easing on down a high-speed road in a luxury car. His name is Noelle Oscar Chance Jr.,. The unhappy look on his face is no mystery to those who know him. His would-be handsome face carries a perpetual frown about everything in his life with the sole exception of money; he has plenty of that, but a smile can be found as he drives and listens to his favorite talk radio show.

The radio show on KNSV 100 FM is called the Money Tree, and

it is hosted by Lester Givings. Noelle loves the host's catchphrase, "Les Givings shows you more for the taking." He listens regularly, but today hears a mistake in programming that results in no sound. A pocket of silence on the radio called dead air, which is a commercial radio station's nightmare and a waste of money that experienced DJ's and programmers try to avoid like a piece of bruised fruit in a bowl, since every second counts.

Noelle makes a living as a financial expert. He finds the ways a business has dead air in their money-making operation, then turns their tables from losing to winning. He could host a talk show about money, but this man of financial brilliance has no interests in a mentorship program. The only way to learn how Noelle finds solutions for his clients is by osmosis, because he blinds you with financial science when he works on your case, and ain't no sunshine when he's gone.

The dead air on this October Indian Summer day provides peace that surpasses all understanding and makes Noelle a passenger, while an Angel he is unaware of takes the steering wheel during the 55-minute ride to the casino. The Angel, present for the sixth sense to perceive, makes itself available to Noelle and touches the soul of everything in his life. Then in the next moment, the once dead air comes to life through a melodic keyboard and guitar riff that charges the visitation.

The sound of the music strikes a chord with Noelle and springs forth the shadow of a forgotten feeling for a certain woman, feelings unearthed from the past that will have to be reburied now, so they may be forgotten again.

And the melody still lingers on...

The dead air from KNSV 100 FM continues unnoticed for a minute, an hour, or a lifetime. Every single second counts, and who knows how much time is given or taken but the father of Time...

If silence is golden, then this visitation was sponsored by the golden time of day, a Spirit of the Past that gives way to a commercial that breaks the moment, allowing Noelle to dismiss the lapse of emotional control and blame it on the boogie, but there is a weakness for this woman.

Les Givings re-enters the scene on his record machine, and instead of saying "ooh papa doo, how y'all do", Noelle Chance speaks in unison with the radio host when he says...

"Les Givings... shows you more for the taking..."

Noelle turns the radio off as he enters the valet parking lane of the lavish Bella Bella Hotel and Casino on the Bella Bella Native American Reservation. The poetry of hot temperatures breaking the Fall Season's grip of cool days and chilly nights, that harken Winter's frigid might are now halted; if only for one day, and it feels so good, if only for one night.

An unusually warm day or series of days after the first killing frost or frosty nights, is called Indian Summer because that's what Indian Tribesmen described to the European settlers, who experienced the conditions themselves and called this phenomenon Indian Summer.

Noelle's cool style will have to pass for excitement when he meets his former Mentor and Boss for the Awards dinner banquet, followed by playing games of Super Bingo, which features big prizes and money jackpots. Noelle calls out to the valet attendants and states he would like the Shuttle to take him to the Outpost Store. He loves bargains and The Bella Bella Trading Company thrived as a store only before the Casino legislation of 1975 made gambling a life-saving financial enterprise for the American Indian Businessman.

Noelle does more than shop. He constantly calculates money moves. The world sees the icy demeanor, but he wasn't always cold.

~

ONCE UPON A TIME Noelle enjoyed having fun with friends. He had a beautiful girlfriend named Millicent, who he met at State University, both being brilliant students. Millicent and Noelle Chance fell in love after graduating from college and seemed destined to be a happy, successful couple, both being in the prestigious Mentorship program of Mr. Price Waterhouse.

Price Waterhouse owns a Debt Collection Agency and other businesses. He is a well-liked family man who is kind, fair-minded and charitable, helping worthy causes. He is a great leader that rewards hard-working employees with top wages, benefits, work schedule and vacation plan. Price Waterhouse has trained people to be financially successful and great Citizen's, all would prosper under his tutelage, but none would become as rich as Noelle Jr.,.

Price Waterhouse favored Noelle, providing him with a rock foundation and guidance to flourish within his company and become an obvious success with his own business. He's famous for his festive Christmas parties, which include an office party for his employees and guests, a private party at his home for family and friends and he organizes a grand event for the general public, which this year will be held at the North Star Village Community Center.

The Price Waterhouse Company provides a Continental breakfast for his employees on Friday's. It's a business perk that he believes builds teamwork. Noelle's drive to the Casino is part of a Price Waterhouse business perk to reward his top performing employees, invited guests and the top businessmen of North Star Village. Noelle Oscar Chance Jr. is tops in his field.

The Bella Bella Trading Company store has come a long way since its niche tourist attraction days as a destination for low prices on beer, alcohol and tobacco products. Native American Reservations were allowed tax relief in the sale of these products. Money cannot buy relief from a sorrowful legacy, but it helps to restore the remnants of the once mighty people. It cannot erase the pain for souls that have gone on to be with the Big Chief in the sky or families left behind. Only the sky Chief can dry the tears of the Native American, numbered over 20 Million people once upon a time, to become less than 100,000 in the mid-1800's, victims of disease and the massacre of war. The rivers of tears from indigenous people still flow on Earth, but now you can add money into the trail, like the money a Reservation Casino makes in a year, day and night.

Noelle was a hurting soul, money could not buy his happiness. You could sense a kindred spirit in the way he responded to the Native Americans, an unspoken bond in their mutual financial successes. Noelle is no stranger on the Bella Bella Reservation, but on this visit, there would be a big difference, for a relaxed dinner with Price Waterhouse is planned as well as playing Super Bingo.

If revenge is best served cold, as the saying suggests, then favor is best just served. Call it favor when Native Americans went from the cold outhouse of second thought, into the warmth of a penthouse within the stroke of jurisprudence; served better late than never, and a pen when taxes are alleviated on all Reservations, by the United States Government. Within this moment, the spirit of good sense visited the Florida Tribe with an idea to offer big jackpots, more money, and more winners to their bingo games. The spiritual comeuppance of this Divine Intervention brought a here-to-for unseen financial success. These moves moved Native American Tribes and Reservations into fortunes, and through the game of Super Bingo, Super Casinos were built.

Noelle has seen the Trading Post store grow into a state-of-the art, mixed use complex, but only applies the theory of luck to the Native American rags to riches story. The blessings they receive continue to flow down this river of redemption, as America celebrates Indigenous People Day, along with the original celebration of Christopher Columbus Day in October, which is the 1492 discovery of the Americas and the Indigenous people of America. Noelle knows dollars and cents, and knows the Native Americans are indeed moving in the right direction, but he is lost in faithlessness, which is far away from his former place of good sense. It's time to catch the next shuttle back to the Casino, but a beautiful piece of wall Art captures Noelle's eye. It's a picture of the mountains surrounding North Star Village at Dusk, titled Dreamcatcher.

"Sir, have this picture shipped to my office", Noelle says to the store clerk, who gladly takes the order.

The clerk states, "The shuttle is waiting for you, thank you for visiting us and supporting our Art. 'The Dreamcatcher' is a great picture, it will help you catch good dreams."

Noelle dryly replies, "I work hard, go to bed early and rise early, I sleep very well..." said while filling out the shipping form with the mailing address, "Thank you and goodbye."

The clerk shakes his head, seeing the name on the shipping form and says, "Wow... N.O. Chance."

Mr. N.O. Chance enjoys the beautiful scenery of the Casino Hotel complex he sees looking through the shuttle van windows, which is part of the people moving system that transports the Casino patrons around the campus. Mr. N. O. Chance is going back to the Valet parking area, instead of the Casino entrance to meet his mentor, then hears a familiar song playing over the valet lobby speakers. He remembered hearing it on the way to the Casino. Once again, the sounds have instant access to buried heartstrings.

There's no chance to reminisce. Price Waterhouse is waiting for his arrival and greeting Noelle warmly says, "Thank you for being prompt. It's time to network with all of my guests."

The dress code is semi-casual for the event that takes place within the semi-private suite at the Bella Bella Steakhouse, sure to entertain the excellent businessmen and woman that he has assembled.

The guests of Price Waterhouse are networking, catching up on business and personal matters. While the staff is serving appetizers, Price pulls Noelle close and says, "I'm happy to see you Noelle. Your company is doing well. You deserve the Award you will receive tonight."

Noelle replies proudly, Thank you, Sir. You taught me well."

Price Waterhouse puts his hand on Noelle's shoulder and states, "I hear some grumblings about long work hours and such. Noelle, let me be forward. I've worked hard, and I thank God for my success. I know you're a hard worker as well. Just remember Matthew; the Disciple of Jesus was a tax collector who loved money but learned to love the Lord."

"Mr. Waterhouse, you are a good man in my eyes, and all of North Star Village loves you." Noelle says with affection, and he continues, "your Bible references take me back to my time as one of your mentee's, the grumblings you've heard must be bad. Which one of my employees do I have to let go?" he said with no affection at all.

"Noelle," Price Waterhouse says sternly, "your employees wouldn't dare complain to me, but wives have their own ways of communicating."

Noelle states triumphantly, "Mr. Waterhouse work is all that I know, and when do you ever have enough money? Everyone constantly complains there's no gladness to be found. As for me and my house, all I can count on is to keep counting money and make as much as I can."

Price Waterhouse states with a knowing confidence, "I believe you are a good man; I have watched you grow over the years, but have you considered Jesus?"

Noelle gets a troubled look on his face, Price Waterhouse immediately interjects, "Please don't defend yourself. This is not an attack. I have no Heaven to throw you out of or Hell to put you in."

Noelle laughs in relief, then states, "Mr. Waterhouse, you are a great businessman, but I think you would be an even better preacher. You... I can believe in, maybe even develop a Church life."

Price Waterhouse pleasantly replies, "Noelle, that is a kind and wonderful thing to say, but to minister the Gospel of Jesus Christ is a whole lot more than what you see on any given Sunday. Your words are flattering, don't put your trust in a person. People, even me, will let you down every time. Put your trust in Jesus Christ of Nazareth, He will never leave you or forsake you."

Noelle always felt good in the company of Price Waterhouse. What would have been forced and off-putting if brought on by others in conversation, was received as mutual edification, indicated by his easy reply. "See, that's what I'm talking about, that right there is good stuff and although I haven't joined a Church or attended a Church service in a long time, I know good preaching when I hear it. My father talks like that," as they shake hands gladly.

Price Waterhouse looks Noelle straight in the eyes and says, "Ah yes, your parents are fine people."

Noelle replies, "Thank you. They are doing well. I call them regularly... and wait a minute, don't say it... I can tell by the look on your face that you're going to say, spend more time with them".

Price Waterhouse notices that the Wait Staff is getting into place to serve, and while gesturing to Noelle that they should move, he says, "The dinner tables are assigned seating. Name cards are in front of each seat. Noelle, you bury your best self in good intentions. You cannot just work and shut yourself off from the world. It doesn't work that way, there is more that is required of you."

Noelle finds his name card. He is sitting next to Price Waterhouse and says, "Sir, I thank you for inviting me to this occasion and for my award."

Price Waterhouse moves to the center of the room and gestures to all of his guests to be seated and returning to the table says to Noelle, "I want you to consider helping me as Co-Host of the Christmas Community Center Christmas party."

Noelle thinks to himself, *please don't try to be a matchmaker*, and at that moment Price Waterhouse says, "All work and no play will turn you into a Scrooge, this Christmas. You need to get out more. You haven't dated since being with Millicent Manor."

Noelle says, "Mr. Waterhouse, it will be my pleasure to help you in any way I can for the Community Center party, but Millicent Manor is a name from a long time ago."

"No need to go back to the past young man," says Price Waterhouse, who knows all too well the sad story of the one-time happy couple. To change the subject, he continues his Christmas pep talk saying, "Don't make yourself miserable Noelle. I know you don't like to talk about that period of time, but it seems like you have lost all of your compassion since those days. I'm going to do my best to change that, so I'm also inviting you to join me for my family Christmas dinner party."

Noelle pulls out his cellphone and confirms each date as an event on his calendar, which will remind him of his new plans for the upcoming Holiday Season. But he fits into Christmas like a square peg fits into a round hole, and you can't make that fit.

For Noelle, who feels he and the Holiday Season do not fit, for the sake of his soul, must acquit Christmas, even though as things stand, it doesn't fit, and he has no love for it.

Price Waterhouse is very happy that everyone he's invited is present. He stands proudly to address his guests, saying, "Thank you all for taking the time to be here today. I'm proud of you and want you to enjoy yourselves here at the Bella Bella Reservation complex. Enjoy our meal. Please keep your table name card and bring it to the cashier, where you will receive $50.00 as my gift to help you enjoy the Casino. Play Super Bingo or both, after we eat."

The room erupts with applause.

Price Waterhouse continues, "For those who rode the Limousine Bus, please report to the valet parking lounge between 11:00 and 11:15. We will be leaving the Casino promptly at 11:30. If anyone stays after we leave, I suggest you stay overnight. There are rooms available to you on discount when you present your name card. Then he says with a straight face, "If you stay, I will pick you up tomorrow, depending on how much you win."

Another moment of silence, then everyone gets the joke and laughs out loud.

"Please let me have your attention for just another moment... this is a serious request that I have of each of you who has driven here. If you drink, please have a designated non-drinking driver. Let's enjoy our night," Price Waterhouse says to applause. Then speaking over the noise he says, "The staff is ready to take our orders. I ask for a moment of silence to pray over our meal. Please let's bow your heads."

And after a moment of silence, Price Waterhouse begin to pray. "Lord, thank you for bringing us together. We offer this thankful prayer that you bless our meal and the hands that prepared it for the nourishment of our bodies. We ask these things in the name of Jesus Christ. Amen."

The guests take their seats and fill the room with sounds of pleasant chatter. Christmas is in the air, Price Waterhouse says, "Even for you, Mr. Chance, there's opportunity for a new beginning."

Noelle humors his mentor with a forced smile, but he doesn't believe it can happen.

Price Waterhouse proposes a toast to Noelle, saying, "May this Christmas be the one that changes your Christmas story."

~

"Noelle, try this steak dinner with me. You work so much it doesn't seem like you get to enjoy the fruits of your labor." Price Waterhouse says as a waitress moves toward their table to take dinner orders. "Order the Royal Treatment," he says, "I think you will like it."

Noelle states, "Mr. Waterhouse, it is your leadership and work ethics I fashion myself after; even if I work too much." Then he asks, "What's in the Royal Treatment dinner?"

Price Waterhouse delivers the contents with the flair and confidence of a world-renowned Chef when he says, "Chateaubriand steak with a Chateaubriand sauce, served with potatoes and asparagus, and for dessert we will have Royal Cheesecake, which is a blend of Blackberries, and for an appetizer, Bruschetta is served with Royal Chambord and Champagne."

A pleasant look replaces Noelle's frowning face, then he says, "That sounds mighty rich, Sir."

Price Waterhouse greets all in attendance, personally welcoming his guests to the unannounced opening ceremony for the Holiday Season. The theme becomes apparent when the waitresses put on red and green aprons and Santa Claus hats. Then a male voice over the public announcement speakers says, "Would everyone please return to their seats. Your dinners will be served shortly."

~

An imperceptible waif of air turns Autumn's fascination with summer's disappearing leaves act into a Harvest Moon that promises to fall, when Winter's cold proves temporary dominance; for Springtime's warmth will renew the cycle.

The cold world breathes death's frozen grip on all it touches. The dormant who heed the miracle of re-creation; that is the birth of the seed of God at Christmas, receives the promise of Spring's re-birth. October will mad dash to the finish of its evil Halloween heyday, which demands respect and will not be moved by man's hand. Yet and better still, there is the forever presence of true believers for goodness sakes. Only God knows the number of these Saints, who will cry out in the wilderness that the Everlasting light shines on the coming Messiah; called Emanuel, the baby who is born King of Kings and The Prince of Peace.

~

The room lights dim. A lighted dance floor comes to life. A giant movie screen descends from the ceiling and the room fills with 12 Christmas themed waitresses, who are followed by spotlights.

The head waitress steps forward and says, "Good evening ladies and gentlemen, my name is Diane and I welcome you to The Bella Bella Hotel and Casino. Thank you for choosing us for your dinner banquet. Your food orders are in final preparation. We would like to take this time to sing a little song to you, karaoke style. We invite you to sing along with us. The words of the song will appear on our big screen. The song is done by the group known as The Waitresses. It's titled, 'Christmas Wrapping'."

The music begins and the Waitresses sing.

*"Bah, humbug! Now that's too strong*
*'Cause it is my favorite holiday...*
*but all this year's it been a busy blur,*
*don't think I have the energy*
*to add to my already mad rush*
*just 'cause it's 'tis the season*
*the perfect gift for me would be*
*completion and connections left from last year."*

The song ends with two lost souls finding each other; helped by the magic of Christmas, and the waitresses sing,

*"Merry Christmas,*
*Merry Christmas*
*couldn't miss this one this year"*

Price Waterhouse rises up out of his seat to give the talented ladies a standing ovation. Each of the guests does the same, even the usually dour Noelle Chance can agree.

"That was great," says Price Waterhouse. "I'm ready to eat, drink and be merry," he said with a laugh. "Maybe the Casino will show us the royal treatment by letting us win."

Noelle dryly states, "Bingo!"

Price Waterhouse replies, "Mr. Noelle Chance, you will have more energy than that, if you win."

"B-4!."

A soulful male voice sings out, "Before I let go!" Maze featuring Frankie Beverly style. Then the next number is called out.

"I-22!"

A sultry female voice chime's in, "Two, two!

Then the next number is, "N-40!"

A man bellows out with an incredulous retort, "Forty!"

The caller proclaims the next number is, "G-52!,"and a high pitch women's voice in a nasal tone breaks through the air, as if in a department store, "Fifty-two!... pick up."

Then another number is picked, and the game host calls out, "Oh-66!"

There's a pause. Then a beautiful baritone voice sings out, "Get your kicks on Route 66!"

"Bingo!" yelled Noelle Chance.

"Well, stand-up man!," the table mates reply, including Price Waterhouse.

This was an exciting conclusion to a rousing Super Bingo experience at the Bella Bella Hotel and Casino. Noelle Chance has just won $1000.00 in a room full of characters. Some, seemingly unimpressed, looked like Noelle did when he first appeared, but that was before his big win.

Others in the room and around his table were happy for Noelle, and happiness; momentarily, sweeps over Noelle. The look on his face prompts Price Waterhouse to state, "Well look who is excited now. It's a pleasure to see a smile on your face. It reminds me of the times past when you were in my Mentorship program. That's good, there is still hope for you."

Noelle excitedly says, "Keep hope alive."

Although winning changes Noelle's demeanor, it's obvious that hearing Mr. Waterhouse say, *there is hope for you*, startles Noelle. Sensing that he has struck a nerve, Price Waterhouse immediately says, "That was then. This is now and my friend, your smile looks great."

Just then, the bingo attendant verifies Noelle's winning game card by calling out each number to the satisfaction of the game caller, who then thanks everyone for participating and welcomes all to come back soon. The announcement dashes everyone's hopes that the person who yelled bingo was somehow wrong. Now verified, that was their last chance to win.

Noelle has won on the night's last game. The bingo attendant gives him a Bella Bella Casino token, signs his winning bingo card and tells him to go to the cashier window to pick up the money.

"Congratulations on your winnings Noelle. I hope you realize how fortunate you are. It's not easy to win Super Bingo, and as you see, there was plenty of competition." Price Waterhouse says. He continues, "I'm sure you know; I remembered that you love competition."

Noelle Chance quickly thanks Price Waterhouse for a great night and hurries the conversation along stating, "I want to go to the cashier window right away and get an early start back to North Star Village." Reaching out to shake hands, he says goodnight.

Price Waterhouse walks with Noelle stride for stride and said, "Goodnight Noelle, drive safe and I look forward to us spending more time together. You really could have ridden here on the Limousine Bus, but this was a great day to drive that beautiful car of yours. Let's talk soon about the Harvest Moon Masquerade Ball."

Price Waterhouse heads toward the main concours to re-join his guests and have fun in the Casino. The Limousine bus is not scheduled to leave for over 90 minutes.

There is a pep in the step of Noelle Chance as he walks to the cashier window. If you did not know him, you would not guess that he has built himself into or better said, torn himself down to a person only a mother could love.

A pretty face and friendly voice greet Noelle Chance at the cashier window. She says, "Congratulations on your winnings playing Super Bingo Mr. Chance. It looks like you played your cards right. How would you like your money distributed?"

Noelle states defiantly, "Try placing all big bills in the middle of my palm."

The cashier, unamused, did so cheerfully and answered his next statement; which was a question with a smile. "Which way to the valet parking lobby?"

"Follow the yellow brick arrows and drive safe. Goodbye," says the Cashier.

Noelle arrives at the Valet lobby and is impressed by the smooth operation of the fast moving, polite attendants. A point he failed to notice on arrival.

"Thank you for visiting the Bella Bella Hotel and Casino," says the head attendant, as Noelle hands him his valet ticket. He senses a familiarity and uncharacteristically begins a conversation by saying, "You look like someone I know."

The Attendant is tall, dark and handsome. His looks puzzle Noelle, who begins to rack his brain for a clue as to why this man looks familiar.

"Sir, you are fifth in line. Your car will be here shortly," says the Attendant.

Noelle replies, "Excuse me for looking at you so hard, but what is your name, young man?"

The Attendant smiles, then answers, "Sir, my name is Cole Bucks."

The answer fascinates the usually stoic and sullen Noelle who replies, "Young man, you have the uncanny look, sound and movements of my late business partner. His name was Khole Cashe. He was a great man, a hard-working person that made a lot of money. We were quite a team, the best in North Star Village."

Noelle reaches out to shake the hand of Cole Bucks and says, "It's shocking how much you resemble my old friend from many years ago. It makes me realize how much I miss my friend," he said with a sigh, and in a huff.

Cole Bucks kindly responds, "Sir, be encouraged, your friend is blessed that you speak so nicely of him. May he rest in peace. Then there was an awkward pause until the silence was broken by Cole Bucks. "Sir, I will get your car now," and he returns in a few minutes.

Noelle, who is always tight with money, proceeds to tip above his usually minimum calculation, based on perpetual irritability, but not tonight. On this October night, the chilling coldness of a frosty heart warms up after a chance encounter. The Bella Bella Hotel and Casino experience has broken the ice on a heart frozen by a series of life's pains; self-inflicted or not, that can cause him to lose his soul and give into the tempting temptations of indifference to right and wrong.

Price Waterhouse evoked dormant feelings for Millicent Manor; beloved former girlfriend, and the awakening continues with thoughts of Khole Cashe, revisited by the sight of Cole Bucks.

~

NOELLE OSCAR CHANCE JR., Mr. No by reputation, has had enough memories for one night and he begins to shut down. But as Cole Bucks shuts his car door, he says, "Money can't buy friendship Sir, don't try to make all the money you can. Slow down a little bit."

"No Chance!," is his instant reply, and Noelle continues, "Cole Bucks, you just repeated line for line what my old partner used to say to me, then he would go out and make all the money. How incredible does that sound!" Once again, they share a moment of awkward silence.

Noelle enables the voice command feature in his car and says, "Play my money playlist." Waves goodbye to Cole Bucks, as the car slowly rolls around the lobby area. He turns up the volume so everyone can hear the sound of a trumpet horn solo from his favorite song by T. L. Williams, titled Gettin' Mo Money Than You. Then comes the vocals.

*They say I need to slow down when I drivin' my fancy car,*
*drivin' my fancy car...*
*See I know why you mad at me...*
*I'm gettin Mo money than you,*
*getting Mo money than you.*

Speeding away from the Casino, there is no happiness to be found for anything but thoughts of getting back to work, to make more money. Noelle sinks into the driver's seat and listens to the tires roll over the road and the sound of music that surrounds him in the sound scape the interior of a Cadillac provides. Thoughts of making money moves are riding in the lap of luxury towards a luxury home, full of the finer things in life. But material things have stopped bringing any joy. Noelle has become lost in the masquerade of the superficial. He arrives home safely, finding his home just as he left it, but lays down to sleep without giving thanks and neither is he thankful.

How long?

Noelle is a man of a certain age, and the saying goes, there ain't no fool, like an old fool.

# Chapter 2

## *The Money Tree*

### Simeon

---

*14. And this is not all that is meaningless in our world. In this life, good people are often treated as though they were wicked, and wicked people are often treated as though they were good. This is so meaningless!*

*15. So I recommend having fun, because there is nothing better for people in this world than to eat, drink, and enjoy life. That way they will experience some happiness along with all the hard work God gives them under the sun.*

*— Ecclesiastes 8: 14*

---

Who looking upon a new day could say that this is a cold, cold world. How long will sleep come easy to Noelle Chance? How long would the fervent, effectual prayers of those who love him go seemingly unrequited? How long can parents or anyone else stand in gap to pray for one who does not pray with you or for themselves? Only God knows how long for anything under His creation, being that God is time and when it is time, it is God who will call a man or women to Him. Since mankind cannot call themselves to God.

Noelle Chance awakens to the sunrise of a brand-new day; one that has never been seen before, healthy, wealthy and wiser by the time he spent driving back and forth to the Bella Bella Casino. If there is a change in the heart, then he is truly wiser but not today, as once again Noelle fails to give thanks for waking up to another day.

Another thing that does not change is his desire to eat a Po-man early breakfast, to break his food fast, called sleep. There is a certain wisdom that can be found in the Po-man early breakfast, which consists of two eggs, toast with butter and jam, sausage patties and coffee. Noelle needs a good breakfast on a crisp morning after a longer than usual night, and his favorite breakfast place; North Star dinner, puts in his regular order and he sits in his regular seat at the counter before heading in to work.

Most days Noelle is the first one in the office, but not today, because Nickolas Kingsly, the brightest asset of the N. O. Chance Financial Agency, is the early bird. Mr. Nickolas Christopher Kingsly is a man of respect. He's the Office Manager and Business Developer, adept at his job of running a Financial Business Services Company.

Kingsly, as the Boss calls him, is a Cocoa skin attractive Black man of average height and weight, in his mid-40s, made distinctive by a well-coiffed small afro and his sideburns that look like lamb chops. Nickolas is well liked in the community, well liked in his Church, loved by his family and friends and well-liked by his Co-Workers, who call him Saint Nick.

Nickolas Kingsly is married to the former Mary Jasmine Goldmill, a beautiful, brown, buxom Black woman, with black shoulder length hair and pretty brown eyes. Mrs. Mary Kingsly is a kind, smart, faith-filled women and the supportive backbone for a family of 5. A working wife that helps to make ends meet as a Tailor and Seamstress. She also has a talent to design and produce women's hats for all occasions.

Husband and wife have three children; two boys and a girl. Hope is a common thread that runs through the family, especially in Christopher Timothy Kingsly, nicknamed Tee Tee. Christopher is the apple of everyone's eye because of his sweet smile and shy disposition on his slim, soon to be 10-year old body. Tee Tee, as only family calls him, doesn't talk much in school and is mistakenly thought to be a slow learner, but he talks when he is home. Christopher doesn't help perceptions of his abilities because he doesn't like to talk in public, preferring to whisper to his family members. He is a shy cutie pie.

Marion Kingsly is the oldest; almost Twenty years old, and a replica of her mother, determined to help the family financially. Marion has picked up her Mother's talent for making hats and is well known for her hard work at Village Hats and Racks—Women's shop in the North Star Village Shopping Center—where she is Assistant Manager.

Simon Peter Kingsly is a good son to Mother and Father; he's a strong, healthy, handsome young man eager to help the family anyway he can. He will soon turn Eighteen-years old and graduate from High School. He wants to further his education, but the family needs a scholarship to send him to College or Trade School. Simon carries a joyful spirit and day by day faith, to work hard to create options for himself. He has done so throughout his young life. Simon keeps hope alive in all things he does and in everyone he touches. He has a talent for gift giving. His gifts always receive smiles. He gives the best gift of all, which is love.

Noelle Chance; Mr. No, is not all bad, but Nickolas would be hard pressed to come up with something good to say about his conversations, demeanor or general outlook on life. There is the good that Noelle hired him ten-years ago, two years after the passing of Noelle's former partner and friend Khole Cashe. That dynamic duo made a great deal of money as Tax Accountants and Financial Advisors in North Star Village.

Khole Cashe had questionable legal tactics, and he tirelessly worked to be successful. He and Noelle Chance Jr formed an odd couple of talent and greed that fed on the misfortunes of other business owners, who needed their expert calculations to get out of tax troubles.

Nickolas Kingsly wasn't the first to apply for a job at N. O. Chance Financial Agency, but getting hired was an answered prayer for a man with a wife and children and a good chance to learn from a well-known, successful man. Staying in the company was difficult to do under stringent work hours, and the just enough pay offered. A few had quit before Nickolas took the job.

Nickolas Kingsly is proving to be a lifesaving hire for Noelle. Saint Nick, as he is called, has done as well or better than Noelle's former business partner in creating programs for all clients. Nickolas helps clients grow, and he does it without questionable tactics, while bringing good tidings to Noelle, who is falling into bitterness and losing his soul.

Noelle Chance enters his non-extravagant but well-done office and is immediately greeted by the kindness of Nickolas Kingsly who states, "Good morning Mr. Chance. Good to see you fine and fit from your dinner with Mr. Waterhouse."

Noelle replies dryly, "Good day Kingsly. Yes, Mr. Waterhouse once again spent too much money to entertain people who could do better things with their time—like make more money."

Nickolas Kingsly says, "Sir, it's quite an honor to be recognized by Mr. Waterhouse and you do work hard... I hope you enjoyed the night and the celebration of your accomplishments."

Noelle moves towards his office, then says in a dismissive tone, "Yes, Mr. Kingsly as you often say, keep hope alive. I enjoyed myself and even experienced some unique memories, but it was pure luck that I made any money."

"Oh! you made money on the Slot Machines," says Nickolas.

"No Chance! I'm too smart to lose any money on those calculated, calibrated collectors of cold cash. I was totally lucky to win at Bingo," Noelle says defiantly. "And it was on the very last game of the night. Surely there was someone there more needy than me. I'm sure they hoped for a win, but it was me that called out bingo! Can you explain that, man?"

Noelle goes to his office saying, "Let's get to work and make more money."

A quiet satisfaction falls on Nickolas Kingsly. The Boss has stated for the first time since he has known him; the phrase keep hope alive. That's one small step for a man, but a giant leap of faith for the spirit of a man.

Noelle's bitterness is imperceptible in the beautiful morning that unfurls itself within glorious sunshine. The office works efficiently, qualifying Financial Accounts, and time moves on in timeless fashion.

"Mr. Chance," says a smooth female voice on the speakerphone.

"Yes, Miss Flowers."

" There are two gentlemen here to visit you... Reverend Avery Mann and Deacon Peoples."

"Thank you, Miss Flowers." says the Boss. "Hold them for a moment while I clear my desk. I will buzz your phone when I am ready for them."

Kristen relays the message to the guest.

Reverend Mann is a distinguished-looking Clergyman in his late 60s, average height with a husky build, short black hair; greying at the edges. He is cheerful, energetic and full of the light of the Lord.

Deacon Peoples is a younger slim version of the Reverend, with a touch of grey hair in his trimmed mustache and a classic high fade haircut made famous by the great Philadelphia Pennsylvania boxing referee, Larry Hazzard.

Nikolas Kingsly is a member in good standing at North Star Baptist Church, where Reverend Avery Mann is the Pastor. He greets the Men of God warmly in the front lobby area saying, "Come into my office, I just left Mr. Chance. He will be with you shortly. I'm thankful to have this opportunity to organize a donation for the oncoming Thanksgiving and Christmas Holidays."

Reverend Mann speaks with the voice of a school principal making an announcement when he greets Nickolas. "Good day Brother Kingsly," as Deacon Peoples does the same.

Reverend Mann continues saying, "Brother Kingsly, you have been good to our Church since you stepped foot in the door. This is just us stopping by to welcome your Boss to our Church, thank him for past support and encourage him to consider North Star Baptist this Christmas."

Reverend Mann, Deacon Peoples and Nickolas, who will soon be elevated to Deacon, stand on one accord and enjoy pleasant conversation until Kristen Flowers comes to the office door of Nickolas and says, "Mr. Chance is ready to see you now."

Prompted by curiosity, Noelle Oscar Chance Jr decides to meet his guests in the lobby area.

Nickolas, seeing his boss approaching says, "Mr. Chance, thank you for coming out to meet our visitors today. Let me formally introduce you to Reverend Avery Mann, my pastor and Deacon Allen Peoples."

Noelle shakes the hands of the Reverend and the Deacon, while inviting them into his personal suite, motioning for everyone to be seated. Then he addresses them with an assertive confidence saying, "Gentleman, what brings you to my office today?"

Reverend Mann immediately responds.

"Thank you for your time, Mr. Chance. I want to introduce you to our new Charity programs we've designed to be more effective in helping the needy families of North Star Village. Our mission is to move the resources people need most to be more directly helpful and give them a hand up from hopeless to hope filled. We know if we can offer hope to help their unbelief, these families of men, women and children can restore their individual lives, and be positive stories of healing in North Star Village."

Noelle nods his head in agreement and states coldly, "Good luck working with those people who have lost their way. If they keep working, then things will get better."

Reverend Mann inhales the indifference of the Owner of N. O. Chance Financial Agency and exhales his own brand of positivity within a calm voice, saying, "Mr. Chance, we're reaching out to those who need a hand, those that could be considered lost sheep out of our herd, and we are the shepherds. We can shepherd in opportunities, help needy folks get back on their feet and show them dignity by treating them as we would want to be treated if we woke up and found ourselves in that position."

Reverend Mann hands Noelle a brochure titled, 'Read And Feed The Need'. Speaking with compassion says, "Mr. Chance, this brochure will explain our mission, provide a structure for donations, ways to volunteer at our events and, of course, all donations are tax deductible. But I don't have to tell you that."

Noelle states dismissively, "Well, we do give to the Community Fund, a program that Mr. Kingsly brought to my attention."

Noelle goes quiet, as thoughts of Price Waterhouse go through his mind and how he reached out to help him become the rich man he is today.

Reverend Mann patiently waits for Noelle to pick up his conversation.

Noelle restates, "Mr. Kingsly has brought different programs to my attention and there are many people who ask me to donate to this or that charity, and why I just give to the Community Fund."

Deacon Peoples joins the conversation stating, "We are proud of the work of Mr. Kingsly. We also help the Community Fund, but it was actually Mr. Price Waterhouse that recommended we speak to you specifically, because he believes your expertise would guide us to success."

Reverend Mann states, "We are blessed to know Mr. Waterhouse. He is a strong member of our Church and generous with his donations. He speaks fondly of you and so does Mr. Kingsly."

"Mr. Kingsly speaks well of your Church, and so does Mr. Waterhouse," says Noelle. Now seeing the hand of Price Waterhouse on this meeting he still doubles down on his doubting ways stating, "Mr. Waterhouse is a good man—although I don't understand how he gives away his hard-earned money to those who have made bad decisions, don't want to work, or can't hold on to a job."

Reverend Mann gently interjects into Noelle's rant saying, "Every man needs help at some time in their life. We give thanks for what we have and try to help our neighbors, treating them like we would want them to treat us if we were in need. But by the Grace of God, it could be me."

Noelle, defiantly says, "I was once in need. I got back up and I will never again go down."

There's an awkward pause once again and the air charges with lightning, that strikes negativity, having found the right conditions to become furious. A storm can strike without warning in your life and force you to practice what you preach.

Reverend Mann exhales and says, "Heed these words Mr. Chance. Be quick to listen. Slow to speak and be slow to become angry." Fighting the negativity storm with prayer, he becomes a living testimony to the phrase, practice what you preach.

Noelle pushing back hard, making you want to argue. Holding your peace is easier said than done. It's not easy in the face of the enemy who shows up as a dark angel, and you are unaware.

Jesus says there will be no more signs for this generation, but by faith Avery Mann preaches under the belief in Jesus Christ's Life, Death and Ascension. The world will find a perfect storm to test your faith and bring about your anger. It can happen in a moment, but peace comes over this meeting and tensions are released.

Avery Mann looks Noelle in the eyes and calmly says, "Mr. Chance, you have acquired obvious wealth. Your talent with money management for business owners is well known throughout North Star Village. We hope you will help us help others, as we prepare for the Holiday Season and Christmas."

Noelle Jr, his heart hardened, says sarcastically, "Gentleman, didn't we just celebrate Christmas in July?"

This one-man joke falls flat, even as Noelle chuckles at his sense of humor. That no one else thinks his joke was funny doesn't bother him at all. Noelle says, "Christmas, no way! Gentlemen, the commercialization of Christmas makes money for me. People spend more than they have to spend, and I help individuals and businesses out of their financial troubles for a fee."

"Thank you for your time today, Mr. Chance. You are most generous. Please consider visiting us at North Star Baptist. We would love to see you," Reverend Mann says, rising up out of his chair to shake hands with Noelle. Deacon Peoples following his pastor's lead, does the same.

Noelle and Nickolas escort the Clergymen to the front door and Noelle says, "Goodbye and have a good day," then returning to his office.

Reverend and Deacon say goodbye, then Avery Mann turns his attention to Nickolas and says, "Brother Kingsly, thank you for all that you do. We can easily see and feel your presence in this office. Be encouraged, and we look forward to seeing you on Sunday."

Noelle, now back in the comfort of his office chair, studies the brochure left by Reverend Mann and notices a small envelope stapled inside. He opens it and reads the personal note signed from someone that cares.

It says, 'The first Noelle the Angel unaware did say, for to certain poor shepherds, his donations would pay. Noelle, Noelle, give peace a chance. Consider helping the North Star Community Fund before getting lost in the Masquerade dance.'

Noelle has a quick reaction to the note from Reverend Mann. He calls Nickolas to his office with intentions to rant about it, but as Nickolas enters his office, discretion becomes a better valor and Noelle beats back his inner Grinch, that is eager to steal this Christmas.

"Kingsly," says Noelle in an irritated voice, "those men are already talking about Christmas, so surely you are too, but hear this, there will be no extra days off this Christmas."

Time moves relentlessly onward, waiting for no one, divided only by day meets night. The two are continually introduced by dawn, as an early light of the new day and dusk, which delivers the news of the day's ending forever, by the darkening of daylight. Dusk signifies a day's demise, giving no promises of life continuing into the brand-new day, which beckoning. Like watching sand fall through an hourglass, each grain, a figment of time that drops, as a clock goes tic tok, and the day's end is close, but so far away...

Noelle fails to see the fortunes of the immediate time he has spent with the Clergymen sent to soften his hard stance on life. They representing good, and he unknowingly representing evil, but only God has mercy. Time has no mercy, none...

Noelle represents the hardness of the world and, in doing so, does like All Hallows Day does. Known as Halloween, the last day of October works to validate evil intentions, even evil that is unknowingly facilitated.

Yes, and it counts. The foul against his soul is another brick to add to a heart's hardness that stands like a wall, blurring the timeline drawn as a dash from our born day to our last day alive. We can see our birth but fear the end of our time, looking at the timeline between birth and the end, which no one knows but God. Our minds want to be in control and some stop believing in the absolute of God and His creation.

A day ends at midnight. That's an absolute death to a day that was, and a new day fetches fast the fasting time—that is sleep—a common denominator all creation must succumb to, until breaking that fast. Awakening with a hunger for breakfast, let us eat, drink and be merry. Although time waits for no one, blessed by the Creator of time for further participation in life, new grains of sand fall through the aforementioned hourglass for Noelle Jr.

Noelle wastes time, which presented itself as a new chance, and even stood still, by the Grace of God, while everyman, Deacon Allen Peoples visited him. Non-fiction sounds like it's the truth and fiction sounds like it's a lie. Knowledge and creativity can turn a lie into the truth, and the reality of the truth can be unbelievable. The upside is down, and the downside is up. There's friction in the air. Non-fiction is true and fiction is the shadow of doubt, but light exposes the truth and it shines on Noelle.

Nickolas Kingsly receives the blessing from the Heaven-sent Clergymen. Blessed to see the good present in every situation but watches in silence, when the spirit of goodness dances past his boss, offering no rebuttal to Noelle's decree that there will be no extra days off for Christmas.

The silence of this lamb proved to be golden when the boss states, "Well Kingsly, it seems we've wasted enough time today. Let's get back to work."

The office of N. O. Chance Financial works smoothly throughout the day that ends with good news, when Noelle picks up a new client named North Star Village Cadillac.

Noelle calls Nickolas into his office to deliver the good news, "Kingly," as he likes to refer to his faithful employee, "this is short notice, but I want you to finish preparing the proposal for our new client."

Nickolas readily accepts the assignment and states, "This account is quite a blessing, Sir," keeping a cheerful disposition. Realizing the next request from the boss will be extra work.

Noelle Chance says, "Kingsly, I want you to work on this through the rest of the week and meet me on Saturday morning at 11am, so we can make sure the proposal is ready for Monday."

Nickolas responds immediately, "Yes Sir, we will get it done," making a note for a Saturday meeting.

Noelle Chance says, "I was in the right place at the right time for this deal. Let's call it a day. I'm sure tomorrow will be busy for us all, because it's Halloween."

Nickolas states, "I'll be busy here and I will be busy at home helping my wife and children get ready for Halloween."

"Kingsly, you surprise me... ," Noelle says spitefully, "a religious man like yourself dealing with Halloween? Man that's confusing... I suppose your children will be out and about celebrating evil just like everyone else!"

Noelle's dry humor again loses its taste and, like old chewing gum, it's humorless.

"Mr. Chance," Nickolas says without raising his voice, "I try to bring joy to a day that celebrates evil and wicked things. I do this by focusing on the good. Good and evil exist together, it is a part of all things on Earth. I enjoy spreading that duality of joy and pain to combat Halloween, that is the evil twin to All Saints' Day, which is the day after and the base of this celebration.

Nickolas pauses, expecting Noelle Chance to continue his Halloween rant, but getting no opposition, he continues saying , "Mr. Chance, I teach my children the truth of life, that there is duality in our lives and there will be troubles, but have faith in God, who created all things of the world. Let us elders remember to always suffer the children, as Jesus instructs us in the Bible."

"Suffer the children to be hypocrites. Man, you can't have it both ways," Noelle shoots back looking Nickolas in his eyes.

Nickolas keeps the eye contact and says, "There is so much to learn," walking over to the window.

Nickolas looks up at the sky and, speaking with joy says, "As for me and my house, we live in this world, but we pray not to become products of the world."

Nickolas Kingsly has achieved another first. This time he has the undivided attention of his boss, who listens to the brilliance of his Office Manager with a measure of respect. Noticing he still has the attention of the boss, calmly states, "Mr. Chance, it sounds funny and looks funny for me to join in on the Halloween celebrations but like I said... suffer the children, which means let them learn and have fun along the way, as we teach them about the mystery of life."

Nickolas changes his tone; still calm, but he talks with the emotion of a father who loves his children when he says, "My children do not celebrate evil. I teach my children to see that some people do celebrate evil, and some purposely do mean things. We must learn to deal with the mystery of life in real ways, teaching the truth about good things and bad."

Nickolas, wanting to end on a positive note states, "My children don't celebrate evil. I teach them to be aware of their neighbor because we may be the only good that they see, or the only truth that they will hear. I pray to do all things in moderation and that we eat, drink and be merry."

Noelle Chance Jr is overwhelmed. He nervously chuckles while gathering the written proposal for North Star Cadillac, then says, "Save your preaching for Sundays, Kingsly. You would do better then. You're on a roll, but as for me, I will stay on the outside and look in, okay."

Nickolas says, "Mr. Chance, it may appear that evil is winning, but there are good souls; young and old, who are out to have fun and enjoy each other in goodness. Whether it's a Halloween party, Trick or Treating or like you are doing, in going to the Harvest Moon Masquerade Ball."

Noelle continues his dry humor, saying, "Halloween is beginning to look a lot like Christmas. You got colorful lights, commercials, and there's a lot of money being made."

Then changing the subject quickly, he says, "This Christmas, I will donate to North Star Village Baptist Church in care of you, Deacon Peoples and Reverend Mann. That should stop everyone else from bothering me for money." Then looking up says, "Goodnight Kingsly, see you tomorrow. You can lock up."

Noelle strolls down the hallway, convinced of his brilliance, but his mannerisms are speeding him down a path to self-destruction. Superficial things are all he can see. He stops to look in the mirror by the front security desk. Not looking any deeper than material things, Noelle does not look at himself truthfully. He stands in the mirror unaware of his feelings and blind to his surroundings. The Security Guard stands in the doorway looking straight at him, but Noelle is closed off from the world. It has been this way since he chased away his would-be fiancé, Miss Millicent Eboni Manor.

"Have a great Night," says the Security Guard.

Noelle waves goodbye.

Noelle is now in a committed relationship with money and the pursuit of it. An attraction that brings satisfaction, but it becomes a hollow victory when thoughts of Millicent comeback after so many years. He lives alone and there has been no woman of interest since the relationship ended. Millicent's name came up at the Bella Bella Casino dinner party when Price Waterhouse mentioned his Mentorship program, where Noelle and Millicent met.

Tough day, tough thoughts and tomorrow is just a day away, but everything seems better riding home in the luxury seat of a Cadillac. A gift that keeps on giving when the dealership he bought it from, North Star Village Cadillac, hires N. O. Chance Financial Agency to plan its expansion.

~

Holly Evergreen is the name that comes up on the caller ID. It's Noelle's beloved older sister who has a pretty face, smile, style and effortless energy. Holly wears her brown hair in natural styles. She has brown skin, brown eyes and looks younger than her early 60s age.

"Hello Holly, "Noelle says from his comfortable Living Room chair.

"Is there a doctor in the house? Oh, I keep forgetting. Dr. No is from a James Bond movie, your Mr. No personality comes from the Grinch who stole Christmas," says the happy voice on the other end of the phone call.

Holly continues, "I know you are busy brother, you're always busy, but I'm calling to remind you to see mom and dad tomorrow and show them your mask and the suit you are wearing for the Masquerade Ball. We're all so glad that you are going, and we want you to enjoy yourself. Jake and I will be there, and I want you to remember to take a picture for your nephew. It's amazing how my son looks up to you."

Noelle responds gently, "Holly, I will see mom and dad tomorrow. I will stop by and spend some time with them before I go to the Ball. Mr. Waterhouse is expecting me early and I guess it's time to get excited about being a Co-Host. I'm only working a couple of hours tomorrow and I'm glad I won't be home to be bothered by anyone trick or treating. I'll see you there, okay..."

Holly speaks to uplift her Brother, like she has done all of his life, "El, I pray for a yes spirit to prevail in your life. You don't have to be that Mr. No character," said with a laugh. "Oh yeah, when I put my mask on, you won't even know me. You can put on a mask and be nice again."

Noelle Chance is cold to the world, perhaps misunderstood, but he tries hard with his Sister, her husband and their son, his beloved nephew Jacob Jr.

Noelle, speaking with determination in his voice says, "Holly I'm going to bed soon, so I'm getting off of the phone, but dear sister, I would know you anywhere. Goodnight, and I will see you tomorrow."

Holly hurriedly replies, "Wait! Thank you for paying mom and dad's home bills. It really allows them some financial freedom and feeling of security. They like the assisted living style. Thank you on behalf of the whole family... okay! I just want you to visit more often. Goodbye Mr. No."

Nickolas Kingsly is ready to leave the office and celebrate his good day. Locking the front door, he pulls out his cellphone to call the wife.

Mary Kingsly answers, "Hey honey."

Nickolas excitedly proclaims, "We picked up a new client today, and I'm writing the promotion."

"Congratulation's honey. I'm thankful to see you get rewarded for your hard work," Mary says.

Nickolas chimes in, "Yes, I'm thankful too. It was a good day all around. Deacon Peoples and Reverend Mann came to the office today, and I think Mr. Chance will donate to the North Star Village Church Charity for the holiday season."

Mary, in a voice of wonder says, "It's amazing that Mr. No said yes. Are you on your way home?"

"Yes, I am," Nickolas says with a big smile on his face. "First, I'm going to the Save More Market Plaza to pick up some candy to pass out for Halloween, and a dinner for two. I got a feeling from our brother-in-law that your sister wants Marion and Simon to spend the night and spend some time with your niece for Halloween. It looks like it will be just you, me, and Chris at home."

"And Chris will be tired from trick or treating, won't he, Mr. Kingsly. No wonder Mr. No said yes. Saint Nickolas is irresistible." Mary says in a seductive voice.

Nickolas responds, "Mary, Mary, I do believe you are flirting with me!"

Mary replies, "Honey, I'm going to let you go now, so you can concentrate on what you are doing. Don't worry about dinner for tonight. It will be ready when you get home okay, bye..."

"That's music to my ears... I will see you when I get there... bye!" says Nickolas. Now talking to himself, "It's a good thing no one can see my face. I believe I'm blushing."

Nickolas Christopher Kingsly is a man in love. "It's time to leave the job parking lot and get to the market," he says out loud, looking in the rear-view mirror. He cranks up the Mini-Van and turns on the radio.

A commercial for Target Department store is the first thing he hears, saying, "Santa is on his way and savings are too. Let the Spirit of Christmas come on in with gifts from you. And we welcome you to be an early bird and get our savings on Black Friday. Doors open at 6am."

The female voice of Minister Kay Silvers booms around the stereo speakers, as she greets the listeners, "Good evening to you. Welcome to my radio show where the beats are paved in gold. The Bible says, suffer the children, so let us provide a safe, peaceful Halloween experience tomorrow. Take it from me, please drive extra careful and let's all be extra prayerful."

The popular Gospel DJ is feeling the Holy Spirit, and she continues, "Good people of North Star Village listen, if you are struggling to see the light of the Lord in these times of darkness, let this song by Howard Anderson Jr show you the way. It's titled, 'Hard Praise'."

"I'm Minister Kay Silver and I want you to remember that sometimes you got to turn your praise up way past 10. Hard Praise right now on KNPR 99.5 FM, keeping the Praise 100."

A strong alto male voice sings,

"Here's what you have to do...hard praise!
Here's what you need to do...hard praise!
It's going to pull you through...hard praise!"

Nickolas turns up the volume and lo-and-behold, there is a praise party going on. Let the good times roll.

The road to Save More Market is more crowded than usual. Nickolas is not the only last-minute shopper for Halloween, but he finds a close parking space when a car begins backing out, just as he approaches. He pulls into the vacant parking space, like it was waiting just for him.

Nickolas says, "Thank you parking lot Angel."

Save More Market is full of shoppers, but Nickolas easily finds everything he wants, including a bottle of BLACKSTONE Cabernet Sauvignon Wine. Shopping is easy as finding a parking space was.

Everything he wants shows up, as he walks down the right aisles at the right time and finds a gift basket that contains an Italian dinner for 2, complete with Florentines for dessert.

The checkout line participates in the win-win-win scenario, when Nickolas pushes his cart of goodies up to a cash register line that opens right up to a pleasant and efficient cashier.

The nametag on the cashier says Cherub. She smiles at Nickolas and says, “It looks like someone is playing their cards right today. Thanks for shopping with us. Have a great night!”

Nickolas is pleased. Ole Saint Nick leaves the Market with time to spare but moves right along, as dusk has turned into dark on the smooth Jazz drive home. He's listening to a Gospel Jazz CD titled Trumpet Sounds by Rod McGaha, given to him by his brother-in-law, Matthew Davis.

Nickolas arrives at the door of his home and his wife; the object of his heart's desire, greets him lovingly. The Kingslys pray that their steps are in order, believing a family that prays together, stays together. Tonight's dinner is fried chicken with mashed potatoes and vegetables.

“Hey guys,” Nickolas says, noticing that everyone is close to finishing their dinners, “we have chocolate chip cookies for tonight's dessert. Tomorrow morning, I'll have breakfast ready before anyone has to leave. Let's all get a good night's sleep, because it will be a long day.”

North Star Village and surrounding communities are planning for Halloween night and the oncoming weekend. All Hallows Day peacefully joins the sands of time; evil passing over onto the next day, which is the first day of November, called All Saints' Day.

Opposites attract. Each is necessary to expose the other, as dawn is the light of a new day and time waits for no one. Halloween has its time, it moves on at midnight, for no one—whether they be bad, or whether they be good—can control time in daylight, or in darkness. Time knows dawn moves to dusk and dusk sings ... turn off the lights.

And the melody still lingers on...

# Chapter 3

## *Trick or Treat*

### Levi

*And moreover I saw under the sun the place of judgment, that wickedness was there; and the place of righteousness, that iniquity was there. 17 I said in mine heart, God shall judge the righteous and the wicked: for there is a time there for every purpose and for every work.*

— *ECCLESIASTES* 3: 16

Nickolas Kingsly is up and at 'em, with the break of dawn's early light finding the man of the house busy with the early birds who look for food, but he cooks the food. Nickolas adds love to the seasonings he puts on the family meal to break the fast of sleep. It's his one ingredient found in all he prepares, and it can't be found in a seasonings rack.

Home is on the other side of town from the office of N. O. Chance Financial Agency and being the early bird on this Halloween morning gives Nickolas the opportunity to set the breakfast table with good food and good spirits for the day ahead. Nickolas and Mary Kingsly are a Church going family that works hard to support three children ages 19, 17 and 10 years old. In their happy home full of love, doing all things in moderation, they eat, drink and be merry.

October 31st is Halloween, a yearly contest between good and evil. A day full of events for all ages that will test the patience of parents, guardians and teachers that must remember to suffer the children. Costume play can turn into frightening reality when evil masquerades undetected among the people, hiding motives to steal, kill and destroy. Halloween, and All Saints' Day that follows, not only collide at midnight but the ways of the world collide every year, as good and evil get to witness their contrasts during this celebration.

Halloween can be a fun costume party time for parents and boys and girls of all ages to walk through their communities, as neighbors handout candy. Children dressing up in costumes and going out house to house with parents or guardians became a popular American tradition in the 1930s, called trick or treating. The trick or treating concept was introduced by Europeans, who brought the mystic celebration with them to America. Our modern-day Halloween strives to be a harmless celebration, but fright night is people; young and old, trying to be scary, dressing up as monsters, decorating their houses in demonstrations of evil, and promoting all wickedness.

Folklore states, spirits of the dead get this one time of year to come out and confront people, who must give them a treat or exchange their souls, hence, trick or treat. The last day of October is All Hallows Eve, known as Halloween. The first day of November is known as All Saints' Day. The good and the bad play out a battle for the souls of mankind.

All Saints' Day is the beginning of the traditional Holiday Season of Thanksgiving, Hanukah, Christmas Eve, Christmas, Kwanzaa, New Year's Eve and New Year's Day. Kwanzaa is an African American Heritage celebration, recognized around the world since 1966, which begins on the day after Christmas, ending on January 1st, New Year's Day.

Jesus Christ of Nazareth is the reason for the Christmas Holiday Season and the Christmas Day celebration of Peace on Earth. A Peace that surpasses all understanding, seen clearly around the World, which stops to observe Mother Mary, Joseph, and the birth of Jesus, as the greatest story ever told. Spiritual eyes can see, and spiritual ears can hear, flowing from the heart, are the issues of the heart. Whether you believe in the story of the son of God or you don't, truth meets denial, fear meets faith, and fantasy meets reality during the most wonderful time of the year.

The Kingsly kitchen is the center of the household, active every morning, but this morning Nikolas is up earlier than everyone else, who will go to school or work except Mother Mary, who gets to sleep in a little longer on this day. Nickolas is busy in the kitchen, but he is keeping the noise low, because he wants the smell of fresh coffee and sausages frying to wake up the house.

The woman of the house and each of her children react like a roll call. Mom wakes up with a smile on her face. The smell of breakfast is a glorious stimulation to the senses and today Nickolas serves her a cup of coffee in bed, watching her come to life after a good night's sleep.

The oldest boy, prodigal son Simon Peter Kingsly, gets the next wake-up call and says, "Breakfast!"

Marion Katherine Kingly, the firstborn, wakes up saying, "This is a great way to start the day."

Christopher, the youngest, jumps out of his bed and runs to the kitchen to see his dad scrambling eggs, then gives him two thumbs up when he looks up from the stove.

Mary Kingsly is the good thing that a man finds when he finds a woman. "Oh! honey, breakfast smells great, and the coffee tastes great," Mary says with a big smile, sitting on the side of the bed. She says, "Let me get dressed so I can enjoy our time together."

"Slow down sweetheart, we have plenty of time before I have to get to the office," Nickolas says

"Thank you dear," Mary replies while drinking her coffee.

"ALTHOUGH WE CAN'T GO the Harvest Moon Ball tonight, I'm putting a request for time off on December 19th, so I can take you to the Community Center Christmas party, and then you can put on your red dress," Nickolas says with a look of determination.

Conversation flows freely around breakfast on the table. Everyone is excited about the Halloween celebrations planned. Everyone looks across the table towards the youngest member of the family, the cute little sweetheart son, sits silently, holding onto the moment until mother Mary says in a questioning voice, "What do you say about breakfast TT?", his family nickname Tiny Tim.

Christopher gets up with a serious look on his face, everyone says, "Hey Chris, what's the matter?"

"Simon didn't say eat," he says laughing, then everyone starts laughing.

Nickolas knocks on the table, stating, "Quiet down everyone," standing up next to his chair at the front of the table he says, "I'm proud of you guys and I want you all to know your mother and I appreciate how responsible you are, but be extra careful today, because it's Halloween."

The proud dad continues to say, "Everywhere you go will be crowded and everyone will be in a hurry. Please be patient, stay positive and remember we celebrate the good in this world that is the Holy Spirit." Everyone nods their heads in agreement.

Mary says, "That's a great speech Daddy. When can we expect you to be back home?"

Nickolas replies, "I should be back here before 5:30."

"Daddy, I can tell by the way you are looking at me, you want to know what my plans are for tonight," Marion says, "I'm glad to say my store is having an employee and guest party tonight, and the theme is disco night.

"I want Simon to be my guest if you guys are okay with it? Sorry for the last-minute notice. I thought I was just going out with my girlfriends, but I want to hang out with my little brother while I still can. Aunt Marie wants to go, and she said she will pick us up and we can spend the night."

Mom gives Dad the, *it's okay, I knew about it look.*

Nickolas says, "It sounds great. Be safe and have fun."

Simon jumps into the conversation, "Dad!! check it out. Simon says dance everybody," as he turns up the radio that's playing a classic Gold Rap song, 'Haunted House of Rock by Whodini'.

Simon and Marion do their disco dance routine and motion for everyone to join in. Simon then says, "Everybody stop!" everyone stops except Marion, who keeps dancing.

Simon states, "Mom, Dad, TT, you're all out." Everyone says together, "Why!"

Simon does his best dance move and yells out, "Because I didn't say Simon Sez stop!"

~

MARION SAYS, "Simon and I are gonna wear the same outfit to look like soul train dancers. Dad, Mom already knows all of this, but check this out."

Marion pulls out an outfit. "My store manager gave me a great costume idea for TT. She said I could design and sew a Karate uniform like the one the Jim Kelley character wears in the movie, Enter the Dragon."

Dad and Mom say in unison, "That is cool!"

Marion continues, "Yeah, I can dig it! But Mom, Dad, check this out...TT loves it! He also will carry a Black Panther comic book to complete the look, and he's got a move and catchphrase. TT anytime someone asks you what character you are, give them your punch line."

Christopher Timothy Kingsly jumps into a karate stance and says the line Jim Kelly made famous, "Man... 'You come right out of a comic book'!"

~

A BEAUTIFUL LATE October sunrise meets the drive into downtown with its obligatory morning rush traffic. Noelle Chance Jr., has every option available on his satellite radio system, but the traffic reports he likes, comes from local radio station KNSV, The Right Choice.

The Personality DJ lives in DriveTime on the radio, and the personality that runs the morning time in North Star Village and surrounding areas is DJ Jack The Rapper. DriveTime radio always has a local and regional need for a Johnny on-the-spot report, with news and traffic updates you can use in the morning and in the evening.

Noelle wants to look over some new client notes and return some phone calls this morning. Many of his contacts will be attending the Harvest Moon Masquerade Ball tonight, Halloween night. Noelle has no interest in partying but prefers Halloween celebrations more than Christmas and New Year's Eve. Wearing a mask at the Masquerade Ball is becoming more appealing as the time gets near.

Nickolas gets to the office after Noelle has arrived, but ahead of the 9am start time and the arrival of his co-workers. As soon as he gets settled in, the boss calls him into his office.

Nickolas enters Noelle's office stating, "Good morning Mr. Chance."

"Kingsly, I'm looking forward to your ideas on the car dealership in our meeting on Saturday. I won't bother you today, but I will remind you to visit the food truck Vendors and advertise our eMobile card processing department. I'm sure you know that I will be leaving early today. I promised Mr. Waterhouse I would Co-Host tonight's

Masquerade Ball and I want to be prepared. I trust you to work a full day, even though you have a Halloween dance, or something planned with your kids."

Nickolas perks up at the mention of Price Waterhouse and states, "Mr. Waterhouse is a wonderful man. I'm sure you will have a good time tonight. It's my hope to be able to attend his annual Community Christmas party on Saturday, December 14th."

Noelle Chance bellows out, "Christmas! Already. No way! That commercial monstrosity begins earlier each year. Christmas is nothing more than another opportunity to get my money. They can get your money Kingsly. Mines... no way!

Nickolas Kingsly, who is referred to by co-workers as Saint Nick, will not allow Mr. No to steal his joy. He refuses to be swayed by negativity, having heard the commercial Christmas rant before. To his credit, Saint Nick has not lost his temper or his job and has kept the peace in these confrontations. Instead of exasperation, Nickolas shows patience to be a virtue, and when the opportunity arises, he will state the reason for the Season, is the birth of Jesus Christ on earth.

Noelle Oscar Chance Jr., lives by the motto, 'Be great today', but he says it with no regard for his fellow man or with any fear of God's judgment. Although Halloween is not significant to him, neither is the oncoming Holiday Season. He bases his life and happiness on money, which has become his god, and he's famous for his catch-phrase, *NO WAY*!

The alter ego of Noelle has earned his nickname Mr. No. He is well known by his actions in past Holiday Seasons and shows indifference to all things Christmas. Mr. No is a North Star Village legend. Noelle Oscar Chance Jr. is Ebenezer Scrooge, the joy stealing character from Charles Dickens, 'A Christmas Story' but he is a Black man.

Noelle is the Black Ebenezer Scrooge, who will tell anyone who listens that Christmas is a Pagan ritual; not understanding the word pagan means to go against Christianity. He has lost faith in God and now believes in pragmatic theology, to explain the mysteries of life and death. He has a cold heart that forgets Christmas is the original celebration and the Pagan ritual is to question the birth of Jesus, as the son of God, conceived by the Holy Spirit to Mary and her husband Joseph.

Noelle Jr., subscribes to manmade logic to understand the mysterious power of God, not caring for much of anything. He loves his mother and father, willingly helping them to pay their living expenses at Wellness Springs Assisted Living Center.

He doesn't show his love outwardly, but he loves his family and the family prays for him, especially older sister Holly Evergreen. The Kingsly family knows faith is the substance of things hoped for, the evidence of things unseen and they know without faith, it is impossible to please God.

Noelle Oscar Chance Jr., is falling into the ways of the world and takes for granted the teachings of his Parents, who led by the example of prayer, believing if you train up a child in the way he should go, when he is older, he will not depart from these ways.

Noelle could not steal the joy from Nickolas Kingsly, who started this day by cooking breakfast for his family and plans to end the day cooking dinner for the love of his life; his wife.

The morning passes quickly at the office of N. O. Chance Financial Agency. Noelle is ready to leave the office and spend the whole afternoon with his parents, but before he does, he visits Nickolas and says, "Kingsly, I'm done, I'm sure you will finish the work we set out to do today, and even though it is Halloween, I expect a full day's work from you and the staff."

Nickolas says, "Mr. Chance, the Staff and I will continue to work hard. Enjoy your day and night."

"I would rather work, but there's always tomorrow," says the boss. "It will get here soon enough. Kingsly, I'm leaving you in charge. Goodbye."

Nickolas follows the boss to the door and waves goodbye, watching him leave the building and the parking lot, then he gets on the intercom and states, "Ladies and Gentlemen, it's lunchtime."

There's a saying; when the cat's away, the mice will play, but this room is full of cool cats who know how to play the game of cat and mouse at the N. O. Chance Financial Agency. For them Nickolas Kingsly is Top cat. Saint Nick has a winning philosophy to work hard and play hard, which makes tough days doable, and this day blow by on a successful breeze.

"Thank you for your work today," Nickolas says to the Staff gathered for the end of day meeting. "Please drive carefully tonight, look out for children Trick or Treating and if you are walking with them, remember to have flashlights.

"Mr. Chance is Co-Host of the Harvest Moon Masquerade Ball tonight, which is why he left earlier. If anyone is going to the Ball, don't be surprised to see him. If there are no questions, we can leave."

There are no questions. Nickolas says, "Goodnight guys, see you on Monday." He is eager to get home and move onto his dinner plan for two. A feeling of confidence moves in, a momentum created by accomplishments that demand a celebration.

Nickolas Kingsly can sense the buzz of excitement in the air because of Halloween. It is easy to see when you look at all the people that seem to be in a hurry to get home or wherever they are going. Misery loves company and tonight it will have the once-a-year Halloween companion to run with in cities and towns across the U.S.A. But the Season of wicked things will close at midnight.

Nickolas listens to the great American Art form, known as Jazz, flowing in sonic excellence from the car radio. Jazz was founded by African Americans in the late 1800s and early 1900s in New Orleans, Louisiana, becoming a noted American music form during the 1920s Jazz Age.

Life is bustling outside his windshield, and art imitates life when 'Life in The City' plays in the background. People look like they have somewhere to go. The Isley Brothers song adds poetic justice to the ride home for Nickolas.

"Daddy is home," Christopher yells as the van pulls into the driveway, and he runs to the front door to open it just as his father reaches for the doorknob and says, "Daddy you are right on time to see me put on my costume."

"No," says Mom, "let's eat first and then we all can get on with the festivities."

"Christopher Timothy," says Daddy, "Mom is taking me out Trick or Treating."

Mary, kissing her husband hello says, "Nick, you can get washed up and catch up to us. I have a chef salad prepared for us. Everyone else is eating pizza and French fries."

Nickolas does his happy dance and states proudly, "I'm ready to celebrate a good day."

Simon says, "Hey Dad, pizza, fries and salad is cool," but he exaggerates while looking at the dinner gift basket, "is this for us?"

Nickolas says, "Son, this dinner basket is just for two. I'm cooking spaghetti and meatballs for your mom and me." Nickolas looks directly at his two oldest and says, "Marion, how's your night shaping up? Are you and Simon all set?"

Marion replies, "Yes Dad, Aunt Marie and Stefanie are going to my company party. Auntie is picking us up here, then we're going to spend the night with them. Uncle Matt is going to take MJ out Trick or Treating around their neighborhood."

Mary interrupts the conversation, "All right everyone listen, time is moving fast. Marion, I want you and Simon to make sure you have everything you need to spend the night with your aunt. She will be here to pick you guys up in about 30 minutes."

The family gathers to eat. Mom and Dad have their chef salad and enjoy the company of all their children together once again at the kitchen table with smiles, laughter, and easy conversations.

Christopher jumps up from his seat and into a Karate stance, breaking up the love festival to ask a question. "Is it time yet? Can I put on my costume?"

Mary replies, "Yes Chris, get dressed and I will too. We'll leave your dad in the kitchen so he can get started with our dinner, but we'll eat after I take you out for Trick or Treat."

Nickolas is proud to prepare meals when he can, and he is a good cook. The wine is chilling in anticipation of an intimate connection of the 5-senses; touch, taste, smell, sight, sound, and a 6$^{th}$ sense of each other's needs—quite a combination indeed.

Dinner for two simmers on the stove in a house of love, where two hearts beat as one for the man of team Kingsly. The object of his desire enters the room, walking sensually through the steam rising from the pots on the stove.

Mary is stunning, although dressed comfortably in a white Karate outfit—beauty is in the eye of the beholder—but she is always stylish. Often sewing her own clothes, creating an outfit to play sidekick to Christopher's little Jim Kelley costume, makes her the coolest Mom on the block.

Marion takes pictures of these priceless moments, asking all to smile for the camera.

The Spaghetti dinner passes with flying colors. "Nick, dinner smells delicious," motioning Marion to give her the camera. Proud Mary continues to say, "Okay guys, I want a picture of you all in costume. Everyone please stand by the front door."

Marion gets in the middle of her brothers and says, "Mom just line up my face in the square and tap the screen."

Mom takes pictures, then Marion says, "Mom you took some good pictures, and you look cute, let me take a picture of you, Karate girl."

Mom gets the Star treatment as she takes several pictures by herself and more with each of her children. The whole gang is at the front door looking at the shots they like when the doorbell rings, temporarily stopping the fun. It's Wonder Woman and Super Girl.

Aunt Marie and her daughter Stephanie, who are dressed as Wonder Woman and Super Girl, are at the door. All are glad to see each other, and Marion continues taking pictures.

"Stephanie, you look great," says Uncle Nickolas, "and it's official. Wonder Woman is in the house," he says greeting his sister-in-law Marie.

Marie replies, "Hey Niko," the nickname she gave her Brother-in-law, "Matt and MJ say hello. They're staying home and Trick or Treating in our neighborhood, but Matt wants me to tell you that they will enter the Metroplex Mall costume contest on Saturday. They will be dressed as the Green Hornet and Kato and they look cute, so maybe they'll win a prize."

Aunt Marie looks at Christopher in his costume and says, "Man, you came straight out of a comic book," giving her nephew a high five.

"Niko," Marie says in a high pitch voice, "dinner smells great. Okay Mary, what do you have cooking for tonight?"

Mary answers with the Wonder Woman signature stance, arms crossed at the wrist, in front of her face and says, "Dinner for two!"

"Wow!" Marie replies laughing out loud, "I had to ask. That sounds great for you two. Enjoy your night. We will bring Simon back tomorrow and get Marion to work on time. Simon, please load your bags in the back of my truck.

"Bye Sis," said with a hug. "I plan on being home and sleep by midnight, but we're going to have fun!"

Nickolas pulls out two small gift bags, each with some candy and a palm sized booklet titled, 'Personal Bible Verses of Comfort', and hands them to his sister-in-law.

Marie gives one to Stephanie and the other to MJ, then waving across the room he says "Steph, thank you for going out tonight with Simon and Marion."

Nickolas, turning back to Marie says, "Thank you, for taking Marion to her Company Halloween party and for letting both of them spend the night with you."

"It's cool Saint Niko. You're welcome," Marie replies, "I love my niece and nephew." Then taking notice of the Personal Bible in the bag, she opens it and reads a passage out loud saying,

"Blessed are they that hear the word of God and keep it. Book of Luke, Chapter 11 Verse 28.

"I shouldn't eat the candy, but this is a great treat Niko, let me have two so I can give one to Matt."

"I have plenty. Please give one to Matt or should I say the Green Hornet," she said as they both laugh.

"I will set up a little table in the front of the house," says Nickolas, "and pass out these little see through bags of candy with the Personal Bible inside."

"That's a good idea, Niko, but I'm disappointed not to see you in a costume. I'm sure we'll see the famous Christmas hat and coat of Saint Nick this Christmas.

"And by the way, my sister is smiling right now. I don't think you'll have to hang any mistletoe."

Mary interrupts her sister to say, "Baebee,... hang all the mistletoe!"

Aunt Marie is dressed as Wonder Woman and niece Stephanie is dressed as Super Girl. Brother, and Sister Kingsly are dressed alike as old school soul Train Dancers and this group happily drives off, as Nickolas, Mary, and Christopher wave goodbye!

Christopher then says, "Mommy, is it time for us to leave?"

"Yes, my child, my Karate champion," says Mom dressed as Karate Girl, "but I want you to go to the bathroom before we leave, then we will catch up to our neighbors."

A warm kiss separates husband and wife, as mother and child go out with the Smith, Johnson, and Bingham families, who also wave to Nickolas when their children run down the sidewalk to his table. The boys and the girls give Christopher a high five, and then they say, "Thank you Mr. Kingsly," as they get their candy bags and run back down the sidewalk to the next house.

The Kingsly house was one of the first stops on their walk around the neighborhood, Nickolas smiles and waves goodbye, noticing all the children have happy costumes on, and he's happy to see some dads walking with the group.

Time passes by quickly. Quite a few children visit Nickolas, keeping him busy. Their parents were happy to see the palm size, 'Personal Bible Verses of Comfort' booklet in their candy bag, smiling and saying thank you.

One of the boys out Trick or Treating stopped by the table Nickolas has set up, and he takes off his werewolf mask to ask what was inside of the booklet.

Nickolas replies, "Young man, inside this booklet are words of inspiration from God, in the form of Bible verses chosen to help anyone through days and nights when they feel like a werewolf."

The young teen says, "I'm not a werewolf."

Nickolas states in a teaching manner, "With that werewolf mask on, you might feel like scaring people and do things that you really don't want to do."

The young teen says, "Sir, when I was younger, I wore all good guy costumes."

"I'm sure you did," Nickolas says as two more young boys come over to the table.

"Trick or Treat!" they say in unison. The three boys are together.

Nickolas answers them, saying, "Good evening guys, I have a treat for you that you can share with family and friends," as he places his candy bags inside their treat bags. "My name is Mr. Nickolas Kingsly. What are your names?"

"My name is Michael."

"My name is Jaime."

The one who walked up first says, "My name is Ben."

The three boys are best friends who have decided to walk around with scary werewolf masks on. They were determined to put the fright into fright night, but Michael and Jaime take their masks off, just like Ben has done and they say, "Mr. Kingsly do you have a son named Simon?"

"Yes, I do guys," is the reply from Nickolas.

"He's our Youth Track Team Coach," said in unison, "please tell him we were here."

Ben says, "Sir, we owe you an apology. We came by to scare you," Ben continues, "the other kids were all wrong. They said you didn't have any candy and that you were no fun."

Nickolas says, "That's okay. I thought you boys were bad guys wearing those masks. Some people may think I'm no fun because I talk about treating your neighbor good and being kind to one another.

"I talk about doing good things in your life, even on a Halloween night, when there are too many people out trying to be scary because they think that is fun. But you boys are growing up and will be young men soon. We have to talk to each other and make up our own minds about people; I want you guys to remember not to judge people by the way they look."

The young boys nod their heads in agreement and shake hands as they say, "Bye! Mr. Kingsly."

Nickolas notices they don't put their werewolf masks back on as they walk down the street.

Mother and son make it back home and say they had a fun filled walk through the community. Christopher is happy and tired with a bagful of candy, and stories about the houses he visited, including the scary ones they just walked past.

Nickolas wonders if the three boys that stopped and talked to him are telling stories of their night with the same joy as his son. Then Mary says, "I'm going to take a shower before our dinner date."

Father and son enjoy telling each other of the costumes they saw, the good ones and not so good ones. Christopher is happy to hear other children enjoyed the Kingsly family table display and special candy bags.

He takes a seat on the couch and says, "Dad, we did good tonight. It looks like you passed out a lot of candy bags. They're almost all gone."

Nickolas hugs his youngest and says, "TT we wanted to do good, and I believe we did. I even met some boys that know Simon. Their names were Ben, Michael, and Jaime." Nickolas continues to tell his story about the boys walking around with werewolf masks on to scare people, and when they came down the street, he didn't know what to expect.

"Ben took his mask off, walked up to the table and asked about the little Bible. It didn't take long for the other boys to come over, and they both took off their masks. Nickolas continues saying, "The three of them were respectful young men. We talked about their mask and how that image could get them to act in a bad way.

"They may have agreed with me, I don't know, but I did notice they didn't put their masks back on when they left."

Story time goes on and on, each enjoying one another's company.

Mary makes her way back into the room and announces that she has pictures from Marion's Halloween party and shows them to Nickolas and Christopher from her cellphone.

"They look like they're having fun," says Nickolas.

Christopher says, "Dad, I don't see anyone with scary masks on."

Mary laughs and says, "Guys, wait a minute." Looking at her youngest son, still in his Jim Kelly costume, and says, "Man, what kind of comic book are you coming out of?"

Nickolas; trying not to laugh, just looks at his wife with a straight face.

Christopher tries not to laugh but starts laughing and laughing. The kind of laugh kids do when they are overtired.

Dad says, "All right Mommy, that was a little funny."

Mary says, "all right, I'LL tell you what ain't funny at all. And that is... I .. am... hungry..."

"Honey, the table is set," Nickolas says, "please start without me. Just warm up the bread and I will catch up to you after I get TT in the shower and into bed.

"Alright Mama's baby, you can bring your candy bag over here. I'm going to keep it. You've had enough for tonight. We will go through the bag tomorrow and see what you can keep."

"Ok," says Christopher, while giving Mom a big hug. "Mommy, thank you for taking me out Trick or Treating. Good night."

Mary has a big smile on her face when she says, "Thank you love bug for making it such a fun night. Make sure you brush your teeth before you take a shower."

Mary yells out, "Simon just sent me a text message. He says everything is fine and they're having lots of fun," as father and son leave the living room.

Nickolas has done more than just cook dinner. He has set up an ambience of peace and love for his off Broadway play he calls candlelight and you.

"Turn on the stereo honey, it's set to the quiet storm of a slow jamz radio show. "Don't mind the candles on the table. I want to light them when I get back," he yells out to his wife.

Christopher is tired and he moves fast, getting in and out of the shower and into his bed. He's ready for sleep, too tired to miss his brother, who will spend the night at his Aunt and Uncles house.

Tiny Timothy is growing up. "Goodnight Dad. Enjoy your dinner," he says.

Nickolas reminds his son to pray, then tucks him into bed before saying, "Goodnight, Chris."

Parents can make all the plans they want to make to spend time alone, but those plans always seem to meet with some other pressing matter of parenting and get postponed. But tonight's plan for dinner for two moves, like clockwork.

Don't you love it when a good plan comes together?

"Christopher is all set," Nickolas says on his return to the Dining Room.

Two hearts beat faster with the adrenalin of love flowing through their veins, and they believe this moment will lead to moments of uninterrupted happiness and togetherness. On this night, the midnight bells will ring in the saints, and the saints of goodness will come marching in over Halloween's night of doom and gloom.

Nickolas and Mary Kingsly; from this moment and on towards

midnight, keep hope alive and nurture a man's love for a woman and a woman's love for a man, on into a new day and beyond.

Nickolas walks into a Dining Room full of the ambience of soft music, candlelight, and the look of love from the face of his wife, which chases away the weight of the world.

Mary, speaking through a beautiful smile says, "Honey, I warmed up the bread and poured us a glass of wine. I decided to wait for you after talking to Stephanie.

"She called to tell us they are home safe, and all enjoyed the night. She said the Halloween party was fun, and she enjoyed being with Simon and Marion."

Nickolas replies, "Marie said they would get home early. It's good to know they are safe."

"So now let's both relax and eat," says Mary. "You light those candles, and I will fix our plates."

Simple pleasures are the best and a simple spaghetti dinner for two tastes great, made even better by soft music, candlelight, chilled wine, and a tasty desert, which can turn minutes into an hour.

"Mary, you can relax in the Living Room. I will clean up the kitchen but be careful not to fall asleep in the chair. The next dance is mine," says Nickolas.

The radio plays a song that becomes one with the moments of the day and then the candlelight flickers.

Nickolas says, "Honey, I hear your song."

*If You Play Your Cards Right* by Alicia Myers flows in the background, then Nickolas, who has played his cards right all day, steps into the groove of this slow jam and says, "Mrs. Mary Kingsly, may I have this dance?"

"Happy wife, happy life."

Mary floats out of the chair and into her husband's waiting arms, where a strong heartbeat is easily found. One body to another body, soon moving to the beat of their own drum.

Nickolas and Mary get lost in their passion, and the beautiful song plays on and on. Time standing still within their slow dance until Nickolas spins his wife around into a dip, followed by a kiss.

It's time to say goodnight to a good day, and this couple will continue to love one another and pray together for the refreshed blessings of a new day.

Halloween promotes a fright night of evil, but as the devil works, so do those who believe in God, prayer and the works of faith and praise.

*Now I lay me down to sleep, I pray the Lord, my soul to keep on this night.* No tricks, just treats.

# Chapter 4

## *Lost In The Masquerade*

### Judah

*The heavens declare the glory of God; and the firmament sheweth his handiwork.*

*—Psalm 19:1*

"Hello Mr. Chance. Welcome to Wellness Springs," is the enthusiastic greeting from Mrs. Luveen Policy, an elegant, tall, well-dressed woman, with a pretty and well-defined face.

Mrs. Policy is well known for hiring quality personnel. Her beautiful silver hair adds a personal touch with the tenants of Wellness Springs. It could be said that she runs a tight ship, which impresses the hard to please Noelle Chance Jr.

"Hello to you Mrs. Policy. I am here to see my parents. I trust everything financial is up to date?"

Luveen Policy politely responds, "Mr. Chance, your parents seem to be happy here. We certainly enjoy them, as do our other tenants. I am scheduled to meet them after the oncoming Holiday Season to go over plans for the New Year, but everything financial is up to date."

Noelle Chance nods in agreement and before he speaks, Luveen Policy interjects, "You and your sister Holly should be proud of your efforts here to honor your parents. You are doing a very good job. Enjoy your visit Mr. Chance."

*Mr. Chance is my daddy's name, and he sure has worked hard enough to retire in comfort.* No time for me to think about that Noelle thinks to himself, while walking through the Townhouse like apartment complex of Noelle Chance Sr., and the former Isabella Queenfield, now Mrs. Noelle Oscar Chance Sr.

Although he has a key and called from the car, Noelle rings the doorbell. Mom, seeing her son through the security peephole, swings open the door to greet him with a hug and smile, which always brings delight to the otherwise dour face of Noelle Jr.

"It is great to see you, son. It's been too long," says Mother Chance. "Your father is expecting you and should be right back from the activity room. He keeps busy fixing things in the building."

"Mom, how do you feel? You look great!" Noelle says affectionately.

Mother Chance says, "I feel fine, just getting older kiddo! I thank the Lord for life, health, and strength. Sit down and catch me up on your life. What are you doing these days?" said while she moves the conversation into the living room.

Noelle proudly reports, "Mom, I work and keep to myself. I just picked up North Star Village Cadillac Dealership as a new client, and oh yeah! I won $1000 dollars at the Bella Super Bingo!"

Isabella Chance reaches out for her son's hand and gives a passionate response saying, "You are a successful businessman and I try to stay out of your affairs, but I want to make sure you give back.

"Please try to find a good Church to attend regularly and put your great heart to work for the Lord. Son, I know I'm preaching at you again, but be mindful of your blessings, and you will gain joyfulness.

"I don't want you to settle. I pray you won't be alone. I'm not so old that I can't remember a time when you were happy."

Noelle Chance has slipped into an uncomfortable place that money could not fix, or work could not hide, he begins to think.

*Mr. Waterhouse mentioned Millicent also,* slipping further, farther into the darkness of a faded painful memory, which time tries to bury, but only God can truly heal.

Once upon a time, this place was love for Millicent Manor and before Noelle Jr., could explore the rare emotions beginning to surface, Isabella Chance does what mothers all around the world do. She moves on effortlessly to another subject.

"Noelle, your sister tells me you are going to the Masquerade Ball tonight, so I know you don't have a lot of time to be with us today and that's all right," says Mother Chance. "I'm so glad you are going out tonight. You should know that you can't just work. You will wear yourself out."

Noelle responds in a carefree manner saying, "Mom, I'm going to the Masquerade Ball only to help Mr. Waterhouse. I guess people are excited for the adult Halloween party," but he can tell his mother has something else on her mind and asks bluntly, "Mom, what's the matter?"

Isabella Chance loves her husband and both of her children have always known this. She speaks lovingly saying, "I want you to talk to your father about his health man to man and find out how he feels. The phone calls are nice, but you're not here much and I want you to be closer to us this Christmas. Your father loves you and I know you love him."

Noelle snaps out of his daze and speaks to eliminate the sudden concern he hears in his mother's voice saying, "Mom, I will talk to

Dad, and I will make every effort to be with you guys more during this Christmas; even though, this Christmas is beginning way too soon."

Noelle glances toward the front door and it seemingly begins to brighten. On cue Mr. Noelle Chance Sr., opens the door and immediately greets his beloved son, gladly saying, "There he is."

Noelle, the son, rises to greet his father and says, "Hey Dad."

Daddy Chance says, "Bella," which is his loving nickname for his wife Isabella, "take a good look at our son. Mr. No, has finally said yes!"

Noelle Jr. looks like his dad, minus the brightness that shines through from the heart.

Mom says, "Yes, is not all he said. He had bingo in the big game at the Casino, and he said, 'yes' to Mr. Waterhouse to be a host tonight at the Masquerade ball."

"Tonight!" Daddy Chance says, "son, that is outstanding!"

Noelle Jr., pointedly states, "I was surprised because it was the last game of the night."

Dad continues, "Noelle, winning is always a good feeling but really, I'm happy that you're going out to have some fun, and at the same time help Mr. Waterhouse, who has been a blessing to you and to this family.

"Hey son let's eat lunch. Mom has some cubed steak and gravy to put over some rice. How's that sound to you?" said with the authority of a doctor.

Daddy Chance has a rich alto voice and speaks with deep intonation and although he walks with a slight limp from a bullet leg wound received; with Purple Heart, from the Vietnam War, he gets around with a pep in his step. Mr. Noelle Oscar Chance Sr., is a distinguished man, as was his father; Grandfather Avery O. Chance; rest in peace, who served with Honor in World War II.

"Dad, that meal sounds like what the doctor ordered. Let's eat."

"Dad, will you show me again how to tie a bowtie," Noelle the son says. He's now ready to fulfill his promise for the man-to-man talk, and time slows down as the taste of a Mom cooked meal settles down in the belly.

Noelle Jr., says, "Dad, you look amazing at 75 years old. Time is moving on and I'm sorry for not being here more often."

Daddy Chance smiles and replies, "I know you work hard son. I'm proud of you. I just want you to be happy. I know your sister loves you. I'm proud of you both, but it's important that you have each other to hold on to in this life, because your mother and I won't be around forever."

Noelle Jr., protests, but Dad makes a gesture to be patient and doesn't interrupt as he continues speaking, saying, "Listen El," the nickname he gave his son, "I want you to have the love of a good woman. That love will empower you and take care of you. Don't give up on love and don't give up on God. He will never give up on you."

Determined to change the subject, Noelle Jr. says, "Dad! wait a minute. It's all right for you to slow down a little bit. I want to make sure that you are keeping up with your scheduled doctor visits and that you listen to your body. Please don't ignore a pain sign or something unusual that goes on with your body, okay?"

Noelle Jr., continues, "Dad, you and Mom have done great by me, and I know Holly would say the same thing. As for love Dad, I love making money and I refuse to be distracted. Please don't waste any energy wondering about me," said, rising out of his chair. Looking out the window, unknowingly towards the hills for help that comes, as he mentions, there is a strained relationship with the Almighty.

Noelle Jr. continues to talk, and says, "Daddy, God knows my heart, but I see people who I question their place in life. There's no way I would live like they do," said with a now common lack of compassion and even less compulsion to help.

Noelle the son is on a roll. The talk to help the father has turned out to be a talk to help the son, and it has worked to open up hidden feelings that flow like a babbling brook.

The son turning back toward his dad and reveals a cold indifference when he says, "Dad, I say live and let live; I keep my emotions in check," Noelle Jr. chuckles.

"I've worked hard for everything I have Dad," says Noelle Jr., "I'm no fool, I have a low tolerance for lazy people, beggars, complainers and the ignorant, because I have faith in working. Now, as many times as you and Mom have taken me to Church, I think that'll preach."

Noelle Sr. seizes this opportunity to speak life to his son saying, "El, God will not be mocked. You could preach one day, remember even a donkey has spoken for God."

Noelle Jr., is all too glad to dramatically respond, "Dad! Mr. Noelle Oscar Chance Sr. there is no way that I would ever, ever, ever be a preacher," said in a full belly laugh.

Mr. Noelle Oscar Chance Sr. rises as if lifted out of his chair to greet his wife entering the room with a Bespoke blue tuxedo for her son to wear to the Masquerade Ball. Mom insisted on freshening up the shirt and tuxedo for Noelle Jr. He is happy to show off his full-face mask.

Daddy Chance, looking on admiringly says, "El this tuxedo is 5-star, but in the matters of your heart, there's some work that must be done. You have been running from your heart since your days with that girl you loved so much! What was her name, Bella?"

"Her name was Millicent Manor," says Mother Chance.

Daddy Chance remembers her name and face saying, "Who could forget a name like that! I remember she was a beautiful girl, inside and outside."

Mother Chance says, "Milli is married now. She had to move on from a broken heart. I think she loved you truly, my son," looking admiringly at Noelle Jr. "Milli is a sweetheart. She still contacts me for my birthday and other times of the year, especially Christmas."

"Mom!" Noelle Jr. says with exasperation, "let's get through Halloween, get to Veterans Day, then the man-made feast fest called

Thanksgiving, and the dreaded Black Friday weekend; with all of its accompanying annoyances, then we can celebrate the commercial success that Christmas is."

Isabella Chance gently but firmly speaks, "My son, that time of your life is over. Everyone has moved on, but you still seem to be so bitter. It's time to get better."

Noelle Jr. states defiantly, "I am not bitter! I am better... and I really do appreciate you guys worrying about me, but don't continue in this way. I will tell you again, I am all right. I have everything I need, and I don't need anyone to mess that up."

Noelle Jr. looks directly into his parents' eyes, sensing he may have gone a little overboard. He tries to ease the tension, fully expecting a harsh comeback because of his Christmas rant, but none comes. Then he calmly says, "I don't need anyone else because I have you guys. I love you, but I have to leave now to be on time. I promised Mr. Waterhouse that I would arrive early and go over my speech since I am the co-host."

Noelle Jr. thinks he has regained control, but what happened instead reminds him of the unexpectedness of life.

Daddy Chance clutches his chest and bends over as if he is in great pain. The son now chastises himself for being so callous and yells out, "Daddy! What's wrong?"

For the first time in his adult life, Noelle the son gets a scared feeling from the reality that says we are not in control and the next moments are unknown.

Noelle Jr. immediately panics. Doom shoots through his mind. *What can I do? I don't want to lose my daddy.*

Panic is not action. It's a waste of time when action is needed and every second counts. Prayer will lead you to listen for and lean on the voice of God, who will tell you what to do in an instant.

Noelle Jr. returns to a child-like state, uttering in bewilderment, "What's the matter Daddy," now getting more confused. Then he looks into his mother's face and cannot tell if she is laughing or crying. Panic has shut down his mind and stopped him in his tracks. This moment has chilled his soul into doing nothing. Mr. cool is totally shook and begins to feel his strength leaving him.

Noelle thinks, let me call for help and then just as suddenly as Daddy Chance bent over, he rises with his hand over his heart and says to his loving wife, "Bella! Bella! Isabella Precious Queenfield... this is the big one honey!" Fred G. Sanford style

Staggering around the room and he says, "Baebee! this is the big one... this is my big finish," and sings a song by The Main Ingredient, 'Everybody Plays The Fool.'

"*Listen baby!*
*Everybody plays the fool.*
*You're no exception to the rule,*
*maybe factual maybe cruel...*
*I ain't lying...*
*but everybody plays the fool...*"

Closing this Doo Wop session with an amazing voice that drags out the word fool... ouu ouu ouu...

Noelle Jr., who now has his mouth wide open, closes it to say, "It is entirely possible that I deserved that!"

Mommy and Daddy Chance, now hugging, say in unison, "Christmas is forever the celebration of Jesus Christ being born on Earth, don't ever forget that again."

"I can't tell if you guys planned that, but I will spend more time here with you but promise me you won't scare me like that again," says Noelle Jr. who has grown cold as ice.

It is well known around town, as his nickname Mr. No is infamous. In his younger days, he was cool and fun to be around. That was before his insatiable quest to be financially successful.

Mother and Daddy Chance have planted a seed of redemption to reclaim their recluse son, who up to now, refuses to receive a rebirth or to repent. The prayer is love will help him speak life in the face of trials and tribulations that will continually come forth.

Holly will be proud of herself for encouraging her brother to get dressed at their parents' home when she hears the story of the Main Ingredients.

Noelle feels the anticipation building for a Halloween Night Masquerade Ball, but he could not know the path he is on, leads to a life-changing intersection. At this crossroad, he must choose a road that will save his life, or he will lose his soul and his life.

He strikes a pose unexpectedly. As he sees himself looking back from the mirror, Noelle only looks for the superficial. He's impressive in a tuxedo that works hard to hide his rough edges.

Noelle Chance Jr. is handsome once again and can fool most any observer until he opens his mouth. That reveals he is cold, but maybe tonight will be different, because the faces will be covered by an actual mask. He has chosen a brilliant mask to enhance the masquerade.

A beautiful sunset meets dusk in a magnificent transfer of daytime turning into night, which on this occasion will reveal a Super Moon; bright and full, empowering the dreams of surrounding clouds that would be dark, if not enlightened.

The clouds are soon to be seen dancing in moonlit unison, mirrored by the uncanny timing of couples in masks, who masquerade while dancing through the night. Halloween and evil; thought to be serendipity, give into the Creators' Will to present a new day, a premise revealed at midnight, moving clouds and humans from darkness into the light of All Saint's Day.

The grand sights, elegance and excitement of a Black-Tie event are framed by the Big Sky Ballroom inside the Palisades Hotel and Conference Center—the Downtown destination for the RSVP guests of the eighth annual North Star Village, Harvest Moon Masquerade Ball.

RSVP is the acronym for the phrase Répondez s'il vous plait, which is French, meaning 'Please respond' as each attendee must do.

Tickets are $100 single or double, if married. Proceeds will go to the Charity Fund program and help the 'Fight Family Hunger' campaign.

*Please consider private donations and/or volunteering to staff our Christmas and New Year's Day family dinner events, organized by Mr. Price Waterhouse and the North Star Village (NSV) social service workers,* says the writing on the back of the tickets.

Noelle is the first Volunteer to appear. Driving up, he immediately observes the Valet parking attendants, quietly looking at their faces for a trace of his former partner Mr. Khole Cashe.

Noelle thinks of the frightful encounter with the Valet attendant at the Bella Bella Casino, but all of that is quickly replaced with peace when he hears the pleasant sound of symphony music.

Noelle uses hand signals that suggest a valet attendant to come to the car and when he receives his valet ticket, begins speaking in a gentle voice saying, "Young man, do you know what music is playing?"

The life lesson delivered by his parents, *that everybody plays the fool,* has softened his hard edges for the night. These movements become the first dance of the Masquerade Ball.

The captain of the valet parking attendants, whose nametag said Vellman, states eloquently, "You are hearing the story of great music. The baroque era symphony theater music and songs.

"We will play Bach, Corelli, Couperin, Handel, Purcell, Rameau, Scarlatti, Telemann, and Vivaldi."

Noelle is once again astounded by song and wonders if this theme will play through the night. An almost awkward silence is broken by the voice of Price Waterhouse, who greets both men with handshakes.

Speaking to the Captain of the Valet attendants says, "Thank you for your attention to detail, Vellman."

"You are welcome, Mr. Waterhouse. My staff is prepared to assist you and your guests. Have a great evening," replies Vellman.

Price Waterhouse walks into the Hotel lobby with Noelle

heading to the event space, then he says, "Thank you Noelle for helping me and my staff as Co-Host. That tuxedo looks great on you."

The look on Noelle's face is priceless. His normal frown falls when blushing turns into a smile. If there is a tug of war for his soul, the smile is winning the fight to emerge from gruff indifference. It's no contest tonight because his invigoration will give way to the masks of the Harvest Moon Masquerade Ball.

The Big Sky ballroom is a stunning picture of beauty, showcased with festive gold and red curtains, among twinkling lights and a unique ceiling that reveals the sky. The Ballroom features multiple skylights, which display the supernatural splendor of the Cosmos. An architectural wonder presented to be an interactive experience with the North Star in the sky.

The entrance doors are attended by two men dressed like Toy Soldiers performing their duties as security. Their resplendent appearance is reminiscent of the ambience of the world-famous Christmas classic, The Nutcracker Symphony.

Price Waterhouse is the perfect gracious host. He is dressed in a black tuxedo with coattails, gold vest and red bow tie on a white formal shirt. He is a regal figure along with Noelle Chance, as they greet each guest on arrival, directing them to pick up their reservations and table number.

The evening begins with a host dinner reception, featuring a splendid buffet assortment of heavy hors d'oeuvres and light desserts set up with serving stations. The Hosts are set up to the right of the ballroom doors, lending elegance to the harvest moon theme. Beautifully incorporated by gold and white napkins on red tablecloths, each table accented with a centerpiece of wildflowers arranged in red and gold colors.

Noelle is taken aback by the beauty of his sister Holly Evergreen, as she and her husband enter the reception area.

Greeting them both, Noelle states dramatically, "Holly, my goodness you look great! Mom and Dad must have taken a lot of pictures," as he hugs his sister and shakes the hand of his brother-in-law approvingly.

On this night, the gruff face and cold demeanor of Noelle Chance are hidden by the spirit of love, returning youthfulness to a once handsome face and warmth to a heart. The once bitten by love, now twice shy heart of Noelle Chance Jr., comes out of one mask and into another.

Noelle's Harvest Moon Masquerade Ball mask hides a poker face that needs a break from hiding all reactions in a self-imposed isolation.

Noelle, speaking to his brother-in-law says, "Mr. Jacob Evergreen Sr., you're looking fit. It seems you're keeping my sister happy. How are Jalisa and JJ doing?", said with uncommon charm, a once common trait.

Jacob Evergreen Sr. is a hard-working Maintenance Engineer for the department of Highways and Bridges of North Star Village and the apple of Holly's eye. He is refined, husky, and athletic with a baby face.

On any other night Holly and husband look younger than her brother, but not on this night. The Harvest Moon Masquerade Ball is a chance for Noelle to wear another mask, and the hope is this experience will open the door to a second chance.

Jacob Sr. responds to his charming Brother-in-law with a smile and says, "Thank you Noelle, you look better than ever. I want to tell you before I forget, JJ is putting his life in order, and he wants you to visit him at his apartment for dinner or dessert.

"He made me promise to tell you, and I have kept my promise. Please, stand in front of the table. Let me take a picture of sister and brother together, to remember this night. Fulfilling my second promise to my son."

The older sister Holly hugs her brother and says, "Once again Mr. No says yes! I'm proud of you El. Mom and dad told me you stopped by earlier today and they said I would be shocked when I saw you. They were right, brother. You look very nice in a blue tux."

"All right everybody, smile. Look at the camera," Jacob Sr. says, while taking more than 1 picture. Then he asks Noelle to take pictures of himself and his wife. Noelle gladly takes the cellphone and directs the happy couple, taking wonderful pictures.

Suddenly, Holly backs away from her husband and begins waving her hands. Then putting them on her hips, she says, "Everybody plays the fool."

Her husband chirps in saying, "Sometimes!"

Holly and Jacob Sr. point at Noelle and they all laugh and laugh together, oblivious to the arriving guests, who look on amused, clapping their hands in approval.

Holly says, "Let the good times roll."

Price Waterhouse is pleased to see siblings enjoying one another's company again, just like in the days when he took Noelle into his Mentorship program. Holly did not have an interest in the program, but Price Waterhouse would advise her on a career choice of business management and fashion design, which followed in the footsteps of her mother.

There was something magical in the air and good feelings abound. Holly thanks her brother and says, "We're ready to eat. See you at the table."

Noelle replies, "Mr. Waterhouse and I will be in soon. We're the first half of the reception team. Our replacements are on the way."

Holly waves goodbye and moves on to greet the awaiting arms of Price Waterhouse.

Noelle continues to greet the arriving guests with dignified curtesy, passing the first task as co-host. The next welcoming crew show up to relieve Price and Noelle Jr., who now can enter the Ballroom together and take in the grand setting.

A beautiful sight it is to see. An elegant buffet style food presentation, with serving tables of hot and cold hors d'oeuvre, temporarily covering what will be the dance floor.

The aromas tantalize everyone's appetite. Price and Noelle take their seats at the round tables set for eight. Their table includes Holly and Jacob, Mrs. Elizabeth Waterhouse and two members from the band named the *Instrumentalist*, who are part of tonight's entertainment.

Chef Lisa enters the ballroom and is given a microphone. She begins by welcoming everyone and proclaiming excitement for the opportunity to feed some of North Star Village's finest citizens.

The celebrity chef confidently congratulates everyone on being invited and returning the RSVP. She notes there is plenty of food for the 250 eating guests, and states she will assign the eating order for tables to enter the food area until each table has come forward, then everyone is on their own.

The California cool chef continues, speaking as if she is auditioning for a movie, stating, "The food tables will be taken down one-half hour before the dancing part of our night officially begins. This will be after our host Mr. Price Waterhouse and our co-host Mr. Noelle Chance Jr., addresses us."

Hearing his name spoken on the sound system surprises Noelle, who now remembers his second task of this night is to accompany Price Waterhouse on stage and address the attendees about the distribution of proceeds from the Ball and read the rules for the mask reveal at midnight.

Chef Lisa continues, "I am proud of our entire menu. You should enjoy what we have to offer. If you have a question about the food, please ask any of my staff. I suggest the California bay area inspired tropical fruit skewers, made of pineapple, papaya, and mango, along with the banana skewers, made with toasted coconut and brown sugar, and a sour cream dipping sauce." A selection that receives 'umm's' of approval.

Chef Lisa walks towards the food area and a spotlight follows her to a serving station, where she states, "Here we feature a Mediterranean dish. Hummus dip with pita, a hummus and tahini dip, surrounded by pita triangles and sliced cucumbers. Tahini is ground toasted sesame seeds, condensed into a sauce.

"I'm sure you will enjoy our assortment of beef, fish, and chicken dishes. Try the Southern specialty dish of shrimp and grits, inspired by Atlanta, Georgia." That receives an energetic applause.

"Thank you for your attention. We're ready to serve you. Please be seated until we pick your table. Now Reverend Avery Mann of North Star Village Baptist Church will pray to bless our food."

Price Waterhouse thanks chef Lisa, as she greets and selects his table and guests to be the first to move to the food area. Her assistant picks the front table on the opposite side of the Ballroom to join them. Great customer service, enhanced by smooth jazz music, provides a warm ambiance to begin a fun night of ballroom dancing.

The guests are completing their feast fest. Pleasant conversations can be heard person to person and table to table. Chef Lisa didn't mention dessert, because the Harvest Moon Ball tradition are usually assorted puddings and sorbet. Holly and Jacob hold hands and smile joyfully, watching intently for Price Waterhouse and Noelle, to make their way to the stage and address the ballroom.

*Did a star just twinkle at me?* Noelle thinks to himself as he takes in the view of the see-through ceiling, which exposes a beautiful night sky.

The DJ, who is also Master of Ceremony, asks for the attention of the room and introduces the host and co-host of the 8$^{th}$ annual Harvest Moon Masquerade Ball, Mr. Price Waterhouse and Mr. Noelle Chance Jr.

The attendees rise out of their seats in applause.

The pressure of the occasion suddenly hits Noelle. He immediately reverts to his cold and selfish heart, falling victim to his inner demon. His inner demon wants him to put on his favorite mask and act out the treachery of Doctor Jekyll and Mr. Hyde for a Halloween night spectacle.

"Oh! that's right, it's Halloween!," Noelle says under his breath, while balling his fists and gritting his teeth.

*Everyone is as conflicted as that fool employee of mine, Nickolas Kingsly, who is so holy he wants to shine his holy light on Halloween night*, Noelle thinks.

Noelle is on the verge of forgetting why he is on stage. He is losing it. His mind is confused, and he continues to have bad thoughts about Nickolas Kingsly.

Noelle mutters, "He better have the Cadillac dealership paperwork all ready for processing or his holiness can look for another job," getting lost in the moment.

Then he looks out into the audience and into the eyes of his sister Holly, who gives a thumbs up signal that reminds him of his task at hand.

Noelle instinctively waves to Holly. His new found charm and right mindset returns just in time to take the microphone and pleasantly say, "Good evening everyone. Welcome to the Harvest Moon Masquerade Ball. I want to thank the Masquerade Ball committee for putting together this beautiful presentation."

A few words on a note card come in handy, "My name is Noelle Chance Jr. I own the N. O. Chance Financial Agency and I'm proud to be your co-host tonight. It's my job to assist you as your event concierge, helping you with any questions you may have."

Noelle adjusts the microphone and continues to say, "Tonight is a great opportunity to get dressed up, have some fun and, at the same time, help the North Star Village Charity Services, with your financial support.

"I donate the price of tonight's ticket and $400.00 on behalf of the employees from my company. You are an impressive group here tonight. You look wonderful and on behalf of Mr. Waterhouse, thank you for selling out the tickets for the Harvest Moon Masquerade Ball in advance. Give yourselves a round of applause.

"Please don't stop your applause," continues Noelle, "I'm proud to introduce our host for the $8^{th}$ annual Harvest Masquerade Ball, Mr. Price Waterhouse."

"I thank you all for being here. This is our eighth time putting the ball together and this year we want to expand our outreach program," Price Waterhouse says with enthusiasm.

"There are just over 250 guests tonight. Please give yourselves another round of applause. I thank you for your support. The night is young, let's have some Halloween fun," said walking across the stage.

Then he points out his wife and while looking at her says, "This is my wife, Elizabeth. Please stand. I'm proud of this woman. It was Elizabeth who suggested we have a Masquerade Ball, and she showed me how to do it. Darling, thanks to you. Here we are."

More applause fills the air.

"Thank you, my love, for your vision," Price Waterhouse continues. "Thank you to our DJ and our MC, Casanova Cocoa Brown,"

Price sounds like the late legendary showman Ed Sullivan, when he says, "Ladies and gentlemen... The Instrumentalist, featuring Marvin Paul."

Applause rises to a cheer when the dance floor, now clear of serving stations, is illuminated.

Price Waterhouse then says, "On behalf of the North Star Village Harvest Moon Masquerade Ball, thank you for your support. Now everyone who purchased raffle tickets, please keep the ticket we gave you at the reception table. We will use the last three numbers on the bottom of the ticket to choose our winners."

Price Waterhouse is clearly enjoying himself. He continues, "Please listen to the few rules for tonight," and motions to Noelle to lead him down the stairs to the dancefloor.

Walking he says, "Ladies and gentlemen, there are no in and out of the Big Sky facility privileges. If you leave, there is a no return policy. We ask you to please stay in the foyer area, where you see couches and chairs and if you leave the ballroom, please remove your mask."

Holding his own mask over his head says, "Everyone please keep your mask on inside the Ballroom until our Midnight reveal. If you have any questions?" waving to the volunteer staff to come forth, "see a staff member. You can readily identify them by our glow in the dark wrist bands."

Price Waterhouse pauses, once again looking at his wife, then says, "Hey, are you guys ready to have fun? I want to dance with my wife. Remember, the raffle winners must be present to receive their prize and everyone will receive our swag bag as a thank you.

"I encourage everyone to freshen up after the midnight reveal and before you leave the hotel. Please take advantage of our presentation of coffee or tea and delicious slices of pound cakes, from one of our wonderful event sponsors, K. Sylvia's Coffee & Cakes. Govern yourselves accordingly."

Price Waterhouse turns towards the band and signals them they can begin playing. "The band will play twice tonight, each time followed by a short intermission. In the first intermission, DJ Casanova will play music until the band returns to the stage.

"After the band finishes its second show, DJ Casanova will take us through our midnight mask reveal and announce our three raffle winners. Now ladies and gentlemen, everyone put on your masks."

The entire volunteer staff gathers on the dance floor holding hands, then raises their arms over their heads so that everyone can see the bright neon purple glowing wristbands. They urge all to join them and begin dancing.

Singer Marvin Paul grabs everyone's attention, saying, "Good evening, ladies, and gents. We want to get you started with some Mid-Western style steppers music. Come on and move with your partner to the Instrumentalists' remix of the great song from the classic movie soundtrack of Saturday Night Fever—done by the Bee Gee's—titled 'More Than a Woman'."

The Ballroom is bathed in synchronized movements and the audience is seduced to step-walk under the pretty lights that highlight a variety of elegant dresses, gowns, suits, and masks.

Noelle has agreed to begin the night hosting the front entrance area of the Ballroom, and happily gives Price Waterhouse the opportunity to dance with his wife. She meets him on the way to their table and Mrs. Elizabeth Waterhouse compliments the host and co-host for their speeches.

"Gentlemen, you both did a wonderful job," says the wife of Price Waterhouse.

"Thank you," they say in unison, as Price leads his wife to the dancefloor.

Holly and Jacob Sr. tap Noelle on the shoulder, stopping him before he goes to the front reception area. They want to make sure he recognizes them in their masks and compliment him on his opening speech.

Holly says, "My dear brother, you did good tonight. I want you to find someone to dance with because all work and Mr. No play will make you a dull boy."

Jacob Sr. jumps in saying smartly, "Hey old man, watch me, just in case you have forgotten. Hold the lady's hand with your left hand, gently hold her by the waist with your right hand and lead her in the dance." laughing as he leads Holly away to the dancefloor.

"Oh yeah, there's one more thing," says Jacob Sr., "don't step on her foot."

Mr. No has become Mr. Yes. The Masquerade Ball is festive, if only for one night, like Cinderella had in her story and All Hallows Eve has when it meets All Saints' Day. Then, like every day meeting a new day, what comes next is unknown. Midnight is the end of a day, and midnight is the beginning of a day. The end of one is revealed onto another. It is within that duality of time, Noelle dances through the hourglass, lost in the Masquerade.

Noelle is an attentive host, dutifully making himself available at the entrance, even gently reminding those who would forget to place their mask back on their faces upon re-entering the Ballroom. The Instrumentalist featuring Marvin Paul, reaches the first intermission, serenaded by genuine applause. They leave the stage to take a break.

Noelle turns to the reception table to instruct the staff and says, "The band is good. We're at the halfway point of the Ball and everything is going along fine. Let's walk around the Ballroom to make ourselves available to the guests, then meet back here in 20 minutes to close the night."

The staff agrees to walk throughout the Ballroom. In that same moment, a woman wearing a mask, beautifully dressed in a purple and gold gown, appears and approaches Noelle. She nonchalantly asks him for the name of the band. Her voice sings in a familiar tone and her stature is reminiscent.

Noelle and the women in purple stare at each other through their masks; the pause has a dramatic effect. Noelle snaps out of the staring contest when their souls meet through the eye contact and unknowingly calls her Milli. Then says, "Excuse me Miss, you asked me the name of the band?"

The woman in purple moves away but nods her head yes to Noelle's question. He moves towards her, which is his second unintended dance of the night. Speaking gently, he says, "The name of the band is the Instrumentalist, featuring Marvin Paul. They will play again shortly."

"Thank you, Sir," she says and surprisingly continues to talk, "they are good. I would love to dance to their music, if I find the right partner." The woman in purple has quickly mesmerized Noelle Oscar Chance, and she talks even more, saying the sweetest things in the sweetest way. Her voice awakening memories of another woman from years past.

Noelle tries desperately to see through her mask. She continues, "Finding the right partner is so important," followed by a question in the form of a statement, "don't you agree?"

A soft, clear, powerfully feminine voice awakens emotions long dormant, thought to be dead and gone. Noelle is enchanted by this familiar yet unknown woman, nodding his head in agreement. He says, "Yes, I agree with you."

At that same moment, a man in a mask appears at the reception table. It's Price Waterhouse. He taps Noelle's shoulder, breaking the enchantment by causing Noelle to turn away from the captivating woman.

Price Waterhouse did not notice the conversation, and shakes Noelle's hand, "Thank you Noelle for being such a great help to me. The night is going great, and I may have danced too much," said while looking at his wife. "I will take over the front area. Please have some fun and find someone to dance with you."

Noelle turns and sees no trace of the women in purple, but the night is still young.

DJ Casanova Cocoa Brown has the dancefloor full of people doing their favorite line dances. The Electric Slide and the Cha-Cha slide. Noelle is off to the races trying to find the lady in purple but doesn't see her anywhere and begins to lose that loving feeling.

Once again, Holly and Jacob Sr. find Noelle strolling around the Ballroom, and they re-inspire him with positivity, laughter, and love. Being together with family and friends is a good thing.

"Mr. No says yes again," Holly says to her brother, having just left the dancefloor. "El, it's nice to see you out here walking around the Ballroom. I thought you were going to sit down all night!"

Jacob Sr. joins the conversation, "Noelle, that neon wristband you have on makes you easy to find, so if a mystery lady makes herself known to you, please dance with her," said as a joke, but Noelle is desperately seeking Susan, like he's a Noir era movie detective.

The husband, wife combo of team Evergreen enjoys the momentary shocked look that takes over Noelle's face. They don't know of the actual mystery surrounding the woman dressed in purple, who has awakened the emotional fire of Mr. No.

Brother-in-law can sense a difference in Noelle, not just a pleasant demeanor, but the look and moves of a man searching for someone. Jacob Sr. tries to find Noelle's eyes behind his mask, but he can't, then says, "Mr. No is on the hunt and looks like he is going to catch up to somebody."

Holly replies in a happy tone, "Noelle Chance Jr., I have a feeling you're going to meet someone nice tonight. Just let it flow and whatever you do, don't say no to a chance to dance."

"Honey," she says to her husband, "the band is playing our kind of music," said reaching for his hand. Holly also searches Noelle's mask for the eyes of her brother, and upon finding them says, "El, we will see you at the midnight reveal." Holly is pleased to see the mean-spirited demeanor of her brother has disappeared; not only hidden by a mask, but gone away, if only for one night.

The DJ completes a successful intermission with the audience, enjoying dancing to his music. The band plays softly to accompany the announcements. DJ Casanova Cocoa Brown has a radio announcer's smooth voice that commands the attention of all in the Ballroom when he turns into the Master of Ceremony and says, "All of the proceeds from tonight's raffle--from the sold-out Masquerade Ball—will help fund the North Star Village (NSV) Charity organizations and the NSV Community Christmas party, to be held Saturday December 19th, at the NSV Community Center.

"The band is ready for their final set. I will be back at midnight for the mask reveal and announce the winners of our raffle. There are three great prizes. Remember you must be in attendance to win."

DJ Casanova Cocoa Brown says, "Our third-place winner will receive a chauffeur driven night on the town for two, with dinner at the Northern Lights Steakhouse Restaurant and a movie at the NSV Showcase Cinemas.

"The second-place winner receives a luxury two-day weekend staycation, right here at the Big Sky Hotel.

"And our first-place prize is called *Hollywood Swinging*, which features a Los Angeles beach resort, two-day All-inclusive vacation for two."

DJ Casanova leaves the stage to walk along the dancefloor and turns up the energy in the room when he says, "Enjoy the rest of your night and remember, you just never know who you are talking to. I'm sure there will be some surprises out there. I hear the band is ready to play. Once again everyone, Let's give them a big applause for a wonderful first set and show them, we're ready for more.

"Give it up for the Instrumentalist, featuring Marvin Paul."

The Band plays magnificently, picking up where they had left off and time moves on to reveal the pieces of the puzzle. We are all a part of the puzzle determined by the Creator of time. In the beginning, all things unknown will be known, in due time.

Time waits for no one on earth, and time reveals the clock is running out for Noelle Chance Jr., who searches expectantly for the woman in purple. But oh where, oh where could she be? The man who believes in luck has no luck finding the woman in the purple dress. She brings back memories of a love lost, buried within a heart made bitter by self-destruction—within a choice to walk away from love.

How did these feelings, buried deep, packed away with purpose, get out tonight? Why did they reappear for the women in the purple dress? *It has been years since that relationship ended*, thinks Noelle, but the woman in purple stirred up feelings of a lover. Lost because of the love of money, Noelle gave her the nickname Milli. She was beautiful in every way. Her name is Millicent Eboni Manor.

Noelle Jr. was trapped within a pride-filled silent pain. How did he turn away from this woman? He saw life dimly through the glass he claimed to be the future, now stained by a cold heart. That cold heart broke the heart of a good woman, he calls Milli. The future for Noelle provided money and financial riches, but at the cost of a heart that now beats without passion or compassion—except his love for mother, father and sister.

Noelle has not recognized this walk through the shadow of the valley of death and would be alone, but God says He will never leave you or forsake you.

Noelle Oscar Chance Jr. taught as a child about the love of God, knows to love Him with all his heart, soul, mind, and strength. But his pursuit of happiness has led him to ignore the signs of worldly temptations, now lost in the masquerade.

A song wells up from the depths of his heart, taught to him in childhood, which sings out like a Canary in a Coalmine.

*Time is full of swift transition,*
*naught on earth unmoved can stand,*
*build your hopes on things eternal,*
*hold to God's unchanging hand,*
*you got to hold to his hand...*

*God's unchanging hand.*

Noelle builds his hope on things of the world, but for all of his selfishness, he has a great business sense. It's an uncanny talent given by the Creator of all things. Noelle senses that the mystery woman is good. This sense moves his feet and enlivens his heart. Reawakened in pursuit of a woman within the Harvest Moon Masquerade Ball, a dream that will end at midnight. The hour quickly approaches.

Noelle walks confidently along the Ballroom dancefloor full of couples skillfully hand dancing, step dancing and getting down.

Virtually dancing with everyone, "Excuse me," he says to one group of dancers on the left, "pardon me," he says to another group on the right, continually moving forward. A walk made easier by his neon wrist band.

*Who knew these silly wristbands would be so useful?* thinks Noelle. "They help in the search for the women in the purple dress, but I give up this chase," he says, sitting down in the lounge of the indoor bar. "I will watch and listen to the Band," says Noelle in exasperation.

The band continues to play great, and their performance takes him away from the distraction in his mind. It was time to get back to business. He could blame it on a fine brandy; top shelf whiskey or Dom Perignon Champaign, but Noelle did not drink, except sparkling water.

"Let me get up and get into position for the raffle. At least I'll be ready to close this night and go home," Noelle says out loud to inspire himself out of the comfortable lounge chair. Walking back through the crowded dancefloor, Noelle looks up and notices the beautiful night sky in the Big Sky Ballroom's glass like ceiling. At that very moment, three stars twinkle in sequence, winking at him in a sight to behold. This brings forth a smile underneath his mask.

"Did anyone see the stars twinkle?" Noelle asks to no one in particular. He spins around slowly. His eyes are now a willing gate, looking for confirmation of the heavenly event, losing faith that he saw anything. Noelle says, "Has anyone else witnessed the stars dancing in the sky?"

She speaks in a voice that is warm like a summer breeze. "That was truly beautiful, wasn't it? The stars winked at me!" It was her! The woman in the purple dress. Their eyes meet without a search through their masks. Noelle's heart searches for calm, only to find more excitement when the woman in the purple dress answers his question saying, "Yes, I saw the twinkle, twinkle little Stars." She continues, "The heavens are wonderful, and the stars are smiling at you and I tonight."

Noelle bashfully states, "Oh, I don't think so! I just looked at the right time." Then, not wanting the conversation to stop he says, "I think me seeing the stars twinkle was just lucky."

Hearing this reply, the woman in purple reaches out for Noelle's right hand and speaks directly into the face on his mask. Now mask to mask, but not seeing eye to eye she says, "Well Sir, do you feel lucky right now? Are you willing to thank the heavens that you found me by luck as you have said, or was it me that has found you?"

Noelle is calming down. He caresses the hand that has reached out for him like a life preserver is thrown to a sinking swimmer, and speaks with confidence saying, "My sister said I would meet someone tonight, and that I should remember to ask her for a dance. Miss, can I have this dance?"

Lead singer Marvin Paul says, "This will be our last song of the night, thank you everyone."

Behind a pleasant mask, the woman's still lovely voice says, "Your sister and brother-in-law love you Mr. No, and because you said yes, I say yes to this dance."

Noelle gestures his hands to say, who me?

And his new dance partner; if only for tonight, says, "Don't be perplexed, I overheard your sister calling you Mr. No during the intermission. I guess you didn't see me."

Noelle leads his new dance partner to the middle of the dance-floor, where they wait side by side listening to Marvin Paul introduce the Band and their final song. "Please enjoy my version of the love song Careless Whispers, originally done by George Michael."

The woman in purple speaks into Noelle's ear saying, "Who is Milly?"

"Do I know you?" Noelle says.

"No, you don't," is the reply from the private dancer in the purple dress, who continues to say, "Back at the table when we met, you called me Milli. I want you to know that my name is Nevaeh."

Noelle confesses to Neveah, "Milli was the name I gave to a special friend many years ago when we both were young and in love, but sometimes Neveah, things don't work out."

The act of confessing to Neveah, who is a stranger to him, releases long pent-up burdens of guilt and pain that leave Noelle's body in a rush when he exhales. Then he continues to confess saying, "Thank you for being kind to me Miss Neveah. I do feel like dancing with you."

The Band begins playing a beautiful sounding mix of saxophone and trumpet horn. The once full dancefloor recedes like tidewater at low tide, but emotions rush into the heart, like high tide. The ebb and flow of blood throughout his body, create an emotional baptism, and in this surreal setting, Noelle's broken spirit begins to heal, watering the seed of love that was planted in his heart.

Noelle has lost his faith in love. Without faith, love is a fleeting emotion. Even so, the heart provides a beat to this feeling that awakens passion, as blood flows through the heart, mind, body and soul.

The Heavens provide a witness by a ceiling skylight that reveals to the soon-to-be midnight sky. They are a couple moving in perfect combination, reconnecting broken pathways of logic through an unexplainable mystery of life, each in the company of an angel, and unaware.

Noelle can feel the moment slipping away, as the dancefloor begins to empty and his dance towards romance, with its niceties of quiet reflection and movements of sensuality, will soon end. Speaking hurriedly, he says, "Neveah, I feel great in your arms. Perhaps we should meet at the midnight reveal and take off our masks and see where that leads us."

Marvin Paul sings, "*Time can never mend, the careless whisper of a good friend, to the heart and mind, ignorance is kind, there's no comfort in the truth, pain is all you'll find.*"

"*I'm never gonna dance again, guilty feet have got no rhythm...*"

Neveah responds gently, "Noelle, we may never see each other again after this dance. Our masks hide our pain, and midnight will reveal our best and our worst. We fight our good on Halloween and our bad on All Saints Day. Let go of past mistakes and you will find that good man you were intended to be. For us, the midnight hour that approaches can be easily remembered and easily forgotten, depending on who wins our soul."

Noelle says, "You feel so right in this moment, but I can feel your disappointment also. Do I have to let go of you again?" Neveah dances with Noelle Oscar Chance Jr., their hearts prepare to re-enter the real world, and careless whispers meet the surreal.

Marvin Paul sings, "Tonight, the music seems so loud, I wish that we could lose this crowd, maybe it's better this way, we'd hurt each other with the things we want to say. I'm never gonna dance again, guilty feet have got no rhythm..."

The song comes to an end, the audience applauds loudly for a performance wonderfully done. In the middle of the cheers, Noelle and Neveah find each other's eyes beneath their masks.

Neveah speaks over the noise to say, "Mr. No, say yes to the test... say yes to save your life... goodbye...!" She turns to leave, the words of the song careless whispers ringing true.

Noelle is stuck, his feet will not move, but he manages to say,"Goodbye, whoever you are."

Price Waterhouse and wife, along with Holly and Jacob, excitedly join Noelle, Holly proudly states, "My brother can dance," and everyone agrees.

Marvin Paul states "Thank you everyone. You have been a great audience, let's do it again sometime. Now it is my great pleasure to do our countdown for the midnight reveal. Everyone please join me... 5! 4! 3! 2! 1! Lights please."

The midnight unmasking of the guests at the Harvest Moon Masquerade Ball always reveals surprises and the 8th annual edition does not disappoint. Noelle struggles between feeling the event was a trick or a treat. His thoughts are of Neveah; the woman in purple, who just appeared, then disappeared from the Ballroom, as midnight comes to take away the day.

Brother-in-law Jacob grabs Noelle's attention and pulls him aside for a private conversation, saying, "El, which way did that woman go? You should meet her during the reveal."

Noelle shakes his head no and Mr. No begins to reappear in his mind, but he's in a trance when he says "Jake, that lady is a mystery, who will stay a mystery."

Noelle goes through the next 90 minutes on cruise control. He follows Price Waterhouse, who personally conducts the Raffle and encourages everyone to enjoy K. Sylvia's Coffee and Cakes. The wind down activity is accepted as a normal closing feature of each event put together by Price Waterhouse. He is determined to make sure all are sober before they leave for their homes.

Noelle's ears were still ringing from the compliments of the party people, still on cruise control he suddenly finds himself in the Valet parking lobby saying goodbye to Price Waterhouse and his wife and goodbye to Holly and Jacob, who have carried the conversation and kept Host and Co-Host company during their closing activities.

Noelle snaps back to his senses as the Valet attendant pulls up with his car, then hands him the keys saying, "All is well. Please drive home safely."

The ride was pleasant. It was great to get home and it won't be hard to fall asleep after a long day and night. The bed and pillow feel better than normal, as do the first memories of the Masquerade Ball as he falls asleep. The event was a complete success with tickets, donations and raffle proceeds climbing over thirty-five thousand dollars.

Halloween turns into a pumpkin, making way for All Saints Day, which opens the door to a brand-new Holiday Season. The Holidays are not important to Noelle, but he did receive a Christmas gift of friendship from the woman in purple named Nevaeh, who confirmed the stars in the sky were winking at him, while they danced, lost in the masquerade.

# Chapter 5

## *Remember November*

### Zebulun

*(For the LORD thy God is a merciful God;) he will not forsake thee, neither destroy thee, nor forget the covenant of thy fathers which he swore unto them.*

— *DEUTERONOMY* 4: 31

The rain from Heaven falls on the good and the evil at midnight of Halloween. The two meet and depart from one another, who is victorious does play out within the souls of man and woman. The midnight countdown on New Year's Eve separates the years, but the midnight countdown on Halloween separates spirits. Halloween, with its cryptic Spirits, tries to mimic Christmas with festive lights but it celebrates evil, including mis-guided gift giving and idol worship, but as October ends, November enters with All Saints' Day. November 1st is a Christian celebration of good things, done in remembrance of loved ones and honoring all saints, known and unknown.

In these two days, opposites do attract and attack each other annually, and this time, the transition falls under a full moon, which moves the ocean tides and light up North Star Village onto the midnight hour.

All of the Saints that come marching into the new day will move good and evil but for Noelle, it's like the story of Cinderella, who rushing to escape the change from Princess to Pauper that midnight will bring, ran out of the Royal Ball, much the same way that Neveah left the Masquerade Ball.

A full moon night gives way to a sunny morning. The clouds are dancing across the sky, some shaped like a lion, some like mountains, others like dragons. You can see this when you use your imagination and look. The dawn's early light, celestial display mimics the midnight sky, when Halloween met All Saints' Day and the Moon; referred to as the lessor light did dominate the transfer, let us remember November.

Cinderella left her glass slipper in her story; Neveah left a piece of Noelle's heart, momentarily healed by her company, as the woman in a beautiful purple dress, then lost within the twelve strokes of the clock at midnight. Dawn of a new day brings forth the morning light. For Noelle Jr., that light also brings back his indifference to life and people.

The old Noelle reappears to erase any feelings from last night's would be romance, as being lost in a masquerade, forgetting that the road to salvation is paved with faith, love and forgiving those who trespass against you, even if that person is yourself. He arrives to the first minutes of daylight on All Saints Day with a soul shaken by the events of the night, but still he must learn that life happily ever after, is lived in thankfulness, missing this opportunity to rise like the Sun and be thankful for what he's got.

Noelle is a man who would be King, who did present to Cinderella her lost glass slipper, as he did present Neveah with his glass heart. The glass slipper turned Cinderella into a Queen, but his glass heart turns Nevaeh into the Queen of hearts, who danced with his cold heart and left it half full of love, by running away when the midnight bells bong.

The alarm clock rang three hours later than it usually would, but there's no need to hurry and plenty of time for a fresh cup of coffee and coffee cake. I'm not as young as I used to be, says Noelle talking to his pillow, understanding the body is reacting slowly due to a late night of playing host at the Harvest Moon Masquerade Ball, staying up late into the early morning hours. The alarm sounds loud, moving him to turn it off quickly and gather his thoughts while sitting on the side of the bed. Noelle Oscar Chance Jr., lives by the motto, be great today but he says it with no regard for fellow man, basing his happiness on money.

Noelle is blissfully unaware of the stumbling block he represents to people around him. Halloween has no significance in his life, but that is made null and void since Christmas is not important either.

Confounded by his lack of morality and poor leadership, Noelle leads any who follow him into temptation, which goes down the wide road of destruction instead of the King's Highway, which is straight and narrow. No matter which direction he goes down the road of life, called the Kings Highway, All Hallows Eve and All Saints' Day will change Noelle Oscar Chance Jr., who now believes in luck and leans on science to explain the mysteries of life. He applies the flexible ideology to take the best from multiple religious beliefs and form logical thoughts on life, death and the pursuit of happiness to be coincidences that can be controlled by good decision making.

Noelle believes he can take chance out of life's happenstance, but he overlooks that every word that proceeds out of the mouth of God, rules all. Noelle has money plans and up to now they are working, but all work and no play made Noelle a dull boy. Last night's Masquerade Ball brought on playtime that causes a late start to the Saturday work plans from the man who would be king.

Noelle is trying to forget about last night and the lady in a purple dress who disappeared at midnight, but not before she struck his heart with electric shock therapy, reviving it back to life with a dance before she said goodbye, Neveah is the mysterious lady's name.

"NO WAY!" Noelle's bah humbug statement, reacting to the first TV commercial he sees of the oncoming Christmas Season. He reads the caption out loud, in a sarcastic voice, stating, "Christmas layaway has already begun. Begin yours tomorrow!"

"That's it for TV. It's time for me to get to work." Noelle starts his trip to the office in silence but suddenly sings a song he made up for the Holiday season.

*"It's beginning to look a lot like money... everywhere I go."*

He turns on the car sound system to listen to the radio to be captivated by the sounds of a smooth bass line, followed by an expressive acoustic guitar. He remembered hearing it on the way to the Casino and winning at bingo but didn't know the title of the song.

Hearing it is a good sign, he thinks, as the mid-morning show called, Great songs returns from commercial, then a smooth professional announcer's voice says, "This is KNSV FM... make it a great day... Yall know money don't grow on trees... This is your man, Lester Givings, here to show you the money.

"Check me out for music and money news you can use. My next topic is additional revenue streams. Take a drive and ride with me... it's the best thing you can do with your money for free..."

The cellphone rings over the radio. It's Holly. She calls her brother often, determined to defeat his Mr. No personality. This is what she calls putting faith in her works.

"Good morning," Noelle says greeting his sister.

Holly replies right back, "Good morning... I thought you would be sluggish after your long night."

"Holly, about last night... all that matters is that Mr. Waterhouse had a successful event," Noelle says quickly, trying to cut the subject off, but Holly jumps right back into the conversation.

"Okay... I get it... your dance didn't turn into a romance," she says, in hopes to make light of the situation.

Noelle doesn't respond.

"Alright El, let me get to the point. Please put Thanksgiving dinner in your planner. Be at my house by 3 o'clock, you can bring a dessert of your choice.

Noelle rarely turns his sister down and responds quickly saying, "Okay 3 o'clock...Thanksgiving feast fest, got it. I will bring a dessert... Holly, I got to go I'm on my way to the office."

"I understand. Be safe and have a great day," Holly says before yelling out, "Wait a minute brother dear... it was good to see you dancing at the Ball and smiling again... I love you... bye, bye!"

The Great songs radio show comes back on the car speakers playing a Target department store commercial promoting online shopping for Christmas and savings on Black Friday that brings on the first full rant of the Season, as Noelle Chance Jr., sarcastically says,

"No way!... Christmas comes earlier every year. It's all commercial, but it won't get me... no way... no way! I know what's next. They're going to play that song over and over and over again, that song I've heard so many times... *Hang All The Mistletoe*."

DJ Angel returns to her radio show and continues to promote the Money Tree topic about additional revenue streams and better use of your cellphone for eMobile internet business.

Noelle is half listening, his mind is on new client meetings and Nickolas Kingsly, his Office Manager, who has put together some promotion ideas.

Noelle turns into the office parking lot and sees the minivan of his office manager is parked close to the front door, prompting Noelle to say, "I have done well to hire a hard-working family man."

Nickolas and staff worked hard to prepare for Black Friday and the Christmas shopping Season.

Noelle enters the office to a jovial greeting from Nickolas Kingsly.

"Hello Mr. Chance, how are you today?" Noelle barely nods his head, while Nickolas continues to say… "Sir, I hope you had an enjoyable time at the Masquerade Ball."

"I had fun for the first time in a long time," Noelle replied before mentioning to Nickolas, "Time waits for no one," as his voice trails off as he enters his office.

Noelle has forgotten the kindnesses he received while working himself up the ladder of success and doesn't give back, as he was given to, by his mentor Price Waterhouse.

Nickolas wants time off to attend the North Star Village Community Center Christmas party, and he enters Noelle's office to make his request saying, "Mr. Chance it's a good thing that you hosted the Harvest Moon Ball. I'm sure Mr. Waterhouse is now working on the details for this year's Community Center Christmas party."

Nickolas has done this dance before, testing the water but not protesting the results of other requests he's made, the answers were always no, prefaced with statements of the importance of getting ahead of work orders, because the boss thrives on work to provide an escape from life.

Nickolas Kingsly states, "Mr. Chance, I have finished my proposal for North Star Cadillac, and I want you to take a look at it. We can go over the details before the business day ends."

Noelle nods his head yes… he's ready to hear the ideas and strategy his Office Manager has worked on for the new client.

"Sir, I will bring you my folder but before I do, please look at a new work schedule, it will keep us from working on a Saturday during the Holiday Season. I've put the shifts together to allow us to keep up with our workload, have time off and go home early for Thanksgiving, Christmas, and New Year's," says Nickolas, catching the boss off guard.

Noelle responds awkwardly, "Well Kingsly, you sure are putting in your request early enough."

"Well sir, it's All Saints' Day and Christmas is right around the corner," says Nickolas keeping the pressure up… "Sir, my big concern is this year's Community Christmas party. It's a big deal.

Last year the whole staff worked on the day of the event, which makes it almost impossible to attend. Please take a look at my plan."

Nickolas Kingsly doesn't ask for much, and he has a determined look on his face.

Noelle complains, "It seems I have been hearing about Christmas this whole morning. My goodness man, it's just a party. Why all the fuss?" Noelle says quickly. "Sure, the Community Center event is a good thing that Mr. Waterhouse does. Alright Kingsly, give me your paperwork on North Star Cadillac, then you and I will get back together before we leave."

"Thank you, Mr. Chance. You won't be disappointed. As I like to say, a happy worker is a hard worker. I left the proposals on my desk. I will bring them to you right now and check back on you after lunchtime."

Noelle is unfeeling towards All Saints' Day and November traditions, with the exception of Veteran's Day, the day he celebrates the family contributions to the United States Armed Forces. Noelle will study the proposals from his Office Manager, but counting blessings is not on his mind, only the mighty dollar.

~

Noelle is impressed with the strategy from Nickolas Kingsly and is ready to discuss his ideas for the North Star Cadillac Dealership and calls Nickolas into his office.

This is a big day for Nickolas. He has quietly excelled for years but today there's something in the air about meeting with the boss. He sees his step are ordered when he entered Noelle's office space, today he senses the Saints' have come marching in before him and the feeling flushes him.

"Come right in Kingsly," says Noelle. "You've done a fine job on these promotion incentives for North Star Cadillac," he said with a sudden smile. Noelle always smiles at the prospect of making more money. "... "This is clever work. I'm confident they will like it and commit to our services as a long-term client."

There's a dramatic shift in the atmosphere. Today the boss gives in and says yes with a sigh.

"Mr. Nickolas Kingsly, you may incorporate a Holiday schedule... I want to thank you for your hard work... you can plan on being off from work on the weekend you want, it just so happens I volunteered to help the Community Center Christmas party, by request of Mr. Waterhouse.

This time it's Nickolas Kingsly who is caught off guard.

"Thank you, Mr. Chance", Nickolas says and takes a deep breath, surprised by what he had heard. Patience is a virtue. Nickolas Kingsly has achieved a Holiday work schedule and a measure of respect in the eyes of the boss.

"Congratulations Kingsly, I will let you tell the staff of the good news and I expect everyone to be up to speed on North Star Cadillac by the end of business on Monday. Also, check out the Food Truck vendors' eMobile processing status. We can gain more clients with them. Call that one food for thought."

Noelle gets up from his desk too pleased with himself. With a smile on his face, he says, "Kingsly, I'm leaving in the next few minutes. Please close up the office."

"It's a good thing that we don't have to worry about working on Saturday. That's going to be a weight off of our shoulders. Have a great day Mr. Chance."

Noelle wants to get to the Big Sky Metroplex Shopping Center, which is always crowded on Saturday. Today will present a parking challenge, but not for patrons like Noelle Chance Jr., who used valet parking.

"Thank you for joining us today. We will take good care of your car sir. We hope you enjoy your shopping experience," says the parking attendant cheerfully.

"Thank you," responds Noelle to the young man.

Noelle stops to watch his car disappear into the valet parking area, then gets lost in memories of Bingo night at the Bella Bella Hotel and Casino. The Valet driver on that night said his name was Cole Bucks, but he resembled the dearly departed Khole Cashe, his former business partner. The interaction scared Noelle.

Khole Cashe worked himself to death, but the flowing sands of time have helped Noelle to adapt the story to be only remembered as a good friend who died too soon.

Noelle refuses to see the true memory of Khole Cashe but seeing the Parking Attendant named Cole Bucks did scare him, and now this daydream haunts him. The daydream is broken up by the festive noises of people all around who are dressed up to enter the "Superhero and Good Guys" costume contest.

The costume show is designed to provide family fun for everyone. All contestants receive prizes and there's a good feeling in the air, but Noelle is determined to hold on to the dark place of loneliness in his heart. The event organizers present the Superhero and Good Guys contest to combat the wickedness of Halloween, which works for Noelle Chance Jr...

Noelle is at the Metroplex to return his tuxedo, purchase two Bespoke white button-down dress shirts and pick up some fine meats from his favorite supermarket. But he finds himself watching the costume contest.

He watches with amusement when a father and child team present themselves as The Green Hornet and Kato and he reminisces of the times when he would ride in his father's 1965 Chrysler Imperial Crown pretending that he was Kato, the Martial Arts Master.

Noelle tries to act indifferent, but the seeds of his dad's love are planted in his soul soil. Suddenly he remembers poking fun at his Office Manager because he projects to the good side of our American celebration of Halloween, and All Saints' Day.

"That's enough of that," says Noelle to himself and moves on from the performance area to do some window shopping and count the number of stores that are presenting Christmas trimmings.

The Christmas Season begins on All Saints' Day is the quiet

revelation of the dour dapper dan, who drop off the tuxedo and purchases the shirts to refresh his stock. Noelle wears a white shirt dress shirt every business day, changing ties, shoes, and dark color pants to match his collection of Fedora Hats. Tonight's dinner for one, only the best Tomahawk Steak Chop will do.

The Angels dispatched by righteous prayer converge on Noelle Chance in an always timely manner and as he nears the entrance of the Wellness Fresh Meat and Produce Market, his cell phone rings. His mom.

"Hi mom," says Noelle, stopping before entering the market. "How are you? What's going on?"

"Hello son," spoken as only a mother can say. "I won't keep you long, but your sister tells me you are coming to Thanksgiving dinner this year, and I want you to be on time. All you need to bring is desert and that coffee you like so much... what's it called?"

"Folgers but I think you are talking about the coffee I brought over to your house, and that's called Sylvia's Best. But mom, I'm at the Metroplex right now. You called me just as I was going into Wellness Market. Can I call you back later?"

"Yes, call me back later," Mom says in a way that sounds like *you better not forget.*

"I will call this evening and yes, I will be at the Thanksgiving feast fest. I will talk to you before you go to bed. Bye for now!"

Noelle can tell his mother is smiling by the way she says... "Bye, bye!"

Noelle was raised to know better, but again he credits the man-made alarm clock for waking him up; giving no thanks to God, repeating a bad habit that has become a daily mistake, instead of his daily bread.

Noelle crossed over the midnight madness of Halloween into the goodness of All Saints' Day. It looks like daylight is gonna to catch him again, neither having respect for evil or good, on an early Sunday morning. Noelle's Newfoundland is a country of self-proclaimed Holy ground he has found in the Faith of pragmatism, but the mind, body and soul, spiritual warfare this causes is not pragmatic at all. There are false hopes on the foundation of pragmatic thoughts, of self-control over life. Fool's gold is not victorious, but it promotes stronger mind tricks.

All of this free will is fine until it becomes time to explain Supernatural interventions in life's dire emergencies that prove to be unexplainable, when practical application of the theories of self-control needs a miracle of God. It's within these times, which we all must face at different times in our lives, that even a small portion of real Faith in Jesus, defeat the practical application of day-to-day living. God Bless the child who has his own, the prayers of the righteous avails much, as did the prayers of Abraham save his nephew Lot, but you got to get your own.

Noelle fell asleep to Jazz music on his favorite radio station, which turned into Gospel Jazz easy listening on a Sunday morning. This pragmatic move works wonders to show the subconscious listener the way out of darkness and into the marvelous light of the Lord.

And the melody still lingers on...

Playing softly in the background, Gospel Jazz provides a music bed for all listeners to relate to the Prince of Peace, heard in the good news of the Gospel, heard in Gospel music.

*Hark the Herald Angel sings, glory to the newborn King.*

K. Sylvia, the owner of K. Sylvia's Coffee and Cakes, is also a Gospel music Disc Jockey. Her radio name is DJ Saint. She is featuring the Men's Choir of North Star Village Baptist Church, who, on this Sunday, sing in real time in Studio B at the radio station, giving all with ears to hear a Mini Concert of Negro Spirituals in acappella.

Noelle is awakened to the Hymn titled, *Certainly Lord.*

*And the voice cries out three times... have you got good religion... three times, comes the reply... Certainly Lord ... And three times the voice cries out... have you been baptized... three times, comes the reply... Certainly Lord... And three times the voice cries out... do you want to see Jesus... three times comes the reply... Certainly Lord*

*All together the voices sing... Certainly, Certainly, Certainly Lord...*

Noelle has no plans to go to Church, and he doesn't listen to traditional gospel music; unless he is with his parents, so today will be an oddly aimless day, for the spirit longs for the Altar of prayer and praise and the body longs for rest.

Noelle enjoys the body resting in a rare eight hours' sleep and he wakes up feeling refreshed. There are things you can do for yourself, to develop your spiritual self, without going to church but nothing comes to a sleeper but a dream, is a story only half told when said dream is indeed a nightmare, and who can you run practically run to, within a dream?

How many dreams does it take to get to the chocolaty center of a tootsie pop?

The wise owl says 3, 1 for the father, 2 for the son, 3 for the Holy Ghost. Noelle, who was trained up in the Church, knows he can meditate, pray, and open the bible to maintain a personal relationship with God.

"Good morning coffee machine. How are you this morning?" says Noelle the would-be dreamer." Would you perk a perfect cup for me today?"

On pops the TV. It's time to catch up on local and business news, while watching time fly like sand through an hourglass. Going to Church is not on Noelle's mind. Noon approaches with images from the past few days passing through a drive-thru window, showing the confrontations had with real and imagined people. The mind gives no rest to the spirit. Noelle's remedy for stress is denial, the TV, and a late brunch to turn into an early dinner at his favorite diner.

~

Nickolas Kingsly redoubles his efforts to be a churchgoing Christian; remember the Sabbath day and keep it Holy. The first Sunday of November takes its place as the herald of the oncoming Holiday Season. Nickolas and Mary Kingsly navigate through life's events with daily prayer, and are unashamed of their praise as they hold on to the Lord's unchanging hand.

*"Peace on earth and mercy mild, God and sinners reconciled, joyful all ye nations rise join the triumph of the skies..." Hark the Herald Angel Sings* is true for Nickolas Kingsly, who finds the new day to be a loving joy. The Kingsly family enters into this Christmas Season full of faith.

A brilliant sunshine. Easy Sunday morning shines on North Star Village Baptist Church and the communion opportunity it offers to those who put up the good fight of faith, against the wickedness of the season of Halloween. The Church is full, the whole congregation is on hand and the sanctuary is under the Holy Spirit, bringing peace to those that partake in the refreshing.

"Govern yourselves accordingly," says the Church Secretary Pearlie Rae Dean, after reading the announcements and welcoming the visiting guests. "Please everyone, let us pass the peace that is the presence of the Lord and briefly greet one another."

A short time passes by, then Pastor Avery Mann asks all to return to their seats. He is clearly pleased to see everyone gathered together and immediately moves along in the order of service, asking Price Waterhouse and the members of the North Star Village charity committee to stand.

Mrs Elizabeth Waterhouse: wife of Price Waterhouse, and two others stand up from where they are in the Church. Pastor Mann speaks directly to them,

"On behalf of your fellow Church members, we all thank you for your efforts and for the donations we are receiving. Your work and results ensure our 'Read and Feed The Need' programs will be able to continue providing Thanksgiving and Christmas dinners, and empower people through our food and literacy Ministry."

The Congregation, which includes the mother and father of Noelle Oscar Chance Jr., applauds the Charity Committee members. Nickolas, who was asked to sit in the Pulpit, gives thanks, seeing his wife and children along with Aunt Marie, her husband and their children. It's a family affair.

Pastor Avery Mann begins to preach about All Saints' Day... saying, "God bless the saints that we pray for. May they continue to rest in Eternal peace with the Lord Jesus Christ of Nazareth. We believe they are safe in the Savior's arms, and we give thanks for our Guardian Angels.

"Brothers and sisters, let no one steal your joy today. Once again evil did its best to prevail and once again, by faith, our father who Art in Heaven, did rise up to defeat evil at midnight on the last day of October. Now the Holy Spirit has gathered us out of the many. Right here and now, let us profess to the Lord that He has done a new thing in us.

"Turn your Bible to the book of Isaiah and find Chapter 43: verses 18 and 19. It reads... 'Remember ye not the former things, neither consider the things of old. Behold, I will do a new thing; now it shall spring forth; shall ye not know it? I will even make a way in the wilderness, and rivers in the desert.'"

Pastor Mann turns around in the pulpit, saying, "The Lord has done a new thing in me, turning around my bad situation, late in the midnight hour, fighting for me as I slept and I can't tell you what it is right now... but I know in my heart, that midnight victory was for me and my situation. Holler if you hear me..."

Pastor Avery Mann pauses to wipe his face and takes a deep breath, as if to inhale the presence of the Holy Spirit, before continuing to preach. "I'm preaching to myself people, but if somebody knows what I'm talking about, let your praises flow. He is worthy! Jesus never fails, not today! And forever more... I say, see the light at the end of the tunnel, see the tunnel as your problem and see Jesus work it out, as the light... Praise His name...

"Praise is a must for Jesus. Remember Jesus said I must leave you now to be with my father. The prince of this world comes and there is none of me in him. Jesus says 'feed my sheep, as I have fed you' and He's coming back to take His believers to a new place, to do a new thing in Eternal Heaven, Hallelujah."

Pastor Mann walks to the left, stating, "Have you got good religion?" and the deacons and Nickolas Kingsly reply with a shout.

"Certainly Lord!"

Pastor Mann inhales and walks to the right and states again, "Have you got good religion?" and the whole Church shouts out,

"Certainly Lord."

"That's good for you. I thought I had lost you all." He starts to laugh... and so does the Congregation.

"It's good to laugh sometimes," says Pastor Mann. "Go'head laugh... Jesus said be merry, so that this life of trials and tribulations is made bearable. Keep your faith. Without it you will not make it home to Jesus.

By faith... the Prince of this world will not stop us from making it back to Jesus. But you've got to have faith. We've got to have faith, because the enemy looks just like us and has mirrored our ways. If you judge a man or woman like you judge a book cover, you will not be able to separate the evil wolf, who wears the sheep of Jesus' clothing, pretending to be Holy, to lead you astray."

"You right, Sir. Pastor. You're in the book," says Deacon Peoples.

And the Church said "Amen."

Pastor Mann continues, "We that submit to Jesus Christ of Nazareth will not be stopped by this adversary. He's to be separated from us says Jesus. Let us not waste any more time trying to be Holy or Holier than the next man. Let us be about the Lord's work, repenting our sins and praying daily for the restoring of His mysterious works in us. Works that make us faithful...Amen..."

"Amen," says the Church Deacons, and seemingly the whole church gets brighter. The air becomes sweet and the smoke from the candles rise, pausing in respect of the Holy Spirit.

"Faithful church, breakthrough the ground that would hold back your talents, which would hold back your praises and dig out your praises like buried treasure. I want to put your minds at ease. The Baptist Church will no longer be stuck within the guilt of association with worldly things. We are in the world but not of the world.

"Shine the light of truth wherever you go and no longer separate yourselves from family, friends, and community under false pretenses. Believe by faith that your steps are ordered by the Lord. Go when He says go. Stay away when He says stay away... And know that you know the voice of my Savior, and your God."

The whole church rocks and sways with praises heard from new voices, from hearts cut free from the bondage to this world, reborn to be with King Jesus. Nickolas can sense Pastor Mann is moving toward closing his sermon, even before he states to the choir director that he is closing...

Pastor Mann claps his hands, says hallelujah, and continues to speak the word God has given him.

"Church... when they say, why are you celebrating Halloween, I want you to know it was they who said to Jesus Christ, why do you eat with sinners? Let your reply be ... my light may be the only light of the Lord that is seen."

"Church," says Pastor Mann with fire in his voice, "I want you to be confident that wherever you go and whatever you do, that you pursue righteousness. Being in the world, but not of the world.

"Remember that the Lord gives sunshine to all. Let no one play the game of, I am holier than you because of this or because of that... Let your light shine from the inside to the outside, and the world will see that light is the light of the Lord inside of you. The light in you is greater than him. That is the evil in the world."

"Amen," shouts the Church.

"Be in the world faithful Saints, not of the world and don't be confused. Know that it is written in the Bible to eat, drink and be merry, doing all things in moderation.

"Church... pray daily. That's our daily bread and the Rod of correction from Our father who Art in Heaven. Prayer will guide you and the Staff of the Lord will lead you, not into temptation... Amen."

"Amen," shouts the Church.

Pastor Mann speaks his closing words with volume, saying, "Now that we who believe, submit ourselves to the son of father God, we are in obedience. Do this in Remembrance of Me, and by doing so, we live life more abundantly until Jesus comes back from Heaven. The time of his return, no man or woman can say the day, or the hour."

And the Church celebrated with praises of hallelujah! and other praises of joyful noise.

"Let us celebrate the birth of our Savior here on earth, Jehovah God by any other name, Christ to the Masses...Christ more... Merry Christmas to the world. Let's celebrate Jesus, the light of life. God Bless, All Saints' Day. Let the church say Amen."

"Amen."

"Let the church say Amen again!"

"Amen."

Pastor Mann walked down the pulpit stairs to the center isle of the Church saying, "The doors of the Church are open. Will there be one to join us today? Make today your day to join the Holy Spirit of Jesus Christ. Hear His voice in your heart and step out on faith. Believe in Jesus, and confess your sins... Jesus is love. Will there be one?"

And the Spirit of the Lord descended on the believers, bringing a breakthrough for five people who got up and walked to the Altar to join the Church, each one stating they want to be baptized.

~

Pastor Mann begins Communion, having had the Deacons pass out the elements of the sacrifice of Jesus, breaking the unleavened bread, which is the body of Christ Jesus and drinking the juice or wine, which symbolizes the Blood of Jesus, shed for our salvation.

"Thank you, Lord," says Nickolas Kingsly, shouting out, "Hallelujah!"

The North Star Village Baptist Church choir picked up the Spirit in the air and sang the hymn Thank you Lord, as they made their way out of the choir stand.

Nickolas and Mary Kingsly agree to meet in the foyer, as they go around the church, greeting the other members and their guests.

AFTER A SHORT COOLING off session for Pastor Mann he appears in the foyer to greet and say goodbye to all who have gathered, Nickolas and Mary greet their Pastor, telling him how they enjoyed the Sermon.

"Thank you. Glory to God!" he said, reaching for the right hand of Nickolas. "Brother Kingsly, next week; Lord willing, will be my Thanksgiving Sermon. Please be here if you can be. I know you rarely miss a Sunday worship service, but on behalf of the Deacons I want to congratulate you on becoming a Deacon of the Church."

Nickolas smiles, nodding his head yes.

Pastor Mann continues, "I will not be here for Thanksgiving weekend and the Deacons will run the service. Deacon Peoples will call you on Tuesday evening and we all will meet with you on Wednesday night, after Bible study."

"Thank you, Pastor. Glory to God!", says Nickolas, I look forward to Wednesday.

"WELL MRS. KINGSLY," says Nickolas on the way to their van, "Thank you for loving me. I know you are excited for me and becoming a Deacon is an important matter and like everything else we do, we'll do this together, but right now I need you to drive us home. I feel like taking in the moment and just ride along with my family and look up at the clouds."

~

And it came to pass that Veterans Day appears on the November calendar and Noelle thinks of his dad, a proud United States Army Veteran, a Buffalo Soldier.

He comes to life in a different way on Veterans Day. *Daddy Chance always buys the red remembrance Poppy flower*, thinks Noelle. *Dad taught us all that the Red Poppy flower commemorates Soldiers who've died in war*. The symbol itself was commemorated as a National symbol in 1921 and we always buy some from the local Veterans of Foreign War; (V.F.W.) post around Veteran's Day.

Noelle Jr. is within a thoughtful moment; sitting in his office chair, gazing into sky, thoughts of granddaddy Avery Chance take their place, and a lasting memory forces its way out of buried emotions to reveal a rare occasion when his Granddaddy would speak of his war experiences to his son. Experience that would help Noelle Sr., fight in a different war, but any war is hell.

Noelle Jr., feels Veterans Day is a day when the sacrifices of his father and the sacrifices of his grandfather; in separate wars for the United States of America, weighs heavy on the heart and mind and although he has returned to his cold ways, there's a crack in the ice.

Noelle Jr., hears his father's voice in his head and writes down the thought. It says, "When you see the poppy flower growing in a field, it is a reminder of life continuing on from death. Every enlisted man has signed up to die; if necessary, having sworn an oath to defend America.

"Memorial Day commemorates the Fallen Soldier. Veteran's Day honors all the Soldiers of our Armed Forces. This is why the Red Poppy flower is held in high esteem."

Noelle Jr. is ready to leave the office, but before leaving, he walks around the office to observe his employees, who are all working hard on this Federal Holiday. But it's not a Holiday at the office of the N. O. Chance Financial Agency.

Nickolas Kingsly can see the boss is getting ready to leave the office and meets him in his walk, saying, "Mr. Chance, I have some good business news. The radio ads we put together for NSV Cadillac are doing very well. They are in position to end the year with great sales numbers."

Noelle dryly replies, "Well, that's good news Kingsly. More sales for them, more financing goals met for us. Come to my office. I want you to relay that information to the staff and take over for the rest of the day. I will be leaving for the rest of the day shortly."

Nickolas Kingsly is a good office manager. He has prepared the employees to work hard throughout the day, knowing the boss would be leaving the office early.

Kristen Flowers, Administrative Secretary to Noelle Chance Jr., buzzes the office phone and states, "Mr. Chance, there's a call for you on line 2."

Picking up the phone, Noelle replies, "Miss Flowers, who is it?", while putting on his sports coat.

"It's Mr. Les Givings from radio station KNSV," says Kristen Flowers.

"Yes, Miss Flowers, this will be my final call for today. You can tell Mr. Givings I will call him back within the next 30 minutes. I will call him from my car. I'm leaving the office now. Any other calls will have to be scheduled for call backs. I will meet with you tomorrow around 11 am. Have a good night, Miss Flowers."

The boss leaves the office to the relief of everyone.

"Enjoy the rest of your day, Mr. Chance," Nickolas said, returning to his desk smiling.

The staff works hard for Saint Nickolas; as they call him, because he treats them fair, respects their ideas and works hard to make the N. O. Chance Financial Agency the best it can be.

Nickolas waits to see the boss leave the parking lot before instructing the staff to finish their projects in the next two hours.

Everyone knows that he will close the office early in honor of Veterans Day.

Noelle Oscar Chance Jr., the boss of N. O. Chance Financial Agency, is also known as Mr. No, who is the Black man Jazzy remix of Ebenezer Scrooge, and the Grinch that stole Christmas.

Mr. No is a hard man to work for, having horrible sensibilities, but a change is going to come.

Noelle Jr., loves his car, he always uses his Bluetooth connection for a hands-free driving experience and using the voice command feature, he calls radio station KNSV.

The Secretary picks up and immediately connects him to Les Givings.

"Hello Mr. Les Givings, how are you today?"

"Thank you for asking, Sir. I'm well. I wish you and your employees a Happy Veterans Day. Sir, I will get right to the point, we here at KNSV appreciate your business and are you pleased with our commercials for your client, North Star Village Cadillac."

"Well Mr. Givings the commercials are working well. Let's keep up the good work," Noelle says.

"That's great Mr. Chance. I'm in the process of putting together a VIP sponsorship package for our broadcast on Thanksgiving Eve, Black Friday, and Cyber Monday. I think you can get sales traction," he said with his great DJ voice.

"No way!", says Noelle," I'm not interested in becoming part of the commercial express that Christmas is. I'm not interested at all, but I do enjoy your wonderful radio show called money tree. Let's talk in December and we can discuss that show for the New year."

"That is good for me. I will call you before the first day of Christmas."

"Very clever Mr. Givings. Thanks for calling me, I must go now... goodbye!"

"Have a great day," says Les Givings.

Noelle has a special Veterans Day lunch date with dad and nephew Jacob Evergreen Jr., Holly's beloved son. All will be together in honor of the Holiday and are going to the North Star VFW post 555 to celebrate. He's driving to meet everyone at his parents' home.

Jacob Evergreen Jr., is 25 years old, single, charming, polite, handsome, and considered a good catch, much like his uncle was at his age. Jacob Jr. is not an accountant like his uncle. He has a Civil Engineer Degree and plans a career in water engineering.

"Hi mom," Noelle says walking into his parents' home and into a warm hug from Mom, who says gladly, "Hello son, I'm so happy to see you. Your dad and JJ will be glad too."

"Hello uncle El, it's good to see you," says Jacob Jr., hugging his beloved uncle as he enters the living room.

Noelle Jr., can't help but smile when Daddy Chance reaches out to hold his hand, saying, "Son, thank you for hanging out with your old man today."

Noelle is impressed with JJ, the nickname he gave Jacob Jr., as a baby, and he has grown up to be a fine young man. Noelle Jr., taking a moment to look at the son of his beloved Sister, states out loud, "Mom, Dad... isn't it amazing how much JJ favors his mom."

Jacob Jr., laughs. "Thanks Uncle El. Speaking of my Mom, your sister wants me to remind you to be on time for Thanksgiving dinner. I want you there to hear my good news announcement to the family. Oh man...I'm excited about this Christmas season."

Mother Chance says, "JJ that sounds good. Don't you know grandmothers love good news in the Holiday season. How about giving us a clue?"

"Grandma it's good news and I want to share it when the whole family is together for Thanksgiving."

"Uncle El, you are hard to catch up to," says Jacob Jr. "I want you to come over to see my apartment before our Thanksgiving family get together, just come over for a little while to see where I live."

"Okay JJ. All of that is good, but there's something on your mind.

You got a look on you. I may be a little out of it, but I remember that look and that feeling, so who is she?"

A shy smile escapes the handsome face of Jacob Jr., who then says, "Uncle El you are sharp. You are always direct. I'm not prepared to talk about that right now, but I do want you to set up a time to visit me at my apartment."

"JJ, your mom has told me that you've been asking for me and I'm sorry it has taken this long for us to get together. I will see your new place sometime soon. You know I like to work and that keeps me busy. I'll plan to have coffee and dessert with you at the place you call home."

Jacob Jr., who is slightly stunned, replies with gladness in his voice, "That's great Uncle El. I live at 5000 Trinity Street, in the Trinity Gardens Apartments, number 556."

Noelle looks deep into the eyes of his beloved nephew and it's like he can see himself years ago. That cool guy returns to speak knowledge, talking slowly and carefully, he says, "JJ, believe it or not, I was once in love and I was just about your age, as a matter of fact. I was working after receiving my Accounting Degree."

Noelle continues to talk straight to his nephew and opens up more about his feelings... "I met a beautiful woman and I thought it would last forever, but she wanted more from me at a time when I felt and knew I had to work harder to get the type of money success I wanted. She became unhappy, and I was unhappy too. I said, maybe it's best that we take time away from each other."

Then suddenly Noelle stops talking. It was almost like he was talking to himself.

Jacob Jr. breaks the silence, speaking clearly and with respect saying, "Uncle El, that story sounds kind of sad. I want success too... I work hard and would like to have my own company, but I want to believe when that right girl shows up in my life, everything else I need will show up with her."

Noelle snaps out of his daze to say, "JJ remember this, you are young, you can have your own company and make a good living. Stay hungry and all things are possible for you. I have been cold for a long time now. I'm comfortable in my money. My focus and my mind are on money. I'm lucky, but I have worked hard to be where I'm at now and I was lucky to work for and to work with Mr. Price Waterhouse. I learned a lot from him. He is my mentor."

Uncle Noelle is excited when he asks his nephew, "Has your mom ever told you Mr. Waterhouse mentored us?"

"No."

"We both worked hard to get ahead, just like your granddad and grandmother taught and showed us."

"Well... Uncle El, my mom and dad told me you still got it. They saw you dancing at the masquerade ball."

Noelle is back to life, speaking with confidence he says, "JJ, it's funny and not ha ha, that you speak of that night at the masquerade ball. It turned out to be strange and wonderful. I guess it sounds like an old-time detective story when I say, yeah it was Halloween night at a masquerade party when I met a mysterious woman."

Noelle Jr., chuckles and says, "I didn't get to see her out of the mask she wore, but she did get me to dance, and I enjoyed her company. JJ, I was having fun for the first time in a long time and get this, it was the last dance of the night."

"Uncle El, your Halloween mystery can turn into a Christmas miracle. I love this time of year. It's the time of miracles for families and a time for families to renew their strength, especially for the kids. It's the season of expectations, peace, and joy. I'm looking forward to putting up lights, building a pretty Christmas tree, singing Christmas carols and I will hang all the mistletoe this Christmas."

Noelle interjects, "This Christmas! Oh no way! Not you too nephew. That song by Donny Hathaway used to be my favorite, now I hear it from November to New Year's Eve. Babe for me, the thrill is gone."

"Uncle, with the darkness of the world every day, I can't wait for the lights of Christmas. Thank God for spreading the light. For me, it's all love, and that's what the world needs more of. Let's celebrate that!"

Noelle Oscar Chance Jr. says emphatically, "No way! Even the new generation has got the same old commercialized religion."

Jacob Jr. becomes concerned by his uncle's disdain for Christmas. "Wait a minute Uncle El, this is my first time seeing your bah hum bug personality. Mom told me about it, but I hear it for myself and it's almost scary. I've heard the stories about your alter ego, Mr. No, but Uncle El, I know the real you, and this is not what I want to remember. Don't chase everybody away. Let people meet the real you."

Daddy Chance gently eases into the conversation, saying, "El ... JJ, listen to me. I'm only going to say this onetime. Reverend Dr. Martin Luther King Jr., may he continue to Rest in Peace, has a famous sermon called the fierce urgency of now. Now is the time for both of you to make your move towards God. I believe that God has plans for both of you. Don't keep putting off a commitment to God. I did it; finally listening to His call, and it's the best thing that I ever could have done."

"You both can make this Christmas season special forever. What I'm saying to you is not to just go to church, but to find out who Jesus is in your lives, and who you are as a servant of the Lord. Do it for yourselves, do it from your heart and if there's a voice telling you why you shouldn't commit, I want you to remember these words from me... the devil is a liar, and he is lying to you right now!"

"Men it's time for you to be reborn, it's time for you to get baptized. Wow! I'm preaching, I can tell because the looks on your faces are priceless."

Noelle Oscar Chance Sr. smiles with cool confidence and says, "Grandson you have met Mr. No now it's time to meet the E-man It was E-man that just took you to the water. I pray both of you will one day have this conversation with people you love; especially men, because men need a real talk about the importance of a relationship with God."

Noelle Jr., and Jacob Jr., have a stunned look on their faces and

Daddy Chance continues saying, "Guys, you can relax. I love you both, I want the best for you. Noelle, I can tell something is going on in your life. Remember this son, no one comes to the Lord, unless they are called by the Lord, take on his calling and choose to be baptized."

Noelle Jr., responds, "I thought I was baptized already dad."

Daddy Chance leans over the table, speaking quietly he says, "El some get called while young, that wasn't you. Your mother and I want you to make that decision for yourself."

Granddaddy Chance reaches for the hand of his Grandson and says, "Jacob Evergreen Jr., my beloved Grandson, I am proud of you, you're on a great path but don't lean on the faith of anyone else, not even your mother or father. You were Christened as a baby, just as your uncle was Christened as a baby. I am blessed to be able to say I witnessed both events and both were joyous occasions. We all love you, but God loves you best. Being Christened is not the baptism I'm talking about. The truth is in the New Testament of the Bible. In the New Testament you will find that baby Jesus was Christened, and later in his life, it was an adult Jesus somewhere between 30 and 33 years old that went to John the Baptist, stating to him, 'You must baptize me.' Jesus said, 'I must be baptized and born again of the Spirit."

Isabella Precious Chance, wife, mother and grandmother; appears suddenly, as an Angel would speaking with a soprano's intonation.

"El, I want you and JJ to listen to me. This is what your generation calls real talk. What is born of the flesh is flesh indeed, what is born of the Spirit is Spirit, the Spirit must be born again, translated by the Holy Spirit onto Jesus, who will translate you onto Father God, onto Everlasting life!"

Daddy Chance joins hands standing in the middle of his son and wife, who reaches out her hand for her grandson, who closes the circle by reaching for the hand of his Uncle Noelle.

Daddy Chance clearly speaks, saying. "Noelle and Jacob, commit this following phrase to your hearts. I want both of you to repeat after me. Say A B C"

"A B C," they both reply.

Daddy Chance explains, "It's as easy as ABC. A, admit that you are a sinner, and all fall short of the perfect man, Jesus. B, believe that Jesus is the son of God and He died on earth, on the Cross, his Blood for our Salvation. C, confess your sins to Jesus and as a Christian follow His teachings written in the Holy Bible."

"ABC," says Jacob Jr. "I can't wait to tell my Mom and Dad, thank you Grandma and Granddad, that was cool."

"Dad, that ABC memorizer is better than the commercialized world, all they want you to remember is cash, check or credit card." Taking a pause, Noelle suddenly had an idea. "Hey Dad! Let's get you to the VFW before Thanksgiving." The men gather themselves to leave, the son pledges to bring his dad back to his mom with a hug.

Jacob Jr. hugs his grandmother and says, "Bye grandma. Thanks for making sure I get to hang out with my uncle and granddad today. I'm looking forward to your sweet potato pie and bean salad on Thanksgiving. I love you Grandma and don't worry; I will watch out for your men."

Daddy Chance simply seals everyone's goodbyes by kissing his wife, and they're off to celebrate the bittersweet Veterans Holiday at the Veterans of Foreign War Post 555.

Noelle Jr. bought the Cadillac for nights like this. The men are enjoying the ride to the VFW, when Daddy Chance reminisces about his dad; Avery Chance, and the struggle of Black men to serve in the Army of the United States of America. He talks in poetic spoken word of serving the Country in a segregated Army, his voice matching the Marcus Miller bass line thumping the Jazz tune titled "Panther" that walks out of the Cadillac sound system, like a cool black cat within a sonic masterpiece to accentuate the story. The eyes of Daddy Chance say hold on to these truths by heart, he tells us to give these truths to our sons and daughters, so they would know these stories by their heart, because that's how it was originally translated.

Jacob Jr. begins thinking to himself, *I've heard my Granddaddy speak of my great Granddad before, this is the first time that I listen with my heart.*

And my ears itch when the breath of history brushes them gently, backed by the bass line connecting this moment into a timeless session; paced by our heartbeats that beat like African drums to announce a Holy Spirit is present.

The presence of the Ancestors has come forth to bless these moments, bringing to life remembrances of things too hurtful to carry daily. These stories of living through hell on earth are now ordained to come forth.

And the melody still lingers on.

And time itself takes its time to show the scenes of life onto the approaching sunset, and into the twilight goes the living dreams of ancestral warriors who ride along, putting all under protection of angels, and an Angel speaks life, saying;

"The Army stayed segregated past the end of World War II in 1945, and stayed segregated until July 1948, when the 33rd President of the United States Of America; Harry S. Truman issued an Executive Order abolishing segregation in the United States Armed Forces forever."

The melody is on beat, with a performer's perfect timing, and I heard Granddaddy Chance say, "Oh thank you Lord, that you would make evil become a footstool to the Buffalo soldiers."

Daddy Chance is one with the ancestors and he double snaps his thumbs and says,

"War is hell. The black man is a part of the history of the United States, the very fabric of the 50 State Union, America and the Black man are joint survivors of the hell from every war fought by the Union of States, our Country tis of thee:"

Hear this prayer and praise with a believer's ear, and never let anyone, of any color, ever take that away from you. I pray in the mighty name of Jesus.

Now hear this! my heart is heavy, for I have seen the eyes of great warriors, and even better men be closed forever to this world, those eyes looked at me for assurance, which I gave, to keep the faith and keep their story for their family and for mines."

Jacob the grandson and Noelle Jr., the son did see through the eyes of Noelle Sr., the Spirit of Avery Chance speaking through his son, who tells us to live this life we are given, and to not let their legacy die.

"They gave their blood, so we could live and speak life as survivors, our bodies would forever be tortured on earth through the blood loss represented by the Purple Heart Medal, through their hearts, received with honor, it's the blood, there is power in the blood, live my sons."

Noelle Chance Sr., paused, inhaling to exhale these words,

"These tears you can now see are the purple rain from the Purple Heart I've carried home. See me, look at me, I am a man, a black man standing on the shoulders of giants."

Noelle Oscar Chance Sr., father and Grandfather star hop through the heavens to deliver the spoken word from afar, and he closes saying,

"We've ridden in the stars, not seeing the moment coming, but catching just a glimpse of it leaving, and like the synoptic Gospels of Apostles, Matthew, Mark, Luke and John, each of us are given our own recollection of the truth from the blood of Avery Oscar Chance. In our recollection we will each state that we have witnessed the fulfillment of a covenant between men of faith, prayer, and God, and Peace."

The radio goes silent. The peaceful moment returns the men to the comfort of a luxury car and Daddy Chance, catching the final breeze of the spirit wind; not knowing where it came from, or where it is going, states...

"I will remember this night. It will be specific to each of our souls, when called on again by the Holy Spirit to deliver our story to future Generations, the seeds of our seeds." "Thank you, Granddad," says Jacob Jr.

Noelle Jr. turns the radio off and says, "Dad, we are here. We made it to the VFW. Your story telling was amazing. I felt wonder and fear and I could also feel the strength of my granddaddy Avery. I could feel his fearless presence in your words."

Noelle Sr. speaks calmly, saying, "That's good son, because I really don't know what I said. I loved my father. I know the war and the experiences of life here in America were hard on him, and men like him, but they carried it off with dignity, style, and strength."

Daddy Chance gets animated with his hands as he continues, "My dad called me Cutty, because I cut straight to the point, but he did not want to talk about the war or any war stories. It was only after I kept on asking him different questions that he would tell me anything at all."

Daddy Chance is on a roll now "No more spoken word theatrics," his voice lightens up as if he's trying not to scare us when he says, "My dad told me the Buffalo Soldiers made up a nickname for him, they called him E-man. They said it was because he represented every man to them."

Daddy Chance chuckles as he continues to tell an intense story of a man-to-man battle.

"Many troops fought and there were many brave Black Men. The War turned because of the will of men of all colors, fighting man to man foxhole to foxhole. He said listen here boy, don't ask me again to talk about this war I was in, then, what he told me, put goosebumps all over my body and raised the hair on the back of my neck.

He told me about a foxhole standoff with an enemy soldier. A foxhole is what you dig in the dirt, so your body can lay flat, and you can shoot your gun and reduce the chances of you getting shot because the only thing exposed was your helmet.

E-man, as they called him, took me to that very time and location. It was like I was there in Europe, in World War II, in a foxhole. I could see the enemy across from me and the enemy could see me. E-man was tired, but he could not fall asleep, or his head would pop up and get out of position. That's when you get shot dead.

E-man said both men traded shots at each other whenever anyone made the slightest movement, and both men had good aim. It was after many hours of this standoff, did my daddy Mr. Avery Noelle Chance; nicknamed E-man, wins that standoff. Man, he told me everything he saw, and I was cheering like it was a dunk in a basketball game, but my dad told me he had respect for the fallen Soldier, and I should respect him also, because it could have gone either way."

Daddy Chance ends his story but speaks slow saying,

"I never asked another question about that World War II, but that story helped me in my time of need, when I was dealing with the demons of fighting in that war, the Vietnam War."

He wanted to continue, but silence again takes over the car. Each man lost in his own emotions from what they had just heard.

Jacob Jr. begins to feel the rush of adrenalin that comes along with hearing of the bravery within his blood.

Daddy Chance praises the Lord, saying, "Thank you Lord for regulating my mind, for bringing me back from insanity and Hell, to be with my wife and children."

"Dad, that's a great story. I'm proud to be your son, and I am sure this is how I'm making my way through life, Dad. It's because of you! Because of Granddaddy Avery,"

Noelle Sr., looks at his son with loving eyes, the eyes of generations before them and says,

"It's not about me, my son. It's not even about my dad, it's about Jesus! I'm thankful for you two, and since we are here at the VFW, let's go in and put this stuff behind us. I want to enjoy each other and salute this day."

~

The family of men laugh easily, eat well, and play bowling games while at VFW post 555. If you take a casual glance at them, you can see three Generations together enjoying the evening.

Daddy Chance has made his way to the bar, where many of the

Veterans have gathered. Noelle and Jacob Jr., look on admiringly, and they see flashes of these men in their youth. It's as if their minds are playing tricks on them. They both wonder what those Men of War are talking about on a day like Veterans Day, speaking in their own private code of shared pains and the encouragements they gained, to keep moving onward day by day.

Daddy Chance and the fellow soldiers have delivered on private promises made in battle, as son and grandson watch the old soldiers, who are gathered around the bar. The bartender rings the old firehouse bell hanging behind the bar. It signals someone is buying a drink for everyone.

"Go ahead, enjoy yourself; I will get you home safely," thinks Noelle Jr., and Jacob Jr., at the same time, as they toast each other.

This great night is coming to an end. Noelle Chance Sr., Noelle Chance Jr., and Jacob Evergreen Jr. have crossed a bridge over Generations. Each in their own way looks forward to being together again, Lord willing on Thanksgiving.

# Chapter 6

## *Black Is Regular*

### Issachar

*Then the word of the LORD came unto me, saying, 5 Before I formed thee in the belly, I knew thee; and before thou camest forth out of the womb I sanctified thee, and I ordained thee a prophet unto the nations.*

*—JEREMIAH 1: 4*

Christopher Timothy Kingsly is naturally shy, and that doesn't help when he struggles with schoolwork, caused by undiagnosed dyslexia. Christopher doesn't know how to explain the problem that creates mixed classroom results, which teachers and counselors misunderstand.

Dyslexia, undiagnosed, is a problem made more understandable when teachers have more than the recommended classroom size for optimal learning, which is 14 to 15 students. Classrooms with more students than that make it easy to overlook transposed numbers, using

31 instead of 13, or thinking ei but writing, i.e., down, as in the word rec-ieve.

Transposing numbers and letters are some of the problems of Dyslexia undiagnosed. Thank God for Theo Huxtable, a black television character who had this problem hindering his schoolwork. Theo is the son of a successful doctor who has all the advantages of wealth but that could not help this child. Perseverance and Divine intervention showed the problem is not psychological.

Children with this problem are not slow as they are thought to be. Dyslexia is cognitive, it is not a mental problem, prescription glasses can be a remedy. General awareness is important to the potential problem of all concerned. Teachers and Students require R. E. S. T., which stands for recess, educate, study and training. R.E.S.T. depends on teamwork, everyone must work together for better results in schoolwork and in the homework required of the student.

Our teachers need the help. The youth in these classrooms are our future leaders. Nickolas and Mary Kingsly are involved with the learning process of their child. They apply the REST theory and have met with Miss Labelle Patience. Teacher and parents working together have found a school sponsored Tutor program to help Christopher, which is the best option until Mom and Dad can afford a specialized school like the Bella Institute for Advance Learning, an excellent option that will have to wait.

Hard work has allowed Christopher Kingsly to pass from grade to grade, but this 10-year-old boy wants to do better, and his best is yet to come, that's the title of his favorite song sung by the North Star Village Baptist Church Choir. Christopher is well known in school because he keeps his teachers and classmates joyful by showing his love of life, his courage, and his kindness, that shines like a light from his inside out to the world.

Aleayah Fields and Jimmy Dewland know these qualities well. They are his best friends and not surprised when he asked them to wait for him in the hallway.

Christopher has saved a delicious red apple from home, to give to his teacher on the last day of school before the Thanksgiving Holiday break. Miss Labelle Patience is pleasantly surprised when Christopher steps forward at the end of the early dismissal day and says, "Thank you for being my teacher, Miss Patience. I like learning with you and the way you help me to know more stuff, so I want to give you this apple I saved for you."

Miss Patience responds with a big smile on her face and says, "Well, this is nice Christopher. Tell your parents that I said thank you, and I thank you for being a good student. I have faith that you will keep working hard and doing all of your schoolwork, so you will be ready for 6th grade."

"Okay! Bye Miss Patience. I gotta line up for the bus. Happy Thanksgiving."

Miss Patience is genuinely touched by the sweetness of her thoughtful student, almost forgetting that she is covering the school front office for early dismissal. Christopher, Aleayah and Jimmy walk together to the bus drop-off, pickup area and are ready to say their happy goodbyes.

Aleayah rides on bus number 4, Jimmy on bus number 3 and Christopher rides on bus number 5, The good friends promise to give thanks for their friendships and say goodbye with their special handshakes. They will be gone until school restarts in 10 days, and then the countdown to Christmas vacation will begin.

~

SIMON KINGSLY IS a senior at Bella Hills High School, and he has the task to care for his little brother today. He also has early dismissal and goes straight home to be there when little brother gets off his school bus and walks home. Simon has planned a brother's day out on the town, so they do more just sit around the house waiting for the rest of the family to get home for dinner.

Mary Kingsly works part-time as a Tailor at the ELOQUII plus size Women's Fashion store in Uptown Village. When she needs the van, she takes over as the family driver, but on today daughter Marion uses the NST; North Star Transit public transportation system, to get to work.

Today is early dismissal day for the school kids; but it's Friday of the weekend before Thanksgiving for everyone else, and this is the busiest food shopping time of the year, so Dad, Mom and Daughter will join each other and the other shoppers' afterwork.

Mother Mary is the Van driver today and the first stop of many for Mary Kingsly is the office of N. O. Chance Financial Agency to drop the husband off at work

Nickolas says, "Honey, we're going shopping tonight right?"

Mary nods her head yes and with a kiss asks, "What time will you be ready to leave here?"

Nickolas states, "4:30 or so. Just call me when you are close. Bye! And have a great day."

Mary begins planning the day, thinking, *I will call Marion at lunchtime to tell her I have to pick her up before her father, then we'll go to the supermarket together.*

Simon Kingsly is glad to spend some time with his brother; he makes sure he gets home first and is waiting in the kitchen, when little brother unlocks the front door with his own key for the first time.

"T.T is growing up," says Simon, as the younger brother makes his way across the house to his big brother, and they exchange their special handshake. Simon is excited about the day he has planned that he could not wait to tell Christopher.

"Hey kid, it's me and you all day, and I've saved a few dollars for us to have some fun."

Christopher is surprised to hear his big brother say they are going to hang out together.

"Really, Sy man. Me and you hanging out? That's cool. What are we going to do?"

"Simon sez we're going to do some window shopping, get some pizza, and check out the Christmas Village, then while we're out there we might as well visit the Wiz Pinball Arcade that all my Senior Classmates are talking about. We've got plenty of time to hang out since Mom, dad and Marion won't be home until about 8 o'clock and they want us to eat dinner together."

"How are we going to do all of that?"

"Simon sez we gonna catch the bus Gus, make a new plan Stan, don't need to fuss much, we will get on the NST cross town express to the mall and I will show you how it's done kid. Are you ready to hang out with your brother all day?"

Christopher nods his head yes.

Simon spins around in a smooth dance move and flexes his biceps; which have gotten muscular; weightlifting with the Bella High track team.

"Little Brother, let's have some fun. If I were you, I'd go to the bathroom and change clothes. It will be dark by the time we get back here, especially since the time just fell back an hour. Go head, I'm going to check the bus schedule to see the best time to leave here."

Christopher begins to feel more confident in himself. He knows big brother is not just showing off, but he's showing him that he's growing up. Christopher looks at his brother, who is looking at the bus schedule, and sees something different about him. He sees the man that he's growing into, and he admires what he sees and yells out,

"Sy man, you think you're cool, you! All right with me. Thanks for planning this day," and he runs out the room.

Simon is taken by the moment, realizing that he now has the responsibility of taking care of mommy and daddy's baby boy, who is growing up. The two of them begin this Christmas in a way they couldn't see coming, but it's right here, right now. Simon, for a brief moment, gets cold feet and wants to change what he has boldly planned. But love for his brother and the way Christopher looks up to him touches his heart, and he laughs it off, shaking his head saying to himself, *Simon sez get it together*.

A partly sunny day chases the chill away, the air carries a slight breeze that promises colder temperatures and snow are on the way, but so is Thanksgiving and the Christmas Holiday Season. Today looks bright and has the promise of a wonderful experience for the two brothers, who are about to ride the City Bus. When you ride the bus in any city in the USA you will see people of different races and different skin colors than yours, people of the world, some good some bad but judge them by their character.

Prejudice is easy if you never see people different than yourself. We are all of the Human Race and have different languages, customs, food and even beliefs, but you can go around the world and find one common joy to the world, which is Christmas. The year speeds through its final two months. New Year's Eve is on the horizon, but in the USA, first comes Thanksgiving, then the anticipation builds up for Christmas Day and the peace that surpasses all understanding.

Simon shows his brother that their home is not far away from a city bus stop, how much it will cost to ride on the bus, what to look for on the bus stop sign, how to wave to the Bus Driver to let him know to stop, how to read a bus map, different bus numbers and the bus routes around the city and how to get on the bus when it stops. The Brothers are ready to go and out the door they go ready to enjoy the rest of the day, and they don't have to wait long at the bus stop, because the bus is running on time today. The Bus Driver greets them both as they walk up the bus steps but directs his attention to Christopher saying,

"Hello young man. I haven't seen you at the bus stop before. Is this your first time on the NST?

"No sir. I have caught the bus before with my mom," Christopher says. "But this is my first time with my big brother."

Then Simon greets the driver and asks for two transfer tickets.

The bus zips along, and in-between the stop and go of picking up and dropping off passengers, each stop offers a new perspective.

Simon tells his brother it's time to get off this bus and transfer to the Express bus, which will take them to the Christmas Village. The hustle and bustle of downtown reminds Simon that next Friday will be Black Friday. Simon says.

"Hey T.T, if you think this is crowded, wait until next Friday, which is Black Friday. It will be super crowded everywhere and then we will start Christmas shopping for real."

The Brothers begin to make their way through the crowd gathered together in different areas, waiting to transfer to their next bus, and Simon challenges Christopher to find their Express bus waiting area.

"Here it is!" he says proudly.

Then Christopher notices that the building across the street is the Bella learning Institute.

"Hey Sy man, that building over there has the name Mom, Dad and my teacher were talking about. Mom and Dad said they're praying for me to be able to go to that school over there. Thanks for taking me with you today. I can't wait to tell everybody when we get home."

Simon is smiling and profiling, noticing that there are pretty girls also waiting for the Express bus, but he stops long enough to tell his little brother about their surroundings.

"Oh man, that is cool. You can see the school," says big brother. Looking eye to eye, he says, "T.T, I believe prayer changes things for real. I have seen things change with my own eyes. The Bella learning Institute has a great rep, but it cost money baebee, let's believe it can happen for you."

The Brothers have a great time window shopping, eating hot dogs and especially playing games at the arcade. Simon doesn't have much money, but he has enough for them to enjoy the day, topped off by visiting the Christmas tree Holiday lights, which have a walkthrough and a drive through exhibition celebrating their grand opening.

Simon says, "T.T, I want you to go over to the counter and get a flyer for us to bring home. Maybe this year we will drive through the Christmas lights show."

Christopher gets the flyer and, walking back to his brother, notices a group of girls and tells his brother in a whisper, "Sy man, those girls are looking at you." Simon turns around and Christopher starts laughing. "Made you look!"

Simon laughs too. "I thought you were talking about those girls over on the other side, cause they been checking me out since we got here. Then Simon; looking at his watch, and says, "T.T, it's time to catch the bus back home. Let's go."

Time seems to fly on by when you're having fun. Simon Peter and Christopher Timothy Kingsly have had a fun day, where even waiting at the bus transfer point was an unforgettable experience. Going back Downtown provided an answer to the question, why did the chicken cross the road. Christopher could tell you about the answer from his own experience, and he would say it was so the chicken could get a closer look at the other side.

The ride back home provided a closer look at the other side of the road. On the other side, there's a unique story to tell, and this time around a dream can be touched, while waiting to transfer buses. On this side of the road Christopher's dream is not a faraway vision anymore, what was across the street can now be touched, and the doors to help his unbelief are opened by faith, when he can see and touch the doors of The Bella Learning Institute.

Christopher can now see himself as a new student that walks up the stairs to the entrance doors, and he remembers what his teacher Miss Labelle Patients said. "You will be ready for 6th grade."

Christopher knows in his heart that prayers are working. He can now see he is close.

The Brothers received help for their unbelief. God Bless the child that's got his own, and this day trip for the brothers will serve as lifelong proof that faith is the substance of things hoped for, the evidence of things unseen.

Simon's cell phone makes a notification sound.

"Hey T.T, Marion just text me to say they picked up Dad and are on the way to the Supermarket. Man, that's what I call good timing."

"Simon, I'm ready for my own cell phone, especially because you won't be going to school with me no more after you graduate. After today you can tell Mom and Dad that I did good and I'm ready for my own phone."

"Simon sez be cool Chris. Tiny Tim is just your nickname. I know you are growing up, just keep doing what you're doing little brother, and everything will be alright."

Simon continues teaching his brother, giving him the bus schedule and saying, "Chris, look at the bus schedule and find the bus that leaves here to go to Scenic Parkway and Mountain Boulevard, then tell me what time it leaves."

Simon sez, "Take your time, get your information, and always be prepared. Remember this, you can always ask the bus drivers for help."

Christopher says, "I can do it, Sy man. I will show you. Alright, don't talk about it, be about it. And Chris, do it for yourself this time, not because Simon sez!"

Christopher replies almost confused, "Sy man, are you trying to trick me?"

Simon speaks with a serious tone when he says, "No little Brother this is no trick. We're out here in the public together. I want you to be aware of everything around you at all times, no joke. So, I will be watching you."

Simon pulls Christopher shoulder to shoulder and leans into his ear to say. "Chris, whenever you are out and especially alone, be quick about everything you do, alright? Go ahead, and concentrate on the schedule. I will watch out for you."

Christopher does a great job, and they get on the bus heading home.

"Chris, I want you to look at our bus route on the schedule and find the bus stop right before Scenic Parkway. Remember to press the rubber strip between the windows after we leave that stop. When you press that strip, it rings the bell and tells the Bus Driver you want to get off the bus at the next stop, which is our stop at Scenic Parkway.

Don't get nervous and if you get confused, ask the bus driver for help, and tell him what street you want to get to. Then you can ride the bus anywhere it goes. I already text Marion back, so she knows we are ok and on our way home."

Simon and Christopher make it back to their neighborhood safely. The walk home is a pleasant evening stroll past many houses that have put Holiday Harvest Wreaths on their doors. It's the Thanksgiving effect; a harvest of thankfulness takes over.

Simon begins to realize the big Thanksgiving Day football game for his High School, will be his last as a student, he states out loud, "Hey Chris, I just remembered the turkey day football game for my school will be my last one as a student. Man, I'm going to have fun. Rain, snow, or shine.

Christopher says, "Am I big enough to go with you this year? Tiny Tim, or should I say Chris..."

Simon waves his hands over his brother's head and taps both of his shoulders and says, "My little Brother is growing up, dub thee boys to men, milk to meat, and big boy let me tell you something, you can go any place with me."

Simon gives his brother a high five and says, "Uncle Matt and Aunt Marie want to go, and I guess Mom and Dad want to go also, so I'm the last one to figure it all out."

Whatever Simon is feeling stops him from walking.

*Okay, deep breath, now I can get my cool back,* Simon thinks to himself and they continue on in silence until arriving at the front door of their home.

Simon reaches into his pants pocket for the House Keys. He's ready to unlock the door but stops suddenly and states, "Little Brother you did good today, really good. Simon sez Chris, you can use your key to unlock the door."

You can tell by the smile on Christopher's face that he appreciates the trust from big brother, and they're both glad to be back.

"There's no place like home."

MARY KINGSLY HAD a busy day of Seamstress work, there are plenty of request for work to do before Thanksgiving, and the Holiday parties of December. Mary is not one for texting, but she texts her daughter; saying I will be there in about 20 minutes. After picking up Marion, it's onward to pick up Nickolas, then shop for Thanksgiving dinner.

The office is empty when Mary calls her husband to say she is just a few minutes away, Nickolas also had a busy day with his co-workers, but all are happy with extra work in preparation for the new Holiday work schedule that will begin in the oncoming Thanksgiving work week. The main goal is to assure the work is done, so the staff can leave early on Thanksgiving Eve and return to work on two hours later than their normal start time on Black Friday, they have met that goal.

Nickolas greets his wife with a kiss and is happy to see his daughter.

"Hi Daddy," Marion says with a hug, while moving from the front seat.

"Please stay in the front. I have the two of you to myself for a while. I don't remember the last time it was just us 3, so don't mind me if I just take it all in," Nickolas said as they drove to the Supermarket.

"Marion, how was your day?" Dad asks, and she is excited to report her day was a successful one.

"Dad," Marion says with energy, "business is picking up after being down since the summer. In our Staff meeting I learned what our Sales objectives are for Black Friday. Last year, the Store had sales numbers that were in red; not good, turn into black sales numbers, which stand for financial profit. Black Friday weekend is the most important time of the year for Retail stores and this year I will be part of the management team."

Marion then turns in her seat to look at her father. Speaking with passion, she says,

"Dad, I want to tell you something that hit me today. Black Friday is a play on words; intentional or not, that relates to cargo ships coming into port to dock and unload, whiskey, clothes, tobacco, spices and other products of pre-slavery trade, making people rich and coining the phrase, 'My ship has come in.' Although it is great for goods and produce, it loses its flavor when the cargo is Humans, intended for slavery. And when you study the Middle Passage, you will find out that slave-trade ships carried over 20 million Black men and women as cargo."

Marion makes a point to her parents, a point she would not make in mixed company, just like politics and religion. Slavery talk does not make for pleasant conversation.

"Over 12 million of the 20 million Humans, made the Middle Passage to the United States. Black people, as cargo from Africa, provided our country with an economic base virtually free of cost, due to slave labor through multiple Generations for over 400 years. Things are better now, but we all have learned to survive by going along to get along, to move the family forward and stay alive," says Marion in a pleasant yet emotional tone.

The Kingsly family achieves book education, street education, world education by real talk, faith, hope and working hard for what you want. The family teaches when gathered together and believe in the words of the dearly departed Reverend Dr. Martin Luther King Jr., who said, "Judge people by the content of their character, not by skin color," and "We Shall Overcome."

"Marion, your Grand Daddy Chance used to say that in the card game of life, 'You got to know when to hold 'em, know when to fold 'em, know when to walk away, know when to run. Never count your money when you're sitting at the table. There will be time enough for counting when the deal is done'.

"It's part of an old school song called "The Gambler" that's written and sung by a white man named Don Schlitz. Where he got it, nobody can say, but it's good advice for any skin color, but definitely for that mean green," Nickolas said to his daughter matter factly.

Mary Kingsly perks up, saying, "Marion, my Mamma said one day as a little child, she was playing with the children her mother, grandma Pimmy, was taking care of. These children just so happened to be white. A white man came to the house to visit while they had been playing in the backyard. He was dressed nice and had blue eyes and nice hair, fixed up like white men do.

"Mamma and the rest of the kids stopped playing and gathered around to hear what this important looking white man had to say. Grandma Pimmy and that man were laughing at the things they were saying, but they couldn't hear. After a quiet spell, that man got up out of his chair and they could clearly hear him talk. He sounded just like black men talk.

"My Momma did something that was considered fresh, and she spoke into grown folks' business, and said to Grandma Pimmy, 'how come that white man sound like he black?'

"Grandma Pimmy took it in stride and said, 'Fresh mouth little girl, I'm gonna deal with you later.' My Mamma got paddled for that, then she said, 'this here man is a Black man'

'But he ain't even light skin, he's white with blue eyes,' my Mamma said. 'Baebee,' Grandma Pimmy said, 'Everything ain't how it looks. Don't judge people by looking at the outside.' She chased them all outside, and they watched that man get into his fine car and leave."

Marion is less agitated when she speaks mother and father don't interrupt her thoughts and she says "I'm not looking for a handout from society or sympathy about the Black people's history in the United States; you didn't raise me that way, but I won't run from the truth. I heard you loud and clear when you said, followers just follow, leaders just lead."

Mary speaks to her daughter with an encouraging tone, saying, "Marion, that's a lot to take in. We can find the positives in a bad situation, and we have to, because so many people don't know what Black Friday means at all. Many will continue to only see it and the Christmas Season, as a commercial to get shoppers to spend more money."

Marion says, "Yes, yes, yes, this knowledge came to me today. I already knew it but couldn't handle it. Those memories are painful and the truth of slavery hurts. Slavery and the vision of the unimaginable misery our ancestors endured terrorized their soul, and are passed down through generations. Thank God for taking away the pain. God's love lifted me. I was lifted in the middle of my distress with these thoughts and then joy overtook all the bad feelings and that's when I realized who the son sets free, is free indeed."

Momma Kingsly says, "Girl, you just said something right there. I like that!"

"My Kingsly queens, you speak the truth and teach the truth. Let's all remember to speak the truth to power, when prompted by the Lord, and that the truth will make you free."

"Black Friday is what it is. Stores are in business to make money, but I never equated the term Black Friday to slave ships coming into Jamestown, Virginia in the sixteen hundred's," says Marion.

The Supermarket is not far from the workplace of Nickolas Kingsly. The drive is made more pleasant by joyful conversation. Mary pulls into the Supermarket parking lot and finds an open space close to the entrance, saying, "Thank you, Parking Lot Angels, for a great parking space."

"The parking lot Angels show you favor, Mom!"

"Amen to that, baby girl. This is a good parking spot," and it doesn't take long for Mommy to move into shopping gear. "Alright guys, for tonight and tomorrow's dinner, we'll get a couple of rotisserie chickens, soup, salad, and fruits. I'm making beef stew for Sunday dinner, so I need beef, and we will get a Turkey. Marion, you check mark the list I have of things we need for our Thanksgiving dinner. We will clean out the refrigerator and eat leftovers for the week ahead, then get pizza for Wednesday night. Now prepare to shop."

Mary looks to her husband and says, "Oh yeah, Nick, I spoke to Simon and T.T after school. They have kept in contact with me all day. Simon last said that they were on the way to the Downtown bus transfer stop and should soon be home."

"Mom, we've been texting each other all day. They are having fun."

"That's good news. I told Simon to keep the communication tight and don't give us too much guesswork.

"He did that," says a proud dad. "Alright my ladies, I gotta get something to eat right now. Do you want a hotdog and something to drink?"

Mother and daughter say, "Yes," and Nickolas happily replies, "Let's do it. Then we can get this shopping done," as Christmas lights appear, and the nighttime begins to settle in.

The lights and decorations add cheer to the atmosphere and for those who love the Season, the festive colors bust out on the scene. The Retail world is ready for the Holiday, and everyone can tell when they begin hearing Christmas music playing on the store speakers; for some, this is a joy but not everyone. There are some who perceive the change over from regular music to Christmas music as an annoyance, but for all there's an undeniable turn to more peaceful times.

A Christmas song favorite, *It's the most wonderful time of the year*, floats through the speakers, coinciding with the feeling Nickolas has, while enjoying a hot dog and soft drink with his wife and daughter.

Into the air floats through the speakers, another song coinciding with the feeling Nickolas has. It's known as the Black people's

Christmas anthem and it is known from the very first notes the song introduction is underway, then together, everyone sings.

"Hang all the Mistletoe. I'm going to get to know you better, this Christmas," and the melody still lingers on.

Together, the three shopping musketeers fill their shopping cart with food for the Thanksgiving feast and have an easy time of it. Even within a supermarket full of people, it's teamwork that makes the dream work for team Kingsly.

Waiting in the checkout line is not a bother at all and the menu is complete, including the traditional turkey, ham, collard greens, string beans, potatoes, stuffing and cornbread; pies were purchased earlier and frozen, but not sweet potatoes. They are purchased when you are ready to make them into pies on the biggest cooking night of the year; a Holiday itself, Thanksgiving Eve.

The close parking space does come in handy, as everyone begins to feel the effects of a long Friday workday. Nickolas says, "Let's go home," and he finishes packing the groceries in the van.

"Honey, I'm going to let you and Marion take care of dinner when we get home. I know Simon and TT are waiting for us, so I will drive, and you guys relax."

"Good. I was getting tired," says an appreciative wife.

Marion turns on the radio to KNSV, the number one radio station in North Star Village, and a commercial is on promoting the radio station's Thanksgiving Eve cooking show.

"Join us for the soul music show that shakes and bakes R&B classics on the radio while you're shaking and baking in your kitchen. It all begins at 10pm on Thanksgiving Eve. We will take your requests and you tell us what's cooking on your Thanksgiving menu. Check out your host with the most, Les Givings, keeping you company along with special guest, DJ Casanova Cocoa Brown."

Marion says, "Mom, I bet you Aunt Marie will be listening, and I know we will, so let's call in."

"Marion, you can call in... but I will be listening to music and cooking," said Mary.

Nickolas pulls the Van into the driveway and Simon comes bounding out of the house with Christopher not far behind. They greet everyone with a joyful noise! Simon says, "Don't worry about the bags, we'll bring them in and put the food away."

"You get no argument from us," Nickolas says. "It's been a long day, so you guys handle the groceries and I'm going in to wash up for dinner."

Mary replies, "I second that emotion. Marion, please put the turkey in the freezer and the food for Thanksgiving away separately. We'll let the turkey begin to thaw on Sunday. I'm going to change clothes and I'll have dinner ready in half an hour." Team Kingsly works together. They always do.

Winner, winner rotisserie chicken, French fries and salad dinner. Who knew it could be so good?

"Thanks for dinner, mom," says Simon before adding, "Hey guys, check this out. Next Friday is Black Friday and we'll still be eating yard bird, but the one you got is big bird."

Simon laughs at his own joke, then says. "Mom, Dad, I just realized today that this year's Thanksgiving football game will be my last one as a High School student."

"Simon sez he's getting sentimental," Marion says.

"Hey brother, snap out of it. You got a long way to go until graduation, just enjoy it and don't stop working hard. I would love to go to the game with you, of course, as a distinguished Alumni student, but I got a feeling I will be cooking. Wait a minute, I haven't heard about your day T.T," turning her attention to the youngest brother. "Do tell us all about it."

T.T has a different look. He's growing up, and he begins to speak with an excited confidence saying, "Mom, dad, thank you for everything you do and thanks Sy man for spending money for me to catch the bus and showing me a fun day."

"Marion," T.T says looking at his sister, "Sy man said that I can go with him anywhere he goes, and that I did good today. I didn't get scared. I talked to the Bus Driver and oh yeah, Mommy I walked up the stairs and touched the door of the Bella School you and Dad said would help me learn better. I like the way it looks, and I remember the bus route to get there, so we can keep praying that I can go to that school."

Marion gives her little brother a high five, and Christopher continues saying, "Um wait, I also gave my teacher an apple, and Sy man bought me some hot dogs, and I saw the pretty Christmas tree lights. It was a long bus ride to get to Christmas Village, but I didn't fall asleep. Daddy, I want you to know I unlocked the door with my house key today, and I won't lose it. I had a good day; the best part was Sy man said I can go to the football game with him on Thanksgiving."

Nickolas says "Boys, I am proud of you. Simon Peter Kingsly, you stepped up big today and I know you could have done other things with your time. Thank you for helping our day go by smoothly, and you kept in contact with us. Chris, you have grown up right in front of our eyes."

Daddy Kingsly takes in the moment. "Chris, I love you, son. I'm glad you came into my life. Each of you are a joy to me and your mom. I guess that's my Thanksgiving prayer but hearing that you guys saw and touched the Bella Learning Institute helps our prayer life and helps us to keep believing in prayer."

Nickolas and Simon exchange their special father and son handshake and a grateful Dad says, "Simon, job well done. I'm looking forward to going to your last turkey day game as a student at the Bella High School Catamounts."

The Kingsly family is stuck in a moment of love. Silence has taken over, and each member takes in the ambience of the sudden quiet in their home. A delicate balance for peace is found between a world of chaos; that attacks daily, and the good fight of faith that doesn't get much notoriety.

MFSB has the theme of the soul Train dance show and mother,

father, Sister, Brother who are the Kingsly family; Mary, Nickolas, Marion, Christopher, and Simon are a team, and their souls dance as one. As one, they are not uneasy about the silence, savoring the pregnant pause in the presence of the Holy Spirit, unaware.

Mary breaks through the smoky haze of silent praise, saying, "I am very glad for you, Simon. You would make any mother proud. Chris, things went well today, and it might seem like it was easy, but you guys accomplished a lot. Marion, thank you for effortlessly pulling us through this day. Maybe when you have children of your own, you will look back on this day and say, 'how did Mom and Dad do it?' but you are a wonderful Sister, a great daughter and you will be a great mother. Thank you, babe."

The loving mother moves to clear the table, but is met by her daughter, who signals she will do it. Mom moves towards the living room and says, "Chris you and Simon had a good day."

Grabbing her husband's hand, Mary continues... "Look at the things you accomplished together," listing them with her fingers. "No problems getting out of school, Chris used his own house key for the first time, and learned about the city bus, even getting a transfer ticket to ride all the way to and from the Christmas Village. Chris, I pray you keep the faith, and now that you have seen The Bella Learning Institute, confirms that our prayers are working."

Nickolas, sensing everyone is tired, says, "Let's all call it a day. You look tired. Mary, all the Thanksgiving frozen food goes in the garage freezer, the kitchen refrigerator is cramp, but that's a good problem to have. Today's memories will be part of my Thanksgiving Testimony."

"Goodnight, Mom, good night, Dad," are the joyous noises ringing out in a roll call from all the children of Nickolas and Mary. They will sleep well tonight.

The older siblings are blissfully unaware of the times, unaware that they have enjoyed one of the final meals together in their childhood era. Marion and Simon look to go out into the world, but home will live forever in their hearts.

Mother and father can sense that this Christmas Holiday Season will be the last of its kind; the children are growing up, but there's no time for melancholy emotions, the celebration of life is just beginning.

And the melody still lingers on. The land line phone rings. Mary answers it in the living room. Not looking at the caller ID number, she says "Hello!" It's her sister Marie on the mainline.

"Hey girl, what time do you want me to pick you up in the morning?"

"Hey Marie. Thanks for reminding me. Let's be at the church at 9:30, then we will help them pass out the turkeys until about noon. Don't worry about breakfast, the Hospitality committee will provide it and I'm sure it will be nice."

"Okay then, I need to go to bed soon. Oh yeah, before I forget to tell you, Matt wants to go with us to help."

"That's great," Mary says, turning on the speaker phone. "Marie, I just put you on speaker so Nickolas could hear."

"Hey Niko, congratulations on your elevation to Deacon. We will see you in the morning. Matt and I want you to know how happy we are for you."

"Thank you, my Sister-in-law. I appreciate y'all and it's all good," Nickolas says with joy. "Please tell Matt I said thank you. I look forward to seeing you tomorrow."

Marie gets a kick out of her Brother-In-law, and replies,

"Yes Sir, Niko. I will tell him."

"Alright y'all we're all on the same page. Sis, I will see you in the morning, please tell Steph and Jr., that Auntie says hi I love you." They both hang up the phone, each saying, bye at the same time.

"Honey, since you are cleaning the kitchen counters, I'm going to do like the kids and go to bed. You're such a good man, Saint Nick, see you when you get there."

Nickolas replies, "I see you looking over your shoulders honey, I'll be there."

THE WEEKEND before Thanksgiving is a magical time across the Country. It quietly announces that a new Holiday Season is upon us with an Evergreen light, which shows us; everyone, the way to Christmas Day.

The Sunday before Thanksgiving week offers the spiritual, the fellowship joy of giving thanks in the Sanctuary through prayer and praise at the Altar. The Sunday before Thanksgiving week also offers the joy of final preparation for Brother Nickolas Kingsly's move into a Church leadership position; as a member of the Deacon's Board, an elevation he did not seek, and neither would he turn it down.

What joy.

A joy that fills the heart of North Star Village Baptist Church, like the joy of children who are out of school with little or no homework.

What joy.

The joy of grownups knowing the work year and domestic year are soon to end with a dual celebration of out with the old, and in with the new.

What joy.

Everyone is not joyful. For some; like Mr. N. O. Chance, this time of year brings forth depression, frayed nerves, and short tempers.

What joy;

There are some in the crowd of people that feel out of the Spirit of Christmas due to family strife, a loved one's death, being away from home, homelessness or just problems with money.

What joy.

JESUS

AND IT CAME TO PASS, Thanksgiving Monday and Tuesday go by as pre-written blessings of a short work week that moves fast, sped up by anticipation of Thanksgiving Day. Nickolas manages a workforce that's eager to be productive, thankful for a new Holiday work schedule that includes returning to work at 11am on Black Friday.

Noelle has agreed to try the Holiday work schedule suggested by Nickolas Kingsly, which added two hours to the Monday, Tuesday workday, which will allow everyone to leave work early today, Wednesday Thanksgiving Eve. The prospect of earlier workdays did not bother the boss. He would work every day if he could and make his employees do the same, not breaking the routine of work for anything and certainly not Christmas.

Everyone that works gives thanks at Thanksgiving time; knowingly or unknowing, for the worker's union had to fight hard for employees to have basic rights with their employment. Before Union's stood up for people, the worker class had no rights for necessities like work conditions, bathroom breaks and eating to name a few.

The Black Ebenezer Scrooge, Noelle Oscar Chance underwhelms everyone with his personality. The cool Joe he used to be in his younger days has disappeared, only recently materializing at the Harvest Moon Masquerade Ball to dance with the woman in purple, and again briefly on Veteran's Day in the company of his father and nephew at the VFW Post 555.

The Black Ebenezer Scrooge is in denial, rejecting the reason for the Season but not the reason for his money season. Wednesday morning, Thanksgiving Eve, is still Humpday and even in a short work week it's just as tough as Monday, and he finds himself talking to himself in a way that's seems strange for a man who has the means to buy anything he wants.

Noelle talks to himself with the gruffness of a drill Sergeant at the beginning of boot camp when he says, "How did Kingsly talk me into this Thanksgiving Holiday work schedule?", while looking at and talking into the breakfast menu. "I'll tell you what I'm thankful for, my money and no woman or kids to take it away from me."

Peace and peacefulness are not on the menu at Sylvia's Coffee and Cakes café, but their spirits are present in the atmosphere.

"Good morning. Welcome to Sylvia's coffee and cakes. My name is Trina, and I will be your waitress this morning. Are you ready to order?"

"Yes," said Noelle almost annoyed. "I will have your regular breakfast and a regular cup of coffee."

"Sir, what is regular coffee?"

Noelle looks at the attractive waitress and begins to think of the voice he heard behind the mask of the woman in purple at the Masquerade Ball. Thoughts of their conversation and dance bring a smile to his face, removing his own mask of cold gruffness when he continues to talk to the waitress, but suddenly with a voice with the smoothness of butter.

The man who would be King reclaims his inner Prince Charming when he says, "Well of course regular coffee is made by adding two creams and two sugars."

Trina's reply continues to wake up the ghost of the past when she says,,", "Oh, that saying is from Delaware. At Sylvia's we say black is regular, not like down south. For you sir, regular is cream and sugar, and black is black."

Noelle smiles at the waitress, who just smiles back and says, "Sir, I'll put in your order and be right back with your coffee."

Thoughts of former business partner Khole Cashe start dashing through the snow on Noelle's one-track money mind; now open to the past, as he whispers, "I miss you my old friend, you always said black is regular."

Noelle wants to be served breakfast today, rewarding himself for being a good businessman and pick up dessert cakes he pre-ordered. He chose a candied sweet potato pound cake and a red velvet cake, two delicious options that keep his promise to bring dessert to what he calls the Thanksgiving feast fest. Each cake is packed within a Holiday theme box and paired with an appropriate wine and/or a non-alcohol sparkling water.

Noelle's cellphone rings and he answers, saying, "Holly. Aren't we both the early birds today?"

Holly responds, "Nice try Mr. No. I'm calling you to cheer you up and tell you somebody loves you babe."

"I'm fine. As a matter of fact, I'm just picking up some dessert for tomorrow," Noelle says proudly.

"My dear Brother, Jacob and JJ are looking forward to spending quality time with you tomorrow. We all love you and want you to be happy, so try extra hard to be nice today and to be on time tomorrow," Holly says, while laughing.

"You are so dry. I think you're trying to be funny but it's, 'I love you more today than yesterday,' but not as much as tomorrow."

"Got cha brother," Holly responds. "You might be on to something El, but like you say no way."

"Holly, I'm excited. If for no other reason, it's because you are excited."

Holly enthusiastically says "El, don't forget to call mom and dad, and give yourself a reminder to listen to Les Givings radio show tonight because your nephew's commercial about the Read and Feed the Need charity will be featured, and he will be interviewed. It's scheduled for 10pm."

"Holly, you sound like my secretary Kristen."

Holly jumps right in saying, "I like that girl."

"Alright, alright look dear heart, I'm getting ready to leave the restaurant. My desserts are wrapped up and I still have to take them home and get to the office. I will call mom and dad, and you can tell your husband and son that I look forward to being with them tomorrow so we can have some turkey. Now Mrs. Evergreen, I will be thankful for you to say bye!"

"Bye," Holly says with a gleeful cheer in her voice.

"Noelle replies with a gleeful bye."

Noelle has a better attitude when he walks into the office, just as Nickolas Kingsly has called for a meeting.

"I want to officially wish each of you a Happy Thanksgiving," Nickolas states to his co-workers. "You guys are a great staff and I want to thank you for your enthusiasm and hard work to make the first part of our Holiday work schedule a success. Thanks for your timely work on Monday and yesterday. Let's continue to win through this short workday. We'll be leaving today at 3 o'clock, so let's take a 20-minute coffee break now and meet again before leaving for the day."

The rest of the morning zips along and lunch time approaches, just as Miss Kristen Flowers approaches the office of Noelle Chance and quietly knocks on his door.

"Come in Miss Flowers. What am I missing?" says Noelle.

Kristen Flowers is the Administrative Secretary for the N. O. Chance Financial Agency, and a graduate of Blackstone College in nearby Chinook County and a lifelong resident of Northern California. Kristen is also a direct product of the Internship and Mentor program put together by Mrs. Elizabeth Waterhouse, wife of Price Waterhouse and a flawless asset to the company.

Kristen has brown skin, brown eyes, black hair and is a well-built Black woman of average height, who dresses office chic; understating her beauty, and is about business. Today, however, she enters the office with a subtle change as she sits down for their daily work briefing.

"Mr. Chance," Kristen says urgently, "I'm thankful for my job and I want to say thank you for allowing me to work here and learn from you and this great staff."

Kristen has entered the office many times, but today is different. This conversation with the boss is one he is not prepared for. He is already on guard, thinking she's preparing to leave for another job.

"Wait right there, Miss Kristen Flowers. There's room for you to grow here. You do not have to leave me. I mean, leave the company," Noelle says, almost panicked. It's the first time in two years of employment that he expresses how much he values her work.

"No sir, I'm not thinking about leaving," she said, trying to hide her smile. "I just wanted to let you know how I feel, since it's Thanksgiving time and a time to give thanks. Mr. Chance, I believe the good things of the world surpass the bad, but you have to put up the good fight and stay positive. I represent the employees when I say we have a good news report and request to present to you."

A look of shock is written all over Noelle's face, and Mr. No, the personality that dominates this time of the year, scrambles to recover, he's trying to regain the emotional leverage he has given to his secretary and minimize what he fears will be financial damage.

Kristen's pause in the conversation was no business strategy, but it was well played. Seeing the reaction of her boss, she quickly says, "Mr. Chance the Staff asked me to speak to you for permission to put together a light breakfast on Black Friday in Honor of Nickolas Kingsly, who was elevated to Deacon at his Church. We want to celebrate his good news and show our appreciation. Please excuse our last-minute request but we just found out, and Black Friday will be a great opportunity to do it. That's what this meeting is about."

The Boss looks relieved when he says, "Thank you, Miss Flowers. I get it, I know I can be hard, but that's why I'm a successful Businessman, I've worked hard to be a success and Kingsly is a great help, and so are you. I'm lucky to have you here as my Secretary and Kingsly as my Office Manager. You both do a fine job. I appreciate this talk." Noelle stands and checks his Pocket Watch, then says, "Yes, Miss Flowers, do the breakfast. Let's congratulate Mr. Kingsly, but I will not pay for it. You guys will have to pay for it, and you have to do it on your own time."

"Mr. Chance, we'll plan the breakfast for 10am on Black Friday morning and make the announcement at our afternoon meeting. Speaking of meetings, you have no further meetings scheduled until Tuesday, December 3rd. Thank you for saying yes, Mr. Chance. Enjoy your lunch," Kristen said, closing the door.

Kristen Flowers delivers the news to Nickolas, and he immediately walks over to the office of Noelle Chance and says to his Boss,

"Mr. Chance the breakfast is a wonderful surprise. Thank you, Sir. I appreciate the gesture."

These are awkward moments for Noelle Chance. He likes Nickolas and fights himself when he treats him badly. Hurt people, hurt people, Noelle Chance is a man in pain that hides it by overworking and burying his feelings.

Nickolas defeats an awkward pause in the conversation and says,

"Mr. Chance, Christopher is coming to the office. He will be excited about the Office breakfast celebration."

Noelle has always been fond of Christopher Kingsly. Even in his coldness, the child breaks through the ice. It seems that he sees himself in the young boy.

"I haven't seen Christopher in a few months. How is he doing now? I'm sure he's growing up."

"Yes, he is growing and learning to show the great young man we see of him at home. He's doing better with his schoolwork and taking on a distinctive personality. I think you will see it, if you are here when my wife picks me up."

Noelle cuts right to the point, saying, "I know you are a Deacon now. Let's see how it sounds on you, Deacon Nickolas Kingsly," says Noelle in a stately manner.

"Sir, that's the first time I've heard my name like that. I like the way it sounds, but I will continue doing what I have always done. Nothing will change."

"Well, that's good to know," replies to Noelle. "Heaven knows you certainly preach enough already, Saint Nick, but good for you. That's your thing. I respect a man's business, and I expect that from those around me. All that Church stuff is silly to me. Whatever, enjoy the breakfast Tribute." Noelle continues to say, "As for your kid, bring him to my office when he gets here. I will be staying late; I have no reason to rush out of here tonight."

Noelle Chance is blinded by his idol, which is money. Saint Nick; as Nickolas is called, is aware that the boss is in a wilderness season of his life, running from the devil.

3 O'CLOCK COMES FAST in the minds of the hard-working staff of the N. O. Chance Financial Agency and the office is full of joyful noises when Nickolas calls an end of the day staff meeting saying,

"Please, can I have your attention? This is going to be a short meeting. I know you all have spent the afternoon getting our Black Friday business in order. We have to hit the ground running to tie into client concerns. We will begin our workday at 11am."

The room fills with applause. Then Kristen Flowers steps forward, stating,

"Attention, attention everyone. I have an announcement," gesturing to Nickolas Kingsly to stand beside her. "Thank you, everyone, for your attention. Mr. Kingsly, I address you properly to congratulate you on your resent elevation to Deacon at North Star Village Baptist Church. We like good news, so on behalf of Mr. Chance and your co-workers, we want to Honor you with a recognition breakfast on Friday morning, beginning at 10am. Our celebration will be off the clock, but we will get a great start on our workday, which will officially begin at 11am. Please attend and enjoy coffee, pastry, eggs, bacon, sausage and juice. Congratulations Mr. Kingsly."

Once again, applause fills the air. A humble Nickolas Kingsly says,

"Thank you, Miss Flowers, and Mr. Chance and all of you. I look forward to seeing you all Black Friday morning for breakfast, and thanks for making our Thanksgiving Holiday work schedule a success."

The office empties fast, each person shaking hands and wishing each other a Happy Holiday until the last co-worker is greeted. Noelle and Nickolas are the only ones left in the office when Mary Kingsly calls her husband on his cell phone to say she's in the parking lot.

Honey, your timing is perfect, Nickolas says, "If Chris is with you, tell him to come to the office. I want him to say hello to Mr. Chance."

Mary responds with surprise, saying, "Mr. No says yes to the children, there should be a news report." Nickolas is stunned to silence, as Mary laughs at her own joke.

The joy of a child during the Holiday Season enters the office when Christopher Kingsly bounces in saying, "Hi Dad, I'm here to pick you up. Wow, there's nobody else here. I like your office Daddy, it's nice, I want one when I get bigger."

Noelle comes out of his office and reaches out to shake hands with Christopher Kingsly, then he says playfully,

"Wait a minute, young Mr. Kingsly. You said the office is empty. Well, it is not I am here. My goodness, young man, you are growing up. I almost forgot how a young boy can be so energetic. I heard you say you want an office too, and you can have one if you work hard enough. Tell me what you want to do when you get bigger."

"I want to be good like my dad and treat everybody good. Do you treat everybody good um?" Christopher forgets Noelle's name? Nickolas says, "Son, you are speaking to Mr. Chance."

"Oh yeah, now I remember," Christopher says. "Mr. Chance, like it says on the door, no chance. Does that mean you give people no chance?"

"Young man, N. O. are the first letters of my first and middle name. N stands for Noelle and O stands for Oscar. I was named after my father," explains Noelle.

"Oh, now I get it."

"That's great Christopher. N. O. are the first letters; called initials, of my name. My last name is Chance. This is my company I call the N. O. Chance Financial Agency. Take my business card and you can see how to set up your own business cards someday."

Christopher takes the card and says, "Thank you, Mr. Chance. My teacher says I work hard, and my mom and dad work hard too. They all want me to go to a new school to help me learn better."

"Alright Christopher, it's time to go home now and get ready for

Thanksgiving," Nickolas interjects. Christopher replies, "Yes, dad. Thank you, Mr. Chance, for being nice to me and being nice to my daddy. Happy Thanksgiving."

Mr. Noelle Chance reaches out to shake Christopher's hand and says, "Keep working hard, young one. Hard work will make you a winner. Mr. Nickolas Kingsly, you have a fine boy here. Thank you for letting him spend some time with me. Enjoy your night. See you on Friday."

"Thank you. Mr. Chance, do enjoy your night and have a Happy Thanksgiving," Nickolas replies as father and son leave together, holding each other's hand.

~

No bah humbug from Noelle Chance Jr. No sarcasm, no coldness or indifference to a man and his child, not on this Thanksgiving Eve, which has an anticipated arrival, similar to Christmas Eve. But it will not be a silent night. There will be music in the air and the sounds of music will include pots and pans clanging and banging along with the sound of food cooking. But Noelle lingers in his office listening to music in solitude.

Dusk approaches quickly, turning darkness into nighttime in North Star Village.

"It's time to go home," Noelle says to himself, after an hour of extra work and an hour listening to smooth jazz on the radio.

Staying in the office late allows Noelle to hide from problems and it provides a quiet meditation space but it's all a facade that is cracking, an act that has run out of time and everyone has to deal with the trials and tribulations of their life.

The next song that plays is familiar, it has a melody that accompanies the saxophone solo and a wonderful male voice mimic's it all in a phrase, singing *don't stop ever lovin' me.*

A KNSV radio commercial for the cooking show breaks through the thought parade saying, "Don't forget to tune in to the Thanksgiving Eve cooking show, with your host Les Givings and our guest DJ, DJ Casanova Cocoa Brown. Tonight, the best kept secret in the USA gets its own celebration of R&B classic music on the radio and what's cooking at home. Tell the Valley about your Thanksgiving menu and give your family a shout out. Get your menu together, call-in and tell us all about it on the cooking show."

Noelle shuts the radio off by remote control. It is dark outside, early evening has settled in; coat draped over the shoulder, Noelle heads to the office front door and begins to wonder is that the Security Guard's footsteps he hears in the hallway. Then opening the door, he is surprised to see no one walking in the well-lit hallway.

Noelle thinks nothing of the strange encounter, the first of its kind, and uses his cellphone voice command to make the phone dial a number.

"Call Chance home," he says.

The slow walk to his car and arm movements make it appear like he's talking to himself, but he is talking through a Bluetooth headphone.

"Hello Dad. I'm glad I caught you. I'm just leaving the Office and I want to know if there's anything you guys need me to pickup for you on my way home."

There are two Security Guards on premise during regular business hours, one takes care of the front reception desk, the other patrols the parking area from an elevated observation booth, both are outside, even though Noelle heard footsteps in the hallway.

Noelle waves slightly to say goodbye and when passing the Security Guards, he seems to be talking to himself.

"Dad, are you cooking anything this year?"

"Yes, I am son. Don't worry, you'll have fried corn and skillet cornbread on the Thanksgiving menu."

"You know that's what I want, Dad. I will see you tomorrow then." He asks again, "Are you sure you don't need anything?"

"Wait a minute El, here is your mother. I will see you tomorrow, son. Be safe out there."

"Yes Sir, good night," says the Jr., Noelle Chance

Mother Chance takes the phone. "Hello son. I went out earlier today with Holly and we're all set. She told me about your dessert choices, and I can't wait to try them both. Holly also told me about tonight being JJ's big night on the radio. Are you at home?"

"No, I'm just getting into my car and leaving the office," Noelle answers with a sigh. "I'm taking it slow, mom. I guess I'm enjoying the very last moments of peace before the Holiday craziness gets on my nerves."

"Noelle, it's too early for you to be worked up about the Holiday Season. This is the most wonderful time of the year. Anyway, listen to your mother. Be joyful on purpose and remember, every day is a gift, that's why it's called the present. On tomorrow, when we count our blessings and give thanks, try to remember the less fortunate who will struggle to eat or struggle to get by. Happy Thanksgiving, son. I will see you tomorrow. I love you, bye."

"I love you Mom. I will see you tomorrow. Bye."

NOELLE IS NOT the only one driving home alone on Thanksgiving Eve, but he drives through the dusk of the day and into Twi-night of poetic justice, for Noelle is slipping into darkness, his ride into the night, mimicking his soul moving towards the dark side of life.

Noelle's ride home is a beautiful one, stress free with little traffic and as everyone heads for their homes, it's beginning to look a lot like Christmas on the streets of North Star Village. The streets are twinkling in Holiday lights that brighten the nighttime with colorful ornaments and the first night of the Holiday is official. Soon there will be chestnuts roasting on an open fire.

Noelle arrives at his luxury home in his luxury car feeling great about the Jazzy Breeze CD playing in his ears. Fooling himself into believing the solitude he's built is a good thing, but once again, everybody plays the fool. Solitude is great for meditation, but when you run away from your problems or push everyone out of your life, it's not good to consistently chose to be alone.

Noelle makes work a substitute for companionship, and when he closes the front door to his home to leave the world behind; as we all try to do, he also closes himself off completely to those around him and most of the outside world. Only occasionally does Noelle even look out of the windows of his home. Only occasionally will he peek out of selfishness and only occasionally will he see anything but his own interests in getting involved.

Noelle sits comfortably in the lap of a luxury chair fit for a king, and the man who would be king sips on fine wine, eats a gourmet tapas dinner and slips into cold indifference, just to spite the warmth of the oncoming Holiday Season. This is a grand scenario, to watch time walk on by like you would watch grains of sand fall through an hourglass, and it would normally bring sleep to Noelle, but Thanksgiving Eve interrupts the serendipity, as he remembers to call his sister.

Holly is excited about cooking the Chance family Thanksgiving dinner. She is also excited about her son's interview on KNSV FM Thanksgiving Eve cooking show and that she's included to speak and wish family, friends, and the listeners a Happy Thanksgiving.

Holly can cook, her Thanksgiving Holiday tradition is a festival of meats, vegetables, desserts, and love, which she puts love into every bite. She will give a shout out to her sister and those who are cooking Thanksgiving meals, then describe what she is cooking and her menu.

The phone rings and Holly looks at her caller ID that shows El Chance calling, answering the phone she says, "Mr. No says yes again."

"Holly, you always surprise me with that saying of yours. You should know that I try hard to say yes to you. Now tell me what's going on because I know you're busy cooking."

"You try hard to say yes to me, Mr. No, and that's okay, because I want you to say yes. So, tell me you will be listening to your nephew tonight, because he will be interviewed on the radio by Les Givings around 10pm.

"They are going to talk about the 'Read and Feed The Need' charity program he's working on, and I want you to stick around for my surprise."

"What surprise?" Never mind that question. "Alright Holly, that sounds good. I like Les Givings," Noelle says. "Oh man, let me get situated. It's already past 8 o'clock."

"Yes, it is. Alright El," Holly says. We're all excited and this is good for JJ, plus my surprise right after the interview. Make sure you tune in and I will see you tomorrow, okay. Then you can tell me all about what you heard. Now I gotta go, bye."

And the march of time waits for no one, though the gravity of time can weigh you down to your very last compound. Pressure bursts the pipes, and it is weight that broke the wagon. But don't you wait until it's too late. Take the time given to you, to be about your best life.

'Happy Thanksgiving' says the business card from Sylvia's Coffee and Cakes, which sits on the small table next to the chair fit for a king. Noelle gets situated in front of the radio, unaware of the kindnesses which time has shown him and the Chance family. North Star Village is about to hear and bear witness to the works of faith that Jacob Evergreen Jr. represents, or JJ as his uncle Noelle Jr., has nicknamed him.

Jacob Jr.'s voice fills up the room, booming through the speakers, commanding the attention of the listeners, and Uncle Noelle Jr. is one of the receivers. He hears his nephew saying, "First, we feed your hunger, then we feed your need. Putting our works of faith into our work to help people who cannot read or who want to read better.

"Illiteracy is a problem in the USA. It's a problem that doesn't discriminate. It means that reading and writing skills are inadequate for tasks that require skills beyond a basic level. We can eliminate this problem and help those who can be helped, learn a skill that they were deprived of for various reasons. This problem dramatically affects your daily life and the ability to make money or make more money with a better job.

"We have a respectful program with compassionate teachers that will teach you the skills to read and write beyond a basic level. Don't wait any longer. Join our program and encourage your friends and family to read. Illiteracy is a curable problem. You will be surprised at the number of people that you love who are just getting by because of this. If you can read, be thankful for what you got and pay it forward."

Jacob Jr. is doing a good job and sounds wonderful, as he continues saying, "Let's get excited. Don't be shy. Step out of the shadows and let us help you to become a reader. Do it for yourself, do it for those you love, and don't let your children suffer this generational problem.

Contact the Read and Feed the Need Program at the North Star Village Community Center Monday through Friday, 10am to 6pm to get more information and setup an appointment. In closing, I must say Les Givings, thank you for interviewing me and have a great cooking show. But I do have a song request."

Les Givings says, "Thank you for what you are doing for the community Jacob Evergreen Jr. It will be my pleasure to play your request. What do you want to hear?"

"Um Um Good, by Men At Large."

THE KNSV RADIO show is an over whelming success. People from all over North Star Village were calling in to proudly talk about their families and what they were cooking to put on their Thanksgiving dinner tables.

Les Givings and DJ Casanova Cocoa Brown did a great job playing Black Classic Gold album hits from the Motown Sound, The Sound of Philadelphia, soul music oldies but goodies and local music favorites, to keep every audience up and cooking into the early morning.

Noelle enjoys the show so much he's starting to get excited about Thanksgiving again, then he hears the song 'What is Hip' by Tower Of Power; a favorite of his, that brings out the college day dance moves, which take the rest of his energy.

He couldn't wait until the midnight hour, and just made it to his bed before sleep came tumbling down just before midnight, as the classic by Wilson Pickett 'In The Midnight Hour' plays on into the subconscious mind.

What is hip for Noelle, is the midnight hour of Thanksgiving Eve came complete with a dance of love through the sands of time, turning its last seconds into the first minute of a brand-new day.

The Saints came marching in again, continuing a celebration that began at midnight on November 1 st, turning All Hallows Eve into All Saint's Day, which humbly is the grand opening for the Christmas Holiday Season.

Thanksgiving Eve continues the love season, as joy fills the air, and everybody knows it's a time for family, friends, food, fun and football.

Happy Thanksgiving. Can anybody be saved by being thankful? The answer to the question is yes. Giving thanks or not, is an annual dose of reality that provides a powerful platform to answer that question about being saved, re-born on earth.

To give thanks or not to give thanks, is not a good question, although Thanksgiving is a non-religious, man-made tradition, it's great and a wonderful supernatural gift, which is based on testimonies of thankfulness to God, the provider of all things.

# Chapter 7

## *Thanksgiving - Black Friday*

### Dan

*For every creature of God is good, and nothing to be refused, if it be received with Thanksgiving: 5 For it is sanctified by the word of God and prayer.*

—*I Timothy 4: 4*

The first Thanksgiving was celebrated in Plymouth, Massachusetts, in 1621. Thanksgiving is a man-made Holiday; as much as anything can be made by man. It is a welcomed family tradition of reunion and spiritual inventory. Giving thanks is woven into the fabric of our National identity in the United States of America, USA.

Thanksgiving Thursday, a National Holiday since 1863, designated by the 16th President of the United States, Abraham Lincoln. Thanksgiving was finalized by President Harry Truman in 1941; having gone through various date changes, it's now a legal Holiday on the fourth Thursday in November.

In the U.S.A, the Thanksgiving Holiday includes Wednesday; Thanksgiving Eve, Thanksgiving Day and Friday following Thanksgiving is a Holiday Season fixture called Black Friday. It is considered the traditional start of the Christmas shopping season.

It has been called Black Friday since 1966 because of the great amount of money it brings to every business, changing sales deficit numbers that are in the red, to profit numbers that are written in black. Thanksgiving Saturday became its own Holiday entity, called Shop Small Business Day, which is a New Millennium tradition to support small business owners.

Thanksgiving Sunday is self-explanatory, then another New Millennium tradition extends the Holiday shopping weekend to Monday; called Cyber Monday, which is a big money Internet business ecommerce day. Consumers shop online for deals on a wide variety of merchandise, which will be shipped to your home.

High School football teams and everyone concerned about them across the country are waking up on Thanksgiving morning, giving thanks for being alive, thanks for football and praying that their team will win. Thanksgiving is not a religious Holiday, but for many it's the equivalent to the Holy mornings of Christmas and Easter, because of the prayer content.

In the Mountain side community of North Star Village California, Thanksgiving morning for Simon Peter Kingsly brings forth prayers for the new day, family, friends, and he asks traveling mercies for all going to attend the last Thanksgiving Day football game he will see as a student.

This year, Bella High School will be the host to their rivals from Chinook County, the Chinook High School Wildcats. The schools alternate location each year. This is the 25th annual Turkey Day game and giving thanks is also true for the prayerful citizens associated with Chinook High. Everyone celebrates the tradition.

The North Star Village civic groups invite people to begin tailgating at 8 in the morning. Both host committees do a great job of making all feel welcomed to the Homecoming family reunion.

The event is well attended in each county and the battle of marching bands at halftime is a show in itself, just as competitive as the game.

The Kingly home is bustling with activity on Thanksgiving morning. Nickolas is making his annual thankful breakfast consisting of his world's best eggs; made to order, coffee, bacon, sausage, toast, fruit juice, oranges, apples, and grapes. The first attendee since he could walk is Simon Peter Kingsly, who every year says, "Good morning daddy. Happy Thanksgiving to you. I'll have some scrambled eggs."

Daddy Kingsly replies, "Good morning, son. Happy Thanksgiving to you. Scrambled eggs coming right up. You want sausage, right?"

Christopher Kingsly enters the kitchen, and like clockwork, says, "I want sausage. Good morning daddy! Happy Thanksgiving."

"Good morning," Nickolas says. Happy Thanksgiving Chris. You and your brother can start with juice and have some sliced fruit, that's on the table."

Christopher says, "Daddy, I want some scrambled eggs please."

The smell of frying sausages wakes up Mary Kingsly, who stayed up late on Thanksgiving Eve, like other cooks have done to prepare their Thanksgiving meals. Mary and the whole family heard their names on the cooking show, when Marie did what she said she would do, and gave everybody a shout out on the radio.

Marie did an excellent job, stating she was cooking a three-cheese macaroni and cheese dish and her husband Matthew is putting the final touch on his famous sweet barbeque pulled pork, then her song request for "Country Christmas" by Patti Labelle went over big time, as she got kudos for it from Les Givings and DJ Casanova Cocoa Brown.

Mary rises out of the bed giving thanks to the Lord for a brand-new day, and smiles when she smells the annual Thanksgiving breakfast. It's time to shower and get to the kitchen because she knows her Sister will be there soon.

The loving Sisters will gather twice today, once to attend Simon's final football game as a student, and again for the family Thanksgiving dinner, which will be at the Kingsly's home this year.

Marie, husband Matthew, 7-year-old Matthew Samuel Davis Jr., and 16-year-old Stephanie Mills Davis are on their way to enjoy the breakfast cooked by Nickolas. Then they will ride together to the Turkey Bowl football game.

Marion Kingsly wakes up about the same time as her mother, immediately giving thanks for the brand-new day. She makes her way to the kitchen, stopping to lovingly observe dad cooking and her brothers talking and eating. Marion smiles and continues to give thanks for a loving family, then suddenly Marion backs away unnoticed, saying to herself, "I better shower and get dressed. I'm sure Aunt Marie is on her way here."

In the Pacific time zone, the famous Macy's Thanksgiving's Day Parade, which began in 1924, starts at the break of dawn. It combines well with the annual breakfast by Nickolas Kingsly, that concludes when Santa Claus makes his triumphant return to 34th street, in New York City.

Simon Kingsly is pleased that his family wants to accompany him to the Turkey Bowl game. He states with joy, "The gangs all here," when everyone packs into the SUV of uncle Matthew and aunt Marie. Then it's over the field they go, laughing all the way.

Americans have many Thanksgiving Day traditions. Every family can add their own flavor to the day. This family is going to the Bella High School Stadium for a big High School football game.

This Christmas for first cousins Marion and Stephanie, is their first opportunity to step into lead roles for the family dinner, and make sure all the preparations for a large family dinner are done.

Practice will make perfect these young women, who will one day lead their own homes. Sisters Marie and Mary leave their Daughter's home alone to take on Thanksgiving dinner, knowing they have taught them well.

Tomorrow stands in the foreshadow of this day. Tomorrow the

families plan to come together again, to begin Christmas shopping on Black Friday, the first day of Christmas shopping.

The football game was exciting. Bella High School won by a touchdown in the final minute of the game. The end of the game caped off another successful reunion and homecoming event for North Star Village and Chinook County.

Simon's emotions are strong. Reality imposes itself into the three-year student dream, that up until this moment has included another school year, but not this time. See you next year, doesn't sound the same and doesn't feel the same. He's heard it said after each game since freshman year.

Tomorrow is not promised to anyone but when you are young tomorrow is just a day away, but today Simon can feel his schoolboy era coming to an end with this game. Everything about it is proving to be a new experience. The combination of the past, present, and future is bittersweet for all of the senior Class.

Simon and his classmates are thrust into leadership roles and see that they must make sure the homecoming reunion tradition of the Turkey Bowl is transferred to the new students. The Thanksgiving Turkey Bowl game is an early Christmas gift for Simon, even with its bittersweet taste of saying goodbye to High School life. He clearly feels it, while leading his family back to the parking lot, waving to his fellow classmates and cheering with them.

Christopher is close to his side, walking along with Matthew Jr., and then he speeds up to walk with his mother and aunt, who have begun discussing dinner start time. The men keep their eyes on everyone as they walk closely behind, talking freely about all things and anything that comes to mind. Enjoying each other's company like brothers and close friends do.

Matthew Sr. congratulates Simon. They have their own handshake, as he gets into the van. Before starting up the engine, Matthew Sr. says, "Hey everyone, this was cool. Now it's time to eat. I haven't watched a High School football game in a long time, and I saw some friends today that I haven't seen in years."

Driving out of the stadium, win or lose for the fans, is a drive into the Holiday Season and along the way Matthew Sr. turns the car stereo down. It seems like he only plays Earth Wind & Fire, Maze featuring Frankie Beverly or Gospel music, much like Nickolas does.

Matthew Sr. asks for everyone's attention and says, "I want to tell you about our good news before we get back to the house. Stephanie will be playing varsity volleyball for Vista View Valley High, and I want us to plan to go see her play, especially you, Simon."

Simon replies from the back of the SUV, "Uncle Matt, that's great. She made the varsity team. I will go to as many games as I can."

Nickolas says "Congratulations Matt and Marie. I'm excited for my niece. She and Marion must be enjoying themselves at the house. We'll plan to go to the games like we all did for Simon's track meets and I want to congratulate Stephanie today, as part of our Thanksgiving dinner."

~

Stephanie looks up to Marion, who is a fine role model. Today they're working as a team and are ready to put the ham in the oven.

"Marion, did we forget anything?" Marion shakes her head no. "I think we did pretty good. The ham should be right on time for our 3 o'clock start time. Let's take a break and talk about all the boy attention you're getting and how you're handling it. I noticed you were getting a lot of attention at the Halloween party at my job. You're going to be a senior next year."

"I'm thankful for my mom and for you being in my life. Your mom is the coolest auntie on the planet. I know you guys care about me. I'm not boy crazy cuz, it's nothing serious. Plus my puppy love moved to San Diego. I'm ready to enjoy this year and be a senior next year. I made the varsity volleyball team and I'm working hard to go to College.

"But Marion all the guys were checking you out in your Super girl costume," Stephanie says, laughing.

Marion cheers for her cousin, saying, "Girl, that is good. I'm glad you're taking advantage of your talent because there are scholarships available for girls' volleyball."

~

In spite of all the travel, Thanksgiving dinner will be served on time. Before eating, all are encouraged to state what they are thankful for; it's a family tradition. The Kingsly family gathers in a circle holding hands, encouraged to state what they're thankful for, followed by prayer to bless the food and this year dad gives Simon the honor to lead the family.

"Our father, thank you for my family. Thank you for everyone being here today and for being with me at the football game. I am thankful for a family that loves openly and, as I was listening to you guys giving thanks, I was moved by your thoughtfulness and that you all pray. Your hearts are exceptional. I give thanks to be able to pray with you and pray for you. This opportunity is special to me, especially this year, and especially today. Today I'm learning to appreciate what I have and who God has put in my life."

Simon pauses to gather himself, he feels the water in his body begin to stir and he feels the Holy Spirit rise in a way he has never felt before. The spirit is moving from the inside, way down deep in his soul. Fight or flight. Sink or swim, but the still small voice of the Lord says just pray.

Simon Kingsly exhales these words, "I just now realized that dad will be leading church service this Sunday as a Deacon of North Star Baptist Church. Let us give thanks to the Lord for that.

"Take your time, son. Pray the prayer the Lord is giving you," Daddy Nickolas says to Simon in hopes to ease his nerves.

Simon Kingsly exhales these words.

You guys are cool. I love you and I want you to know that I am not ashamed to praise the Lord, Hallelujah, I'm growing up. Thank you, mom, for your patience.

"Alright, before I get all carried away, I was asked to pray for a blessing on our food. Dad, you always pray so hard for us all. Let me say thank you, Lord, for all that we are to receive today.

"Please bless this food with your Holiness and your kindness, that it will nourish our minds, body and soul and give us the strength to fight the evil one. Lord, we ask that you bless the hands that prepared our meal. We believe there is power in the Blood, and we ask for these blessings on this food in the mighty, magnificent, majestic name of Jesus Christ. Amen and Amen."

Mother Mary remarks with a heart full of joy, "Thank you for a wonderful prayer son," as everyone together says, "Amen."

Simon sez, "Let's eat."

"Nick, we're going to serve you and Matt first," Mary says. "The collard greens and the sweet potatoes are on the stove, MJ, Chris, let your sisters serve you, and everybody remember we have pecan and apple pie for dessert and there is vanilla ice cream in the freezer."

Knives, forks and spoons do a soul food dance on the plates around the table. Food moves down the table like they are in a soul train dance line. The mac n' cheese gets an applause at each stop and the collard greens are hopping on the scene.

The meats move to their own beat and the cranberry add a chilly sauce. Feet don't let me fall asleep at the table, everyone's soul sings, *let's get up, mind, body, and stomachs, to the rear, march to a seat, there's a train coming, called sleep, don't get it twisted, this party of 9, won't tap dance like Sleep 'n' Eat, Thanksgiving gives rest to those working feet, and the Collective soul says, yes.*

"Hey who made the pulled pork?" says Nickolas.

Matthew Sr. smiles the smile of a satisfied chef. Nickolas continues saying, "Thank you Sir."

Nickolas, looking at Matthew sitting on the opposite end of the couch, speaks in a jolly tone, rubs his belly, and laughs with an unintended ho-ho-ho.

"Matthew Davis Sr., the deep-fried turkey you cooked was delicious."

"Okay, roll call! Can I have everyone's attention?" Nickolas continues to say. "Everything was delicious. Thank you, Mary and Marie. I know we all appreciate Marion and Stephanie, who did an excellent job setting up and cooking, while we were at the football game."

Hand claps and cheers run through the house, followed shortly by the unmistakable quiet that comes just before sleep, as the professional football game on TV serenades all. It was the night before Christmas shopping and all through the house, there was no movement to be found and without a doubt, the food so good, has put everyone out. A sweet and restful sleep, sleep, sleep.

The party is over here, and all have found their own comfortable spot in the modest house of Nickolas and Mary Kingsly. It's easy to do in this home full of good spirits, even though all good things must come to an end. The end of this peaceful time provides all with a win, win, win.

Mary daydreams about days gone by, when mommy would sleep, when the baby falls asleep, feeling at last a moment of peace. Call it a power nap, women take advantage of all that!

Mary has her favorite chair, and her sister has a comfortable favorite there. Although the sleeping could have gone on, the sweetest voice and loving hands fall on her neck, then fall on her shoulders and then fall on her arms, waking her from this peaceful place. Sleep is over, but patients abound. Out of the mouth of her babe comes a familiar sound.

"Christopher," Mary's baby boy, gently says, "Mom, you sleep?"

Mary replies with love in her eyes, "Hey baby. It looks like everybody is asleep, except for you and MJ."

Looking through puppy dog eyes, the boys say in unison, "Can we have some ice cream?"

*How can an hour go by so fast and give back so much!*, Mary thinks.

Mary gets up from her chair in unison with her sister, who gets that same old feeling when her son Matt Jr., races over to help his mommy get out the chair.

Marie says, "Power nap good!", in her best cave man impression, as the sisters laugh together.

Now fully awake, Marie says, "Alright girl, I'm down for some coffee and cake, then we're going to call it a night. Me and Steph will be early bird Christmas shopping on Black Friday. We going to begin our search for bargains at Target and work our way back here to pick up the boys and bring them to the Balloon parade."

Like the movements of a fine Swiss watch, Marion and Stephanie enter the room right on time. In that moment, Marion says, "I wish I could go with you guys, but I will be part of the working crew on Black Friday opening our store at 8 am."

"I'm part of the opening crew for my store, but I will be working 8am until 5:30pm. Nickolas will be the man about town, bringing me and Marion to work and picking us up. We'll miss the early bird shopping, but we can rest up and hit the stores early Saturday," Mary stated.

"Can we all get together for Shop Small Saturday, and go to Scenic View Plaza?" Stephanie asks in anticipation. All the Women agree.

"That sounds like a plan, Ree Ree. When you bring the boys back tomorrow night, we'll get our Saturday together," Mary said to Marie before turning to go to the kitchen.

"Alright Chris and MJ. Let's get you some ice cream."

The Kingsly house comes to life just as quickly as it went into silent night's restful sleep. Big Matt has one eye open and so does Nickolas, stretching out of his sleep.

"Oh, my goodness, that nap was just what the doctor ordered. Nick, I have just enough room for some coffee and dessert, then we are going to hit the road jack. Tomorrow morning, Marie and I will pick up the boys to go to the Black Friday Holiday Balloon Parade. We'll keep them busy hanging out with us all day and bring them back home tomorrow night."

"That sounds great, Matt. Thank you for helping out with the day. I know my boys will appreciate it."

The brothers-in-law do their own special handshake, and agreement flows through the whole family.

NOELLE OSCAR CHANCE JR. may have a bah humbug attitude and a cold demeanor, but you couldn't tell by the way he was dressed. He looked cooler than a fan in a rich gold color tweed sport coat, goldenrod suede dress slacks, chocolate leather and suede half-boot shoes, chocolate Kangol cap, silver turtleneck, with scarf that match, and brown leather gloves.

Noelle has just finished watching his favorite Holiday movie, "Trading Places" and he's singing his favorite line from Deion Sanders song "It Must Be The Money it must be the money, that's got me rolling on strong he says walking through the mist of one of his favorite cologne's "Money" he just sprayed in the air on his way out the door.

It is said that pride goes before you fall and don't let his smoothness fool you. Noelle could be a good catch for the right woman, but he has a hard heart, once bitten and twice shy.

Noelle has packed the desserts and the Champaign he promised to bring to the family gathering he flippantly calls the Thanksgiving feast fest. The Chance family will give thanks with him or without him. He can smell the aroma of his neighbor's Holiday cooking, as he strolls down his hallway to the lobby entrance into his luxury Condo and he must admit the Thanks-giving feast fest thereby, is a sweet test on the senses.

Noelle presses the button for his automatic car starter and he's ready to drive out of his parking spot. As soon as he gets into the car, the phone rings and the caller ID shows Waterhouse.

"Hello Mr. Waterhouse. How are you today?", says Noelle.

"Hello young man. Happy Thanksgiving. I hope I caught you at a good time. Your sister told me she is hosting your family dinner this year."

"Sir, your timing is impeccable as usual. I just got into the car and I'm on my way there now, with some desserts and Champaign."

"I'm sure your selections are impeccable. Noelle, I won't keep you, I just want you to know the Mrs. and I are hoping you can accept our invitation for our Christmas dinner party next weekend. Come over, eat, have some fun with us. During the night, we'll go over my plans for the Community Center Christmas party coming up in about two weeks."

Noelle immediately replies, "Sir, I look forward to visiting you and your wife at your lovely home next weekend. You can count on me to help you in any way necessary for the Community Center event, just like I did for the Masquerade Ball."

"That's great Noelle. Do check out the invitation. Look carefully for the directions to a home I'm showing on my Real Estate listings. I will tell the Mrs. you're coming, and we will expect you around 6 for cocktails. Bring a guest if you like and dinner will be served shortly after that. Thank you, Noelle. I'm thankful for your friendship over the years. Have a great day. Goodbye."

A warm feeling comes over Noelle, but it's met with a subconscious effort to bury all emotions and stay in control,

"I need to get tougher," Noelle says out loud. Ignoring his own heart that unbeknownst to him, responds to the Wonderful Counselor Jesus Christ, who being all things is the comforter.

Jesus Christ is no respecter of man, meaning He chooses all who come to Him. Even a wayward child who would be saved by the prayers of others. And He is a respecter of His covenant to those who love Him, as the Chance Family has prayed for Noelle Oscar Chance Jr., in the name of Jesus, believing by faith. Those prayer avail much.

Just as the father of the seeds of the covenant; Abraham did pray for and protect his nephew Lot, and those prayers were the fervent effective prayers of faith. The faithful Chance family does pray, and those prayers avail them much for their son, brother, uncle, Noelle Oscar Chance Jr.

But how long does anyone have to wait, leaning on the righteous prayers of others, not knowing the next moment and learning now or later that each day is not promised.

Noelle leans into his luxury leather seat and sighs.

"Let's get this day on and over with," he said while turning on the car radio and tuning into radio station KNSV. That will be his passenger on the drive to the Chance family Thanksgiving dinner at the home of beloved sister Holly Evergreen.

Noelle tunes right into a Christmas commercial to visit the International Christmas tree plaza at the North Paiute Outlet Mall, which features unique gifts, Christmas decorations and trees from around the World.

Noelle states out loud, "No way would I waste my time or waste my money with that madness." Then the radio plays a Reggae style Christmas song by Paul Allen; also known as Saint Paul, titled 'Celebrate'.

*It's Christmas time again... we gonna celebrate.... this Christmas... celebrate... with Jesus... celebrate... let's all go celebrate... celebrate, celebrate, celebrate, celebrate, celebrate ... sing... Ra pa pum... ra pa pum pum... ra pa pum pum pum... this Christmas...*

NOELLE WAS STUCK in the magic of the season. He let the whole commercial play, enjoying the music when the voice of Les Givings filled the air saying, "The staff and management of KNSV would like me to thank you, our listeners, for making our first Thanksgiving Eve cooking show a success. Thank you and Happy Holidays from our radio station family to yours."

Noelle wasn't ready for the next song; with its famous musical introduction, known by every Black family in America, followed by the voice of Donny Hathaway singing....

*"Hang all the mistletoe... I'm going to get to know you better... this Christmas... "*

And the melody still lingers on.

Noelle doesn't want to hear this song, knowing this song and all of its renditions will be heard countless times before this Christmas. He can't wait for Christmas to get here, and like so many other people, he can't wait for Christmas to come, so it can be over.

"Christmas," Noelle says, "oh man, this is going to be a long season." He immediately plays his More Butter Jazz music compilation CD, and all is well when he hears the song 'Mr. Magic' by Groover Washington Jr. Now jazz music will play on his drive to the Thanksgiving feast fest.

Jacob Evergreen Sr., greets his brother-in-law in the front yard saying, "The... first... Noelle... the angels did say. Made sure that he beat his son here today," and started laughing.

Noelle Jr. couldn't help but laugh when the first Noel came out the door next saying, "I heard you were bringing a red velvet cake and a sweet potato cake. I'm here to bring them in, son."

"Come on in man. I'm glad to see you and you know your sister will be glad too. Let me introduce you to JJ's guests he invited to celebrate with us. He left to get his date,"

Noelle replies, "A Thanksgiving date? Well, well, it seems my nephew is making matrimony moves."

Jacob Sr., seems surprised at that realization, but just says, "JJ is a good young man."

Holly Evergreen and Isabella Chance; daughter and mother, are in the kitchen keeping the food ready to be served. They both come out to greet Noelle in the living room.

"Hey Holly. Hi mom," Noelle says. "The food smells great.

Holly hugs her brother. Giving him a high 5, she says,

"Thanks for being on time brother my dear. Let me introduce you to who is here."

Noelle is glad to be in the house, in the company of family.

"Mom, no matter how many times we do this, it just doesn't get old. It's so funny that I don't feel any excitement until I see this moment. Mom, why can't I keep this feeling?"

Mother Chance, the Matriarch of the family, the pride and joy of Noelle Oscar Chance Sr., senses the struggle within her son and says,

"El, you look good and you're here on time. Give thanks from your heart on this Thanksgiving Day. Just as every single day prior to this one was a blessing, this day is a blessing, too. Your father and I take them as they come and enjoy them for what they present. El don't think about it too hard. Give thanks to the Lord for all that He has done. He's worthy boy, I love you, I'm glad you are here. Now where is that red velvet cake?"

"Dad brought that cake in, and Jake has the sweet potato pound cake. I also got 2 bottles of Champaign; Moet, of course, and some sparkling water."

"Of course, El. You're a brother of distinction. Everything is a yes about you, until that Mr. No personality shows up. Mr. No is as cold as the wind in a winter storm. Maybe this year there will be a new you. After all, I did see you dance at the Masquerade Ball," Holly interjects.

Jacob Sr. joins the conversation, stating, "El my Brother, I wouldn't have believed it, if I didn't see it with my own eyes. You bury it way down, man. But you still got some moves and I remember you dancing with that mysterious lady in the purple dress."

"Come with me, brother dear. I want you to meet JJ's friends he invited to share the day with us. Give me your Sport Coat and hat and follow me," Holly said as she grabbed onto Noelle's arm.

When Brother and Sister enter the living room, Holly grabs the attention of JJ's friends.

"Guys, I want you to meet my Brother Noelle Jr. You've already met my father Noelle Sr., now you can see the Generations of men in our family."

Gesturing towards Noelle, Holly continues, "El, let me introduce to you to Miss Carrieann Gant."

"Hello Sir. Happy Thanksgiving," Carrieann politely responds.

"El, this is Jacob's best friend for life, Mr. Amir Landison."

Amir reaches out to shake Noelle's hand, saying, "Hello Sir, Happy Thanksgiving. JJ has told me so much about you. I'm glad to finally meet you."

"Are you two a couple?" Noelle asked, noticing how attractive these two were.

"No. We're friends of Jacob," they both reply with a smile.

"Very well. I'm glad to meet you both. Any friend of my nephew is alright with me."

There is commotion at the front door when Jacob Jr. enters the house with his date. Immediately seeing his uncle, he greets Noelle with a hug and says,

"Uncle El, I want to introduce you to my date."

Out from behind him steps forward a beautiful woman who takes his breath away.

Noelle Jr. has the biggest smile on his face when he recognizes his Administrative Secretary, his valued employee Miss Kristen Flowers is the fair maiden making matrimonial moves.

"Well, that went way better than I thought."

Uncle El, who then shakes the hand of Miss Flowers, as he is accustomed to addressing her, turns up his charm as he greets her.

"Happy Thanksgiving Uncle El. I see you have met the rest of my guests for today and of course you already know Kristen," Jacob Jr. said while taking off her coat.

Holly gives Kristen a warm hug. Jacob Sr. turns to Kristen saying,

"Hello. Happy Thanksgiving."

"Sweetie," Holly says to Kristen, "Come with me to meet my mother and father. Everyone else please go to the dining room and my husband will seat you, so we can eat."

The Thanksgiving feast fest has only just begun, like the classic Carpenters song sings, and looking at life through the eyes of his beloved nephew, Noelle can believe again that the gift of love can be found, and the man who finds a wife, finds a good thing.

Miss Kristen Flowers is that good thing found by his nephew, and now with his mind freed, the rest of Noelle follows Holly and Kristen into the kitchen to hear the introduction of Kristen to his mother and father, to see their pleasure in her Spirit.

Noelle Jr., speaks, "Mom, Dad, this young lady works for me. She has effectively run things since she arrived. In her I am well pleased."

"Won't he do it!", says mother, Grandmother Isabella Precious Chance.

"Won't he do it!", says father, Grandfather Noelle Oscar Chance Sr.

"Yes, he will," Holly replies.

Noelle Jr., doesn't realize what he just said or how he said it, but everybody else does... and a confirming silence rest, rules and abides in the house of Holly and Jacob Evergreen Sr.

The dining room table is set with a traditional Thanksgiving dinner, at the center is a roasted turkey, stuffing, gravy, mashed potatoes, sweet potatoes, yams, string beans, cranberry sauce, cornbread and an Evergreen family recipe for lobster bisque and lobster macaroni and cheese, there's juice, soda and adult beverages including Champaign, it's time to give thanks.

Jacob Sr., states, "Lobster is an Evergreen family tradition. My mother and father send their love. They're spending Thanksgiving in Napa County with Jalisa and my son-in-law Barry Bridgeman, enjoying being with their great grandchildren, Bobby and Lisa. We all have reasons to be thankful. Please join hands and help me pray for a blessing on our food."

As per his request, everyone gathers together.

"Take this moment to clear your minds and tell the Lord what you are thankful for." After a moment of silence, Jacob Sr. says,

"Thank you for this moment, Lord. Big Daddy, I love you. Will you pray for a blessing on our meal?"

Noelle Oscar Chance Sr. does not hesitate.

"Oh, gracious and wonderful God, we come before you today in awe of your mercy and grace over our lives. We come together by your Will, to break bread and fellowship one with another, family, and friends. Lord, we are thankful for this food that you have provided in abundance today. Lord, we ask that you add your Blessing to this meal, that this food, prepared out of your love, will nourish our bodies and feed our hearts and minds with loving kindness. We ask in the name of Jesus Christ. Let's eat."

Smiles and laughter flow with good food. Everyone is hungry, and everyone did eat, football plays on the TV, but it's not dominating the atmosphere. There is the high feeling of expectancy in the air. The light seems brighter, and the moments have a sense of defined purpose, like something good is happening, even Noelle Jr., feels it, as he locks eyes with Kristen Flowers.

Holly states, "There's plenty of food. If you want more, let me know. Right now, we're preparing for dessert, and we do have ice cream."

Jacob Jr., then moves to the center of the room and asks that the TV be turned down.

"Thank you everyone for being here. I have my other Grandparents on the phone and I'm going to put them on speakerphone. Hello me-maw, can you hear me?"

Both Mamie and Benjamin Evergreen respond with hello's and everyone else in the house does the same.

Jacob Jr., continues. "I'm thankful to have both of my Grandparents in my life," he said looking at Noelle Sr., who he calls Big Daddy and Isabella who he calls Grandma. Before anyone can get to the next thought, he says, "I have a girlfriend. She's here now and I want everyone to know we're dating. Her name is Kristen Flowers and you guys will meet her this Christmas."

There's a momentary pause as Jacob Jr. hugs Kristen, then

everyone begins cheering, and you can hear cheering on the phone too, then a new voice cracks through the air. It's older Sister Jalisa who says,

"Hello everyone. Happy Thanksgiving. JJ, please send us some pictures and you guys enjoy your dinner."

"Jalisa I will send some pictures before I leave here tonight, and I look forward to seeing you all this Christmas."

"Okay JJ, please do," Jalisa replies.

"Okay. Everybody that can hear my voice, enjoy the rest of your night, thank you for being there for me and for Kristen. Bye, bye for now. I love you all. Happy Thanksgiving."

Uncle Noelle is stunned into submission. Love does conquer all and his love for his nephew will not allow the Mr. No personality out to play. Jacob Sr., directs all to their seats and everyone is settling down to eat when Noelle Jr., pulls his brother-in-law aside for a private talk.

Noelle Jr., speaks in a sincere tone saying,

"Hey Jake, I think this is a good thing for your son. Kristen is good at her job and should be a good influence on JJ."

"I believe you Noelle," says Jacob Sr., as the two shake hands.

Thanksgiving dinner at the home of Jacob Sr., and Holly Evergreen brings family and friends together in a special way, the family gathers around Jacob Jr., and Kristen Flowers to congratulate them on being an announced couple.

"JJ is following your footsteps, son," says Big Daddy Chance. "JJ and Kristen look at each other with loving eyes. That's a look I've seen before. It reminds me of your mother and how she looked at me and still does. I can tell you this much. JJ looks up to you, lead him right El."

Big Daddy Chance takes a bite of cake and says, "Boy this glazed sweet potato pound cake is the real deal. I can't have much, but I can sho-nuff have a bite," he said looking over to his wife, who is at the dessert table cutting slices of cake.

"Ella, bring me some water, please?"

Mother Chance brings her husband a glass of ice water and takes a bite from a slice of the red velvet cake.

"El, this cake is delicious. I heard your daddy talking to you, and he's right about JJ. He does look up to you. He's happy and everything is working out for the good. Now I can see why you brought Champagne and Sparkling water. It's time for you to cheer up, son. You have a beautiful soul, and I will be glad when you let it shine. Let's toast it up."

"Things must be going right over here. I heard my mamma say let's toast it up," Holly says joining in on the conversation. Everyone laughs, and Holly continues saying, "We're going to dance tonight. Everyone has to dance down our soul train line. Call it Christmas Steppin."

Noelle Jr., wants a few minutes alone with the couple and suggests that Jacob Sr., get the Champagne and be ready to make a toast to the couple. He's ready to congratulate the new couple, but first some questions.

Jacob Jr., Kristen, Carrieann and Amir are at the table enjoying the lobster macaroni and cheese, when Noelle Jr. makes his way over.

"Excuse me young people, I want to take the new couple away for just a moment." Noelle turns his attention to Jacob Jr. and Kristen. "Would you two come with me to the den?" The two immediately get up, hand in hand, as they follow Uncle Chance into the den.

Noelle Jr. sits in a lounge chair, while the new couple sit across from him in a love seat. He wants to show the new couple a side of his personality they have never seen before until Thanksgiving.

"Miss Kristen Flowers, tomorrow will be our first time working together with me knowing that you guys are a couple. Whether your co-workers know is not a point I want to make, because I believe you two are professionals. JJ, you are good at your job as a water engineer and Kristen, you are good at business management. I will count on you both to see to it that your personal relationship does not interfere with my company."

Jacob Jr. nods in agreement, knowing there's more to come.

"First, let me tell you guys I'm pleased that you have found each other," he said in such a way that the new couple blushes together. "Miss Flowers, as I am used to calling you, I will continue to address you that way during work or in any situation that involves work. That works for me, at work or not. Young Lady, I am fond of you. I've made no secret of that. You do a great job for me, I'm sure your co-workers want that to remain the same. You have always addressed me as Mr. Chance, that's how we communicate at work and that will work, but please refer to my dad as big daddy, which I think he will like."

Uncle Noelle Jr. begins reminiscing. "JJ, this is my poor excuse for an apology. I can see now how you've been trying to tell me something about your life. That's probably why you made a point for us to be together on Veteran's Day with my dad, and why your mom kept on telling me to call you. It's all starting to make sense now."

Noelle turns to Kristen to address her directly, "Miss Flowers, I thank you for taking the time to prepare me for today. I now know why you came into my office yesterday. It was to make sure that this point we are at right now would not be so awkward. I thank you both for patently inviting me into your lives. I'm in my own world and I didn't see the signs, even though I profess both of you are important to me."

Noelle gets up and stands on the side of his chair, saying, "Let's start over. I can't change who I am, and if I am Mr. No it has served me well. No one else has to walk in these shoes and people are going to see what they want to see. I will tell you I've worked hard to be where I am, but within the matters of love, maybe I gave away some things that hurt my heart and soul. If I did, I gave my all to be successful. Seeing you two together reminds me of me when I was your age."

Noelle stops talking and you can almost see a wall going up. All of a sudden, it seems like a new program is being installed. "Never mind about me. I'm set in my ways. I guess it's silly of me to ask how you guys met, but how did you meet?"

"Uncle El, meeting her was great. It's not a long story, but I will let Kristen tell you from her perspective, because what I remember is that the stars in the sky winked at me."

"Mr. Chance," Kristen says with a broad smile on her face, "We met after Church service quite a few months ago. We literally bumped into each other while greeting Pastor Avery Mann. Neither one of us had a regular attendance pattern, but we would sit in the approximate same section. One Sunday, we were both there and once again greeted each other on the way out. We introduced ourselves to one another and wished one another a great rest of the day. One day Jacob saw me at Sylvia's Coffee and Cakes and said the sweetest thing to me. He said, 'I made him feel like life was trying to tell him something and I knew what it was.' I just smiled and said, 'are you sure it's not just coincidence?' Jacob said he doesn't believe in coincidence."

Reaching for Jacob's hand, Kristen continued, "Mr. Chance, your nephew has a way with words. He asked me who was I getting cake for? I told him my mom and dad, then I asked him what are you doing here? "I want coffee," he said, 'but I will get my mom and dad a cake as well. "Then he gave me his phone number and said 'Please let's talk more about what life is trying to tell me about you, over lunch.' Obviously, I called."

"Uncle El, I know that look you are giving me. I live in a nice condo complex, but we do not live together," as Kristen and Jacob Jr. chuckle together.

"That's cool. Hey, you guys are grown, as I said earlier. I'm glad you told me that. Let's get back to the dining room and open the Champagne."

~

Re-entering the living room, they can see everyone has gravitated to the TV; but not to fall asleep. Instead, they are enjoying a family movie that's become a Thanksgiving classic, "The Wiz." Noelle Jr., interrupts to say,

"Please excuse me. Let's join in and toast to the new couple. Jake, are we ready? We have Champagne and there's Sparkling White Grape for anyone who doesn't want Champagne."

Holly brings out long stem glasses, making sure everyone has a glass for the toast. Mother Chance says she will have Sparking White Grape, so does big daddy Chance. Jacob Sr. perfectly pops the cork and begins to pour Champagne. Holly pours Sparkling White Grape for her mother and father, and both state they will look forward to having Champagne on New Year's Eve.

Holly states, "Before we toast, I want to thank you all for sharing your day with us. Thank you, mom and dad and my brother. It's great to be with you, Kristen. Jake. My husband, the floor is yours. Go ahead with your toast."

Jacob Sr. begins to sense this moment is bigger than ceremony and more like a blessing on a future daughter-in-law. He looks at his wife and they sense it together.

"I want everyone to help me toast this wonderful Holiday of Thanksgiving," Jacob Sr. said as they all agreed.

Jacob Sr. rises to the occasion and says, "Who knew that Champagne would be on time for tonight. We've toasted to each other before, as a warm-up for New Year's Eve, but this is the first time we've toasted to a relationship for Jacob Jr., or JJ as we call him. Please raise your glasses.

Thank you to my father-in-law for being such a great example to our son and thank you to my mother-in-law. You two make us all so much better with your spirit. Thank you, Noelle Jr. for being gracious under pressure and showing us your kindness. Thank you, Amir, and Carrie-ann for being good friends and better people in our son's life. Miss Kristen Flowers, we are glad for you. We salute your family for raising such a beautiful young woman. We can see your influence on JJ. His manhood flourishes in your company and it's a good thing.

Jacob Benjamin Evergreen Jr., we believe in the Lord, and we give thanks for you in our lives. We're proud of you. Thank you for announcing your relationship with Kristen to us. We all wish, hope, and pray for you both to be happy, healthy, and successful. When you think back on this moment, let it be cherished for the simple love God has shown us. A toast to us all," and everyone drinks.

"Before anyone leaves, please take home some food. I have Styrofoam boxes you can use. Mom and Dad, since you cooked for yourselves, I'm planning on eating with you after Church on Sunday. I already put some food and dessert away for both of you."

Amir and Carrieann are well mannered and polite. They brought spirit and energy to the festivities. They are told this as they stop to greet each person and say goodbye. Kristen does the same, accompanied by Jacob Jr.

"Grandson, I think you have some good friends. you all be safe in your travels tonight. And Miss Kristen Flowers, keep helping each other to be great and don't worry about my son, the notorious Mr. No, you are good for him too. Jacob's grandmother and I are on one accord with our feelings about your new relationship, and tomorrow at work, don't you stop smiling, like you're smiling now. Enjoy your workday," said Big Daddy.

"Thank you, sir," says Kristen Flowers, a blushing brown beauty.

"You can call me Big Daddy."

Then the grace of Grandmother Isabella Chance enters the equation by smart conversation. When she says,

"Kristen, sweetie, don't you call me Big Mama."

Everyone holds their breath. Then mother Chance starts laughing. "Look at your faces. That was supposed to be funny," she says as the whole house erupts in laughter. "Sweetie, call me Mrs. Chance, or Grandma."

"Alright everybody, we are about to go. I don't have to work tomorrow, but I want to go with Mom and Dad, to do some Black Friday shopping," Jacob Jr. says, heading to the door.

Get here at 7 in the morning to have some coffee and cake, then we will head on out. We won't catch any door busters, but we will find some sales at the Metroplex."

Kristen says, "I'm going Black Friday shopping with Carrieann, after I get out of work.Amir is going out with his whole family, starting with the 6am door buster sales."

The goodbye moment stuns Kristen, who begins to recognize that she has shared Thanksgiving with 3 Generations of men, a grandfather, his son and Grandson. Even though the son, Noelle Chance Jr. is her boss, the father of her boss said she's good for his grandson, her new boyfriend Jacob Evergreen Jr., and good for her boss. Kristen smiles now that she meets the approval of the mother, grandmother and father of Jacob Jr., although a relationship must stand on its own. It's good loving somebody, when somebody loves you back.

Kristen and Jacob Jr. have a great feeling as they leave the house, and everybody knows a turkey, and some mistletoe makes the evening right. Kristen happily thinks ahead to her family meeting Jacob Jr., on Thanksgiving Saturday, shop small business day, but it's a big day for them.

The Flowers family will break bread with the new couple and Jacob Jr., will meet Kristen's father and mother; Russell and LaChristian Flowers, and her older Sister Kathleen.

Kristen and Jacob Jr. have taken the time to get to know each other and their relationship has grown strong without interference from either family, but the time has come for all to know. Thanksgiving weekend is built for family and friends to gather and count their blessings, it also begins the Christmas Season and love is in the air.

"Dad, I know you still like to drive," Noelle says, "but I'm glad you relaxed today and let us drive for you and mom. Holly and Jake do a wonderful job helping you out, and I want to be more available for you. I get so wrapped up in my work that before you know it, a week has gone by. Please charge it to my head and not my heart."

"Son, I'm thankful for all that you do," Daddy Chance replies.

"It's nice to hear that you care, but I've said this before, and I will say it again, you can't buy your way into heaven."

"Got it Dad. I have heard you and Mom say that before. I didn't bring you here, but I will be taking you guys' home when you're ready."

"I think we are ready to go. Let me check with your mom and Sister."

"Thank you, Jake, for all that you do," says Noelle Jr. to his brother-in-law, just coming back into the house, after watching his son and guests drive off."

Noelle shakes his brother-in-law's hand, saying, "I ate well. This was a good day. I will tell you this though, I was caught off guard when Kristen walked in with JJ. For a moment, I thought I was at work and that I had forgotten some important meeting."

"El, we're family. Man, I'm glad you enjoyed yourself. I think everyone did. I do what I can to make your sister happy, then I do what she tells me to do, he says as they both" laugh. "Uncle El, as my son calls you, all kidding aside, I'm sure you were surprised by JJ's announcement, but you handled it well and I'm thankful for that."

"Jake, your son is grown. You guys are great role models for him, but I wouldn't want to hurt him in any way. JJ and Kristen are good young people."

"Your sister knows more than me. That's mommy, JJ loves his mom, and they talk. I knew he was dating but I didn't know she works for you. That, I just found out."

"It's all good Jake. Shoot, I was like JJ when I was young. They got me to thinking of my first love and how I had to let all of that love stuff go, to get to my success."

"Those two young people are into each other right now, and I'm sure they were nervous about tonight, but you pulled them through. You did a great job, my brother, you were gracious."

The two men, who were close by law, get closer and develop their own handshake.

"El, I've heard you say that you let go of love for success before, but now is the time to break those chains that bind you, my brother. You think you're talking about the love of a woman, but I believe you're talking about a relationship with God." Jacob braces himself for the cold wit and sharp tongue of Mr. No, but it doesn't come.

Noelle just breathes and instead of a sharp tongue, he just exhales for the first time in a long time, then clears his throat to say,

"Jake, man that's cool. I'm getting tired and I know my mother and father are getting tired too. I want to thank you for bringing them here, but I will take them home and you and Holly can enjoy the rest of your night."

"Thanks, El. We're going out early tomorrow and do some Black Friday shopping."

"Bah humbug. I can't go for that. No can-do. I'm going to work and then relax at home, Noelle Jr., says. "On Saturday I'll take mom and pops out to do some of their shopping. Then on Sunday I'm going to the Bella casino," Noelle Jr. says motioning to his sister to join them.

"Holly, it's been a stone gas man. Good job on everything, especially keeping your son's secret. You got me. Mr. No says yes, you got me good. Don't say anything, let's just kiss and say goodbye. Thanks for a good day. Goodnight now," he said with a sly smile.

Love peace and hair grease, says the happy couple of Evergreens, laughing all the way.

Noelle's Cadillac glides along the road to mommy and daddy's house as they go, and he is even enjoying their conversation, which is a not so gentle nudge to come to the Lord. A true gift from your child is their acceptance, belief, and confession that Jesus Christ is the son of God, born on Earth to save the world. God bless the child that has their own, their own faith, their own love, their own relationship with God, for their own sake.

There's an unmistakable magic on the first day of Christmas shopping and despite the hyper commercialism of every aspect, you will find an undeniable excitement to the traditional beginning of the Holiday season. Christmas is a spoonful of sugar, spice, and everything nice to help the medicine go down; "Do This in Remembrance of Me," it's medicine for our souls.

The world takes notice of Christmas, and there will be peace on Earth. No longer is peace an unobtainable fantasy, it becomes the air we breathe. Christ, thy Savior is born, a real medicine we take once a year, and it's a spoonful of the mystery of God, best taken with praise water.

Mother Chance is feeling the joy of the Season and wants to encourage her son with her talent for spoken word, and she reads a poem titled Upon His Murder She Wrote...

*Here is a riddle within a rhyme,*
*just for you to crack your egg head.*
*I've scrambled together the yolk of some thoughts,*
*consider this with your smarts...*
*As we travel through space,*
*on this third rock from the Sun,*
*whether you consider yourself an Astronaut,*
*or a beach bum,*
*whether you consider yourself a believer in God's son or not, call we,*
*call us, call me Astro-nuts,*
*and everything we do is on the 1.*
*Be in the know,*
*don't just sit on your brain and spin around the universe,*
*soon you'll get old and allow your heart to grow cold,*
*to the son.*

And Daddy Chance; ever the smooth operator, lets the moment stand, knowing that times are changing, and almighty time waits for no one. Then he speaks with expectancy to his son,

"Noelle, you're a grown man, but it's time for you to snap out of your funk. Your mother and I are still waiting for a grandchild from you, Lord Willing. My son," Daddy Chance says, "watch the Generations come together tomorrow. Look at the people and see the miracle of the Holiday Season."

I want you to take note of Holiday traditions and be thankful for old family traditions like ours. El, if you pay attention to your surroundings, you'll find Generations of men shopping for their wives, girlfriends and, of course, their mothers. Look closely and you will see a father shopping with his son. I can still remember the wonder you had in your eyes at this time of year."

"Black Friday has a greatness. Look at the people and you will see a family of sisters together. Keep looking and you will see a grandmother, daughter and granddaughter together shopping," says Mother Chance.

"We're here," Noelle interrupts his mother and father as he pulls up to their home. "Mom, your poem is good. You got skills. I 've enjoyed this drive like the one I just had with dad and JJ on Veteran's Day. Dad told an amazing story of Grandpa Avery and I'm happy that you both are happy. I enjoyed our family Thanksgiving. I think Holly and Jake did a great job.

"El, you are getting older, but you will never catch up to me. Don't be so mean. In the meantime, try to have more fun this Christmas. Be joyful on purpose, my son."

"Son, did you hear that? Your mother is a poet, and I think she knows it," Daddy Chance chimes in.

Noelle is stunned into silence. "You guys are too much for me. I'm going to take your goodies from dinner inside and put everything away."

Noelle escorts his parents into their home and says, "I won't be shopping at all tomorrow. I will be home right after work and call you sometime tomorrow night, but we have a date on Saturday. I'm taking you guys out shopping. I'm going to get in my bed and get some sleep, so goodnight."

Noelle sinks back into the luxury seat of his car and turns on his CD, which begins playing a classic song from the Commodores titled "Zoom" and zoom he does, moving through the streets of North Star

Village. Look at the people, he remembers his parents saying and looking into the beautiful night says to himself, so this is Christmas; now seeing the pretty lights of the season, that compare to no other night but Christmas Eve, which is incomparable.

Thanksgiving Eve and Thanksgivings night are close by prayer, it's an event that touches all the senses, and Noelle; now in emotional cruise control, is trying to take back his emotions that were taken aback, bombarded by food, wine, song and love, not to mention the new relationship of his nephew and his secretary. Life happens fast, right turn, left turn, straight ahead, stop and go fast and slow, now home in bed, sleep comes even faster.

Midnight once again delivers a new day unto Noelle Jr., and sweet sleep once again rules the night. The art of the deal, according to Noelle Jr., who built a fortune, is the cost of his money moves, which could be the expense of his soul. A mind is a terrible thing to waste, and your soul should be priceless, but by subtlety and trickery, Noelle is a soul that has gone cold. He is now naughty by nature when it comes to money and making money moves.

Noelle, like people in the business world, gets excited by Black Friday; money is the driving force behind the Thanksgiving Holiday weekend shopping picture. Modern times have extended Thanksgiving Friday into an entire weekend that generates several Billion dollars. Black Friday and the entire Christmas shopping season drives the USA and the Global economy with 100's of Billions of dollars, taking several companies into surplus, hence Black Friday.

Back in the day, when he was a college boy, Noelle began to turn away from Christmas after learning of the USA history of slave trade. Now aware of the obvious tangent to Black people putting plantation owners and manufacturers in the Black; meaning owning slaves, making money from the fruits of the human cargo of Africans brought in, bought, and sold to work.

Money and the pursuit of it, would make for strange alliances and works of evil, some subtle and all wicked, developed by a world scheme and enforced by skin color oppression. Black skin in the game of domination by White skin are strangers in a strange land and could never blend in when their skin color could not hide anywhere in the USA. Nowhere to run, nowhere to hide, always an outcast by skin color but inclusive in the industrialization of America. The financial wealth of our country was built on the backs of their Black slaves, who could not reap the harvest of their blood, sweat and tears.

And the melody still lingers on.

Awakening to the morning light brings renewed thoughts of the money to be made, Noelle Jr., is thankful that after the morning after, work begins at 11am. A 5-hour workday is on the schedule for Black Friday, curtesy of the Holiday work shifts put together by Nickolas Kingsly. Today Noelle must get to work for the 10am breakfast, put together to honor Nickolas being ordained a Deacon at North Star Baptist Church.

Noelle is catching his breath from an emotional Thanksgiving Day with family. The reality of the new day is sinking in with each sip of coffee inhaled. His nephew has officially announced a relationship with Miss Kristen Flowers to family and friends. Noelle plans to be the first one in the office and greet Miss Kristen Flowers warmly, hoping to avoid any awkward feelings that could wreck their business relationship.

The drive to work for Noelle Jr., gets an assist from smooth jazz music and classic Christmas Symphony music, as Victor Herbert "MARCH OF THE TOYS" from Babes In Toyland, flashes across the digital display on the Cadillac CTS stereo, followed by "My Favorite Things" by Julie Andrews. Radio station KNSV has put together a wonderful soundtrack for the Holiday Season, which is playing background to the images of life passing by his windshield.

Black Friday brings a different traffic pattern. Cars are turning into parking lots that are normally empty. *Look at the people* Noelle remembers his parents saying, as his intensity to get to work is met by the intensity of Shoppers in a new Christmas Season. The intensity should be joy filled anxiety, but everyone is not cheerful, some have broken hearts from losing a loved one, some are out in the early morning to fight loneliness, others only have thoughts of saving money on gifts. People will wait in lines for early morning doorbuster sales, many taking advantage of their only time off from work to shop during the oncoming Holiday season.

Noelle is excited to be an early bird, but today is also the day for the breakfast tribute to Nickolas Kingsly, he's surprised to see many of the staff are already there, when he turns into the office parking lot, then the radio flashes the title of the next song "Christmas Comes but Once A Year" by Mahalia Jackson.

Noelle says, *Christmas comes but once a year, but I can't wait till it's outta here.*

Nickolas Kingsly woke up in his right mind, giving thanks to the Lord for the new day. Today his co-workers will honor him with a tribute breakfast and he, ever the thoughtful husband, is up early to prepare a Continental breakfast for wife and Daughter who are part of the Retail world that will open their doors for early bird Black Friday sales.

He's the family driver today and breaks the brisk morning air with hot coffee and tasty pastries.

"You guys enjoy your coffee. I want you to have a great day," Nickolas said, kissing his wife good morning. "Fill your coffee mugs and bring your pastry with you."

Marion, already at the table eating, says,

"Dad, you are always right on time."

Nickolas loads up the Van and drives off into the darkness of Black Friday morning, not having to rush. There's plenty of time to get to both of their stores that open at 8am for doorbuster sales. The rest of the morning moves on quickly.

*I have to save some room in my belly for my tribute breakfast,* Nickolas says, returning to a quiet house. His sons are still asleep, and he can relax.

Simon and Christopher will have a smorgasbord of meats from Thanksgiving to enjoy for breakfast, along with daddy's famous eggs, when they wake up.

One hour of extra rest does go by quick, but it's appreciated by all parents who can find it during the Holiday season and now ready to start his day again.

"Uncle Matt is on his way to pick you up. Simon, make sure you and Chris have gloves, and I want you to wear your heavy coats because you will be standing outside for a long time watching the balloon parade. It's a little chilly outside."

Simon and Christopher nod their heads in agreement, their mouths full of apple pie...

"Oh yeah," Nicklas says, "go to the bathroom before you leave. I have to go now."

The boys to men story in the Kingsly kitchen could be a picture on a Holiday postcard. Simon sets the 10-second delay on his camera phone and encourages dad to stand in the middle of his sons, then the phone beeps its 5-second countdown of time, to capture a moment of love.

Simon and Christopher are happy to see Aunt Marie and Uncle Matt, fresh from Target's 6am doorbuster sales, when they drive up in their Oldsmobile Enclave. Simon invites them in; by instruction of their dad to enjoy the smorgasbord breakfast he put together.

Nickolas calls Matthew Sr., on his cellphone.

"Hey Matt. I want to thank you and Marie for taking the boys out with you today. It's a gift.

"I hear you man, thank you for breakfast. I know your boss is a hard man to work for, but this tribute breakfast for you is a step in the right direction. Marie and all of us are proud of you Deacon Kingsly. I know things are going to work out just fine for you, no doubt.

"Thank you. I'm on my way into the office now. Tell everyone I said hi and enjoy the parade. We should be home by 6 tonight. Simon can take care of Chris if you need to bring them home before that. I will talk to you later."

"Alright Matt. We can hit the road and get a good spot for the parade. I can tell by the way you were talking that ole Saint Nick is excited about today at his job," Marie says matter of factly

"He sounds excited," Matthew says. "There's a first time for everything and Nick will always remember his job recognizing him, personally and professionally. Alright everybody, let's get on the road to the Holiday Balloon parade."

Riding with Uncle Matthew is always interesting when it comes to music, today he's playing a CD titled "A Step Music Christmas." Matthew suddenly turns the music down to say... this is the first time that I can remember not working on Black Friday, look at the people, then sonic art imitates life as the song titled "Christmas Steppin" by Marvin Cole, begins to play.

"Let's get to steppin," Matthew says as he pulls into the downtown parking garage. "We got portable chairs, so let's go and find a good spot to watch the parade."

The first day of Christmas shopping looks like the first day of Christmas, everywhere you go the signs of Christmas are on display. Take a look at the people on the way to the North Star Village Holiday Balloon Parade, a city-wide event to begin the Christmas and New Year Holiday season.

~

Nickolas is not surprised to see the boss is already at the office, and he's glad to see the familiar black Dodge Charger of Kristen Flowers pulling into the parking lot. Kristen is in charge of coffee and donuts and, as efficient as she ever was, motions to Nickolas to meet her at the car.

"Good morning, Miss Flowers. You look like you had a good Thanksgiving. That's a wonderful smile on your face," Nickolas states cheerfully.

"Thank you, Mr. Kingsly," Kristen replies as she hands Nickolas a box of Sylvia's Best Coffee. "You can bring the coffee in. I will bring the donuts. Breakfast will be catered by Sylvia's Best food truck, which is pulling into the parking lot now."

Noelle Jr. is surprised to see a food truck but pleased to see Nickolas enter the office early with Kristen Flowers. The moment he had prepared himself for, comes and goes in a blink from the joy filled eyes of Kristen Flowers, she's in love, shining from the inside to the outside.

"Good morning to you both. I appreciate your professionalism and acumen for financial work. Black Friday is a big money day, the biggest of the year. We've done a great job so far. Please relay that to the staff during the tribute breakfast, Miss Flowers," Noelle Jr. states in a low tone.

Turning to go back into his office, Noelle adds, "Miss Flowers, after you oversee the setup of the breakroom, I would like you to meet me in my office. Bring your coffee if you like."

Nickolas states, "Well Miss Flowers, I believe that was a compliment from the boss."

"I want to compliment you, Mr. Kingsly. Because of our Holiday work schedule, I was able to do a little shopping early this morning, and I was very excited to buy a gift for my new boyfriend," Kristen said with a big smile on her face.

"That is cool. I love it when a plan comes together," Nickolas says. "And your new relationship is right on time to share your first Christmas together. So, who is this lucky young man?"

"Thank you, Mr. Kingsly," Kristen says.

"Thank you for what?" Nickolas replies as they walk to the breakroom.

Kristen sets up the coffee and donuts alongside the buffet style breakfast setup by the food truck caterers, who are ready and waiting for the 10am start time.

"Mr. Kingsly; Deacon Kingsly, I'm thankful for you in my life. I want you to know about my boyfriend because you have prayed for me, and I have prayed to find a good relationship and be happy."

Kristen is nervous in a way Nickolas has not seen before. It reminds him of his daughter. He knows to be patient, as she relays the message that her boyfriend's name is,"Jacob Evergreen Jr."

"I know that name," Nickolas says. "That's Mr. Chance's nephew."

"No one knew we were dating. We wanted to take it slow, and we did just that until he announced it to his family last night. We will meet my family for dinner on Saturday."

"He seems like a very nice young man, Miss Flowers. The Lord is still in the blessing business," says Nickolas.

"Yes. He has never stopped," Kristen replies with a sigh.

"That's spectacular Miss Kristen Flowers. It's a shock to hear at first, but it makes so much sense for you. I have met Jacob Jr., along with his mother and his father, at my Church. I'm happy for the both of you. I think you make a great couple," Nickolas continues. "Congratulations young lady and don't worry, everything is coming together for your good."

"Thank you so much, Mr. Kingsly. As a couple, we don't want any distractions for this office. In time, everyone will know. For now, it's only you and Mr. Chance. I'm sure that's what he wants to meet in his office to talk about," Kristen said joyfully.

"Well alright Miss Flowers. I'm going to drink some coffee and enjoy a donut. You can go on and meet Mr. Chance. I will finish putting out cups and napkins. It's not often that a person gets to set up their own tribute breakfast," Nickolas said as he greeted the staff beginning to pile into the breakroom. "Thanks for telling me about your good news, Kristen."

Kristen is happy, and it shows. She knocks on the open door of the boss, and he motions for her to enter, stating,

"Come in, Miss Flowers and close the door. Seeing you today feels like a regular business day. Your relationship with my nephew doesn't feel like it will be a problem between you and me. Is there anything that you would like to say on the matter?"

"Mr. Chance, I'm thankful for my job. I put forth my best to be an effective administrative secretary for you and the staff. I don't want to let you down and I certainly don't want to let Mrs. Elizabeth Waterhouse down or the business training program she pioneered, which I represent. That being said, I know you love your nephew, and he feels the same way for you. JJ, as you and the family call him, respects me as a businesswoman, just as you do, by allowing me to grow right here at N. O. Chance Financial Agency."

Kristen waits for a response from Noelle. When she notices that he has nothing further to add, she breaks the silence by saying,

"Sir, if that will be all, let's get on with Mr. Kingsly's breakfast tribute, then get on with our business day as usual."

Noelle Jr. quite relieved by the meeting, responds quickly,

"Very well Miss Flowers. I'm glad we had this talk; that will be all for now," and they leave his office together.

"Good morning Mr. Chance," says 2 employees who have come to enjoy the breakfast tribute.

"It certainly is a good morning for the early birds," Noelle replied.

The breakroom is setup to serve, and the boss says,

"Kingsly, I've come to try out the coffee and I want to hear what you have to say. This looks good."

"Sir, the coffee box and cups are on the conference table. You will find cream, sugar, and spoons there too. We also have donuts, pastries and a brunch buffet prepared by Sylvia's Best food truck catering. I'm going to say a prayer now to bless the food, and I will speak just before our staff meeting at 11."

"Come with me to my office after the prayer. I want to brief you on our point-of-sale advice for our clients today," Noelle replies.

Nickolas can tell the meeting with Kristen went well, there's no tension with the boss.

The majority of the staff is now present. Nickolas greets everyone and asks all to bow their heads in prayer to bless the food.

"Our father, thank you for a brand-new day. Thank you for safe travel. We ask that those on their way make it here safely. Father God, please bless this food and the hands that prepared it for us today. Let this food nourish our bodies, as you Lord feed our souls. We ask for this blessing in the name of Jesus. Amen."

Kristen immediately says, "Thank you for your prayer, Mr. Kingsly. This breakfast tribute is in your honor and is now open until our 11am meeting. Please help yourselves, the food is set up buffet style. Any food questions, ask our catering attendants."

Nickolas waits for the boss to head back to his office and freshens his coffee before following him, and as more employees make their way to the tribute breakfast, it's easy to see the joy all around. The Holiday schedule is a success.

"Kingsly, close the door behind you," the boss says. "I want us to be proactive with financial tips and reminders today. Let's help our retail clients be more efficient with their transactions and checkout lines. We can remind them that efficiency on the cash registers will add more profit, and advise them to keep the floor managers engaged, by giving them decision-making power on the sales floor. Today, we want to supply our clients with great customer service. I commend you on developing this Holiday schedule. It fits well. Let's do it again for Christmas and New Year's since so many people are determined to celebrate the overblown commercial that this season is."

"Very well Mr. Chance. We all will appreciate the extra time to celebrate with family and friends," Nickolas said, thanking the Lord from his heart. Let's make this a great Christmas," reaching out to shake hands with the man known as Mr. No, who turned into Mr. Yes on Black Friday.

The workday goes by fast, Nickolas; also known as Saint Nick, delivers an early Christmas gift to the efficient staff. They get to leave early today and one by one they reach out to shake hands with the man with a plan, office manager Nickolas Kingsly. Noelle Jr. looks cold and indifferent sitting in his office. There's a strange look on his face, half mad, half amazed, as he halfheartedly waves goodbye to his employees when each one walks by his office door to give their farewells.

Miss Kristen Flowers is happier now than when she entered the office. Jacob Jr.'s meeting with her family awaits. Waving goodbye to the boss, she happily states,

"Enjoy your weekend Mr. Chance," smiling in wonder at the thought of calling him Uncle El.

Noelle looks up from the papers sprawled across his desk and realizes his personal relationship has changed with Kristen, but their work relationship was not affected. The thought causes him to pause in response to Miss Flowers, giving the moment a dramatic effect.

Kristen, looking into the eyes of Uncle El, saw the wonder of life dash in a flash across his face. Noelle is remembering his first love; Millicent Eboni, and he sits up straight in his chair surprising Kristen with his voice, full of emotion.

"Young lady," Noelle Jr., says, "I wish for you an enjoyable weekend in all that you do, and Monday morning we will start all over again, anew!"

As quickly as the light of kindness did shine, it went back out, like it never shone, but Kristen did see and as a blind encouragement she replies,

"Mr. Noelle. thank you."

The office has emptied out. The employees are now happy campers out and about their Holiday weekend excursions in a variety of styles, different strokes for different folks. Kristen is on the move but feels she must stop again to say thank you to Nickolas, who was waiting patiently in the front of the office.

"Mr. Kingsly, I don't want our personal lives to affect our working conditions. I know you try to keep the office clear of politics and religion, which can become points of distraction and contention, but thank you for allowing me the exception to celebrate your elevation in the Church."

Nickolas looks at Kristen, again with the patience he has learned as the father of a daughter, and nods his head yes in agreement, because this young lady has something else to say.

"We call you Saint Nick around here out of respect for your thoughtfulness. That's why we celebrated your promotion to Deacon.

I will not be going to North Star Church on this Sunday, but I hope to see you there at another time, Lord willing."

"Thank you, Miss Flowers, for putting this together. Now enjoy your weekend."

LOVE BLOSSOMS FOR KRISTEN FLOWERS, who bounds down the hallway at a brisk pace. Happiness is a song tapping along in her shoes, no reason or rhyme, hang all the mistletoe, it's kissing time.

Nickolas feels his cell phone vibrate. It's a notification of a text message from Matthew stating, *I just pulled into your parking lot, the boys wanted to surprise you, so I told them I would text you to see if it's okay to come up, call me back when you get this message.*

Nickolas calls Matt right back, "Hey Matt, what a great surprise. The kids can come on up, no problem. I will be listening for them in the hallway, your timing is awesome. We will be out of here in just a few minutes."

Nickolas opens the office door and in no time at all, there is a wonderful sight in the hallway.

Simon Kingsly says,

"Hey dad, if you hear any noise, it's just me and the boys." Walking fast behind him are Matthew Jr., and Christopher, who both get a welcoming hug.

"I know you are ready to get home, eat and get a little rest on the couch tonight!"

I'd like that son. I'm hungry," Nickolas says. "Did you guys enjoy the balloon parade?"

"It was good," says the young ones in unison.

"It was fun, we had a good day."

Youth is a tonic to lift up the spirits; suffer the children it says in the bible, and it's a joy to see the joy in their faces, every child is excited at Christmas time.

Your Uncle Matt text me that you guys wanted to surprise me. I'm glad you're here. My boss is still here and I want you guys to say hi. Wait right here and I will let him know you are here. First things first, who has to go to the bathroom?"

"I do Uncle Nickolas!", Matt Jr., says, and Christopher agrees.

"Simon, go with them to the bathroom. Follow me, then let me introduce you to my boss before you go."

"Mr. Chance, I'm sure you heard these young men. They came here to surprise me today. You remember my oldest Simon. Standing next to him is my nephew Matthew Jr., and you just saw Christopher."

Noelle Jr. is glad to see the young boys and greets them by firmly shaking their hands and welcoming them to the office.

Nickolas quickly interjects, saying,

"Mr. Chance, they need to use the bathroom," pointing Simon in the direction they need to go. "I will make sure it's clean when they get out," he said as the boys turn and hurry out.

"Nice looking boys there Mr. Kingsly."

"Thank you. I think we did well today. I'm sure our clients were happy with our customer service. The early numbers I saw show the Christmas shopping season is off to a flying start. Mr. Chance, the staff was effective. Happy workers work better and now we can get our clients more involved with Cyber Monday online sales."

"I agree with the money tactics, Kingsly, and our work productivity. Everyone was motivated today," Noelle Jr., states confidently.

"Sir, we say work hard, play hard."

"If that's the playbook, then I co-sign that emotion." Noelle thinks his sarcastic wit is funny and continues almost singing. "Kingsly, check out my favorite song of the season... I'm dreaming of a green Christmas, like that one I had so many years ago," Noelle laughing at his joke.

The new favorite song of Noelle gives Nickolas a strange thought of the world-famous Radio City Music Hall in New York City and their fabulous dancers; the Rockettes, dancing across the Apollo theater stage to kick Noelle off of it, using their famous leg kicking routine, this thought causes him to laugh with the boss.

"Kingsly, or as the staff calls you Saint Nick, I agree with you about the staff. As a matter of fact, consider the Holiday work schedule a Christmas gift," Noelle Jr., says. Before he could say anything else, Noelle was startled by the sound of the boys returning to his office, having forgot the boys had gone to the bathroom.

"I couldn't imagine for the life of me what that noise was. I forgot about the boys," says Noelle Jr.

"Yes sir. They are here with my brother-in-law. He brought them to the Holiday balloon parade, then I think they went to the Warehouse for Christmas cards. I know they wanted to buy some mistletoe. I will let you fellows meet and greet, while I check the bathroom."

Simon Kingsly steps right up and extends his hand to Mr. Chance.

"Hello sir, I'm Simon."

"Simon Kingsly, I haven't seen you in a long time. You've grown up young man. What grade are you in now?"

"I am a senior at Bella High School."

"My goodness, time does fly. Do you have any plans after graduation?", Noelle Jr., asked.

"I'm going to North Star Technical Community College," Simon states with confidence. "I'm not sure exactly how, but I qualify for some scholarships. I will know how much money College will cost and how much help I will get, early in the New Year. I already work part-time when I can, and my family will help me. We're praying together, that I get to go to College."

"That's very smart young man," Noelle replies. "I have a bachelor's degree in Accounting. Do you know what courses you want to take?"

"I've been advised to start out in Liberal Arts until I'm sure of my direction, but I'm interested in water management. Mr. Chance. Why did you name your business N. O. Chance Financial Agency? It seems like people wanting to work with you would get the idea that they have no chance."

"Now that's funny, young man. Stay blunt and straight to the point just like that, and you'll go far," Noelle says while chuckling. He then sits up straight in his chair and says, "Young man, no, as you see it, stands for my first and middle name, Noelle Oscar."

"Oh! now I get it. Simon sez, that's kind of cool."

Christopher Kingsly is now ready to join the conversation and steps up to Noelle Jr., extending his hand saying,

"Hi Mr. Chance, you remember me?"

"I do remember you," Noelle Jr., says. "Your nickname is T.T. Who is the young man with you?"

"Mr. Chance this is our cousin Matthew Jr. Just like you, he is named after his father."

Nickolas enters the office and says, "Alright you guys, did everyone greet Mr. Chance?"

Noelle gets up from his chair to shake the hand of Matthew Jr., and says,

"Mr. Kingsly, you have a fine group of boys here. Thanks, boys, for taking time out to talk to me. You enjoy the rest of the day. Keep working hard in school and you can have your own business one day, just like me."

"Mr. Kingsly, thank you for your suggestion to get involved with small business Saturday. I will investigate some stores on tomorrow when I take my parents out and about. Let's set aside some time on Monday to discuss what I find. By the way, Miss Flowers reminded me of your Deacon program on Sunday. I congratulate you on your accomplishments and wish you the best of luck."

"Thank you for the tribute breakfast, Mr. Chance. I will see you on Cyber Monday." Nickolas and boys head to the door and down the hallway, making a joyful noise...

Matthew Sr., opens the doors to his SUV and says, "Nick, how was your day?"

"Everything was good, Matt. By the looks on the boys' faces, everything was good for you too."

"It was a great day for us. Lots of fun. Me and you can catch up on it tomorrow, my brother. I know you have to pick up Mary and Marion from work, so go ahead and do that. I will bring Simon and Christopher home now, so they can be there when you get home. Me and MJ are going to our house to eat dinner and get some rest."

"Sounds like a plan. Thanks, Matt, for all that you have done today. You are too cool."

On the road again, they go in different directions but on one accord, for the Davis family Matthew Sr., Marie, Matthew Jr., and Stephanie, there's a harvest of love, as Black Friday went off without a hitch, childcare, shopping and having fun in the mix.

The Kingsly family, Nickolas, Mary, Marion, Simon and Christopher, have gone back and forth to work and home it has been a busy day, but it closes with these couples in each other's arms, and this season of love has not lost its charm... Black Friday, Black Friday.

~

Noelle's cell phone lights up and vibrates on his desk. Seeing the caller ID, snaps him out of a bad state of mind, and out of his chair of despair to answer the phone.

"Hello," he says quietly.

"Hello, hello! El, can you hear me?"

"Holly! Stop yelling, I can hear you. If anyone else were here, they could hear you as well. There must be something interfering with my reception. What's going on?"

Holly responds in a calm voice, "Oh my goodness, I'm just checking in with you. Tell me about your first day at work with Kristen. I want things to be good. Relationships can change fast, and she is dating your nephew. So is everything cool?"

"Cooler than a fan. Hey sis, if you keep trying to make me out to be the Black Ebenezer, then that would make you out to be his sister Fan," Noelle replies sarcastically.

"Yea fool. Only thing is, by the Grace of God I live, and I pray that the Lord would say well done to me on that day we meet!

Brother, I love you dearly, but you must speak life to me. Fan, in the Christmas Carol story was dead!"

For all his cold demeanor and sharp tongue, Noelle doesn't cuss, but it sure seemed like he did when he realized that he hurt his sister.

"Oh snap. Hey Holly, I love you. My mouth is hard sometimes, but I was trying to be funny. Please forgive me. I apologize," Noelle says sincerely.

"El, I want you to do better. You can't stay in the middle of this unrighteous road." Almost abruptly, Holly changes the subject saying, "Why are you still at that office? Get out of there. You guys closed over two hours ago. If you're not going to shop today, get out of there and go home."

Noelle responds with his typical sharp wit and says,

"I'm leaving. Let me get out of the office and go home, because there's no way I'm getting pulled into today's commercial Christmas madness."

"Drive safely. I know you're taking mom and dad out shopping tomorrow. Enjoy your time with them, and I will catch you later, alligator. Bye bye."

"Goodbye," Noelle says as he heads out of the office, Christmas steppin' into the season.

# Chapter 8

## *Dance Of The Sugar Plum Fairy*

### Gad

And David was clothed with a robe of fine linen, and all the Levites that bare the ark, and the singers, and Chenaniah the master of the song with the singers: David also had upon him an ephod of linen. 28 Thus all Israel brought the ark of the covenant of the LORD with shouting, and with sound of the cornet, and with trumpets, and with cymbals, making a noise with psalteries and harps.

—I CHRONICLES 15: 27

December, the perfect ten; except we moved the calendar again, the great conductor allowing the wind section to blow life into our lives, providing a musical bed for the beloved December baby. The year has gone by and now prepares to say aloha, which means hello and goodbye, hello January and February too, two months added onto the perfect 10 to throw you off again.

The great conductor knows how, knows when, in creating a wonderful symphony of laughter, tears, victory and fears; to be borne out by faith or faithlessness, each year its own song sung in time, kept by the greatest gift ever gave, which is time metered by heart and heartbeat.

November is the new December, and it closes with Thanksgiving, and lights to highlight the light of life, which we celebrate, born on a Winter night. December arrives with colorful lights that decorate the day and twinkle the night, closing Autumns' Summertime fling with a cold winter's sting, which the Winter solstice brings. Thank God, Intricate subtleties find a common denominator in Him, the Great I AM THAT I AM; Creator of all whims, not a thing that was made, was made to chance, which coincides within a myriad of circumstances, riding on the thoughts of mortal men, Heaven forbid.

One man whose whims would bend our will to win against the odds is by chance named Chance; Noelle Oscar Chance Jr., whom despite favor, even unknown favor of the Creator of all things, is a dour sport, a sour sort lacking in passion and compassion and given to bouts of thanklessness. Noelle exists now in a prolonged status quo, just living through the seasons as though the seasons each have no reason... how long? The mystery of God has no bounds to the grounds we walk on, or the sleep He gives, or the wakeup call, metered by heartbeats. The peaceful sleep of no consequence has met its match through the prayers of others, though time waits for no one. Yet each heartbeat has its own time and December baby has a yearly date, mankind has a unique weight, pulling loves heartstrings playing a symphony of life.

The symphony plays in the background. It's Tchaikovsky, what a strange way for the soul music radio DJ to begin the day with THE NUTCRACKER Overture on the airwaves, followed by The Dance Of The Sugar Plum Fairy.

And the melody still lingers on...

Normally introduced by Jazz, Christmas follows a tradition path now heard in a symphony by the Philharmonic Orchestra, this spiritual coincidence awakens Noelle with a heart on fire, Sugar Plum Fairy is a secret desire, wake up, wake up, wake up, wake up get up, get up, get up get up!

Hope springs eternal, fascination powers the knees. Noelle jumps out of bed with speed, not with thankfulness, but with greed. Getting used to talking to himself, he says,

*For goodness sakes, I don't listen to symphony music enough. I haven't heard much at all since Christmas last year. But why am I still thinking about that dance at the Masquerade Ball.* Smooth Jazz is on the radio, but symphony music surprises him as he awakes.

The first workday after Thanksgiving meets the Christmas Season with a return-to-work zeal and it accomplishes its task for Noelle, who returns to the work routine but not before breakfast that includes hot coffee and pastry left over from the long weekend.

School buses are on the scene and the hustle and bustle brings out the familiar rhythm of stop and go traffic. Noelle overlooks the surrounding Holiday Season decorations, which blend into North Star Village like a best friend that fulfilled a promise to be home for Christmas.

Once again Noelle is first to the office on this first weekday workday.

"Good morning," says the security guard from behind his desk. A beautiful Christmas tree stands out to his left.

"Good morning to you, sir," Noelle replies. Walking and talking, he continues the conversation, saying, "Let's make our good better and our better the best. Well, I guess this tree has some purpose, but that purpose escapes me sir."

Coleman, the security guard, smiles and says, "Spreading cheer with a friendly atmosphere. It's got to be good for business, Mr. Chance."

The office is familiar to Noelle and comfortable, being away since Black Friday feels like a long vacation, the comfortable chair and desk are inviting, being alone here is not loneliness... *Let's get back in gear,*

Noelle thinks, while pulling out notes collected from a working vacation on Shop Small Saturday with mom and dad.

The quiet of the empty office and the big chair take Noelle effortlessly through his notes and the thoughts they invoke of a successful date with mother and father. Too bad there's no one to witness the smile that peeks out from his poker face. Noelle smiles from pleasant thoughts of quality time spent escorting mom and dad to the North Star Village Plaza, where they began filling a Christmas gift list, checking it twice. The plaza consists of small business specialty shops; these business owners have great reputations for quality products and customer service.

The splendor of the gift of time, shared with the parents, escapes Noelle, who instead views the experience solely through the eyes of working to gain new clients. All work and no play does seem to rule the day. Hard work is necessary, and faith without works is dead, but know that faith is compassion, even compassion for yourself.

Ego for Noelle Jr. once again is to edge God out. He's blind to the Lord's hand in all things, blind, and only the Lord can give sight to this kind of blindness. Noelle is not given sight and cannot see who the author of all promotions and the giver of every good and perfect gift is. Noelle's joy is lost for Christmas and life. He can find no joy in the Season but he is always charming for business reasons. His wealthy reputation precedes him. When he introduces himself to business owners, Noelle can find cheer and goodwill when it comes to talking about money.

Now at his office and sitting in the morning sunlight he awaits his employees, it wasn't all work for the dull boy, as thoughts of mom and dad pop into his mind and how he enjoyed lunch and the day spent together, that ended with dessert and relaxation at their home to close a good day. The remembrances continue to flow seeing Mom and Dad bought a movie for themselves titled "Undercover Brother" from a record shop named The Under Cover Brotha, where the owner, who was about Noelle Jr.'s age, said with a deep voice,

"Watch this movie tonight with your son. Enjoy it and have fun."

Noelle Jr., didn't notice that mom and dad purchased a gift for him, the owner whose name was Reed Moore, suggested a gift to give someone who has everything would be a vinyl album titled Strange Fruit, by the great Jazz Diva Billie Holiday; known as "Lady Day."

On Sunday, family and friends gathered together at North Star Village Baptist Church to end Thanksgiving weekend in prayer, praise, and song, but no Church for Noelle Jr., as he fulfilled his getaway plans to see the Bella Bella Casino.

And the melody still lingers on...

The Cyber Monday morning sunshine warms the office space, sunlight attempts to light his face, but Noelle's Thanksgiving weekend memories are smiles turned upside down into frowns, and the thrill is gone and there's no joy to be found.

What Joy?

Ban fun, ban toys and all the unknown blessings that were bestowed for safe travel to and from all destinations, every last one. Ban thoughts of the Casino and Blackjack card games, some lost, some won. Thoughts of the lonely begin to rise, blended in misery that fell into the stem of a Champaign glass filled to the rim, tiny bubbles disappearing like fake friends.

Mondays' mourning of days gone by is a poor substitute for a Monday started by giving thanks, nonchalance will not change the charge put on Noelle's life. Christened; blessed as a baby, he must choose the Lord of his own free Will as an adult, that's the way mother and daddy Chance said it must needs be... Now as an adult, Noelle Jr., is unable to hear the Word of God, unable to see the Light of God and unable to understand who is the enemy that places stumbling blocks in the path to his salvation. Noelle Jr. stopped listening to the voice of God, to lean on his own understanding, now believing that man's hands make all his success by serendipity, coincidence, circumstances, and luck. But the God of Mercy is faithful to His Covenant with His Children; of whom He said He will never leave or forsake, even when we run away.

But when you get lonely, the office will be aflutter with the activity of a business dance between supply and demand but for Noelle Jr., "What Do The Lonely Do At Christmas", is not just the title of a song by The Emotions. Emotion for Noelle is an illusion in all the confusion, droplets on the windowpane and I can't stand the rain, looking out the window in a daze, dreading the days ahead, considered a pain.

MONDAY MORNING HITS hard at the Kingsly home, this day is tough for everyone after the long Thanksgiving weekend and although you can see Christmas coming, the work and school week demand a return to routine. There's no continuation of sweet dreams for Nickolas Kingly, who by routine must leave a warm bed, no snooze on the alarm button, it's out of bed in a series of dance like moves to clear the head.

First, giving thanks for awakening in the right mind, collecting his thoughts on the side of the bed, up goes the arms over the head and the feet touch down firmly on the ground and a system check of the body muscles up and down. Give thanks again and more praise for the new day, searching the sky for the strength necessary to begin. A prayer to make it through, trusting the Lord in all you do, everyone is taught to pray, pray again, and pray some more, in this family.

The power of a hot shower adds muscle to the hustle to get dressed, and teamwork makes the routine work for husband and wife, a bathroom dance that produces no strife, Nickolas keeps pushing forward and the coffee smells great. Daddy wakes up the whole house and all his children begin to stir about, Marion joins the dance as part of the routine, she prepares breakfast for the Kingsly team, and the most important meal of the day sends the team on its way.

The routine allows for prayer together at the kitchen table and even when time and schedules get in the way, they pray separately for one another, with the loving understanding of the phrase, a family that prays together, stays together... Nickolas says,

"Alright guys. It might seem like just another day, but there are only 25 days left until Christmas. Today we begin the Kingsly family countdown and this weekend we'll go to Simeon's Evergreen tree farm to pick a Christmas tree."

"Dad after school today, I'm going to shop online for Cyber Monday bargains, even though I knocked out a lot of my Christmas list on Friday and Saturday," Simon tells his father.

"Simon, your gift giving is a talent. Your thoughtfulness is on another level. I know you have saved up your money from raking leaves and other things you do, but on my next paycheck I will help you." Nickolas, now looking at Christopher, says, "Yes Chris, you too. I will give you some money to go shopping for your mom," he tells him with their special handshake.

Nickolas turns his attention to his daughter and says, "Marion, my dear heart, thank you for sending us all out into the world today with love, smiles and full bellies." He sings to his daughter... *isn't she lovely, isn't she wonderful, isn't she precious, less than 1 minute old...*

Marion hears her dad recite the classic Stevie Wonder song "Isn't She Lovely" in the style that the Deacons of North Star Baptist Church use when they chant hymns. Hymns have been carried forward throughout slavery times for the ears to hear coded communication of times to escape on the Underground Railroad, made famous by Harriett Tubman. Singing hymns into the wind worked in the past, it works in the present and it will work in the future, they are power filled spiritual tunes for the soul, that can send chills up and down the spine... Marion says,

"Thank you, daddy. You got skills. I hear you."

Mary says, "Saint Nickolas is in rare form. Deacon Kingsly, let me take you to work."

"Dad, that was awesome," says Christopher. "I'm going to tell my best friends Jimmy and Aleayah and my teacher Miss Patience that I had a good vacation with food and fun and that my daddy is a Deacon at my Church."

Simon speaks with excitement, saying, "Oh yeah, dad that's right.

Deacon dad, I should say. We're proud of you. That isn't she lovely song style you used, is poetry. It's spoken word, from a man that speaks the Word."

The whole house is stunned by the words coming out of Simon's mouth... the family enjoys a wonderful moment together... Simon, in the brilliance of youth, doesn't know the depth of what he just said, and he continues to speak... breaking the unintended silence...

"Hey dad, you know that song would be alright if you used the line isn't he lovely," he said as he does his cool walk to the door. "Goodbye everyone. We've got to catch the bus. See ya later."

Marion goes to her room to finish getting dressed for work and so does Mary, who will drop husband and daughter off as part of her workday. Nickolas watches the boys walk down the street and looking through the front window of his house of love, memories of Thanksgiving weekend form in the morning dew, looking like drops of rain.

The morning dew on the window reflects the morning sunlight in a reverse butterfly effect, like dominoes of positivity that would fall forward, but these reflections cascade light backwards for Nickolas to see a deeper spirituality of God, family, and work. The reflections of window water enlighten Nickolas to see the prophecy; be fruitful and multiply, is fulfilled in Great-Grandfather, Grandfather, Father, Sons, and Daughter.

The sunlight warms further thoughts of a wonderful Saturday spent home alone, because Simon and Christopher shop with Aunt Marie, while wife and daughter go to work at the same time, having the same schedule.

Why are you smiling like that honey?" echoes the wife's voice blowing through the chasms of his mind, like a summer breeze.

"Babe, I'm going to be a couch potato, watch TV, eat turkey, and wait for you to get back," Nickolas says. More memories come... all the shopping that could be done on Black Friday and Shop Small Saturday was done. Now husband and wife must pick up the gifts put on layaway in October, having planned well, they will clear their layaway accounts within the next 2 paychecks.

Thanksgiving Sunday they patiently did wait to make Nickolas Kingsly a gospel cake, using spiritual milk to bake a deep dish of understanding. God is meat, made from the bread that is the Living Word of the Bible. Thanksgiving Sunday memories find room within this dance of the dominoes in the light of understanding, seen through the windows of a house made from love.

The mind's eye can see Simon and Christopher walking down the street, on the way to school within a Christmas wonderland. North Star Village is within this sunlight of peace that is right outside the front window, right outside of the house, giving Nickolas something he can feel.

The spirit man catches the sunlit drift, and at North Star Baptist Church they did lift a family man that found favor being with the Lord. It is the Lord who moved him from the background to the forefront, to stand as a newly Ordained Deacon and testify at the Thanksgiving Sunday Testimonial service, a Testimony well done that uplifted everyone.

"Honey," Mary's sweet voice did say, causing her husband to jump in surprise. "I didn't mean to startle you."

As Nickolas turns from his window reflection, sunlit reflections of the Thanksgiving weekend, Mary continues to say, "Nick, it's time we get on the way!"

"Mary, you've awakened me from the sweetest daydream and into an even sweeter reality. Seeing you," Nickolas says, "Smiling like the Cheshire cat."

"Mr. Kingsly, the work world awaits your re-entrance. I will take you there in our chariot. We will keep hope alive, believing that your boss will have a smiling face and dare we believe, even a Seasons Greeting!"

Nickolas laughs at his wife's jokes. "My honey is funny, but you keep praying for Mr. No, a name so many people in North Star know him by. Even though he has well-earned that bad reputation."

Mary, in agreement, says, "Yes dear, prayer does change things. We pray Mr. No says yes to the Lord. I'm going to start up the van. You can tell Marion we're getting ready to leave."

Nickolas looks at his wife walking towards the front door and states, "Mary, you sure are fine. Thank you for all that you do. We're going dancing on the first day of Christmas this year, so put on your red dress and I will hang all the mistletoe."

Marion stops in her tracks, speechless. "My, my, my, I believe you're blushing," Nickolas says.

Thanksgiving is over, the Christmas Spirit rushes in with good tidings, colorful decorations and peace that will grow stronger each day in a countdown to Christmas Day. The atmosphere shifts in North Star Village and all over the world, but there's work still to be done, work still until the Eve of Christmas comes. It's time for North Star Village and the world to get back to work and the routines of life, but it will not last, the greatest story ever told will come true again.

The traffic is as heavy as any other Monday and Cyber Monday is no different for Mary, the family driver and chauffeur for today. Nickolas turns down the car stereo; tuned into the morning show on radio station KNSV and looking in the back seat at his daughter says...

"Hey babe girl. I just realized I didn't ask you how your store did over the Black Friday weekend."

"Daddy, it's amazing to see how the business world works. You know I didn't work yesterday, but just from what I know from Friday and Saturday, no I stand corrected. Just considering the Friday sales numbers, the store is in the black. Literally Black Friday put us in the black numbers."

"My store went from deficit to profit for the year in one day. Being a store manager helped me to see business from the business side and the store will do good business today. In the store and with online sales. I'm thankful that you taught me the reason for the season. It's easy to get caught up in the excitement and forget why we celebrate Christmas, then make it all about money and material things."

"Marion, these are the days I try to practice what I preach and remember that the spirit of gift giving is the thought behind the gift. Money doesn't have to be the determining factor in gift giving. I believe people are pleased in their heart by a gift that is given to them in a heartfelt way. But we ain't silly babe, money is a hell-of-vah drug," Mary said to her daughter

The familiar sounds of a favorite song fill the background with music, and Mary turns the radio up. Nickolas says,

"Oh babe, it's the official Black man Christmas song. Come on and sang that song man. Donny Hathaway sings, *hang all the mistletoe I'm going to get to know you better*, and everyone sings the next line together, *this Christmas*.

The radio station plays back-to-back great versions of the song, "This Christmas," each one sounding wonderful. The Kingsly family van is full of cheer when it pulls up to the front door of the office of N. O. Chance Financial Agency.

Nickolas says, "Time to make the donuts. Hey daughter, be careful taking the bus home today." As they hug one another, and she moves from the back seat to the front seat.

Mary rolls the window down as her husband approaches and says through a big grin, "Nick, it doesn't look like you beat the breadman to work, but I got you here on time to make some dough."

"Enjoy your day, sweetheart. You can pick me up after 5. Let the Christmas Season begin," Nickolas said, kissing her sweetly on the lips.

"Good morning. Merry Christmas," Nickolas says to the security guard at the front desk, who returns the greeting. Nickolas looks at the Christmas tree in the hallway and says, " that's nice," and he turns his mind to the workday ahead. We are back on our regular work schedule until the office Christmas Party, then back to the holiday schedule, 9-hours Monday, 9-hours Tuesday, 9-hours

Wednesday, 5-hours Christmas Eve and repeat that schedule for New Year's week.

Nickolas enters the office, not surprised to see the boss, and says, "Good morning, Mr. Chance. Merry Christmas, sir."

The boss seems almost bothered by the greeting and replies, "Well we'll see how good a morning this is, when we look over the client sales numbers from the Holiday weekend."

"Kingsly, I took notes on the businesses I observed on Shop Small Saturday. Let's talk about it and come up with a plan. Maybe that will make me feel better. The morning is slow. I did have a good cup of coffee, but I guess it's this Christmas thing. No way will I get into the commercial mess you call Christmas."

"Mr. Chance, Christmas can be a trying time. There are many distractions, and the emotions are high. Let it come to you naturally, sir. See the season for the peace it can provide," Nickolas says with kindness. "Sir, I smell coffee brewing, which means Miss Flowers is here."

Nickolas asks to close the office door, and the boss nods his head yes.

"Mr. Chance, before we get started, I want you to know that Miss Flowers has confided in me and spoke of her good news about dating your nephew Jacob Evergreen Jr. She has not told the staff. I believe we're the only ones who know and I respect her privacy. What I know of your nephew is that he is an outstanding young man."

"Kingsly, I was surprised by the announcement and a bit confused, but they looked happy together. It's a good thing, as long as Jacob Jr., doesn't let it stop him from achieving in business." Getting up out of his chair to stand in front of his office window, Noelle continues, "I'm sure you know my sister Holly Evergreen and her husband Jacob, since you all go to the same Church. Jacob Jr, tells me he attends often."

Noelle Jr. gathers himself and says, "I hope going to Church is wonderful for you all, but in no way does it work for me. Don't be offended, but I don't want to be a hypocrite just for holidays. I'm not holier than anyone else. No, you guys can have it... God knows my heart."

Nickolas could argue, still fired up from his well-received Thanksgiving Sunday testimony, but he knows that no man can come to God unless God calls that man forth. He can see there's a change in the boss and believes the seeds of peace are working, because the boss started this tirade off much different, this time he stated... *don't be offended.*

"No one on earth is perfect, Mr. Chance. We are all flawed and less than perfect. There's only one man who walked on earth, as the perfect man."

"Yes, yes, the invisible man. The one who can't be seen."

"Mr. Chance, it sounds like you had a wonderful Thanksgiving weekend. I'm happy for your sister and brother-in-law, your nephew and Miss Flowers. It sounds to me that you showed the young people how to be graceful under pressure, it was not easy to be surprised like that." Heading for the office door, Nickolas turns to Noelle and says, "Thanks for your time, I wanted to tell you that I knew of their relationship. It's coffee time. Call me when you're ready to discuss the business owners you met on shop small Saturday."

Noelle Jr. is not quite ready for the world and closes his door to wait for the routine entrance of his Administrative Secretary and brief her on the things to do for the workday ahead.

Kristen Flowers is earlier than usual today, Nickolas is sure it's to share good news from the Holiday weekend, since her family was to meet her new boyfriend, she enters the break room and immediately greets Nickolas.

"Good morning Mr. Kingsly. How was your Holiday?"

"I'm thankful to report the entire weekend was a pleasure," Nickolas replies, surprising her with the lyrics of a popular Christmas song, using the flow of a poet at a spoken word café. "Miss Flowers, it is great to start this day off with you. *Have a holly... jolly... Christmas, it's the best... time of the year, I don't know... if there'll be snow... but have a cup... of cheer...*

Kristen Flowers smiles with joy, good news was written all over her face. A new Christmas season full of wonder has begun and she claps her hands for the poetic rendition of "Holly Jolly Christmas" and says,

"Mr. Kingsly, that was very good. Merry Christmas. I wanted to get here a little early today and I am glad I did. How about we put some coffee in your cup?"

Nickolas smiles broadly, not saying a word... coffee joy was written all over his face.

"I want to thank you for your encouragement, Saint Nick. You are a blessing to me, and I can sense a difference in you. It's a good thing," Kristen says. While Nickolas pours himself a cup of coffee, Kristen continues, "Deacon Nickolas Kingsly, your Thanksgiving Testimonial Sunday service went well, didn't it?"

Nickolas continues to smile, not saying a word. Coffee joy was written all over his face.

Kristen thinks of the breakfast tribute in honor of Deacon Kingsly and says, "Your smile says Thanksgiving Sunday went well. Good for you and good for those who were there. I will be back to North Star Baptist Church, but for now I want to show Jacob my home Church, where my family still attends. Meribah Baptist Church in Chinook County."

Nickolas replies, "I want to thank you for encouraging me. I'm happy for you and that you choose to grow your relationship with each other, through your relationship with God."

The office of N. O. Chance Financial Agency begins to come to life as the full staff arrives. The coffee and the good cheer is a boost for morale. Cyber Monday doesn't have to wait until after lunch time to wake up. Christmas has changed everything. Kristen knocks on the door of her boss and enters his office as she has done by routine since she was hired and as their eyes meet, their business relationship resumes effortlessly.

"Good morning, sir. Happy Holidays to you."

"Good morning to you. What will make this a happy Holiday for me is the midnight hour when Christmas leaves."

"Yes sir, let the Christmas countdown begin and let us begin our workday." Sensing the time is right to speak now or forever hold your peace.

"Mr. Chance," Kristen asserts with positivity, "I think we have a good work relationship. I want it to remain that way. This will be the only time I bring my personal life with your nephew into our business conversation, but it's important that you hear this from me. Jacob and I had a great weekend together. My family likes him a lot and we will be spending more time together."

Kristen briefly pauses, looking eye to eye. She inhales and exhales, saying, "Mr. Chance, I want business to be business and to keep our private life out of the office."

"Mr. Kingsly tells me that you have taken him into your confidence about your relationship with my nephew," he said pulling a gold pocket watch from the inside pocket of his sport coat. "I wish you both continued success and that you stay focused, because distractions will hold Jacob Jr. back. In fact, it would keep you both from being successful. Now shall we get on with our day."

"Mr. Chance, I have put together a promotion idea," she says. "Please take a look at it and tell me what you think," she said, handing her boss a written proposal for a financial advice newsletter, titled Money Chance & Circumstances.

Noelle is immediately taken aback by what Kristen has presented.

"Miss Flowers, that is a good title and concept," he says, rubbing his chin. Money Chance & Circumstances. "I will study your proposal and concept. I may want to implement this as soon as possible," said as Noelle snaps his fingers with both hands, just as poetry patrons do when they delight in a sonic sonnet of a spoken word artist.

Kristen leaves Noelle's office and makes an intercom announcement, "Good morning, everyone. There will be a full staff meeting at 9:15."

Nickolas walks over to her desk and smiles. "Thank you for coffee this morning. By the look on your face, Miss Flowers, I believe you had a good meeting with the boss. I'm looking forward to my meeting, right after the staff meeting."

At 9:15am sharp, Nickolas makes an announcement. "Good morning, everyone. Attention, attention," and the room quiets quickly. "Let's get our meeting started. I want to thank you all for your hard work leading up to Thanksgiving weekend. I hope everyone had a wonderful time." Before he could get another word out of his mouth, the entire staff cheers.

Kristen Flowers yells over the noise to say, "Thank you for your efforts, Mr. Nickolas Kingsly. We all appreciate your hard work on our behalf."

Nickolas is humble, as he effortlessly thanks everyone for their kindness, saying, "Let's keep our momentum going into the Christmas season and finish the year strong." While pointing at the big clock on the wall, he continues, "Hey everyone, it's Christmas time in the city and by your hard work, Mr. Chance has agreed to repeat the Holiday work schedule for Christmas and New Year's." This, of course, leads to more joyful cheering for this wonderful surprise.

"You guys are a great staff," Nickolas says, now waving his hands to ask for quiet. We are making money and helping our clients to make money. The Holiday schedule worked well and getting out of here early in the day was good. I'm meeting with Mr. Chance in a few minutes to plan our new offers. Let's concentrate on the eMobile strength of our clients today and meet again around 4. Let's have a great Cyber Monday!

Nickolas doesn't waste any time in getting to Noelle's office. The door is open, but he gently knocks on it to alert the boss of his arrival.

"Kingsly, that was a rousing meeting you had there. I wouldn't call it the spirit of Christmas though, no sir. I would call that the spirit of money, cash, or credit," Noelle says with his sarcastic wit.

"Sir, can I close the door?"

Noelle nods yes.

"Mr. Chance, you have a good, talented staff. They work hard, and I believe we all are putting in the effort to remain a valued partner with the client."

Completely ignoring Nickolas' remarks, Noelle replies, "Anyway, we can build content and develop a strategy for advertisement and promotion within a financial newsletter called Money, Chance & Circumstances," he said with a confident smile, like the smile on the face of a cat that has secretly caught a mouse.

"How do you like the idea of a newsletter with that title?"

"Yes, that's a great title for a newsletter. I like the whole concept and the staff can get creative with this as a finance promotion platform."

Noelle gets up from his desk; drawn to the sunlit window that is full of his daydreams, good and bad. Good, that a glimpse of light can be seen as a way out of his tunnel of despair. Bad that he feels scientific theories will answer all questions of life. Then the office phone buzzes breaking through the sunlit moment, and Noelle puts the phone on speaker saying, "Yes Miss Flowers."

"Mr. Chance, I have contacted Mr. Price Waterhouse. He said that he will be available to talk to you at noon."

"Thank you, Miss Flowers. Give me a 5-minute advance notice," and turns his attention back to Nickolas. "Now, where was I?"

"Mr. Chance, we were about to discuss the newsletter," Nickolas responded quickly.

"Kingsly, it was Miss Flowers who gave me the idea to begin a newsletter, and she developed the title Money, Chance, and Circumstances. I want to put our financial muscle into writing, and I want to produce content to make this idea work. I will have to commend Miss Flowers to my sister and to my nephew."

Noelle Jr. was blessed to have mentorship and training to maximize his talent, which flourished when the doors of opportunity opened to put him in the right place at the right time and allow his hard work ethic to lift him into financial success. All of these factors in combination have helped Noelle Jr., to build a great business, but he now believes himself to be more special than other people and cannot see that his soul is in a dark place.

Noelle cannot see the Lord's Hands in the prosperity of his company, having no thankfulness to God, from whom all blessings flow. He cannot see the new newsletter idea as a gift from God, a Christmas present. His heart swims in the waters of self-praise and grandiosity, instead of the sweet water of gratitude.

Noelle's selfishness does not lack brilliance. He's pulled the idea out of his head and is ready to lay it down on paper.

"To make the vision plain, let's begin with business tax tips and customer service strategy. Then feature our most influential clients," he says.

"Sir, that's good. The staff will be excited. I suggest contacting small business owners and offer them a questions and answers interview, as an ad space."

Noelle agrees without hesitation. "That's very good Kingsly. I was inspired this morning by Miss Flowers. She gave me her idea to form a newsletter, and she came up with the title, but an idea in the wrong hands can float forever. Serendipity placed Money, Chance, and Circumstances in my hands. This is the right time for a newsletter, and I will show her how things get done."

Noelle sits back in his chair; clearly pleased. "Have the staff write about their particular area of expertise. Assign someone to devote space for start-up businesses and offer free initial consultations. Miss Flowers will put the information in press release to be sent out this afternoon."

"Mr. Chance, Miss Flowers is a talented businesswoman," Nickolas says bluntly. "We are blessed by her warm-hearted presence in the office. This newsletter is a gift for you sir, one that you will have to open your heart to truly understand, especially since it includes your nephew who finds Miss Flowers to be a treasure."

"Kingsly, what you said is well stated. Let's hope the luck stays good for my business and my nephew. If he takes after me, falling in love will prove to be a detriment to his career. Furthermore, did you say Christmas gift? No way is this newsletter going to be considered a Christmas present by me. I don't need it, I don't need anyone or anything," he said, leaning forward in his chair. "Keep trying Mr. Kingsly. You still have a way to go," laughing in a Ho, Ho, Ho like a Santa Claus would.

Nickolas offers no immediate comment, letting the air deflate all the way out of that unfunny balloon, and his silence is golden.

"Mr. Kingsly, I can see why the employees call you Saint Nick. Let's go over my notes and get the press release ready," he said while buzzing his Administrative Secretary, who answers immediately.

"Yes, Mr. Chance?"

"Miss Flowers, as for your newsletter idea... I like it. I want you to prepare a press release to announce the formation of the Chance Financial Advice Group, and our newsletter, Money, Chance, and Circumstances.

"Put the announcement on our website to celebrate Cyber Monday, then email our clients this afternoon. Contact the Newswire and the North Star business newspaper tomorrow. We want this information released to the public on Thursday."

"Thank you for accepting my idea, Mr. Chance. I will have the press release ready right after lunch. Will that be all?"

"After you're finished with the press release, contact the small business owners I met on Saturday. Make appointments to meet by phone... Thank you, Miss Flowers."

Kristen virtually becomes a ballerina, dancing as the sugar plum fairy on the first workday of the Christmas season, on the wings of love, and on the paradigm shift.

The first day of work after the Thanksgiving Holiday moves back into routine, the worker bees are doing what worker bees do, then jolly ole Saint Nick changes the music from classics to soulful Christmas music and 'This Christmas' by Donny Hathaway begins to play. The Christmas music season now begins, with a favorite song that always wins, and a soulful Christmas starts in the hearts and plays in the wind, again and again.

Saved by the buzz of the office phone, Miss Flowers' voice comes through needing his attention.

"Mr. Chance, would you like me to call Mr. Price Waterhouse now. It's almost 12 noon."

"Thank you, Miss Flowers. Call and alert me when you get through."

Getting up from his desk to change the music on his personal speaker from Christmas music, thinking to himself... *I've learned to choose my battles, and a Christmas music battle with Saint Nick is not a winner. Kingsly says it helps office morale, so let them play with their imaginations. I mean they do earn me a pretty penny.*

"Brother, can you Paradigm," says the song by George Clinton. Noelle is saved from the hypothetical proposition, when Kristen Flowers says, "Sir, I have Mr. Waterhouse on line 3."

"Mr. Waterhouse. How are you doing today?", Noelle Jr. says with a hint of excitement.

"Noelle, it's good to hear your voice, young man. How was your Thanksgiving?", Price Waterhouse said in a jovial tone.

Noelle doesn't notice his hands aimlessly massaging the desk when he says, "I had an enjoyable time with Holly and my brother-in-law Jacob, who played host for the whole family at their home. Everything turned out well and everyone is healthy."

Price Waterhouse joyfully says, "Yes, Holly can cook. I remember from the days of you and her in my mentorship program. Noelle, you were one of my best students and you would be a great teacher. I would love to help you start up a mentorship program."

Noelle pushes his head back into his chair and begins shaking his head no.

"Mr. Noelle Chance, you can stop shaking your head. I

remember how you did that in my office when anyone distracted you."

"You know me well, but I have always respected you and your advice. So, I promise to give your thought careful consideration."

"Noelle, every day is a new day, a refreshed opportunity to do things better than the day before. This is the season for changes. This is the season to believe in miracles. It's Christmas time around the World. Noelle, I can tell that you are troubled, but I did see a spark of the great person I met so many years ago, when I saw the old you dancing on the ballroom dance floor."

Swiftly trying to change the subject, Noelle replies, "Mr. Waterhouse that's one of the reasons I had my secretary call you today. Everyone in North Star knows you have the best Holiday parties, and I did promise to help you with the Community Center Holiday party."

"First Noelle, you must attend my ugly sweater Christmas party on this Friday. And Noelle, you can bring anyone you like or come alone."

Noelle has no date to bring and desires to date no one. He's happy to attend the ugly Christmas sweater party, as a party of one. Noelle tries to make a joke out of not bringing a date with his sarcastic sense of humor and says, "Mr. Waterhouse I can find an ugly Christmas sweater to play along with everyone else's ugliness," he says, laughing at his own joke. "Oh my, this is like Elf the movie, and connecting at Christmas time. You can bet that I will be at your home alone, just like the giant elf was in the movie." Although he laughs, his sarcastic-ness fails to pass the good humor test.

"Noelle, just bring your appetite because I'm having my Christmas party catered by Chef Lisa. You should remember her from the Harvest Moon Masquerade Ball. I'm excited, as my party will also be a showcase for the new house listed on my Real Estate business. The directions are on the invitation."

"Sir, I haven't opened the invitation. I will open it right after we get off the phone. Before we hang up, I want you to know I'm beginning a financial newsletter for my company, and you should receive a press release with the information by e-mail before the end of the workday. Thank you for including me in your big weekend."

"That sounds great Noelle. See you on Friday night, then we will do it again for the North Star Village Christmas party. Thank you for saying yes and thanks for calling me. Enjoy the rest of your day."

"Goodbye Mr. Waterhouse," Noelle said hanging up the office phone. Then the first hunger pangs of the new Christmas season makes a stomach announcement... it's time for lunch.

Noelle pulls out the Christmas party invitation from Price Waterhouse out of his desk drawer and reads the directions. "Take Scenic View Parkway from the North or from the South to the North Star Blvd exit and follow the sign that says Country Inn. Continue to follow North Star for 5 miles until you reach the County Inn Estates on your right. Turn into County Inn Estates and continue going straight until you reach 1225 Manger place. Turn right into the driveway and park in front of the garage. It looks like a barn."

And the melody still lingers on.

The melody is the same, but the lyrics float out the speakers into the air, sincere voices in a pitch of divine harmony sing... "*don't stop, ever... lovin' me... don't stop, ever... lovin' me... I love the things you do... my happiness comes from you...*"

Then.... ring, ring, ring! goes the cellphone. This sudden change startled Noelle Jr., to turn and look at the caller ID which says, Sister.

"Hello Holly, I'm surprised it took so long to hear from you today," Noelle states in the way only a brother could do.

"Well hello to you, dear brother. It seems I caught you in the nick of time. Saint Nick of time for you El, or has Mr. No come out to play today," Holly says, laughing at her comedy.

"Holly, my dear sister. It's always a pleasure to hear from you."

"Oh, my goodness that's good to hear. I won't keep you long El, but I got to know how your day is going with Kristen," says Holly speaking as a concerned mother.

Noelle, in all of his cold splendor, immediately melts like frosty the snowman on a bright clear sunny day and speaks gently saying, "Holly, there's no need to worry. Kristen came to work early today, and we had a good talk. She told me JJ was a big hit with her parents, and we agreed to keep our business and home lives separate. I can tell you that things are almost the same as they were before their big Thanksgiving announcement."

"Well, his father and I knew they had started going out on dates shortly after the Masquerade Ball, but he swore us to secrecy because he wanted to tell you himself. He would of, if you had visited his apartment like he begged you to do."

"Holly, I've been busy. I relayed that to JJ when we took dad to the VFW on Veterans day. Now that I think of it, JJ was trying to tell me something that night. I remember talking to him about my past, and how falling in love didn't work out for me and not to allow a relationship to hold him back."

"Noelle Oscar Chance," Holly says with authority, "You've found success in business, but no one can say you would not have found the same or better had you stayed with Millicent, who was your true love.

"El, you know I love you, but Millicent Eboni Manor was a good person. Before you tell your heart any more lies, remember she waited for you, but you would not change and wait for love. I'm glad she moved on to find a good man and a husband, because you are a good man. Milli moved on but you're still single and it is time for you to break the chains that bind you brother dearest. I don't want you to be alone," she said with a loud sigh. "Oh man, El, you got me preaching again."

"Holly, I love you anyway. I know you care but listen to me, I am okay, really, I'm okay. Listen... I will not be the reason JJ and Kristen break up. If they break up, I love my nephew and Kristen is a fine young lady. In many ways she reminds me of Milli back in the day."

Brother and sister have taken similar paths on this first day back to work after the Thanksgiving weekend, Holly; just like her brother has done, spent some early morning time in reflective thought, nurturing her soul in the sunshine.

Holly yells out happily into her cellphone, "Hallelujah, El, I'm glad to hear you say that about Kristen. For you to compare her to Milli, that's a wow."

Holly's venture into the sunlit window and the soul reflection of that meditation was help for her unbelief in the works of her prayers for her brother, prayers that are being confirmed by hearing Noelle speak with compassion, when it appeared that he would never change.

Noelle doesn't even know that his Mr. No persona is changing. Holly knows in her heart a change; even the size of a mustard seed, has come, and she has confirmation to help her unbelief. A quiet peace settles down on this phone call between brother and sister, and it would serve as a perfect wind down after a long workday; except this is the middle of the day.

Noelle breaks the sudden meditation with a cheerful voice, "Holly I got to go. I've got to get off of this phone. Before I do, I want you to know that Kristen came into the office early today and talked about an idea she had for me to form a business newsletter. It was a good idea. So good that we're putting out a press release to announce the startup of the newsletter later today. I won't even tell you anymore because I want you to see it for yourself. I will send you the press release by e-mail. Check it out and call me at home or catch up with me sometime tomorrow and tell me how you like it."

Holly is cheering in her heart; being careful not to interrupt her brother, because he's happy, and he knows it but doesn't clap his hands.

"Man... that's good news. I'm happy for the new couple, and JJ seems to be pleased with Kristen and her family," Holly says with joy. "I just had to call you. I wanted to hear from you on how the new status of boyfriend and girlfriend was working between you and your Secretary...

"El, I have just one more thing. Before you go, remember to call mom and dad, and make some time to stop by to see their Christmas tree before Friday. Also, El please mark your event calendar for Monday night, December 7th. We will commemorate Pearl Harbor Day and have our own Christmas party with mom and dad. I have reservations for all of us to have dinner at the North Star Seafood & Grill Restaurant."

"That sounds great. I will buy the dinners and you guys can buy dessert and drinks."

"That's fine," Holly replies, "The reservation is for 7pm. Jake and I will pick mom and dad up and meet you at the restaurant. Please be there no later than 6:45. Mr. Waterhouse invited Jake and I to his Christmas party on Friday night, but we're going to spend time with Jalisa, Barry, and our grandchildren. I know you are going, and I want you to wear an ugly Christmas sweater and have a good time. If you're not careful, you might have some fun."

"Okay, okay Holly. I got it all together and I will talk to you later. Thank you for calling me. I gotta to go."

"Thank you for being there," Holly says. Now get out of the office and go to lunch because it's lunchtime, and that's what I'm going to do right now. I love you, bye!"

IT'S lunchtime at Memorial Middle School and at Bella High School, but the first day back from Thanksgiving vacation is one of the longest schooldays of the year. Lunchtime takes forever, but finally it's time to eat. Christopher Timothy Kingsly says, "After all the time that has gone by, the day is only halfway over."

Chris is what everybody calls him, but he just outgrew his family nickname TT, which stood for tiny Tim.

Christopher and his best friends, Aleayah Fields and Jimmy Dewland always sit together for lunch. They're excited to make it to lunchtime today and even though baked chicken, mashed potatoes and string beans are not their favorite, it looks good today.

Christopher says, "Hey guys, there's apple pie on the menu for dessert."

"I don't know about you guys, but this is the first-time baked chicken, mashed potatoes and strings beans looked good for lunch," Jimmy says as they move along the cafeteria food line. "I thought I saw the clock go backwards today. I can't wait to sit down and eat."

"I thought it was just me. I know the clock stood still for an hour," Aleayah said as the 3 amigos head over to their favorite section of the cafeteria, a window seat that's next to the heat in winter and air conditioning when it warms up outside.

Christopher begins telling everyone about his Thanksgiving break, which included the Bella High football game, the Holiday Balloon parade and taking the city bus with his big brother to see the Christmas tree village.

The slow and sleepy morning gives way to food, fun and laughter when the three amigos trade Thanksgiving stories... then just before lunchtime ends, one thought runs across everyone's mind at the same time. They look at each other and say, "Christmas vacation is just 18 days away."

Christopher says, "Wait guys, it's time to start our Christmas vacation countdown. There's only 14 school days left."

Aleayah says, "I want you guys to root for the school choir. We're giving our Christmas concert on the last day, right after lunch."

Jimmy says, "Look, there's a picture of the countdown Christmas tree on the wall. It says fourteen days of school before vacation and twenty-five days until Christmas. I didn't even notice it till now."

Christopher says, "Okay guys we had to wait until the last lunch period, but it's beginning to look a lot like Christmas. It's time for the countdown to the last day of school and Aleayah don't worry at all about singing. You're gonna do good."

Chris, Jimmy and Aleayah are big kids now, as they head back to class, but the thoughts of Christmas time still bring out their smile. They've been good year-round, now they'll be extra good, because Santa Claus is coming to town.

IT's lunch time across town at Bella High School, and for the senior students; like Simon Peter Kingsly, there's no slow start for Cyber Monday. They're ready on the first day back from Thanksgiving vacation. Only freshman students show signs of sleepiness. The senior class celebrates being one day closer to graduation and their Thanksgiving Day Turkey Bowl victory over the Chinook County football team.

The game is the talk of the morning throughout the entire student body, and it continues into the lunchtime period. Simon is in the cool crowd; even more so now when the senior students recognize that this is their last time together as classmates for Thanksgiving, and it's right then that thoughts of Christmas and New Year's begin. The world can begin to countdown to Christmas day, but the seniors of Bella High begin their countdown with 12 days until Christmas.

Simon tells his friends from the track team that it's time for him to mingle. He's made quick work of the meatloaf, mashed potatoes, corn, and string beans served for lunch, and leaves the table to see what there is to see. He flows easily through the cafeteria, speaking to the teachers, student-athletes, regular students, boys, girls, bookworms, wallflowers, and everyone else there is, but he has one very big exception... no bullies.

Simon sez, "No bullying," and he does speak up whenever he sees it.

"Attention, attention," flows a sweet voice out of the intercom. "Good afternoon to all teachers, students and faculty." The voice stops Simon Peter Kingsly in his tracks.

"This is Ameenah Mauritius, President of the Bella High Catamounts Christmas Savings Club. All Seniors, I remind you that your savings club accounts are available for withdrawal from today until Friday, December 11th.

"Please visit your favorite branch of Village Bank to close your account or transfer the funds to another account. We all congratulate our football team and the fans that cheered them on to their Turkey Bowl win over Chinook County. I hope that everyone had a wonderful Thanksgiving.

"In closing, I have a message from Principal Deerfield, that says as follows, 'Thank you teachers, students and staff for being great so far this year. I know we will continue to work hard right up to our Christmas vacation break. Let's finish the year strong.'

"Principal Deerfield, faculty, and staff, I speak on behalf of the students when I say thank you for being great. Welcome back to all students, thank you."

Simon Kingsly is Johnny on the spot. He stopped right in front of Principal Randolph Deerfield, a husky black man with a neat afro that is always well kept; like a picture on a barber shop poster, but he has no facial hair. Principal Deerfield is about the same age as Simon's father and sounds like Don Cornelius, the founder of the great music show called Soul Train.

"Hello Mr. Simon Kingsly," says Principal Deerfield, "It's great to see you in such a good mood and I know you are happy to be in the Christmas club. I would be surprised if you didn't hit your savings goal. Young man, while I got your attention, I want to encourage you to keep up the good work by helping you to file for scholarships to continue your education, either to college or a vocation institute."

"Thank you, sir," Simon responds in his usual manners.

"You know, Simon, some Christmas miracles can materialize in the Springtime. Remember Christmas time is a time of hope and hope springs eternal."

Simon stands still, shocked by the directness of his principal. He looks at him straight with unflinching eye contact, and replies with maturity, "Mr. Deerfield, my family and I are looking at all options. I'm flexible, but I don't have a definite direction now. I just want to do something."

"Simon, you bring me joy. It's been a joy to watch you mature during these past school years, young man. I have watched you work hard, and you have made a difference here since entering these doors, much like your sister before you. Listen to me, you've got a great family. Your mom and dad have supported me throughout the years. I want you to remember this I say to you.

"Don't you ever give up and keep hope alive. I want you to make an appointment to sit down with me in the New Year. Before the end of January. We will discuss scholarships and find the best financial options for you to continue your education after you graduate.

"I want you to go to my office right after lunch, says Principal Deerfield, pulling out the ever-valuable hallway pass from his sport coat. "Take this hallway pass, go to my office, and make an appointment for the week after MLK's birthday holiday. If my secretary is not there, wait for her. She will be there soon."

"Thank you, Mr. Deerfield," Simon says, as the principal shakes his hand, just like he would do after receiving his diploma at the graduation ceremony.

Simon Kingsly moves onward to the principal's office to schedule a meeting because of bad behavior. Not bad meaning bad but bad meaning good. Lunchtime is over and so too is talk of Thanksgiving. Santa Claus is coming to town and the students feel it in the air, heading back to their classrooms to finish the schoolwork day. Simon is feeling the pull of the most wonderful time of the year in a way he's never felt before, and a song rises from his soul.

Simon sings, "*I got a feeling, a real good feeling... everything is gonna be alright. Alright, alright, everything... is gonna be alright.*"

Simon repeats the song in his heart but stops abruptly at the sight of the President of the Christmas Savings Club; Ameenah Mauritius, walking towards him, moving with the grace of a ballerina dancing across a stage towards the principal's office.

Ameenah Mauritius has a black girl magic presence that Simon has been able to ignore through the school year, but this time when their eyes meet, so do their souls. Like dancers in the ballet of the Sugar Plum Fairy.

The Dance of the Sugar Plum Fairy is a Christmas time favorite of the Nutcracker Ballet. It is a dance that proceeds the

'March Of The Toys' which depicts toy soldiers coming to life, a scene that Simon is re-enacting walking towards Ameenah Mauritius.

"Hi Simon. Are you visiting the office?", Ameenah says.

Simons hears a voice more captivating than the one heard over the intercom for the Christmas club announcement. He's in the Christmas club and knows Ameenah but missed her individual excellence until now and immediately his dating strategy; that was playing the field, changes as the thought of getting to know this young lady breaks through his poker face.

"Hi Ameenah," says Simon, feeling awkward. "I think you did a great job with the Christmas savings club and your announcement was really cool."

"Are you just saying that to be nice?", says Ameenah with a straight face.

"Oh no, no. I wouldn't try to be nice to you," says Simon. "What I mean is I'm not trying to be nice to you...wait, yes I am but not because I'm trying to be nice. Oh boy, let me start over, I think you're cool."

Ameenah laughs and her beautiful face falls into a joyful smile and says, "I was only kidding. I know you are a nice guy, Simon."

All things were working together for his good. "I think you are nice too," Simon responds. "Principal Deerfield told me to meet his Secretary and I'm glad he did. It gives me the chance to talk to you."

Suddenly, Simon Peter Kingsly is the black cowboy dealt a promising hand but he now must gamble with his original plan, which was not to get serious with any girl before the Senior Prom. That plan to go to prom with a group of classmates is changing faster than the fortunes of a card game.

The Kenny Rodgers song titled, 'The Gambler' comes to mind... *you got to know when to hold them, and know when to fold them, know when to walk away, know when to run...*

Simon changes the last line to know when you've run into a good thing.

"I'm meeting with the Secretary also. It seems we've been put together," Ameenah says.

The office administrator, Mrs. Griffin greets the not so odd couple and tells them to wait outside the principals' office and the Secretary, Mrs. Johnson, would see them shortly.

Thinking to himself, *Simon sez... time for some action*, then a smile replaces any nervousness.

"Wow Ameenah, it just hit me that I'm making an appointment for next year and soon we will be graduating. Time is moving so fast, I haven't even thought about the Senior Prom," he said so fast that the innocence was noticeable and returned just as quick.

"Me neither," Ameenah says, looking into Simons' eyes. "I haven't really had time. I've been concentrating on schoolwork and working part-time, but I do want to go to college or something."

Simon doesn't know what to say. Ameenah has taken over his thoughts.

"Principal Deerfield told me to come to the office to make an appointment to discuss plans for after graduation."

"We are here for the same reasons," she says.

"That sounds great Ameenah, I would love to talk over plans with a girl that's got it going on like you do. Can we talk later?"

"Yes," was the reply, before phone numbers were exchanged.

The rest of the school day flies by, and the month will too. Hang all the mistletoe Christmas decorations without them, just won't do.

~

AND THE MELODY still lingers on.

After a slow start, the first workday of a new Christmas Season moves by fast at the office of N. O. Chance Financial Agency. The day is a productive one for Kristen Flowers, spent doing her usual administrative office work and the added task of developing the press release for the first company newsletter titled Money, Chance & Circumstances.

Nickolas is excited to officially announce the details of the newsletter to the employees gathered together for a late afternoon meeting.

"Attention. Attention everyone," he says as the room quiets. "I want you to know that your hard work has paid off. We're set to close the year at or above our sales goals. I turn the floor over to Miss Kristen Flowers who has more good news."

Kristen immediately speaks with confidence. "Let me get right to the point. We will begin to produce a monthly newsletter that will feature finance and point of sale promotions, along with your specialized business advice. The newsletter will be titled Money, Chance & Circumstances.

"Everyone will have an opportunity to advertise your department promotions and your VIP clients. Please submit to me any promotion or story ideas and I will present them to Mr. Chance. It will take two weeks after your promotion is accepted to receive a publishing date.

"We want our first issue to be ready for the Martin Luther King Jr., Birthday Holiday. The first issue will feature stories on the staff and our strongest clients."

Kristen hands out copies of the completed press release and states, "Read this and send it out to your best clients and prospective new accounts today."

Kristen walks around the room, stopping in front of Nickolas Kingsly and states, "I will send out the general press release to all media outlets on Thursday. This V.I.P announcement from you will serve as our contribution to Cyber Monday."

"Thank you, Mr. Chance, for accepting my idea and helping me to put this together. I thank you Mr. Kingsly, for your support of the entire staff. I turn the floor back over to you."

The employees of N. O. Chance financial agency give Kristen a rousing applause. The boss, listening from his office chair, is impressed by his secretary's speech.

"Thank you, Miss Flowers. This is good news," Nickolas tells Kristen.

There's lots of chatter in the office about the newsletter when

Nickolas says, "But wait, there's more good news. Mr. Chance says we can use the Thanksgiving work schedule for Christmas and New Year's week."

A voice from the left side of the room shouts out, "We wish you a Merry Christmas." A voice from the right side of the room shouts out, "And a Happy New Year." Laughter fills the air from the excitement.

"The Holiday work schedule was a success," Nickolas shouts over the laughter. "It allowed us more time for everything and the 11am start on Black Friday was a great way to return to work. The new schedule will work the same way, but it won't begin until Friday, December 18th.

"That way we can enjoy our ugly sweater Christmas party, right after work, then get ready to do it again at the Community Center Christmas party on Saturday night, December 19th. On monday December 21st through Wednesday the 23rd , we will have 9-hour workdays. Christmas Eve we'll work a 5-hour day. We will repeat that schedule for New Year's Eve week. Okay, let's contact our clients and go home. We've had a long day."

Funny how time flies when you're having fun, sending out the newsletter press release was fun and it made the time go by fast, but the staff was ready to go home at quitting time and emptied the office quickly, knowing tomorrows' workday awaits.

"Good night, Mr. Chance, Nickolas says as he prepares to leave the office for the day. "I'm the last one to leave. Everyone else is out of the office."

Noelle Chance Jr. is in no hurry to leave; slipping into darkness, he continues a recurring theme of staying in the office long after the workday is done. Noelle is captive within the vanity of his mind and speaking up to the boss could cost ole Saint Nickolas his job, but it's by faith that he speaks the truth to the power that is Noelle Oscar Chance Jr.

"Mr. Chance we've had a good day. I think Miss Flowers has a wonderful idea with the newsletter and all of the early feedback from our VIP clients is good. We're on the good foot heading into the Christmas season."

Noelle Jr., sitting grandly at his desk, replies, "Well, I believe the Christmas Season began a month ago. Certainly, I've heard Christmas music for that long. My goodness, *hang all the mistletoe I'm going to get to know you better*," he sang sarcastically, although in a beautiful tenor.

"Well, Kingsly, if you say that now is the Christmas Season, that means I can begin my countdown of the days until it is over!"

Nickolas Kingsly has a strong and gentle spirit that Noelle excitedly tests regularly, and with a special zeal around Christmas, but once again to no avail, as Nickolas replies with a joy that cannot be taken away saying, "Sir, I look forward to a peaceful night at home with my wife and family. I believe we will have a productive work week. Thank you for extending our Holiday work schedule.

"Mr. Chance, my wife is here to pick me up... so I will be leaving now. I will tell the front desk that you are still here," Nickolas said, waving goodbye as he exits stage left.

Noelle spins in his comfortable chair, reaching for the stereo remote control.

"No need for me to hurry, I will not fall victim to Rudolf the Red Nose Reindeer, jolly ole Saint Nick or any rendition of Silent Night, Holy or otherwise," Nickolas said, ranting to himself. Soothing the savage beast with jazz music; the great Black American art form, which plays through the speakers, now at a preferred higher volume.

Noelle exhales and there's no change of heart but as he inhales, the winds of change are signaled in the music of a Sam Cooke song called, 'A Change Is Gonna Come.'

The song gets louder, the words become clear to Noelle, but it's not the voice of Sam Cooke he hears. He thinks it is the voice of his dead former business partner Khole Cashe, saying, "It's been too hard living, but I'm afraid to die 'Cause I don't know what's up there beyond the sky. It's been a long, a long time coming, but I know a change is gonna come. Oh yes it will"

And the melody still lingers on.

The Twi-light zone of this day brings dusk to the sky, preparing it to turn day into night, a silent night that falls into the office room and nothing can be heard, but peace has no chance.

Noelle inhales: having forgotten to breathe and as he exhales, the silent peace is shattered by the loud sound of dress shoes tapping rapidly down the hallway and moving past the office door.

"Who could that be?" Noelle says running to the door, but the sounds fade away. Then the office phone rings, startling Noelle to quickly pick up the receiver, "This is Noelle Chance."

"Good evening, sir. This is Ira at the front desk. I'm on security tonight and I just want to know if you will be staying much later."

"My goodness man, you sure do make enough noise walking in the hallway."

Ira, chuckles, and states, "Mr. Chance, sometimes my keys bang against my flashlight. Maybe that's what you hear."

"It sounds like you're going dancing after your shift, with those dress shoes I heard."

"No sir, I always wear regulation footwear. They have soft soles for all the walking I do, and I haven't walked down the hallway yet. Mr. Chance are you going to be staying much later tonight?"

"Thank you for your good work, Ira. I will not be staying much later. I will be leaving in about 5-minutes."

"Sir I will be waiting to escort you through the parking lot," Ira says.

Noelle leaves the office and looks around, wondering about the noise he heard, but when he reaches the front desk, it looks like he will walk on past without stopping.

Ira leaps out of his seat saying, "Mr. Chance allow me to open the door."

Noelle notices the security guard has on soft sole work boots. *Well, I heard something. Let me get out of here. Tomorrow will be here soon enough*, he thinks to himself.

Ira locks the building doors and walks across the parking lot with Noelle, who goes to his car, as Ira waves goodbye.

Both men move on as two ships passing in the night, Ira floats on... Noelle heads home.

The Symphony Conductor brings music and lights and Thanksgiving to begin anew the world party known as Christmas, a celebration season based on love. The birthday party for the son of God, born on earth. The son of man, this anniversary increasingly misunderstood, manipulated by the manipulator of evil who directs man's hand into mischief. But there ain't no misbehaving for those who adhere to and hear the Director of the Heavenly Orchestra.

In the life of Noelle Oscar Chance Jr., the symphony of the heavenly orchestra represents a commercialized conglomeration of spirituality, bathed in sweet music and the distractions of sensual hints from beautiful ballerinas dancing to mesmerize you. But anyone who had a heart would love me too... is the invisible sign language used by The Conductor, moving the world to see the male as a bridegroom and the female as the bride in this symphony of love, even called the mistletoe jam.

The world dances to the promises of a Holy Kiss from the reason for the season, but not Noelle, who has a cold heart that doesn't dance, yet sings of remorse.

"*The love I lost was a sweet love, the love I lost was complete love...*" he sings.

"*it looks like another love TKO... taking the bumps and the bruises of a two-time loser, trying to hold on, I think my faith is gone, it's just another sad song, I think I better let it go...* sings Noelle,

"*Like a waterfront New Jersey boxer who could've been a contender, knocked down the rabbit hole, seeing further heartache...*" singing remorse.

"*I wish I never met her at all, even so, I love her so...*"

"*How did I fall in love with that women driver of the love taxicab, who takes her riders in a streetcar named desire, and her fare is not fair, when she charges you with unrequited love?*"

And it's said that hell itself has no fury like a woman whose love has been rejected, as the countdown Noelle hates to begin, has begun. There are 25 days until Christmas.

And it comes to pass... all are carried unto Friday December 11th, when loves super intuition will beat in all hearts. Love to love, or love to hate.

And the melody still lingers on.

# Chapter 9

## *The First Day Of Christmas Steppin'*

### Asher

On the thirteenth day of the month Adar; and on the fourteenth day of the same rested they and made it a day of feasting and gladness. 18 But the Jews that were at Shushan assembled together on the thirteenth day thereof, and on the fourteenth thereof; and on the fifteenth day of the same they rested and made it a day of feasting and gladness.

— ESTHER 9: 17

North Star Village looks like a Christmas town postcard, it's covered in 5-inches of pristine snow that lines the streets and sidewalks, which have been cleared, making way for an unmistakable magical feeling in the air. It's the most wonderful time of the year, and the Sun rises faithfully to wake up a glorious new day.

Thank God it's Friday that finds Noelle Oscar Chance Jr. the early bird in the office. First as usual, he turns up the heat and turns on the radio, and feeling the heat feels good, it rises in unison with the morning sun. The confluence draws an unappreciative Noelle to the window, but he cannot see the beauty of the Village, for the coverage of the snow.

Noelle stands in the face of adversity, but it's not by faith. He leans on his own understanding of the world, which is failing him in the pursuit of happiness. He is blissfully unaware of the evil captivating his soul, and he can't get no satisfaction.

The Mr. No personality has no wish list to check once or twice, no preference of people naughty or nice, but he does have a desire in his heart for Christmas to be over, as soon as it starts. Never satisfied, Noelle loses faith, but the warmth of sunshine on his face has a voice that says... store your treasures in Heaven.

Noelle puts faith in the material world, living in a careless state detached from feelings. In this place, he can choose to overlook things. In this place there will be no Christmas Rap or Christmas wrapping for Mr. No. Instead of that comfort and joy, he finds pleasure breaking the happiest time of the year down to its last financial compound.

Noelle's subconscious takes a trip in his reflection from the office windows. He rediscovers the feelings of joy and pain, only to leave them both behind. He is excited to tell the staff that N. O. Chance Financial Agency is a sponsor of the S&G, R&B Gala, taking place on the seventh day of Christmas. The Silver, Gold, Red and Blue Christmas party is a traditional event of colorful outfits, held at the North Star Village Community Center.

Noelle looks away from the window and is startled to see the staff has begun their workday, then he turns his personal music down to answer his cell phone. The caller ID says nephew Jacob.

"Well hello nephew. I hope everything is alright, your call startled me," says Noelle.

"Good morning, uncle El. There's nothing wrong. I'm just calling you to say hello. I haven't talked to you since Thanksgiving, but Kristen tells me you seem to be alright. She also told me that you followed her suggestion to publish a newsletter, and let me tell you something, I love the title Money, Chance and Circumstances. It's good, Uncle El. Thank you for giving her this opportunity. She is a great girl and it's important to me that you two keep a good business relationship."

"Thank you, JJ. You know I like to work, and I have kept myself busy. That's not an excuse, it's just the way that I am. I'm sure you know your mother keeps me informed. She tells me you have a good relationship, and that is a good thing for you."

"Uncle El, it's going to be Christmas soon and you haven't been to my home yet," JJ said in an inviting tone of voice. "I know you're busy, but please come by before Christmas. Let's share some coffee and cake like we had planned, when we went out with big daddy."

"JJ forgive me," Noelle says without hesitation. "Thanks for not giving up on me nephew. Your phone call was right on time today. I'll tell you what, let's meet on the day of the Community Center Christmas party. I can visit you at your home on my way to the event."

"That sounds great uncle El. I'm glad you're getting festive. I won't be able to make it to that party though. I plan to take Kristen to dinner as part of our seventh day of Christmas celebration. We're excited about our first Christmas as a couple. I will be home until five. You can come over for a late lunch. Just call and tell me you're on the way."

"Seventh day of Christmas celebration? No way nephew."

"Yes way, Uncle El." Then Jacob Jr., sings, "*On the seventh day of Christmas, my true love gave to me, seven swans a swimming, six geese a laying and a dinner... partee!*"

"JJ, you remind me of my dad. Your Grandfather is a great man. He loves to sing," Noelle said with his voice trailing off.

"You're trying to make me laugh man. You do make me laugh at times," Noelle said chuckling. "I was just going through the motions today, but you woke me up. I need to go shopping today, to beat the other last-minute shoppers, since we're near the twelve-day countdown. I need to get my shopping business out of the way.

" Uncle El, keep your head to the sky. I see a good man and I believe you can be happy, even if you don't. I encourage you not to give up because you always encourage me. Now take your own advice and keep working to get your happy life back."

"Nephew," Noelle says with confidence, "some say praise is what they do. I say work is what I do."

"Uncle El maybe the Community Center Christmas party will surprise you like the woman in the purple dress and mask did at the Masquerade Ball. You said her name was Nevaeh."

"I met someone. She was a mystery to me," Noelle replies. "I remember your mom and dad got quite a kick out of me dancing that night, but there will be none of that at this party."

"I told Jalisa the story. She said the name Nevaeh is the word heaven spelled backwards, and she was happy to hear that her uncle could still dance. Uncle El, we both believe that was a good sign for you, so don't give up... Okay Uncle El, that's enough about the future, we still have a full day ahead of us."

"Jalisa is a sweetheart and I do have my grandniece and grandnephew."

Realizing that Noelle was struggling to remember their names, Jacob Jr., says, "Lisa and Bobby."

"Thank you, JJ. Man, you wait until you get older. Names don't come to you so fast, but Lisa, Bobby, Jalisa, and her husband Barry are on my gift card list."

"You are generous Uncle El, but this Christmas we're hoping to get you together with everyone so we can take group pictures. We want to make this Christmas very special."

"Alright then JJ," says Noelle. "I got to get off this phone. Time flies when you're having fun and today is my lucky day. The early bird is winning. You can tell your sister that I'm amazed to learn that heaven spelled backwards is the name Nevaeh," his voice trailing off in wonder.

"Uncle El," Jacob Jr., says to cut off the silence. "I won't call it luck, as I'm not superstitious, but I will call it a spiritual coincidence."

"Spiritual coincidence. I will take it nephew," says Noelle, sounding better than he did at the beginning of their phone call.

Jacob Jr. plants the seeds of love and prays that they will grow to soften a stone heart.

"I look forward to visiting your home," says Noelle. "Thanks for calling me."

"Goodbye Uncle El. Have a great day," and they both hang up, feeling better from the encounter.

Noelle Jr., looks over his desk to find the rough draft of the Money, Chance and Circumstances newsletter; pleased with what he sees... says to himself, "Shake it off El. Let's get to work in the real world," but as he looks through his office door window, it looks like a movie screen that is showing the faces of his employees, and how their lives are interwoven with his.

Noelle Jr. limits the harvest from this garden, which is his employees. He doesn't care about the impact his success has on their lives, except that he must pay them to work. The blessings that are these wonderful souls are now on parade right in front of his face. He has ignored them until this moment. These are beautiful people inside and out.

Noelle Jr. hears his inner voice cry out. Instead of reeling in this catch of beautiful people as a fisherman for the Lord, he only reels them into his net for worldly gain. Those gains are the things that have no stock in Eternal treasure. It's fool's gold. Noelle knows the truth of the Lord, but buries this treasure.

And a tangled web we do conceive when first we practice to deceive. Lying to ourselves to achieve, believing our own lies that we weave. But how long? Not for long, it's not for long that we can look at the mirror on the wall and not be true.

To thine own self, you must be true or soon you'll see a fool staring from the mirror, back at you. Lies destroy your soul. Lying takes up space in the garden of truth like weeds, and turns your soul into an undesirable soil for planting or for harvest but justified by faith, our good flowers grow.

The voice of enlightenment comes by visions from a daydream that seems to be a nightmare for Noelle. He now sees true life through his office windowpane and the window on his office door reveals the lives of his employees in this sunlit vision.

These truths are made self-evident when Noelle comes down from his high horse. A forced motion that proves to be a bumpy ride through clouds of self-deception, providing a rough landing back to life, back to reality. Gravity, earth's reality, makes Noelle dizzy to the point of fainting at his desk, when he sees everyone disappear and a vacant rundown office appears before the employees reappear.

Noelle's reality trip, now gone with the wind, sent him knocking on Heaven's door. Life's realities are normally given in small sips to receive and believe, or not to believe, but this big gulp of reality overloads the body's senses. Noelle, stunned in disbelief, immediately fights back because of the adrenaline that rises to give his muscles strength. Then his inner voice says get a drink of water and he adheres to it now like the good son who listens to his father.

"No way! No way," Noelle says, now looking at his watch. *Where did the time go,* he thinks sipping a bottle of spring water. The office phone rings to break through all the confusion.

"Yes Miss Flowers."

The sounds of laughter enter his speakerphone, followed by the cheerful voice of Kristen Flowers. "Hello Mr. Chance. I'm getting ready to shut down the switchboard for lunch time."

"Please note, I will be leaving the office for the rest of the day."

"Yes sir," Kristen replies. "Enjoy the rest of your day."

"Enjoy your lunch," Noelle immediately says as he gets up from his desk, moving quickly into the main office. This time, his sudden entrance doesn't startle the staff, and as he walks across the room, he feels a spirit of peace in the air.

The break room never seemed so far away, as he passes by the faces of his employees, literally taking notice of them for the first time. Today the boss takes in the collective brilliance of the staff assembled over the 8-years since he hired Nickolas Kingsly. There's Inez, Perry, George, Audrey, Ben Ray, Tahir, Jason, Aretha, Ronnie and Letitia.

Noelle Jr. walks by the pictures of his employees with their families and wonders how has he missed seeing them before today, because they're easily seen on their desks and cubicle walls. He glances towards the front of the office and notices Kristen Flowers wave goodbye. Waving back, he continues to wonder about the past, thinking to himself... *how did I miss these pictures.*

Next stop is the office door of Nickolas Kingsly, who is looking out the window at the beauty of North Star Village, then noticing the boss says, "Hello Mr. Chance. Are you ready for our meeting?"

"Yes, I am," Noelle says. "I almost forgot, but almost doesn't count. I'll meet you in the break room," he says, returning to his office to get the updated sales numbers. All eyes are on him as he goes back and forth, but awkward interactions are replaced by easy greetings, as the boss picks up his notebook from his desk, then hurries back through to the room.

"Kingsly, I will be leaving the office early today," Noelle immediately says to Nickolas, who beat him to the break room.

"Time is moving fast today, but we're ahead on all accounts. That's a good thing to know for your staff update, along with the news that our company is one of the sponsors for the Community Center Christmas party. I will encourage all who can attend to do so. I'm attending out of respect for Mr. Price Waterhouse and his wife, who are working hard to make this event a success."

"Mr. Chance, the staff will be excited to take part in the Community Christmas party. I look forward to the festivities and a chance to dance with my wife. Everybody knows that Mr. Waterhouse puts on the best parties, especially the S&G, R&B Christmas Gala."

"Alright there, Mr. Kingsly," Noelle says almost joyfully. "I remember our talk a while back. You requested the day off to attend the Christmas Gala, since you could not go last year or in the past.

The Agency worked overtime on the nights of the Christmas party, and I was right to do so. We have had profitable years, which makes it possible to keep your jobs."

"Prayer changes things, Mr. Chance," Nickolas says in a gentle voice, to remind the boss that he is a believer in prayer, and things have changed for the better.

"Prayer changes things, so you say. I think things happen, good or bad, by the luck of the draw and hard work, like the work you and the staff put in this year. It's your work that I reward by renewing the Holiday schedule. It worked out so well, we will do it again. I know you and the staff are looking forward to your office Holiday party after work on next Friday. That will begin a busy weekend," Noelle says handing Nickolas a folder. "Look over our client sales numbers, Kingsly. Let's talk about them tomorrow. I'm leaving the office early today, so take over."

The meeting ends and the boss quickly goes back to his office for his briefcase, coat, and gloves before heading directly out of the office.

"Elvis has left the building," Nickolas says to himself, listening for the sound of Noelle's shoes tapping a beat as he walks down the office hallway.

Noelle is a one-way street, which supposes life is managed by luck, good or bad. He's a black cat hypnotized by urban legends and superstitions, not realizing the irony of being a black cat that crosses your life path by fate, not luck.

A mind is a terrible thing to waste, but the fears of others must be respected. Our tongue can twist up myths like a pink tornado and turn them into beliefs that destroy the truth. When you don't understand the things of life, then you can suffer from superstition.

Tomorrow is just a day away. Nickolas still has the work of this day in front of him. Who knows yet what this day can bring, but the hours go by without a hitch. Nickolas is good at his job. He brings an intangible Spirit that enhances the N. O. Chance Financial Agency with good tidings for Christmas and a Happy New Year.

After lunch, Nickolas tells the staff the boss has left the building for the day, focus on customer service so everyone would be ahead of schedule before quitting time. Nickolas is keep it real wrapped in faith. The type of person that reassures you there are still good people in the world. That's why he's affectionately nicknamed Saint Nick.

Kristen Flowers makes an announcement over the intercom, breaking through the music. "Attention, all staff. We will be meeting in the break room in 15 minutes. Department Heads, please be ready to report."

The break room is full of happy conversations when Nickolas Kingsly steps forward to speak, "Can I please have everyone's attention."

The noise settles down quickly at his request.

"Thank you all for your hard work this week. If you didn't see the bulletin board, let me remind you that next Friday, we begin our Holiday work schedule. Immediately after work, we will have our ugly sweater Christmas party. Please plan to stay for a little while, so we can exchange our secret Santa gifts.Mr. Chance is excited."

"What!" the whole staff reacts with immediate laughter that fills the room.

"All right guys. Mr. Chance is excited to be one of the sponsors for the North Star Village Christmas party at the Community Center. I had already requested the day off from work to attend, but that won't be necessary this Christmas, because we will party as employees. That's a good thing, ain't that right?"

All agree and give a cheerful applause.

"I'm looking forward to going and I expect to have a good time. I hope to see us all go together but for now, let's go home."

"THANK *God it's Friday during the best time of the year. Christmas time is here, happiness and cheer. The cheese pizza is fun or ravioli for some,*" sings Simon Kingsly.

"Hey pizza dude," motioning to the cafeteria worker, "party over here."

Simon pulls out his black shades from his shirt pocket and says to his best friend, Cary Ward, "Hey Cary the kid is in rare form, tonight."

"What gives bro? No, Simon sez today?" Cary has noticed a change in Simon since they returned from Thanksgiving school vacation. "Hey Simon. Come back man, something has got you shook."

"For real, for real. You know I don't do superstitions. I don't talk about being lucky neither. I'm about that free your mind and the rest will follow. Stevie Wonder said it the best, 'if you believe in things that you don't understand, then you suffer.'"

Cary, who is nicknamed Care Bear says, "I understand that you lit today, so give your best friend the scoop. Who is she? Also, why do they call me Care Bear?"

"Because you care, and you're big like a bear," says Simon.

"Come on man let's sit down and talk," Cary says.

The best friends don't sit in the middle of the cafeteria action today, instead they choose to sit at the table next to the lunchroom monitors where they won't be bothered.

"Man, look at you all excited. It's cool but what's up?", Cary asks.

"I really don't know, but when we came back to school after Thanksgiving, I was cruising through the cafeteria saying what's up to everybody. A voice on announcements about the Christmas savings club stopped me in my tracks."

"Is that all? Just a voice got you open like this?", says Cary.

"Not just the voice," Simon says. "But the principal stopped me when she finished talking and said 'thanks for doing a good job in school.' He invited me to his office for a conference after lunch, then set an appointment after vacation to talk about my college options after graduation."

"Way-minute, why are you talking about next year? What about the girl?" says Cary.

"I'm trying to tell you. It's Ameenah Mauritius. I was walking to the office, and it was just me and her in the hallway. We both were meeting the Principal and began to talk. Before I knew it, I was just running my mouth and asked her could I call her, and she said yes."

"Okay, y'all on each other's radar now because she and some girls just sat down on the other side of the cafeteria monitors," Cary says. "She is fine, man. What you gonna do?"

"Care Bear, I'm going to get to know her better. I'm going to meet her after school and walk her to the bus stop. I have to wait until next week to go on our first date," Simon says.

"First date on the weekend before Christmas? That sounds kind of serious, man. So, I guess waiting until after prom is no longer a thing."

"We had talked before. She's the president of the Savings Club, but this time was different. I was nervous, and she was cool. The next thing that popped into my head was the Gambler song, and I said you got to know when to hold em."

"Okay. It doesn't look like you're going to be able to play poker with her," he said laughing. "Remember, the beautiful ones break the picture every time. Look at your face Simon, I just cracked your face, boy. I was only kidding, man. I got you good. So, tell me why is the kid waiting for next week to go out on a date?"

"Man, tonight the family is driving through the Christmas Tree Village and tomorrow is too soon. Next Friday, when we get out of school early, I got to chill with my brother, but Saturday is all mines. We'll meet at the Metroplex Mall for lunch."

"Simon sez he got plans. It's okay, take it slow. Don't trip, slip, and bust your hip," Cary says as they both laugh. "We still gonna hang out tho' and I want you to give me a call tonight. Simon, take my advice, finish lunch and just wave hello when we go by their table. I don't have a girlfriend, but I have girls that are my friends. Now is not the time to start talking. She's probably telling her girls the same thing you telling me."

The school day moved fast after lunch, and time flies for the senior's that are now taking in every moment of their last Christmas together as classmates. Simon and Ameenah are becoming friends and have learned more about each other from pleasant phone calls. They have agreed to meet after school on a Friday. It will be their first-time meeting outside of phone conversations. Ameenah agreed to be escorted to her bus stop, a short walk away from the front of the school, just down the road.

Simon is happy to see Ameenah, and she is happy to see him, especially after the big smile and wave she got in the cafeteria.

"Hi Ameenah," Simon says. "I hope I didn't keep you waiting. Life changes fast. You and I go through half a school year without seeing each other much, then on today I see you after school."

"I just got here, Simon. I'm sure you know I wasn't going to wait long," says Ameenah.

"Ameenah I would never keep you waiting. I would always try and be early to meet you anywhere and anytime. I just realized how far I had to go to beat you here, and I was trying not to run."

"Simon," Ameenah says gently, "I believe you. Now let's go. I'm going to catch the bus that stops down the road at State and Main Street. When we were texting, you said you wanted to ask me a question in person, so what's on your mind?"

"I would like for us to spend some time together on a date. I want to take you to lunch at the food court in the Metroplex Mall on next Saturday," Simon says walking along in wonderland. "I asked my dad to be my taxi, so your parents can meet me and him at the same time. It doesn't have to be all serious, but I just want them to know who you're meeting, when we come over to pick you up."

Ameenah is a well-dressed young lady. She effortlessly carries her backpack and glides alongside Simon in this wonderland ballet. She is covered up, but her dark skin pretty face shines through a smile that overtakes the beauty of the light snow-covered surroundings.

She is wearing royal blue winter slacks, a dark blue cowl neck sweater, chestnut color tall Ugg boots, long white hooded parka and her scarf and gloves match her boots.

"Simon Kingsly," Ameenah says as she stops walking, "I thought you were just playing a game with me, but you ain't no gambler. Just keep playing your cards right man and everything will be alright with me. I'll be finished with my work by nine. Call me then and we can talk more about your plans for a lunch date," Ameenah says as she begins walking.

"I would love to call you, but I will be out with the family at that time. We're driving to see the Christmas tree Village light show tonight. Can I call you sometime tomorrow? I'll be home most of the day and all-night," Simon says with sincerity.

"Simon," Ameenah replies, looking him straight in the eyes, "a lot of guys are interested in talking to me, but you're the only one who has a plan for a lunch date and that is cute. Plus, you want to bring your dad to meet my parents. No one knows the future, but next Saturday is a firm maybe.

"It sounds like you and your family are going to have a fun night driving through the Christmas light show. Thanks for walking with me. I see my bus is coming, so I will say goodbye now," she said through the cutest smile Simon has ever seen.

"Walking with you was cool. We kind of made it past the awkward stage, but you never said if I could call you tomorrow," he said with a smile.

"Oh, call me around eight tomorrow night. I gotta get on the bus. Thanks for making today a good day," Ameenah said, waving goodbye.

"Today was a good day, Ameenah."

Simon watches her closely as she sits at a window seat, then a cool breeze blows by his ears, reminding him that it would be cool to stop staring and start walking.

~

The Metroplex Mall is a Winter wonderland, decked out in Christmas ornaments, Noelle Jr. is surprised by the volume of joyful noise from the small crowd. He's not happy to be in the crowd, but the Mall is the closest place for Nordstrom Department store Company, his favorite destination for gift cards. Giving out gift cards for Christmas is a tradition he developed for anyone on his short gift list. This method of participation is quick and painless in every way.

*Look at the people El,* Noelle can hear the voices of his mother and father say in his mind, as he observes the great combination of shoppers, young and old.

Dinner for one at a table for two is what Noelle Jr. wants to do. More time alone, not yet feeling the effects of loneliness, and with shopping done its time for an early dinner, Chicken won't be the winner. It's steak, lobster and shrimp.

Where do happy thoughts come from, and who is the original author? Don't look any further. Why wrestle against the spirit that brings forth the recent memories of a joyful time spent with family at the North Star Village Seafood and Grill, in celebration of Granddaddy Chance on the Day of Infamy, Pearl Harbor Day.

"Surf and Turf, that'll do. I'm on my way," the heart heard Noelle's mouth say.

*I see people spending too much money,* Noelle thinks. Walking through the Mall in observation, look at the people rushing here and there.

"I guess you're going to buy an engagement wedding ring, young man," said passing the jewelry store, with its diamonds sparkling in their showcases. *Not me,* Noelle huffs and puffs. *But I remember the time.* He can't resist the chance to see what fancies the young man's stare.

Noelle moves around the jewelry store, turning down help from the saleswomen.

"Oh no, I'm just looking," he says. His gaze contains the thought. *Could it be that it was all so simple, then?* Glancing back at the young man, he can see himself once upon a time.

"Let me get to my car. It's time for me to move on and get to the restaurant," he said, hurrying away from the Tiffany & Company Jewelry Store, away from that memory.

"Sir, there will be a 20-minute wait," says the receptionist. "Would you care to wait here in the lobby?"

Reminiscing about Christmases of the past take over the present-day task of eating out, when waiting for a table brings memories and once again Noelle can hear the voices of his parents... but this time its laughter he hears.

And just a few days ago, he remembers the voice of his sister saying, 'Your niece and her bunch are spending Christmas with us. Me and Jake are looking forward to having everyone together.'

"Mr. Chance," says the receptionist, breaking Noelle's thought pattern. "Grace will be your waitress this evening, Sir. She will be right with you. Do enjoy your meal."

By Grace... Grace served the Surf & Turf dinner of Noelle's desire, and kept his loneliness at bay with pleasant repartee, by chance according to Noelle, bringing love and happiness his way.

The happiness shown by his waitress named Grace, pays itself forward with a joy that resurfaces in remembrance of a great meal, that Noelle Oscar Chance Jr. now savors through a leisurely ride home, rolling by the festive city lights of North Star Village at night.

Noelle finds his spiritual footing by standing on the outside of Christmas. He is content to count the Holiday Season days down alone and will only celebrate when the Season comes to an end. The past days and months have pulled his emotional strings in ways that coincidence cannot explain, and running from these occurrences is wearing him down. Nothing he does keeps these emotions from showing up.

Lord have mercy on my child, is a parents' prayer but the Lord will not turn a stone heart into bread. Although Jesus is hungry by fasting in the wilderness, now tempted to use His Power to win over mankind, The Lord says they must love me by Faith. Noelle will have to choose to be born again; baptized by water in a public proclamation.

He has lost his way, made bitter by the death of a cherished love from a woman and the death of his beloved business partner, which turned his heart to stone. Now standing alone at the crossroad of denial and submission, Noelle rejects the voice of the Lord, that says ease on down the straight and narrow path to peaceful prosperity, instead choosing the wide road of self-indulgence, that leads to self-destruction.

The sleeper has been awakened and once again moves within a routine of thanklessness, neither recognizing the perils overnight, or the unknown dangers of the oncoming day. For Noelle Jr., it's been a long time coming, but a change is gonna come.

Give us this day our daily bread. Noelle doesn't give the air that surrounds him a clue of his good health or pain-free body. In his mind, he's just lucky, and he goes about the morning preparing for his busy Saturday.

Noelle has made several promises to mother, father, sister, brother, nephew and dear friend Price Waterhouse, that he wants to keep, but first coffee. Noelle's affection for coffee is a clue that thankfulness can be found in him. An old dog can learn a new trick. Coffee is indeed a clue that he's aware of the air and has a sensibility to the order of things.

The pleasure Noelle derives from coffee is his ode to thankfulness. It's a thankfulness that the world may miss, but the Creator of all spirits does not miss this act of sensibility, that our bodies willingly perform. Unknown to our senses, the body cries out like a rock to praise God, but that will not take the place of baptism by water and submission to Jesus. Unspoken thanks won't do. Noelle's measured tones of unwillingness to evolve as a seed of the Covenant from God to Father Abraham must meet the melody maker, be reborn, and build his hope on things eternal.

The Lord works in mysterious ways. Noelle's subconscious mind receives the positive message on the to-go cup of coffee from Sylvia's Coffee and Cakes. The message states... 'Coffee is fruit', the coffee bean comes from a coffee tree that yields beans, born with a seed inside, which is the definition of fruit. The bean takes its place as part of the grand design of fruit from God. Noelle never reads the cup message consciously, but his subconscious has absorbed the positive vibes poured out of many cups of coffee to-go. Be fruitful and multiply.

It is sunset and doing all right on a Saturday night is Noelle Oscar Chance Jr., as another daylight falls behind the mountain range surrounding North Star Village. It announces dusk is arriving to the cusp of this fall day. No longer home alone, Noelle dines alone in this natural Twi-light zone, because he's eating good in an uptown neighborhood. He orders Spaghetti lobster for dinner at the Elite Gentleman's Restaurant Club.

No dinner for two, and I shall not be moved, is the vibe emanating from a man who would be King but the Duke of No, puts on quite a solo show. No man can be King without a Queen, and a Queen for this moment, is a beautiful waitress named Dawn.

"Thank you for your order. Sir, will you be having dessert tonight?" Dawn the waitress asks.

"No," flows out of Noelle's mouth with a chill to soothe the savage beast and his cold heart. Then the manners of a cool cat flutter to the surface, revealing a Black Butterfly, free of its cocoon.

Noelle utters in a new tone that destroys the first impression he gave. The new man that doesn't have to be alone says, "Excuse me Miss Dawn," bringing out a beautiful smile from the waitress. "On second thought, I'd like spring water with lemons, served with my dinner. Grand Marnier and champagne in the cigar room, with a Macanudo cigar."

"That's good Sir. I will bring your water right out with our warm breadbasket. Your dinner will be served shortly. After your meal, I will see you to the cigar room," says the blushing waitress.

The Elite Gentleman's Club has a jazzy ambience with photography art on the walls, which features famous attractions from around the world. A man can feel comfortable here dining alone, so can a woman. It all works well until reality comes in to say, you can't end the day this way, another conversation that must be had, gets in the way.

Another night out and another ride against the blowing winds of correction. This dining experience is behind him, but a man has got to do, what a man has got to do, and Noelle Oscar Chance Jr. has got to call his mother.

Noelle calls his mother from the car. "Hi mom. How are you doing?"

"Hello son. Everything is well here. How are you?"

"I feel good," Noelle says. "I'm calling to tell you that I am looking forward to Christmas dinner with the family, but I am not going to be able to go to Church with you this Sunday. I'm on my way home from eating out for dinner. I plan on going straight to bed."

"I'm glad you're getting out and about El. It's never too late to catch the spirit of the season. Don't feel pressure from me or anyone else about Church. God will call you into His House in His own time. Sunday, Lord willing, your dad and I will ride with Holly and Jake to Church.

"Many of our family members said they want to get together every Sunday before Christmas. JJ says he will be there tomorrow with Kristen, and Jalisa is already in town with the kids. She is staying with Holly, which means I get Christmas with my Great grandchildren. Their father won't be able to get here until the Eve of Christmas Eve."

Interjecting, Noelle says, "Thanks Mom, I will see Jalisa soon. I'm going to Symphony Hall to see the Nutcracker Symphony. I've been invited as a guest of the producers, a gift for my company sponsorship of the Community Center Christmas party. I will call Holly tomorrow to invite her, Jalisa, and the kids to my office, and treat them to lunch."

"El, did you enjoy eating dinner alone?" says Mother Chance.

"I guess I'm getting used to being alone. I did have a nice waitress, and I bought a dinner to go, so I will be all set tomorrow," Noelle joylessly replies.

"Son, I believe you will come out of this down season in your life. You can't see it yet, but there's more to life than work and I don't want you to be alone for the time you have left. You don't fool me with that kind of talk, you're only fooling yourself," said as only a mom can say.

"Mom, I will always have you. I don't need no one else," Noelle says sincerely.

"Listen to me good. I won't be around forever, and I want to know that you will be happy."

"I hear you, mom," emotion rushing in, "I will talk to you tomorrow. Bye for now."

The first day of Christmas is December 13th. Christmas is in the air and, like Savior Faire, it's everywhere. On the first day of Christmas, North Star Village went to pray, on a beautiful bright, clear sunny Sunday.

Noelle Oscar Chance Jr. chose not to go, although he would have been received with no thoughts of faults past, just tidings of comfort, joy, love, and happiness. The Lords Mercy and Grace offer Noelle Jr. a pass, but how long will it last? We all must stand alone and it's time for this one to go home.

On the first day of Christmas, my true love gave to me a Partridge in a Pear tree. On the first day of Christmas my true love gave to me math without a problem to solve in a countdown to Christmas. There are eleven shopping days left and Christmas Day twelve days away.

Christmas Day also begins a Christian festival called Twelve tide, which is a twelve-day celebration of the Nativity of baby Jesus, ending on January 5th. January 6th is known as Epiphany and it is celebrated around the world as three Kings Day, the day the three Kings of the Bible visited baby Jesus.

The Spirit of Christmas lands on your shoulders like a dove from heaven. It is felt in many ways throughout the season and makes itself known to young and old, too bad or good, but be good for goodness sakes.

Good cheer is in the air. It gives those who are in despair access to the eternal light of hope to replace hopelessness and destroy darkness. Joy to the world the Lord has come, by the birth of Jesus Christ. Let Earth receive her King.

There is no joy to be found in Noelle Jr., on this Sunday, and he will not visit North Star Baptist Church with his family. He has denied Church attendance today, but if Jesus is to be denied, then it is Jesus who is denied, not Santa Claus.

Christmas blues are heavy burdens to carry, but they can be beat. It is what it is, when it's time to come to Jesus, who is time. One day, late in the midnight hour, Noelle will not be able to plead ignorance, because he knows the truth in his heart.

The North Star Symphony Orchestra; directed by Halbrooks Jarreau, Sunday matinee concert features P. I. Tchaikovsky 's The Nutcracker in 7 Acts. The orchestra will perform selected classics, including a contemporary orchestral remake of "Hang All the Mistletoe" sung by American Soprano, Leontyne Princess.

The concert begins with three songs by G.F. Handel, which are "Overture" from "Messiah," "Lift Up Ye Heads," and "Pastoral Symphony." Then The North Star Ballet Company performs in V. Herbert's "March of the Toys" from "Babes in Toyland," followed by intermission.

The intermission flow of the sold-out crowd is well accommodated by the large mezzanine and main floor reception areas. Noelle walks into the main lobby and is greeted by the man who invited him to be a guest, Symphony Hall Chairmen Steven Land.

Steven Land, reaching out to shake hands with Noelle says, "Thank you for coming out to be with us today. I hope you are enjoying the concert, Mr. Chance."

"Yes, I am," Noelle says, pausing for a moment. Mr. Land, I apologize. I couldn't remember your name. Then it came to me that we met at the Masquerade Ball. I'm honored to be your guest."

"It is a small gesture of my appreciation to you for being a sponsor of this year's Christmas Party at the Community Center. Mr. Price Waterhouse thought a personal invitation would get you to come out and see our show." Turning to his wife beside him, he continues, "Mr. Noelle Chance, please meet my wife, Charity."

"Good afternoon," Noelle says, nodding his head politely. "I am glad to be here. I thank you both for inviting me. The seat you have provided me with is great. I am in the company of some very notable business leaders."

"Please join us for refreshments," Steven Land says, "and tell us more about your new newsletter, Money Chance & Circumstances. My wife received a promotional email, and I must tell you, we are definitely interested."

"Well, that is gracious of you," says Noelle, who appears to lack social grace because of a cold demeanor, but he turns on a cool sophisticated charm when business enters into a conversation.

"Mrs. Land, please tell me which one of my associates contacted you."

Mrs. Charity Land and her husband Steven are in their late 30s. They are quite a few years younger than Noelle and make a pretty picture as a power couple. Charity is an attractive woman, shapely like a model, with a caramel skin tone, brown eyes, and black natural hair, coiffed and styled elegantly.

She is dressed well in a St. John Evening by Marie Grey two-piece suit with a button-down jacket blouse, trimmed with gold. The sleeves have matched gold trim cuffs and the matching skirt is trimmed at the hem in gold; she compliments the confident look with elegant black leather, square heel ankle boots.

Charity Land speaks with authority. Her voice is deep in tone but not harsh, and she smiles easily. Noelle is impressed, as she looks in his eyes while answering his questions about the newsletter.

Charity Land states, "Mr. Chance, I was contacted by Miss Kristen Flowers. She has an idea for a story on the Symphony Hall to bring new membership and concert attendees through co-op business ventures. It sounds promising. We want to sit down and work out the details after the New Year. I will have my assistant call back to set up a meeting at your office."

"That sounds good, Mrs. Land."

Mr. Steven Land interjects saying, "You two keep your conversation going and I will get us something to drink. Sparkling water for us dear," and the Mrs. nods her head yes. "Please allow me to get a drink for you, Mr. Chance. What will you have?"

"I will have a sparkling water also," Noelle says, then returns to the discussion with Charity Land. "Miss Flowers is my Administrative Secretary. She engineered the Newsletter concept. Her plan of action for your outreach program will get my full support. I'm sure she will be glad to hear that I've met you and your husband. We will both look forward to meeting in the New year."

"That's great Mr. Chance. I will consider this meeting with you an early Christmas present," Charity says with a smile.

"A Christmas present," he said with a huff. "Okay Mrs. Land, we will be sure that you don't have to return this gift to the store," Noelle says bluntly.

"Christmas time is a Season of hope, and I am sure Symphony Hall itself will have many returns in association with your company," she said just as her husband returns with the drinks.

"I heard the word appointment. That means good things for us, Mr. Chance," Steven said as he hands Noelle one of the three San Pellegrinos.

"I believe the coincidence of our meeting will lead to good things for all who will come in contact with our joint venture," Noelle says with confidence.

"When you put it like that, Mr. Chance, my husband and I were charmed at our first impression of you as co-host of the Masquerade Ball, and we were pleased to see you again at the Christmas party of Mr. Waterhouse. It was there that we asked Mr. Waterhouse how best to meet you. He suggested we send you a solo invite to our Symphony production."

Steven Land immediately replies, "That's right, my dear, we've come a long way from seeing you at the Masquerade Ball, to setting an appointment. Good luck trying to follow the variables that make up those connections."

"Well, you two make an effective team," Noelle says. "I will look forward to our meeting."

"Thank you for your time, Mr. Chance. Do enjoy part two of the concert. I think you will like it." Steven turns to wife and states, "Dear, I see the Mayor, let's go over and greet him."

"Oh certainly," Charity replies. Turning back to Noelle, she gracefully says, "Mr. Chance, it has been a pleasure to meet you. Thank you again for accepting our invitation. Happy Holidays to you and your family."

Charity reaches out to shake hands with Noelle. Her husband does the same as they both say goodbye.

Noelle says to himself, "Speaking of family, let me call my sister right now," and he moves just inside the entryway to pull out his cell phone. Holly picks up the call immediately and says,

"Hello, is this my brother, Sim Phony," with a laugh.

Noelle is caught off guard and almost laughs himself. "Holly dearest, what would I do without you? I am at the Symphony Hall, and it is intermission. The concert is good, I recommend it to you. There's even a performance of ballet dancers and as I look at the program, part-two will feature a Prima ballerina and a Soprano singer."

"Okay brother dearest, I get it. I might check it out and if I do it won't be my first time around. El we had a good time at Church today. Mom was something else. She told me that you wouldn't be there, but you would call me and I'm glad you did. Everyone did lift up your name in prayer."

"We can all use prayer, Holly. Thank you for always being patient with me. You are a wonderful sister. Intermission will soon be over. I wanted to call now instead of waiting until I got home. I know Jalisa is there and Barry plans on arriving the day before Christmas Eve. I want you, her, and the kids to meet me at my office tomorrow and I will treat you all to lunch, okay?"

"That's great El. Jalisa, and the kids will be excited to see you. Let's make it happen captain," Holly says with the same laugh that she began the conversation with.

"Holly, I would say you're in rare form, but you are always in rare form. It looks like intermission is ending. I will see you tomorrow."

"Bye, bye Noelle Chance Jr."

Noelle makes it to his seat and notices his seating partner is a woman, who is sitting next to Charity and Steven Land. He addresses all cordially. It is then that he wonders; have I been so far into my own world that I didn't even *notice the scent of a woman.* Then the lights dim as part-two of the concert begins.

Noelle has intrigued himself into the mystery of his soup for one attitude towards dating, rarely questioning aloneness, verses an intimate connection with a woman. He peeks over his left shoulder to spy on the space invader who sits down beside him, and quickly notices the lack of tension. An aura of delight appears in a pretty face that glances at his eye contact and smiles before the movement on stage takes her attention away.

Noelle boggles his brain thinking of the last time he paid attention to the opposite sex, it was the dance at the Masquerade Ball with Neveah, a memory that leaves him shaking his head no, as he reaches into his sport coat to see the lineup after first intermission.

The program lists The Nutcracker Suite, with Ballerina Misty Danielle performing Dance of the Sugar Plum Fairy, to open the Act, returning to dance The Waltz of the Flowers. Ballarino Glenn Allen Ailey will perform in selections 3,4,5, the Arabian Dance, Chinese Dance and Russian Dance, then selection 6 features the North Star Ballet in Dance of the Reed Flutes.

The second intermission will feature Platinum Contributors and a giveaway of Christmas gifts, followed by the closing Acts of the concert.

*The Skaters Waltz, Pata Pan, Jingle Bells, Leontyne Princess Sings, Hang All The Mistletoe.*

Noelle counts the time left in the concert and plans his exit, then a beautiful ballerina dressed in purple appears on stage, striking him with elegant movement. He's mesmerized by love at first sight, and time flies in a straight bee line to the finale. Noelle returns to consciousness and gets confused when he cannot find the ballerina, who has left the stage to thunderous applause. The color purple she wore so well, brings back the spirit of a hand dance, now lost in a masquerade.

Noelle looks for the exit sign, only to find The Conductor Halbrooks Jarreau center stage. "You were a great audience. I enjoyed bringing this concert to you. Merry Christmas. We will close the show with a special performance from our divine Soprano and her Operatic Orchestral rendition of, Hang All the Mistletoe."

NOELLE DRIVES HOME to the sounds of the road, the magnificence of a Soprano singing the verse "And this Christmas will be, a very special Christmas for me," stands out in his mind and mixes fine with thoughts of the ballerina.

"How did I miss the rest of the concert?" Noelle says aloud.

The sounds of silence include the drone of car tires rolling and air rushing by the windshield view of North Star Village at Christmas time. Noelle arrives home to eat dinner alone, but this time the thrill is gone. Sole satisfaction of living in luxury with no one to share it with has found its exit stage left.

"I will win," Noelle says to the still quiet voice calling him to change his ways, but he wishes for the end of the Christmas days.

Now I lay me down to sleep, without a prayer for the Lord to keep, taking in a breath deep, he exhales and puts his head on a quality pillow, on a comfortable bed with lots of memory foam.

Noelle is home sweet home on his perfect sleeper. It's a peaceful sleep, but for how long?

The Spirit of Christmas flows from the North Pole to the South Pole and from East to West. You can see the world's behavior go from good to better and better to best.

Monday returns and resets the work routines. Nothing has been the same since Black Friday hit the scene. It took 365 days to reappear, but the happiest time of the year is here, and the world counts down to Christmas Day.

Monday comes with no extra sleep in North Star Village but hardly a frown can be found. They are turned upside down into smiles from town to town, because everybody knows a turkey and some mistletoe will Make the Yuletide Gay. But not everyone will be happy to see this time of year, some like Noelle Jr., will fight depression and get caught up into the commercial hustle and flow of material things that have no rhythm or rhyme and only add financial debt to your misery.

The mystery of life steals your heart away and takes your breath away too. Why this, why that, and why is God born in my season to mourn. To each one, heavenly peace will be granted in their due season, when God reveals every reason, teaching us the universal math that makes up our coincidences and truth that gives you peace. We all will have problems in life, whether we are naughty or nice. Be grateful that the Star light shined over darkness to lead us out of troubles.

~

The early bird gets the worm is the logic all over North Star Village, as last-minute shoppers check their lists twice. Holly Evergreen checks her list and wants to add a few things. Since the grandchildren and daughter Jalisa are home for Christmas, she wants to fill their stockings with surprises and hang them by the tree.

This Christmas will be very special for Holly and Jacob Sr., and it is they who are the early birds preparing a breakfast that includes hot oatmeal, cold cereal, bacon, sausage, eggs, grits, hash browns, pancakes, coffee, assorted juices, and fresh fruit.

Jalisa wakes up before her children, sleeping in a separate bedroom, and gives thanks for a new day. She immediately makes her way to the aroma coming from the kitchen.

"Good morning," she said with hugs and kisses for mom and dad. "Daddy, I'm glad to be home for Christmas. The breakfast looks good and smells great. It won't be long before little Barry and Lisa run in here ready to eat with their grandma and granddad."

"We came to your house for Thanksgiving but I'm glad I get to be grandma and mom at home for Christmas and I get to watch my grand babies open gifts," Holly says, tasting the fruit.

"Mom, Barry is going to bring a few gifts when he gets here right before Christmas. We need you to hide them until we put them under the tree, after the kids go to bed on Christmas Eve."

"I look forward to seeing Barry," Dad says. "I got a place picked out for you to hide the gifts, don't worry about that. I would love to hang out with you all today, but I have to be at my job. I will be on vacation by the time Barry gets here.

"Jalisa, I know you guys plan on shopping before you meet with your Uncle Noelle and you got other things on your mind, but please remember to tell him that we are looking forward to seeing him for Christmas dinner."

'Tis the Season to be jolly for Holly, her daughter and grandchildren, who all believe the reason for the season is the birth of Jesus. A miracle for everyone of faith, and to those of little faith, His light shines to help their unbelief.

Miracles come in every size and shape, and mean different things to different people. It arrives with your name on it, to tell your heart that the gift given was made for your eyes only, because no one else would consider it like you.

Holly watches her daughter shop with the children, as they look for a gift to give the man in their life on Christmas day, a gift from a loving wife and children that love their father.

Jalisa Bridgemen, speaking to her son and daughter, says, "Guys, the Mall is crowded. Let's shop together and we should be able to find everything we want here at Macy's. I have our gift list and we'll shop in this order. Grandmother's, grandfather's, your dad, uncle Noelle, then we'll meet back up with Grandma."

The early shoppers are successful. Holly went off on her own to find the stocking stuffers she wanted. Jalisa and the kids found the gifts they want to give, and they meet in the front of Macy's right on time to get to their lunch date with Noelle Jr.

Holly, who has only been waiting a short while, joyfully says, "Hi guys. By the looks on your faces and your bags, you found what you were looking for. We need to be leaving soon, so we get to your uncle Noelle's office on time. He wants to spend some time with us before taking us to lunch at City Market."

~

The staff of N. O. Chance Financial Agency have moved past the Monday slow start blues into their work routines and the second day of Christmas was unremarkable until the unseen Spirit of Christmas present arrives to take over the hearts of the hopeful. The moment moves in without a notice, but you feel it in the air, as person to person finds a song to sing happily to themselves. The same old Christmas songs that had become background noise, are sentimental favorites again.

Nickolas can feel the Spirit of the Season take over and leaves his office to visit with the office of the boss and when he knocks on his closed door, Noelle motions for him to enter.

"Mr. Kingly, I'm sorry that I missed your meeting this morning. I'm trying to get as much work done as I can before my sister, niece, and her children meet me here. I am treating them to lunch, so please fill me in."

"Mr. Chance, we are doing well. Our clients are happy and the sales numbers you gave me to look at are great. Sir, I want to thank you, and the staff wants me to commend you for allowing us to have an office Christmas party at the end of the week."

"Well, Kingsly. I'm happy to report that I have begun a countdown to Christmas. I can't wait until it is over. Just thinking about that makes me happy," says Noelle. I guess I should just say, bah humbug but that's so old fashion."

At that moment, Kristen Flowers buzzes the speakerphone. "Excuse me, Kingsly, while I take this call," says Noelle. "Yes Miss Flowers," Noelle replies to his secretary.

"Good day Mr. Chance. Your sister and niece are here," Kristen says.

Noelle replies, almost giggling, "Thank you Miss Flowers, please send them to my office."

Nickolas, thinks to himself, *there is hope.* Mr. No Chance doesn't even know the Spirit of Christmas just hit him. "Sir, it's great that your sister is here."

Holly Evergreen enters her brother's office space like a breath of fresh air. Nickolas is pleased that brother and sister are so different, as he stands up to greet the guest of the boss.

"It comes to my attention that you already know each other because you attend the same Church, yet this is the first time the three of us are together."

"Hello, my dear brother. Merry Christmas. And hello Deacon Kingsly, it is a joy to see you here today," Holly says, while returning a gentle handshake from Nickolas.

"I want to take this opportunity to congratulate you on your elevation to Deacon at North Star Baptist. My husband and I are pleased with your selection. We are looking forward to being with you for the Christmas morning service. I believe you know my son Jacob Jr., and yesterday you met my daughter Jalisa and my grandchildren."

Nickolas Kingsly is ever so gracious and humble. He effortlessly removes all awkwardness from the impromptu meeting, with kind words, stating, "Mrs. Evergreen, you and your husband have greeted me with kindness since I joined the Church. You and your husband encourage Pastor Mann and empower the congregation. I give thanks that I received the call to serve."

"Can I say that all things come together for the good of those who have no chance. Won't he do it!" Noelle says with a dry laugh.

"Mr. Chance," Nickolas replies, "Working for you has been good for all of us. I know Jacob Jr. is a fine young man. I will say goodbye now. Enjoy your time together."

"El," Holly says triumphantly, "It is quite a blessing to have that man as your office manager. I can tell that you like him, but you don't want anyone to know. I'll tell you what else I know, prayer works. What I saw with Mr. Kingsly helps me keep the faith. It is the evidence of things I have hoped for in your life, my dear brother."

In a spiritual coincidence, separate lunchtime meetings by Kristen and Noelle Jr. have snowbound ties to Christmases past, present and future, when Kristen pulls Nickolas Kingsly aside to confide in him.

"Mr. Kingsly, I got a feeling this will be the best Christmas ever. I can't say exactly what it is, but Jacob's mother and sister have treated me so well this weekend. As a matter of fact, the whole family has been so kind to me, even the kids. I am kind of overwhelmed. I wonder am I putting too many feelings into these things. Jacob is nice to me too and I really like him. My heart is beating so fast right now, I have to calm down,"

"Miss Flowers," Nickolas says, pausing as he looks into her eyes, "I look forward to seeing you two together at our office Christmas party. You are a sweetheart, and a man would be blessed to have you in his life. I think Jacob is a lucky man. Mr. Chance has a hard demeanor, but he loves Jacob, and he respects you.

"It has got to be tough to be in a relationship with the nephew of your boss, but you pull it off. You told me that Jacob has met your family and they like and respect him, so calm your heart, be yourself, keep your prayer life strong and listen to God for your answers. He will not fail you."

In that moment, the tangent lines of conversation coincide and parallel park with the spiritual mind, to line up over the matters of two hearts in separate places that beat with the one blood of love power. These parallel talking points intersect when Jalisa sits down to speak to her uncle Noelle about Kristen Flowers and Jacob Jr. at their restaurant, creating an intimate connection connect 4.

The duality of the love connections, one at the office, the other at the restaurant, has a made to order feel, beating the odds against Kristen and Jacob Jr, who are touched by an angel.

Noelle Jr. motions to his grandniece Lisa and grandnephew Barry Jr., to come to his table and says, "I have something for the both of you," as he pulls four envelopes out of his sportscoat.

"These are gifts for you and your family. Barry, give your mom her envelope and Lisa, I want you to give your dad his envelope when he gets in town."

"I'll take those envelopes and hold them until we get home," Holly interjects.

Then Barry Jr. and Lisa Bridgeman sound like angels singing together when they say, "Thank you, Uncle Noelle."

"Jalisa honey, I'm going to take the kids on a walk around the Christmas displays in the plaza. I need to work off this lunch. I'm going to enjoy the sights with my grands. We will be back in a few minutes. Thanks, El. This location is great. We all have enjoyed every minute."

"Okay Mom, they are ready to explore." Turning to her uncle, Jalisa says, "Thank you, Uncle El. You always remember us, and I appreciate that," she said as her children hug her before leaving with Grandma.

"Uncle El, I'm glad we have some time to talk," Jalisa says.

"I am glad also. So tell me what's on your mind?"

"Oh, it's nothing to serious," Jalisa says in a way to assure her uncle. "I am happily married. My husband is happy, and we are blessed in our life together. I want to talk to you about my brother and his girlfriend, who is your Secretary."

"I saw you at my office talking with Miss Flowers," Noelle says in a serious tone. "It looked like you two were long-time friends."

"Uncle El... Jay likes that young lady, and I think she is cool. I've spoken to her on the phone a couple of times but didn't get to meet her until yesterday after the Church Service, when we got to spend some time together. She passes the early tests for me, and I think they make a good couple, but it's Jay's thoughts that count. He loves you Uncle El and I love you too, but as a man, he values your opinion. Please tell me how you really feel about your secretary and your nephew having a relationship."

"Young lady," Noelle says sternly to his niece, "I told JJ about my young love experience, how I chose my career, focused on success, and that a serious relationship was not for me at that time. I told him that Miss Flowers is a lovely woman and since their announced relationship, I have not seen any disruption at the office with my secretary or have I had a problem with my nephew. I respect JJ as a grown man. He can make his own mistakes, and just as direct as you are with me right now, your mother has been like that from the start. I can't go back to the past. Even if I could, I wouldn't change a thing. My sacrifices have worked out and I am a successful businessman, okay my dear."

"Uncle El, you are a trip. You can go to the Symphony by yourself, but I don't believe you want to be alone. You're a fine old man," Jalisa says with a chuckle. "Barry and I had that conversation on future success when we began dating, but instead of pushing me away or me pushing him away for the future, we said let's be together in the present. Barry said his best success was going to be with me, and we haven't looked back Uncle El. I know that you love us, and I believe you gave my brother good advice. At least Mr. No didn't come out to say no way."

Noelle begins to smile at his niece and says, "So Jalisa you say your uncle is a fine old man?"

"Uncle El," Jalisa replies, "we all love you, but you have got some cold ways. No one wants to see you end up being alone. My kids are getting up there in age now, so is your sister and my dad, and so are Big Daddy and Grandma. Time is moving on."

The rest of the day unfolds like a map, each moment connected to the next by a point in time. Noelle and Sister finish their lunch date, having found time and space within the busiest time of the year, to get to know each other better. Quality time shared in moments, each placed perfectly by spiritual coincidences made to occur within an ocean of unforeseen action and reaction to various circumstances, impossible to forecast and undeniably made manifest this Christmas.

The commercialized status of Christmas begins to fade into the light of unexplainable majesty, which Noelle can see better. Now back in the office, he looks into the faces of his employees, who are putting on their coats to go home. The Winter Solstice brings with it the longest nights of the year but Noelle, a bachelor by choice, stays in the office a little while longer tonight.

All the King's workers, the men, and women of N. O. Chance Financial Agency, make their way by the door to acknowledge the boss before leaving for home. 'Goodnight Mr. Chance' is repeated by each of the smiling faces. A change for this Chance is gonna come, the winds of change are stirring destiny for Noelle, and he begins to think back on the words of his niece, then pictures her husband Barry leaving his job in a hurry to unite with his wife and make home where the heart is.

On the third day of Christmas, melancholy offers thee, more work galore, but before you get bored, it's plain to see a New Year is coming.

On the fourth day of Christmas, do you know what day it is? Call four of your friends, and big kids and small kids get ready to play, be smarter work harder and an egg you will not lay.

On the fifth day of Christmas five times golden are the days, and seven more days of love are on the way. On the sixth day of

Christmas your ship is coming in, it's halfway there, keep looking to the horizon.

On the seventh day of Christmas a week is made complete, get your rest your almost there but catch up on some sleep.

On the eighth day of Christmas everything is new, keep hope alive because dreams do come true. On the ninth day of Christmas dance the night and day away.

On the tenth day of Christmas, it's the Eve of Christmas Eve, everyone tends to be leaping and there is a lot less sleeping.

On the eleventh day of Christmas, it's sho-nuff Christmas Eve, strike up the band, toot all your horns, the very next day Christ thy Savior is born.

On the twelfth day of Christmas let the drumming all day begin, it's 24 hours of peace and love that continually wins. The day goes fast, hold on the last, because it will be 365 days until we can do it again.

# Chapter 10

## *A Change For A Chance Gonna Come*

### Jacob, named Israel

---

Iron sharpeneth iron; so a man sharpeneth the countenance of his friend.

— PROVERBS 27: 17

---

And it's Winter in Bethlehem, Palestine and Israel, and Israel rejoice; connected above the Northern Hemisphere Equator line, where The Prince of Peace can hear from the womb of the universe, the sounds of silence from a falling snowflake.

And now it's Winter in America. It's Winter in America and all the healers have been killed or betrayed, yeah but the people know, people know it's Winter. Lord knows it's Winter in America and ain't nobody fighting because nobody know what to save. Save your souls...

And the booming voice of Les Givings rings out from the radio saying, "Good morning world. Good morning, North Star Village and good morning to you wherever you are. Thanks for waking up with

100 FM KNSV. Now playing in your ear is music by Gill Scott Heron and Brian Jackson, from the classic album titled 'First Minute Of A New Day.' The song is titled Winter in America.

"The original single came out on 45 rpm record. It was rereleased on the CD Album only, that's titled Winter In America. The original vinyl album doesn't contain the song. The 45 rpm (revolutions per minute) 7-inch record was developed by RCA Record company in 1949. Les, is giving you more butter music on your Friday morning rush. There's only 7-days left until Christmas, and I know for some of y'all, that means it's go time."

Noelle Jr. rolls over and turns the volume down and sits on the side of the bed to collect his thoughts and as usual he has his mind on his money and money on his mind, it's 6am and a full day of work is ahead. Another peaceful night of sleep comes and goes by without recollection, without a peep. Once again there is no thanks given for the gift of another day. New thoughts do enter Noelle's mind, *today we begin our Holiday work schedule, and the office will have its ugly sweater Christmas party after work. Get up Noelle, shower and leave here in an hour. We will pick up some coffee on the way.*

Noelle Jr., also known as Mr. No, is beguiled by fool's gold, the greed for it turns him away from the love of all things. Mr. No. says no to the voice of the Spirit, this disobedience is turning his heart into stone, but Jesus is the constant gardener who plants love as a seed and He will reap what he has sown, in a harvest for the world.

Noelle spends this day working in seclusion, sporadically attending to his faithful clients, like a constant gardener of business. He is the constant gardener of business and an angel unaware, that has lost his way, now believing his success is made only by man's hands. Noelle has the gift of discernment, a talent that has led him to be a business leader who has led his clients and his employees to a better financial life, but with great power comes great responsibility.

Noelle can clearly see that N. O. Chance Financial Agency provides employees a living, but he could pay them better, the voice inside him demands that he perceive their hard work as more than a means to his profit margin, but Noelle doesn't acknowledge it. He doesn't believe the prosperity he has is a gift from the Lord. Thinking like that is a long way from his mind, but he can no longer plead ignorance to what he has heard from the voice and that it is the Lord.

We all fall short of the perfection of Jesus; in Heaven as it is on earth, but Noelle now applies theories of science and pragmatics as his beliefs. He believes you must be able to prove things of life and live by what you can reasonably expect, forgetting what he has previously learned about the Holy Trinity of Father, Son and Holy Ghost. Pragmatic theories test the foundation of faith, since faith is believing in an unseen power and there's no room at the Heart Inn to believe. Noelle, by faith, could become a fisherman for the Lord, casting his net into the water of life to not only lead people to financial prosperity, but the road to spiritual prosperity as well.

Noelle can only see a man's hand in success and cannot see the business world could reject him, but prayer power has empowered his moves. Noelle is unaware of his talent. He says no to the still quiet voice encouraging him to a higher purpose; he wants a ticket to ride on the runaway train of pain. Constant thoughts of self is the only reflection that can be seen looking back from the mirror. These are the reflections that edge God out. This is an E.G.O. that sees no truth.

Noelle tells anyone who listens that the birth of Jesus is a lie, and he twists the Christmas story of baby Jesus; the Son of God/The Son of man, who was born in Bethlehem, with the true story of a Saint named Nickolas, which became the myth of Santa Claus. He is beginning to believe Jesus was only a Prophet, and he is losing faith, but the facts are researchable within The Holy Bible. Hope is the evidence, but believing in Jesus is by faith, not by sight, it defies all pragmatic logic. A hard truth to pragmatically accept is, that it is impossible to come to God without faith. Another truth is God can leave you to the whims of your desire, called a reprobate mind. A reprobate mind cannot discern what is right, from what is wrong in the eyes of God.

What do the lonely do, at Christmas?

The watcher feels that he's keeping the world an arm's distance away, and looking out of his office window, Noelle can do just that. He is getting fond of staying in the office alone, hiding from society, but today is ugly sweater day and he promised to participate. Noelle can see his reflection in his office window that overlooks North Star Village, but his view stirs no emotions and he moves back to the desk to look over paperwork. He pulls his notes across the desktop and begins to organize his thoughts for a meeting with Nickolas Kingsly and the after-work office Christmas party, then notices a note that is circled at the top of the page.

The note says, "No one knows the date, no one knows the hour, no one. Oh, why won't you repent? Instead you fixate on money spent."

Noelle raises his eyebrow and pounds the table, saying, "This is damn strange. The handwriting looks like the writing of Khole Cashe, and I didn't write it."

*How did this*, he says... almost cussing, *get in my notebook?*

Noelle will get to know himself better, *This Christmas.*

BUILDING GREAT MINDS TOGETHER is the theme of the New Year and every student in the school system of North Star Village is saying thank God it's Friday and the last school day of the year. Today is a half-day of fun Christmas parties, then students and faculty are dismissed for Christmas and New Year's vacation.

Miss Labelle Patience kept her students busy with a classroom inventory and cleaning before going to the auditorium. No one is more excited than Aleayah Fields; except maybe her best friends, Christopher Kingsly and Jimmy Dewland, gathered in the auditorium for a pep rally and Christmas concert by the Memorial Middle School Select Choir. Aleayah is lead singer for the first song, O Holy Night, by Mahalia Jackson.

Chris and Jimmy know she is nervous, but they all did their special handshake, and she was calming down before leaving the classroom to prepare for the concert.

Miss Labelle Patience, who was chosen to be the host of the pep rally, says,

"Quiet please. Let me have everyone's attention," then she looks at the Choir members who are sitting together in the front of the stage. "Memorial Select Choir, it's your turn. Please come to the stage and take your positions. Students let's give them an applause," and everyone cheers.

Miss Patience continues to talk over the cheers that calm down as she says, "We only have a short time left before school will be dismissed for your Christmas vacation. I want each of you to have a safe and fun Holiday. Merry Christmas to you all and don't forget the next time we see each other here at school, it will be a New Year. Thank you for your enthusiasm for our pep rally. We have a spirit of friendship at our school and great school spirit. Please give our Principal Mr. Thurgood Marshall an applause for coming up with this wonderful idea for all of us to celebrate the Holiday Season," and more cheers flow from the students.

Miss Patience says, "Let me remind you today we will have 3 lunch periods. The first lunch is immediately following the concert. Everyone will go back to your classroom and your teacher will tell you which lunch period you have."

Miss Patience turns to the Choir and introduces the Director, whose name is Misty Copeland. Once again, the students cheer.

Misty Copeland says, "Thank you everyone. We're going to sing a few Christmas songs for you, and we hope you enjoy them all. These singers are your classmates I've chosen for this choir. Our first song will feature Miss Aleayah Fields from the $5^{th}$ grade. She will sing 'O Holy Night." She turns to Aleayah and hands her the microphone.

Aleayah Fields looks all over the Auditorium at Memorial Middle School and stops her eyes on her best friends Christopher and Jimmy, as the Choir Director announces her name and gives her the microphone, and the little angel sings...

'O holy night, the stars are brightly shining, It is the night of the dear Savior's birth, Long lay the world in sin and error pining, Till He appeared, and the soul felt its worth, A thrill of hope, the weary world rejoices, For yonder breaks a new and glorious morn, Fall on your knees; oh, hear the angel voices, O night divine, O night when Christ was born, O night divine, O night, O night divine, Night divine.'

Aleayah and Choir finish the song to a silent Auditorium, then after a few seconds everyone claps their hands, cheering loudly and you could feel in the air that it's Christmas time. The choir went on to sing 4 songs, all received well by their classmates. The final song was an encore led by a young man named Jariel King, who sang Hang All The Mistletoe and encouraged everyone to participate, to end the Christmas music concert on a high note.

The Auditorium is dismissed, but Christopher, Jimmy and Aleayah's classroom is scheduled for the final lunch period of the day. Back to the classroom, Aleayah, who stayed behind with the choir, meets with her dad, the Choir Director, and her fellow singers before going back to class. Aleayah is escorted back to her classroom and tries to quietly enter the room, but the whole class was waiting to give her a big cheer as soon as she opened the door, and they did.

Miss Patience, unable to hold back her enthusiasm, says to Aleayah,

"That was quite a performance you put on. We are all proud of you and the Select Choir. I spoke to your father, and he was so proud and happy he was able to leave work to see you sing. You will be happy to know you can see your performance, because your dad filmed it for your family to watch at home." Miss Patience turns her attention to all of her students and says, "I'm proud of each of you. The first half of the school year has been good. We have had some fun and we will do even better next year. We have 45 minutes until lunch, then we will get ready for dismissal. I have a homework assignment for you while on Christmas vacation. I want you to draw a picture of your favorite vacation moment, then write a short story that tells us about what you have drawn. Does everyone understand their assignment? If you don't understand, come to my desk and I will explain more. In the meantime, please clean out your desks. I will play music until it's time to go to lunch."

The Christmas songs resume from the Boombox she brought in for the occasion.

What is better than pizza for lunch? Only early dismissal for Christmas vacation. The 3 amigos sense they are parting ways for quite a few days. Aleayah, Jimmy and Christopher sit together as their fellow students get their coats to head for home. Some walk, some ride with a parent and others catch the bus.

Christopher Kingsly says, "Let's go get on our buses, you guys get the party started. I hope we all get what we want for Christmas."

"It's time to go," Jimmy says. "I promise to call you guys. Let's all promise to call each other, okay!"

The 3 amigos get together and do their special goodbye handshake.

Aleayah says, "We waited all year. Now Christmas time is near. Bye guys."

As they each turn to leave one another, the best friends say Merry Christmas at the same time, making a joyful noise... it's a spiritual coincidence in a three-part harmony of voices and waves.

~

AT BELLA HIGH SCHOOL, everyone is excited to go on Christmas vacation, but Senior classmates around the world are happy and sad that they are saying Merry Christmas to each other for the last time as High Schoolers. Simon Kingsly is once again stunned into silence when, after a loud beep, he hears the voice of Ameenah Mauritius over the intercom; she interrupts the party going on in his 2nd period English class.

"Good morning, my fellow students. This is Ameenah Mauritius, Merry Christmas to each of you. Good morning to the Staff, faculty and Teachers. On behalf of the students, we wish you all a Merry Christmas and Happy New Year. I want to remind everyone that Christmas is just 5-days left. Shop for last-minute gift ideas and support the Senior Class bake sale and flea market being held during lunchtime. We hope you purchase a snack and find a gift to fill out your list. All the proceeds will help our Class Day jamboree. Look for our sales tables next to the main entrance to the lunchroom. Thank you."

"Your face is lit up like a Christmas tree, Sy man. You got it bad," says best friend Cary Ward.

"Am I that obvious? We've been talking on the phone a lot lately and tomorrow is our first date. I want to find a gift from the Senior sale and surprise her with it. I'll tell her it's for my sister.

"Tomorrow is the big day, huh? It looks like you have a date for the prom, but I'll go with you to the sales table and help you find a gift. If you need a few bucks, I will help you out. You can call it a Christmas gift from your best friend."

"Thanks man," Simon replies. I'm gonna have to move fast so I can beat my little brother to the house. I'm trippin cause this will be my last Christmas to do it like this. Next year will be a big difference for him and me. Care Bear, you think you're funny, stop thinking I didn't hear your crack about the prom, but man things are changing. This Christmas is changing the game."

"I hear you Sy man. It's cool. We growing up. It seems like Ameenah is a nice girl, but me I'm going to keep it moving tho. "It don't matter Sy man. Me and you going to stay tight, alright!"

Simon notices the look he gets from his best friend Cary, and he gives in, saying, "Alright man. I get it, we tight, and you want some details, so here's the plan. My Dad is the chaperone, he is going to bring me to Ameenah's house and then we both will meet her parents."

"Man, that's big!," Cary quickly interjects.

"We are going to the Mall and my dad will let us have some alone time in the Food Court. We're going to walk around, pick the food we want, then have ice cream for dessert at the Cold Stone Creamery. My dad will pick us up there, after he goes shopping for about 90 minutes."

"So, Deacon Daddy is going to be all up in your business, baby boy," Cary asks point blank.

"My Dad is a Deacon, but you know him, he's cool,"Simon says with a smile on his face. "My mom too. Everyone at my house is excited. The whole setup is kind of my dad's idea because without his help, man this don't happen. My dad said everything will be cool, unless we leave the food court area. He also said that I should not leave her alone at any time, even if I go to the bathroom, and to point her out to a Security Guard." Simon, shaking his head in disbelief continues, "this all started about three weeks ago. I know the Mall will be busy, but we'll be together and get to know each other better."

"That sounds like a plan, man. I might copy you someday, but not anytime soon. Of course, I'm a player. Care Bear will be available, you heard," Cary said laughing.

Simon says, "We got one more class to go. I'll meet you at the lunchroom entrance."

~

Noelle Jr. is spending a lot of time in the window today but cannot see the look of indifference that gazes back at him through the reflection, and he does not recognize the gift of sunlight. Sunshine is soup for the soul of every living creation. Today it brings Season's Greetings that refresh the willing, like a summer breeze, blowing through the mind.

Noelle backs away from the window and time slips into the future, daring him to look into the past, that reflects a present-day soul on empty. Noelle stares into the glass but fails to see the true picture of a man standing on the edge of a cliff, soon to fall off into doom. His heart, once bitten, is twice shy. No man is an island, no one can keep running away from their feelings, and as Noelle continues staring, he sees headlights coming towards him. It's not a car, it's a train.

Pragmatic deductions have no chance, remembrances are removed. Time itself is moved by the dream maker, who allows sight, touch, and sound to return to Noelle as ripples from spiritual coincidence, that combine with the timeline to create the first effect, of the butterfly effect.

Noelle returns from places and spaces with a hit parade of awareness. The change makes you want to hustle, but a soothing sound comes around that now he has ears to hear. The radio plays a familiar tune that fills up the room.

And the Melody still lingers on...

*"Don't stop ever loving me,"is sung sweetly, sounding like a Church choir would sing. Then a male voice sings alone, "Jesus, I love the things you do. My happiness comes from you."*

*"Oh Lord, don't ever stop doin,' the things you do. Cause Lord, I know you know our Sin. No, I'm not ever worthy of you loving me, but don't stop ever loving me."*

Noelle grabs the radio remote control, turns the volume down and looks with fascination at his employees happily working. Relieved to rebound from the reflection trip, "Hello world, I'm back!", says Noelle, getting up from his desk to stretch.

Kristen Flowers knocks on the door. Noelle waves his hand for her to come in,

"Welcome back," she says. "I want you to try some of our food. It's good. You must be hungry."

"My goodness, Miss Flowers, it's good to be back. Has anybody here seen my old friend time? Can you tell me where it's gone?"

"Wow," Kristen says. "I was at the Under Cover Brother Record Store last week looking for a Christmas gift for my dad. The Owner suggested the "Consciousness of the 60's" CD set, and I remember the song you just referred to, because the lyrics are very moving. That song is titled 'Abraham, Martin and John.' The store owner said it was sung by Dion. It's funny now," she says with a chuckle, "because I told him the singer doesn't sound like a girl. Then I found out he was talking about Dion the man, and he has another hit song on the CD titled 'The Wanderer.' Mr. Chance, I know my dad will like my gift now. Most of the time I don't understand you because your sarcastic wit is hard to keep up with, but that was clever."

Noelle responds immediately, as he looks at his watch, "Miss Flowers, I have no idea what has happened to me. The last time I looked up, I was in the office alone. I'm glad you're here. Tell me what's on your mind."

"Thank you for wearing a sweater and supporting the office party theme. I've been watching you this morning, and it looks like you've been in deep thought. I do want to talk to you before your nephew gets here. Today will be the first time you see us as a couple since our Thanksgiving announcement and I want you to know that we are happy together."

"No worries, dear girl. I am happy for you and my nephew. I will mingle at the party briefly, but mainly stay right here in my office. That will be all the happy I can stand. Now let me get to the breakfast you have set up."

"Good morning, Mr. Chance," says Nickolas Kingsly standing at the office door, waiting for them to finish their talk.

"Kingsly, I believe it's true. The early bird does indeed get the worm. My mind is fresh, and I'm ready to make my clients an offer they can't refuse," Noelle said in a huff. "They can call it a Christmas present."

"Tis the Season to be jolly," Nickolas says. "Please have some coffee and enjoy our breakfast."

Nickolas is happy to see the Holiday Schedule is working, and the co-workers are wearing their Christmas theme ugly sweaters, even the boss.

Funny how time flies when you're having fun, and as the final workday of the week comes to its end, the office of N. O. Chance Financial Agency is a picture of Holiday joy. The staff gets overjoyed when Chef Lisa arrives to set up for the Christmas party. Her food menu includes a hot and cold buffet of tasty finger foods, chips, dips, coffee, assorted beverages, and dessert cake.

Nickolas contacted Chef Lisa to provide the food services soon after the Masquerade Ball, where her food was a big hit. He knew the boss would enjoy her food again. The day goes by fast. Soon it is quitting time, and it's time to relax for the first time in a long time and certainly for the staff of the N. O. Chance Financial Agency. Nickolas gathers everyone to the front of the office for a short meeting and a message from the boss before the festivities get started.

Noelle Oscar Chance Jr., steps to the front of the assembly and begins speaking with his familiar on and off indifference, saying, "I'll make this short. N. O. Chance Financial has become one of the sponsors for this year's Community Center Christmas party."

The employees burst into applause...

Noelle holds his right hand for quiet, then continues, "Mr. Price Waterhouse is my mentor. He and his Charity staff have put together an exciting event this year and I would be pleased if you would attend as representatives of this Company. I'm not a man that believes in excess, such as office parties, but Mr. Kingsly helped get me past my objections. This Christmas party is due to his persistence and your hard work, which has made this company the best in North Star Village. I'm sure you saw the notice on the bulletin board about the sponsorship. The Event is tomorrow. Let me say thank you right now to anyone that plans to attend, and I will have tables set up for you as a group. Tonight, Mr. Kingsly and Miss Flowers insist that I partake in our merriment, but the best I can do is make a plate and jingle all the way to my office." Laughing at his own joke, he says, "Let the festivities begin."

Nickolas quickly steps to the front clapping his hands, appealing to everyone to applaud, which they do.

"Thank you, Mr. Chance, and all of you for another productive work week. Please stay a little while and enjoy your Christmas party. Let's eat, drink and be merry."

Christmas parties are fun and so is this one that marches on beyond Noelle's sarcastic wit, who retreats into his office, as the staff celebrates. Nickolas is staying until the end of the party and will be joined by his wife after her workday, but some co-workers are already receiving guests. Kristen smiles when Jacob Evergreen Jr. arrives 30-minutes into the party. She is proud to introduce him to her co-workers, who are excited to meet the nephew of the boss. "Thank you, JJ for being so patient with my co-workers. You are a sweetheart just like your mom and dad, and so different from your uncle," Kristen says with a laugh. "That's the first time I mentioned him by a name other than Mr. Chance."

"Kristy love, my uncle likes you a lot, but he shows the world his hard side. I admit that he is convincingly cold and has a sarcastic wit, but I have seen him be wise and gentle also."

"I've seen flashes of kindness, but not at Christmas," Kristen says. "Go spend some time with him. He's in his office. I'll let you two have some alone time. I promised the Security Guard I would make him a plate. Mr. Kingsly is going to help me bring it to him, then I will be right back."

Noelle Jr., is excited to see his beloved nephew approaching his office and gets up to greet him saying, "Well nephew, I see Miss Flowers made you a plate."

"How can you tell?", putting his plate down on the desk to give his uncle a hug.

"You wouldn't fix your own plate that neat JJ. I still remember a women's touch,"says Noelle.

"Uncle El, you remember a women's touch?", Jacob replies. "You should take a plate home with you. My Mom tells me you stay late in the office too much."

"JJ, I get my work in. Lately I like the peace I get here all alone. I certainly don't miss getting into this so-called Holiday traffic," Noelle says to his concerned nephew.

"Uncle El, you haven't caught the Christmas Spirit yet?" Before Noelle can respond, Jacob Jr., continues to say, "I like your sweater. I guess you gonna look good, even in an ugly sweater."

"My employees worked hard this year, so I gave in just a little bit to wear this sweater and keep them all happy. Take note for when you have your own company," Noelle says.

"I'm thinking of a master plan, and Kristen is helping me put it all together. She is an amazing woman," Jacob says with obvious affection.

Affection and compassion are passions Noelle Jr., keeps tightly wrapped up. He loves his nephew but fails to hear his heart, then he recklessly responds,

"JJ, keep your heart out of any financial decisions you make. When I was your age, I made a choice to dedicate myself to be successful. It was a hard decision to make, but I didn't let my heart stop me. I know times are different now than my younger days, but I had to focus on myself to achieve."

Miss Kristen Flowers looks at Jacob Jr. with obvious affection as she knocks on the door and enters the room. It's noticeable, but Noelle has lost that loving feeling. Kristen says,

"Mr. Chance, Coleman, our Security Guard says thanks for the food. He wants us to call him when we are ready to close up and leave."

"Well, tonight my uncle may be last to leave again, but I hope not."

"Miss Flowers, I'm glad you both are here. There's something I want you to know. When you announced your relationship, I wasn't sure our business relationship would continue to work, but it has. I'm glad that your relationship with my nephew is working and that your work here is flourishing. Like I would say back in my younger days, everything is cool. Can you dig it?"

"I can dig it Uncle El," Jacob Jr. and Kristen say, as the happy couple bring their hands together.

"You two are clever, but trouble comes when you try to make it last forever."

"Mr. Chance, your nephew loves you. He told me there's more to you than what I get to see in business with you, but today is personal. I thank you for giving your blessing to us."

"Call it a blessing. For me, it was a curse. All I wanted was to be rich, and I didn't let anything, or anyone, get in the way of that," Noelle states defiantly.

"Of course, it's a blessing, Uncle El," says Jacob Jr. "Merry Christmas. I hope and pray for you to share your life in a good relationship. I know you have the heart because I love you, and you have shown me love, so don't get too cold," he says, walking over to Noelle's favorite spot by the window. "Speaking of blessings, Uncle El, my Mom made me promise to remind you that the family will be going to Church again as a unit, on this Sunday."

"Oh, my! And you said you're going to Church on Christmas morning?!" Noelle says sharply.

"We don't normally have Church on Christmas Day, unless it's on a Sunday. This year we will and we're going to celebrate, yes Sir!" Jacob Jr. replies with a smile.

"Not this Christmas for me, nephew, no way! But for all it's worth, you can say a prayer for me," states Noelle. "I will see you at the family dinner."

Standing on the wings of love, the happy couple sees another couple that appears to be enjoying each other's company. It's Nickolas and his wife, Mary, as they approach Noelle's office.

"I see Mr. Kingsly and his wife. I want them to meet us as a couple," Kristen says to Jacob.

Noelle puts forth his strange mix of indifference and charm when he greets the wife of his Office Manager.

"Hello Mrs. Kingsly. It is great to see you again. I guess Christmas is useful for more than commercials, but I won't be staying long. I'm sure your husband and the co-workers will make the evening festive."

Mary Kingsly didn't disappoint. Matching her husband's Christmas sweater was more than a fashion point, and another point Kristen Flowers didn't miss, Mary was glowing with happiness.

"Hello Mrs. Kingsly, it is good to see you again," Kristen says as she approaches the couple.

"Hello Miss Flowers, I'm so glad I get to see you again. My husband tells me you are progressing here and are a big help to him. Thank you for all you do."

"Yes ma'am, I appreciate your kindness. Let me introduce you and your husband to my boyfriend. Jacob Evergreen Jr., meet Mrs. Mary Kingsly and her husband, our Office Manager, Mr. Nickolas Kingsly."

Jacob Jr. turns on his charm, greeting the Kingsly's warmly.

"Hello Mrs. Kingsly," he says while reaching out to shake hands with Nickolas. "Mr. Kingsly, my Uncle Noelle speaks of you often. I'm glad to be formally introduced. You may recognize my last name because my mother and father are members of North Star Village Baptist Church."

"Yes, I recognize your name, young man. Your Parents are outstanding members of the Church," Nickolas pauses and says approvingly, "So you are Jacob Evergreen Jr."

"Yes sir. Kristen has told me that you are now a Deacon, congratulations. I want you to know we are planning to be at the Church Service on this Sunday," Jacob Jr. says with confidence.

Nickolas effortlessly comforts the new couple when he says, "Young man, I'm sure you're no stranger to North Star Village Baptist Church and Miss Flowers has visited before. Whenever you do attend, please greet me. I'm happy for you both. Enjoy your first Christmas together. I have fond memories of Christmas past and my girlfriend then, who is my wife now."

Oh, what ah night, late December at N. O. Chance Financial Agency, what a lady, what a night, sung by the heart of Jacob Evergreen Jr., and Nickolas Kingsly, both men had the look of love in their eyes for the woman in their lives.

The Kingsly's are a team on one accord. As they talk and laugh the night away, the party was a stone gas, and everyone left promising to meet as a group for Saturday's R&B, S&G Gala.

The ride home for Nickolas demanded peace, which the sounds of the road rolling under the tires provide in a bliss that two can share, because love is in the air. The office Christmas party and drive home provide a break that gives Man and wife a second wind. No more waiting to exhale, they are in chill mode. Nickolas says,

"Hey lady, I'm going to take the scenic route and take in the Christmas lights. I had fun tonight. I'm glad Mr. Chance left early. It gave Kristen a chance to relax with her man."

"Nick, Kristen and Jacob make a good couple. She has the look of love, but what stands out for me is the look in his eyes. That's how you looked at me, and you still do, old man."

"Thanks for helping me put the office back in order. Monday will be a long workday that will start early. Our janitors do a good job, but I know the office was in good shape when we left." Nickolas inhales gently and says, "I know you have Simon's date on your mind. Our son is growing up. He wants this girl to be his girlfriend. Tomorrow I get to meet her parents and drive the Teenagers to the Mall."

"I asked Marion to coach him up. I think Simon likes this young lady, too. I know he's thankful for this Christmas gift," Mary says, looking at her husband drive. "Nick it's a gift to your son that you offered to be his chaperone. Even Auntie Marie is excited about Simon's date. All of that travel and we still have another Christmas party for us to go to tomorrow. Right now I'm going to relax and take in the night lights, and their Christmas show."

"We all need help from time to time. I'm glad I could help him on this date," Nickolas says to his wife as peace and quiet returns to the excursion and team Kingsly, this Christmas.

Up early in the morning, Nickolas Kingsly is the protector of the pleasure principle today and the principal of pleasure is a fresh haircut, followed by a trip to the car wash. Star Barber Shop is the first place they want to be, to see the father and son team of Michael and Gabriel Fields.

The Saturday sunrise is received with joy, and if you hear any noise, it's just Nickolas and the boys. The gang is all here, boys and the men are back together again, Nickolas and sons with Brother-in-law Matthew and his son. They're on their way to get haircuts.

Nickolas turns down the volume on the 'soul Train Christmas Starfest' CD and says, "Guys, we're here. I want you to hear some of my speech I've prepared for tomorrow's Church Service, while we're waiting for our Barbers." All agree and pile out of the Van and into the Barber Shop.

"Good to see you, Deacon Nickolas Kingsly," Michael said with a yes head nod. "Congratulations on your elevation in the Church."

"It's good to see you too Matthew."

Simon, Christopher, and Matt Jr., say,

"Good morning Mr. Fields." As they walk by, each one tap fists with his son Gabriel Fields who says, "Good morning. Welcome to Star Barber Shop."

Michael says, "Nick, there is 1 in front of you, and 1 in front for Gabriel. I will take care of you and Matt. My son will take care of the boys. Take off your coats and get comfortable."

"Thank you, Sir," Nickolas replies. "We're going to gather in the back of the room. I'm going to read a portion of my Christmas speech to my group."

"That sounds great, my friend. When you are ready, I will turn my music down and if you don't mind, please bless us all with your words," Michael says sincerely.

Nickolas smiles and says, "Alright, Mr. Michael Fields. Let me get it together, then I will speak."

Nickolas alerts Michael and Gabriel that he is ready to speak. They turn the volume down on the TV's and the music when Nickolas steps to the front of the Barber Shop.

"Good morning, everyone, please bear with me. My name is

Nickolas Kingsly, I am a Deacon at North Star Baptist Church. Before you think I'm going to ask you for money, I want you to know that I'm here with my family to get a haircut. I told Mr. Michael Fields I was going to read my family a portion of the speech I have prepared for Church Service on tomorrow. He asked if I would stand and deliver to everyone here, and so here I am. You know when you work for the Lord it's said stay ready, so you don't have to get ready. Now I know why that is said. Please join me in prayer, and when we pray, we begin with our Father. Our Father, thank you for waking us up this morning. It is for your purposes that we are here together. I give thanks for each ear and heart you have put in this place. Oh Lord, have your way. Let each be touched by your Grace, Mercy and Love. I ask this prayer to be heard in the Mighty name of Jesus Christ."

Everyone leans forward in anticipation of something good and the room says, "Amen."

"The first day of Winter is called Winter Solstice in the Northern Hemisphere, which is roughly at the top half of the world. But in the Southern Hemisphere it's Summertime, at the same time. What a wonderful world God Created. Christmas Day is the jewel of Winter, celebrated around the world for the birth of Jesus Christ, believed to be the Messiah. The seeds of Jacob; called Israel, have prayed for over 500 years, through 42 Generations, to come forth as the Savior from Heaven. His birth date has become a ball of confusion, misinformation and lies about the little town of Bethlehem, which is a Palestinian city in the West Bank of Israel near Jerusalem. The confusion begins when Israel, the Nation, is mistaken with Israel, the son of Isaac, named Jacob, who was renamed Israel by God. The children of Israel, sons of Jacob, are the 12 tribes of the Covenant, plus the unknown number of Levites, who are caretakers of the Church."

Nickolas takes a breath before continuing on. "The Covenant of the Rainbow to Noah, is the Covenant between God and the Grandfather of Jacob, who is Abraham. Abraham, Isaac, and Jacob, called

Israel, in modern times we said, "Peace in the Middle East." says Nickolas looking around the room.

"We did not know that we were saying Jesus, the Prince of Peace, born in the Middle East to bring a dead world back to life. The wickedness of mankind was struck down by flood, but by the Mercy of God's Love upon us, brought man back through Noah, his wife Naamah and their sons Shem, Ham and Japheth, who re-populated the Earth through their wives. But Mankind's wickedness returns within the re-population, and God would again turn away from the world. Even so He loved us so much that He would give us His only begotten son, born on Christmas, who was named Jesus and called Emmanuel. God could once again look upon the world He Created with loving Eyes, through Jesus, and see a New Covenant." Nickolas has everyone's attention but stops there and says, "There is more but that's all I got for now."

Simon says, "Dad that's good to go."

Matthew Sr., and Jr., give the thumbs up sign.

Christopher says, "Daddy you should write that down. I want to show it to my friends."

Michael says, "Well Sir, you said that right there. I will try to hear that in person," as a few of the patrons shake hands with Nickolas. Michael motions to Matthew Sr., and says, "I can take you now, Matt. Your Brother-in-law called me and told me you guys were going to the R&B, S&G tonight, so let's get you shaped up and he will be right after you."

Gabriel points to Simon and says, "Who's next?"

Simon brings Matthew Jr., to the Barber chair and says, "This is my Cousin Matt Jr. He wants a small Fro, with faded sideburns. My Brother wants what I get, a light fade, brush length for waves. Alright let's do it, we all got things to do today."

Time, space and coincidences cross personal intersections on this Saturday, the last weekend before Christmas, as husbands and wives do the same things in opposite directions, with the common link being beauty care. Beauty care for the men includes a hot shave, but for women it's hair, nails, eyebrows, and everything gets done.

Mary Kingsly likes what she sees looking back at her. The mirror on the wall agrees and if it could talk, it would say, *put on your red dress*. Hair Poet Tree is the name of the Salon, La Que is the owner and Head Hair Stylist, everyone calls her Dee. Mary and her sister were 2 of the first ones in the Salon chairs on this morning. Saturdays are always busy personal care days but more so on this day, due to the excitement of Community Christmas party going on tonight.

La Que says, "Mary, you know you need to come in and see me more often, but you look marvelous, darling. Your man is going to light up like a Christmas tree when he sees you. Marie, you look ready to go Christmas Steppin tonight. Hair Poet Tree will be there too, our last appointment here is at 3, so we will be looking for you ladies."

Mary and Marie are pleased at what they see looking back at them from the mirror and Marie says,

"Jake is wearing a gold suit and I'm wearing a gold dress, but I can't wait to see you and Nickolas both in red. I know you're going to have fun. We all work hard and haven't gone out in a while, so we both will be dancing on cloud 9. Girl I know you're hungry because I am. It's going to be too many shoppers out here for us to stop and get something to eat, so come over to my house for a quick bite, then I'll take you home."

"Okay, that sounds good," Mary says. "We are eating dinner at home, then Nickolas wants to be at the Community Center right after they open the doors. Nick is busy today. He's the chaperone for Simon's lunch date and he will meet her Parents, before he drives them to the Mall."

"My Brother-in-law is right on point with all that. Matt told me all the guys would be together this morning to get haircuts. It looks like the boys are taking care of business."

"Don't you love it when a plan comes together?" Mary says as she gets up to leave.

"Merry Christmas," La Que says, walking over to say goodbye to Marie, who is a regular client.

"Onward Dasher, crank up some heat and take me home," Marie says as she starts up her shiny SUV the husband cleaned for tonight's party, Sunday Church Service, and the Evergreen family tradition to drive-thru the Christmas tree Village light show.

The butterfly effect of the pleasure Principle continues in waves of positivity that stream in every direction through the Kingsly's and the Evergreen's interactions from the Barber Shop to Breakfast, the Carwash and getting Matthew Sr., and Jr., back home, work in perfection.

"Nice haircut MJ. I will see you at the Christmas party," Nickolas says to Matthew Sr., as they get out the Van to head into their house.

Matthew Sr., says bye to all, then to Simon says, "I have a tip for you on your lunch date."

Simon is speechless when his uncle puts 5 dollars in his hand and says, "You're smart. Figure it out."

7 swans a swimming and a Saturday love is complete with 8 maids a milking for Simon Kingsly, who asks his date,

"What would you like for dessert?"

Ameenah looks at the Cold Stone Creamery menu and says, "I'll have a Signature Creation Falling in Chocolate Sundae."

"That does look good Ameenah." Simon turns his attention to Pat the waitress to put in their order. "We will have two of your Signature Creation Falling in Chocolate Waffle Bowl Sundaes please."

"Ameenah, I got to tell ya, I was nervous all day until I saw you answer the door," Simon says. Speaking with confidence, he continues, "It's funny but I haven't been nervous at all since then."

"Simon, I'm glad you put this together. I wondered how it was going to work, but the Food Court was a great idea. I got to go around the world for food and I enjoyed my Gyro and Orange Julius," Ameenah says, smiling. Lightly laughing, she says, "Let's call it our first date."

Simon instinctively reaches across the table and holds her hand in a way he's never held hands with any other girl.

"A date it is. Ameenah I like you and I'd like to date you right up to the Senior Prom."

"That sounds like boyfriend and girlfriend, Simon Kingsly. We'll take it slow, but if you play your cards right, everything will be alright," Ameenah replies, the two looking into each other's eyes.

Their date has perfectly fit into a busy day. It is like Angels have paved the way, a tender moment ends when the waitress breaks the stare trance dance, but they only stop to start all over again.

"Here you go... two Falling in Chocolate Sundaes," says the waitress in a chant.

"Thank you, Miss," Simon states to Pat the waitress, then says to Ameenah, "Your parents were nice to me and my dad. I'm glad we all got a chance to meet and talk for a little while."

"Simon, your Deacon Dad is cool. I thought he would be different. I could tell right away that my parents liked him, and it's cool that he lets us have this time alone."

"Ameenah there's no doubt that my dad checked on us. I text him where we were sitting, and he told me again not to let you out of my sight. He also said if you went to the restroom, to wait in the waiting area, and if I had to go, to ask you to do the same," Simon said, laughing through a smile. "Wait, is that too much information?"

"No, my dad said the same thing," Ameenah says tasting her Chocolate Sundae. "Mmm I see why they call this Falling In Chocolate. I love it."

The new couple finds a way to slow time down by savoring each second and taking their time for the near three hours they were together, then Simon finds himself back at Ameenah's front door.It's time to say goodbye to his new girlfriend. He reaches into his coat pocket for a Christmas card and says, "Ameenah, I almost forgot to give you this." He then places the envelope in her hand.

"Simon, wait here, I will be right back,"Ameenah says, darting into her home. She returns quickly, and hands Simon an envelope, then says,"I didn't get you a Christmas card, but I have a gift for you. Promise me you won't open it until Christmas Eve night."

Simon says, "Thank you, I won't open it until then."

The date is sealed with an innocent kiss from a happy young lady, who then waves and says, "Bye Simon! Merry Christmas!"

Simon momentarily losing his cool, yells out, "I promise I will wait until Christmas Eve to open my gift, but I will call you tomorrow around seven!".

"It's a date, don't wait too late!" Ameenah says, smiling as she goes into her home.

Simon floats back to the Van and shuts the door with a sigh and says, "Thanks for everything, Dad," holding on to his gift that smells as sweet as his date was. Nickolas looks at his son and sees the vision of the baby boy born onto him, and the big boy he has become. That young man sitting next to him is growing into manhood. Nickolas drives away from Ameenah's home and opts for a quiet ride home again, this quality time is with his son.

A late day Sun falls into sunset, but its sunlight burns bright to show the daytime beauty of Christmas decorations hanging in North Star Village. The proud Dad breaks through the quiet of the drive and says, "Son, I'm proud of you. I believe you are in the elite gentleman's club, and I think your friend and her parents were impressed with you. I'm impressed, son. I didn't think your date location was a good idea, but it seems to have turned out good for you. It worked out for me too. Everything I went shopping for was sitting there, like it was waiting just for me.

"Dad, even though our date was on one of the busiest days of the year, we found our own place in it together, and things just fell into place. We enjoyed each other's company and the awkward stage just disappeared. It was too cool, and she gave me a gift, a blushed faced Simon says.

"And a kiss it seems," says Nickolas.

"Oh, you saw that," Simon replies. "I didn't plan that, it just kind of happened, then I remembered to give her a Christmas card. It's the funniest thing Dad. I picked up some Christmas cards when Chris and I went shopping with Uncle Matt after the Thanksgiving Balloon parade. Who knew that one of those cards would be perfect for today?" Simon's voice trails off into the windshield, his eyes turn to the passenger window that reveals new sights of life in the city this Christmas.

Nickolas leaves well enough alone and lets the drone of rolling tires and the peaceful sounds of air rushing by, finish their conversation. He's sure Simon's mother will get all the details from her son when he tells her about the day, as will the rest of the family at dinner tonight.

The normally relaxed Saturday dinner at the Kingsly home is replaced by a formal gathering at the dining room table. Even Marion adjusted her work schedule to be home and help her mother get dressed for the R&B, S&G Gala, called the Community Center Christmas party.

"Alright guys, it's time for me and your mother to get dressed. I'm not sure what time we'll be back, but it should be before midnight. You can contact us if you need to and remember that your aunt and uncle are going to the Christmas party also, so please call to check in on your cousins," Nickolas says with a big smile on his face.

Mary says,"Okay my daughter, let's get this party started! I'm ready to get dressed and put on my dancing shoes!Nick, I'll be ready in less than an hour. Are you all set?

"I got it together, go ahead and get dressed. I will get dressed in the boy's room and Simon volunteered to shine my dancing shoes," Nickolas says, as everyone gets up from the table.

Christopher pulls out his portable game unit and heads to the Living room. Simon follows his father to the bedroom and says, "Hey Dad, I want you and Mom to have fun tonight, like I had fun on my date today."

Nickolas turns to his son and says,"You invited your friend on a lunch date and impressed her." Simon, folding his arms and rubbing his chin, nods his head yes, and a proud Dad continues to say, "Well, now it's my turn to impress my date. I will tell your mom about meeting Ameenah's parents on our way to the party, and son, it's a good idea to get your sister's advice on how to move forward with this young lady."

"Okay, I'm going to do that before I call Ameenah tomorrow, and Dad, her parents are also going to the Christmas party."

Nickolas likes what he sees when he looks at the man in the mirror. He immediately gives thanks that his prayers have changed things from last year and days gone by. This year he can escort his wife to the Red & Blue, Silver & Gold, North Star Village Christmas Party, and he is ready to celebrate in grand style. He is wearing a red fashion suit that matches Mary's dress, black dress shoes, black shirt, red tie, and tops it off with a black Modern Conductor Hat. The mirror smiles at Nickolas, as he picks up a black London Fog Trench coat and heads to the living room.

Marion and Simon are in the Living room talking about Simon's earlier date with Ameenah, and Christopher is still playing video games when a presence fills up the room, then everyone stops what they are doing to marvel at their dad. It's been quite some time since the children of Nickolas Kingsly have seen him dressed up to go out on the town, and although he wears a shirt and tie to work, and suits to Church, on this disco night, daddy is Dapper Dan.

Marion stands up and says, "Daddy you wear a Santa Claus outfit every Christmas, but you are serious in that red fashion suit, you and Mommy will look great together."

Right on cue; as if a movie director yelled action, Mary Kingsly the sophisticated lady, enters the hallway. All heads turn towards the sound of feet walking, and her presence fills up the house. "Thank you for putting on my makeup Marion, you're a Makeup Artist my girl," said Mary, effortlessly soaking up the attention.

Nickolas loses all his cool and gushes out, "Mae, Mae... you look beautiful."

"Mom, you're making me nervous," Simon says, "I'm buggin out... you are fine"

Christopher runs over to his mother, hugs her and says "Mommy you look like a model!"

"It's picture time!" Marion says, "I want you both to move to the Christmas tree."

The happy couple admire each other and hug adoringly in front of the Christmas tree, as Marion takes a few pictures with her cell phone. "Mom, Dad you make a great couple!" Then looking at her brothers, Marion says, "Guys, you can take notes from dad."

Mary cheers for her sons and says, "Simon, your dad is quite a gentleman and quite a catch, I'm sure the Parents of your date were glad to meet both of you. We'll talk more about your date later, but right now It's My Turn, as she sang the words like The Boss Diana Ross, as everyone claps and cheers.

Christopher says, "Hey Mom and Dad, look over your head,you're standing under the mistletoe."

Nickolas says, "Hang all the mistletoe, this is a great time to kiss my wife," then all saw Mommy kissing Santa Claus.

"It was my idea to hang mistletoe in front of the tree, mistletoe is a sign of friendship and love," says Chris. "Good job Chris." mom says. She immediately turns to her husband and says, "Alright prince charming, you can take mamma to the dance. They leave the house in a flurry of goodbyes from the children, to ride to the Christmas Gala as the last light of the Sun falls behind the mountains of North Star Valley. North Star Village is more beautiful today, but not as much as tomorrow. It's Christmas time in the city, there's love in the air and the best is yet to come. Christmas music plays on the radio and suddenly the Holiday rush slows down, as a man and his wife enjoy the romantic seclusion, they find driving across the City at this time. Nickolas and Mary are on one accord. They have waited for a night like this without complaining. Then all traffic lights in their life turned green, revealing new wonders on the way. Tonight, the stars are twinkling in Mary's eyes with a confirmation that says what they have is still a thrill.

All roads lead to the Red & Blue, Silver & Gold, Gala Christmas party and the excursion to the community center complex has come to an end. Nickolas says, "I'm so glad I get to take you to the party. Everything I want is what you have brought to me, this moment is about you and me. I'm mesmerized by you, my Angel in a red dress."

Mary says, "Honey, there's an open parking space right in the front. It looks like your parking lot angel says park here. Look at the people," she says, as the Kingsly's turn their vehicle into an open parking space. Then Mary says, "They are all so beautifully, dressed in their colors!"

Nickolas, always a gentleman, is proud to escort his wife to the front door entrance of the community center. They unknowingly strike a pose every few feet, as their blood red outfits perfectly match their heartbeats and footsteps.

Price Waterhouse designed the coat check area to function as a meet and greet space. Nickolas and Mary make their way inside and check their coats with the attendants. The entrance looks like a courtyard, the community center is transformed into a dancefloor in the clouds within a mountain glen, that is hidden from view by tall curtain partitions in the red, blue, silver and gold color theme. The entrance and exit corridors blend into the scenery of the gala, as do the security team, dressed as toy soldiers.

Nickolas and Mary hear the sound of Christmas Dance music when they enter the room, and now they're walking into a festive winter wonderland of color.

Mary says, "Look at the people."

# Chapter 11

## *A Change For A Chance Gonna Come - Part Two*

### King Solomon

He that hasteth to be rich hath an evil eye, and considereth not that poverty shall come upon him.

— Proverbs 28: 22

The Butterfly effect for a change comes to Noelle Chance Jr.. Even now as he goes over the river and through the woods to spend the morning with his mother and father, from there he will call his sister. It's a family affair.

"Merry Christmas El," says mother Chance as Noelle Jr., enters her home. "Merry Christmas son," says Daddy Chance. Noelle's rush immediately slows to a crawl, as the hustle and bustle of the season catches even those who swear not to participate in it. Call it the magic of the season.

Noelle Jr., says, "Thank you Mom, Dad. I'm glad you're merry about the spend fest. I see you have gifts under the tree."

Mother Chance replies, "El, this Christmas I want the family to gather around the tree and sing Christmas carols, drink hot chocolate and love on each other. And yes, you'll find some gifts from me and your father, under the Christmas tree."

"Well, you could have saved your money, I have everything I need," says Noelle Jr.. Then he goes to the kitchen, placing a bag on the table he continues to say, "I brought breakfast like I said I would, and regular coffee."

Daddy Chance says, "Black is regular."

"Yes sir," Noelle replies, "Just like you taught me, and like my old business partner Khole Cashe used to say. I call black coffee regular. Dad, I swear you taught him that also."

Big Daddy replies, "I probably did son. You two were thick as thieves in those days. All you did was plot and scheme, God rest his soul, but your friend worked every angle until his death. Noelle, I pray that you learn from his demise and come out of the cold, and you can take that look off your face. I'm not going to preach today, but I will eat. Come on Ella, let's eat this breakfast our son has brought."

Mother Chance says, "El, I am so glad that you're busy doing things for others this Christmas. I'm thankful that you are helping with in town charity work, and that you haven't been too busy like in the past years. I want you to consider coming to our Christmas morning Church Service. We are having a special program that begins at 10am.

Daddy Chance replies, "That's right Ella, we better get it all in now or we won't see him until Christmas night. El, I'm glad that you're taking time for us today. The community center Christmas party has got to be on your mind. I'm thankful that Mr. Waterhouse has made such an effort to work with you this Holiday Season. I'm also thankful that you're taking time out today to visit your nephew. JJ wants to bring his girlfriend here to visit with us this evening, instead of going to the community center Christmas party."

"Well, I'm sure you and Mom will enjoy their company. Oh yeah Dad, thanks for reminding me, I told Holly I would call her." "Then Noelle Jr.," says Mom. "I'm not going to make any promises about going to Church on Christmas morning, and I hope you guys don't have any songs or routines planned for me today." Said El, with a wide-eyed look on his face. "You got me good last time and had me going before you sang everybody plays the fool."

Mother and Daddy Chance laugh out loud at that memory. Daddy Chance says, "Son remember, the best is yet to come."

Noelle Jr. puts on his wireless earbuds and calls Holly, "Good morning, my dear sister," he says. "I'm calling you from Mom and Dad's. How are you doing today?"

Holly replies joyfully, "I'm so glad that you're there! I know Mom told you that the family will be together at church tomorrow. The Christmas Day family dinner is at my house. I want you to be there by 2 O'clock. That will give us plenty of time to take family pictures and sing Christmas songs together. So please be jolly."

"Holly, I need a secretary just to keep up with you, and speaking of that, what's going on tonight with JJ and Kristen? Dad tells me they plan on spending some time here instead of attending the community center Christmas party. What do you know about that?" Noelle asks.

"Kristen and JJ seem to be happy together, El, and I am happy for them. He wants to share his joy with his Grandparents." Then Holly continues to say, "I wanted you to call me so I could tell you Jake and I are excited about tonight. We are looking forward to seeing you as a host of the gala, so get it together and not just your clothes. We want to see a repeat performance of you dancing."

Noelle says, "Don't count on me dancing tonight, Holly. I will watch you and Jake get down, but right now I've got to get to going so I can spend some time with your son. I'm going to get off this phone and get ready to leave here, but I will see you at the community center."

"Bye, bye El," Noelle hears, and says bye, putting his phone away. "Hey Mom, Dad," he says, "I got to get going so I can spend a little time with JJ. I know you will enjoy your time with him tonight, and I will talk to you tomorrow night or Monday."

The early bird gets the worm, Noelle thinks, pleased to get back to his home with plenty of time to prepare, before visiting JJ at his home. Noelle Jr. is barely moved by thoughts of the Christmas party gala, but he is excited to keep a promise to his nephew and see where he lays his head.

Now, after his cross-town excursion to Trinity Garden Apartment Homes, Noelle exits his car and walks up to the entrance where Jacob Jr. is waving at him from the front of his apartment.

Noelle Jr., always the well-dressed man, strikes a handsome pose in black dress pants, white shirt, black tie, silver cufflinks with black Onyx, silver tie clip and chain. A Black Cole Haan half-boot dress shoes, charcoal grey full length Houndstooth Topcoat, with black smooth leather gloves and scarf, topped off with a black all weather Sullivan Crusher dress hat. He calls out to greet his nephew and says, "Well, I'm finally here JJ, this looks like a nice place you have."

"Thank you, Uncle El. Come with me and let me show you the community room. From there you can see the tennis courts and swimming pool. The maintenance crew put the Christmas lights up and I think they did a good job; it looks nice at night. I live on plot number 5. Each section contains 5-apartments with garages in the back. There are 8 groups of homes in this complex."

"Uncle El, you look great man! Come on inside and let's sit down for a while. I'm sorry I can't go to the R&B, S&G Gala this year," Jacob Jr. says with a smile, then continues to say "with the Lord's Blessing, I'll be able to go next year."

Noelle replies, "Well, JJ, things just didn't work out that way this year. Who knew you would be dating Miss Kristen Flowers now? Who knew that you two would celebrate your relationship on the day of the Gala? Not going is not by coincidence, it sounds like a plan to me."

"Yes, it's a plan," says Jacob Jr., pleased by the prospects of spending time with Kristen Flowers, He continues, "call it the seventh day of Christmas gift Uncle El. Christmas will be here before you know it. Enjoy it now or you'll have to wait a whole year for it to come back, and not even tomorrow is promised to us."

Noelle interrupts saying, "I know, I know JJ. That's why today is called the present. Every day is a gift, I get it. I'm not trying to steal your joy. I say to each his own. Believe me when I tell you I'm happy for you. I just want you to keep working hard, and you will make your own luck."

"No luck for me, Uncle El. All promotions come from God. He Blesses us without our consent or acknowledgement. He is love and the true meaning of Christmas. Uncle El it has taken you awhile, but I think of your visit today as a Christmas present to me. Let me take your coat and give you a tour of my house."

Jacob Jr., goes into realtor mode stating, "This is a two-bedroom, split level apartment with 2 and a half bathrooms, a living room, dining room and kitchen."

"The bedrooms are upstairs," says a proud nephew, as he gives Noelle a full tour of his home.

"Uncle El, I figured you would be in between meals, so I ordered your favorite steak dinner from North Star Diner and got one for myself. Just let me warm it up and we can eat."

Noelle Jr. is caught off guard by a rush of emotions that hits hard. His heart sends out a reminder that he has loved his nephew since he was a baby, and now he thinks back to what was just said, that today is a gift, that's why it's called the present. "My goodness JJ, how can I refuse such a gift!" Noelle states emphatically.

Uncle and nephew enjoy each other's company and the conversations flow freely as they talk about work, money, and family.

Jacob Jr. says, "Uncle El, time is moving on. I know you have to leave but before you go, I want to tell you that I appreciate how you have treated Kristen since you found out we were dating. It means a lot to me. I'm thankful that your business relationship with her has not been disrupted, and it was cool to meet her co-workers last night at your Christmas party. We had a fun time."

"Party?" Noelle Jr., says sarcastically, then continues to rant, "JJ,

Christmas is financial wood for a commercial fire. There's so much money flying in the air, I can almost see it. Christmas is a big rip off, and the people don't have a clue about what's going on. They just follow the crowd like sheep follow the herd."

"Slow down, Uncle El. You're getting ready to go to the community center party put together by your mentor, Mr. Waterhouse, and I know that you had fun at his annual private Christmas party. I hope to hear that you had fun at tonight's Gala. I'm glad you've been active this Christmas. You spend too much time alone, and at your office." Jacob Jr. says in one breath.

Noelle Jr. calms down and says, "You're right JJ, it's true. I spend a lot of time at my office, but it's comfortable and I get lots of work done. I work for my success. It's the only reason I'm at the top of my field. JJ, you've got a nice start. Give yourself a chance to make some money, don't get too serious, too soon.

Jacob Jr. says, "Kristen is good for me. I'm glad this Christmas will be a special one for me."

"I haven't always been this old. I told you I had a love of my own back in the day," Noelle says. Then, putting his hand on Jacob's shoulder, he continues, "Try to make great decisions and remember that you'll have to make some hard choices. I've made a lot of money since my days of young love, and JJ, I like money. JJ, I have had a great time with you. Thank you for not giving up on me, but I should go now to be on time for the party."

Jacob Jr. nods his head yes and says, "Uncle El, I'm glad we had some private time together. I'm going to tell Kristen how sharp you look. Let me get your coat and walk with you to your car."

On the way to the car, Jacob Jr. says, "Uncle El, I forgot to tell you that I spoke to Grandma and Granddad earlier. I asked Grandma if me and Kristen could stop by, and she said she would make dinner. She's making chicken stew, which is my favorite."

"I love the way she makes that," Noelle replies immediately.

"Uncle El, tomorrow the whole family is going to be at North

Star Church. I'm sure you already know, but I want to say to you that it would be great to see you there."

"Well, thank you JJ. You won't see me there tomorrow, but you can say a prayer for me. It will make us both feel better. Tomorrow will be a day of rest for me, but I will be staying in the house," he said as he gets into his car, saying goodbye with a wave of his hand. Onward goes the man about town. Next stop will be the R&B, S&G Gala.

DESPITE A DAY MADE busy by keeping promises made, in a minute Noelle Oscar Chance Jr., will be right on time for the Christmas gala. He arrives at the community center parking garage with time to spare, pulling his car into the valet parking lane, where the parking attendants instruct him to pull forward and stop. Noelle gets confused when he looks directly into the bright flashlight from the figure of a man approaching the car, and as the man bends down to the driver's window, he sees the face of Khole Cashe, his dead business partner, which scares him stiff.

Noelle gasps, holding his breath and tensing up his body. He begins to remember this feeling from the first encounter of the third kind he had in the valet parking lot at the Bella Casino. The man motions for Noelle to roll the window down, then the voice he hears sounds familiar.

"I apologize for startling you. I told the other attendants that I wanted to greet you, and that caused the confusion, with me running towards you with my flashlight," the man says with a smile on his face. Then he continues, "Sir, you don't remember me, do you? I met you at the Bella Casino celebration dinner, given by Mr. Price Waterhouse. I remember you well because you told me I reminded you of a friend. My name is Cole Bucks.

"I remember you now," says Noelle. Then Cole Bucks opens the car door.

"Merry Christmas Mr. Chance. I've been expecting you," said with courtesy by Cole Bucks, who continues to say, "I told Mr. Waterhouse that I would be your parking lot angel tonight," as he hands Noelle a valet parking ticket. "I'm proud to take care of the Christmas Gala staff. I must say that you guys have out done yourselves this year with the look of the community center. It's a Red, Blue, Silver and Gold Winter Wonderland."

Noelle Jr. replies dryly, "At least you're enjoying it. I'll be glad when everything returns to normal, and we get back to work. I'll be glad to get my car back like I give it to you, young man."

"And a fine car you have sir. I will take good care of it Mr. Chance. Please follow the employee entrance signs and enter through the employee only door. I will alert my staff that you are on the way. You should find Mr. Waterhouse in the coat check courtyard," says Cole Bucks.

The North Star shines over preconceived notions of despair, and Christmas fatigue. Depressions of all nature disappear, flying away on the wings of love from the prayers of saints elsewhere. And prayer changes things. Lifted past the clouds in the sky, when the sound of your own prayer voice is unknown, the sound of these prayers have a holy tone. A soul belied, relies on prayers of others to survive, Winter, Spring, Summer or Fall. All they do is call on their friend, and oh what a friend you have in Jesus, he is after all the reason for the Season.

Jesus removes a total eclipse of the heart from the dark, into the light of life, born in a manger on Christmas night. Hang all the mistletoe for spiritual kisses too, that deliver a promise made by the greatest story ever told and believed in your heart to be true. North Star Community Center is a surround sound of Christmas music filling the air and the Spirit of the Holiday is everywhere.

It's Christmas love at first sight when you step into what was the community center lobby that's now transformed into a courtyard. Centered is a pretty 7-foot Douglas fir Christmas tree standing on a red-carpet, with a step-up banner for picture taking. The main event space has an ambiance of silver and gold LED lights that illuminate the hanging art tapestry covering the scaffolding built to look like a mountain range. The elevated stage has an overhead trestle of special effects and lighting, to make it appear to be flat land inside a mountain. That will also serve as the dancefloor.

The dancefloor will light up like the checkerboard floor made famous in the Saturday Night Fever movie to brighten the clouds. It's the entertainment centerpiece for the R&B, S&G Christmas Gala, built to imitate the scenery of a Winter Wonderland in the clouds, twinkling under the stars. The Staff is requested to wear black pants and white shirt, with the organizing committee providing a multicolor, buttonless coat vest in the red, blue, silver and gold theme.

Noelle picked up his vest at the private Christmas party given by Price Waterhouse and his wife. Although he hasn't spoke of the party, it was a grand affair. Noelle is greeted when he enters the lobby by Price Waterhouse, then his eyes take in the Christmas imagination of his mentor.

"Noelle, you're as reliable as a Swiss Watch. "How do you like the courtyard design? The entrance has red and blue lights, the exit is silver and gold," Price Waterhouse continues. "You are quite the well-dressed man. I hope tonight goes as good as you look. Let's get on the red-carpet, and take a picture. Then we'll go inside the event room so you can see the work we've done in there."

Noelle Jr. is at a loss for words, when he sees the inside of the transformed community center.

"Noelle, you surely are an accountant," Price Waterhouse says. "I can almost see the numbers floating over your head, as you count the money spent on all that you see. I assure you that I'm a spendthrift, but I want to show my appreciation for the support the people of North Star Village have shown me in all my endeavors, be it business or charity work. Great progress has been made over the last few years. Business is good, generous donations from the community and from businesses like yours, have helped me to help others.

Noelle replies, "Well Mr. Price Waterhouse, you have always

thrown great parties and tonight it looks like you've outdone yourself. I neither have the will or the patience with Christmas, but for you my friend, I make myself available to help."

Price Waterhouse says,"Good, that's good Noelle. This setup cost extra but it's worth it, to show my appreciation. I hired the mPed Event Planners to help me with my vision for the Gala. I wanted it to look like a Winter Wonderland and they gave me a fair price," he said with a smile. "The DJ's name is Calvin Brown, known as DJ Casanova Cocoa Brown. You might remember him from the Masquerade Ball."

"Good evening young man, my name is Noelle Chance. I remember you from the mask reveal at the masquerade ball," said Noelle, looking around the room. Then Noelle continues, "This is impressive, it seems we're in the middle of the mountains," he says shaking hands with the DJ.

DJ Casanova says, "I had a great time at the Masquerade Ball. You two did a good job, but tonight is something extra. I'm finished with my soundcheck Mr. Waterhouse. Let's walk around the stage so you can get a good look at the scenery. We have tables and chairs setup on the exterior of the stage, single chairs are setup facing the stage, and they're roped off to form a walkway around the whole setup with the main dancing area in the front."

DJ Casanova says, "Mr. Waterhouse, this is the schedule I have for tonight. Doors open at 6:30, music until the Business Award presentations at 7:15. Mr. Chance, you and Mr. Waterhouse are scheduled to welcome guests at the entrance, until the staff calls you to the stage, where you will announce the winners. I will take over after the ceremony, then we will begin Christmas Steppin.

Noelle states, "What is Christmas Stepping?"

Price Waterhouse replies, "For me and my wife, it is hand dancing, but for the sake of your question, I'll defer to the DJ."

"Men, lead your partner with a one two beat, Steppers start walking, matching the strides of their feet, it's really easy to do, great exercise, fun too. This dance is created for everyone, even you!" Casanova says in a rhyme. Then he clears his throat and continues, "Tonight we will be steppin around this wonderful stage, just like we're walking around the stage right now, then I will call out dance moves for the steppers to do like, step dance side by side, Fancy Step, Do Si Do and some other moves.

DJ Casanova walks his guests around the stage, pointing out how well the mountain scenery is lit, then states, "Tonight we'll be walking in a Winter wonderland Mr. Chance, and if you want to learn how to step dance, my dance team teaches here on Thursdays. The next class begins in the New Year, on the last Thursday of January. Now back to the front of the stage," DJ Casanova says with excitement. "Please gentlemen, step up on the stage and let me turn on the dancefloor lights for you. Everyone that wants to will get the chance to dance on the checkerboard squares," says the DJ. "It looks like the Disco clubs in the 1970's and 80's. Now back to the front of the stage," DJ Casanova says with excitement.

"Price Waterhouse," says Noelle. "I bet you danced the night away in your younger days on a dancefloor like this. The discotheque craze passed me by. I like having party lights but tonight will be my first dance on this kind of dancefloor.

Noelle nods his head yes in agreement but has no intention to dance tonight. He gathers his thoughts to say, "Mr. Waterhouse, North Star Village is a far better place by all of your efforts." He then turns to DJ Casanova and says, "Thank you Mr. DJ for the tour."

Price Waterhouse replies, "The Staff will be on stage to begin the night. We will hand out awards and sell raffle tickets at 9 O'clock. At 9:30 we'll clear the stage, then at 10 Noelle and I will give away our gifts. DJ Casanova, we shut down at 11" he said, checking his watch.

There is more to see throughout the event space, transformed to be a Winter Wonderland. You can feel the excitement in the air. Tonight, couples will dance in the clouds and hearts will soar. Some will restore the love, together again, like it's the first time they danced at Christmas.

Price Waterhouse looks at Noelle and says, "It's time to meet the rest of the staff. I've asked all to be here at 5:30, so they should be meeting with my wife in the Manager's office. Let's get there so you can see who we are working with."

It's quite a sight for Noelle Jr., greeting all who walked through the courtyard and into the lobby, finding lights, cameras, and action. He looks at the people making their way down the red and blue hallway to enter a Winter Wonderland. Beautiful party people have come dressed in red, blue, silver and gold, full of the brilliant theme colors, and they begin to walk around the stage. Chestnuts are roasting on an open fire. Hot peanuts and a variety of soups, chili, fruit cocktail, assorted fruits, cold cuts, meatballs, chicken wings and drumettes are plentiful. Plus there are assorted teas, all soda for free, and a cash bar with something for everyone. Desserts are available, and first come first serve sea food wraps, go to the first who purchase raffle tickets for a taste of North Star Village.

So many faces; none that he knew made Noelle face his loneliness too. 30-minutes have passed since the doors have opened, but it seemed much longer. Then the faces of his employees appear in a group walking in, and Noelle began to grin. It was the grin that found Christmas.

Noelle states, "Good evening. I'm glad to see you here together!" All could hear and see his excitement.

There was Nickolas Kingsly and wife in red, so was Inez, Audrey's husband too. Aretha, Letitia and Ronnie, with their husbands that wear blue. Ben Ray, George, Jason, Perry, and their wives dressed in silver, and Tahir and his wife are wearing the color gold.

Price Waterhouse enthusiastically greets Noelle's staff and says, "Merry Christmas and thank you for coming, as they present themselves to him."

Noelle, still grinning, says "Mr. Waterhouse please excuse me while I escort my employees to their tables." They did eat, drink and be merry, but not Noelle.

Noelle Oscar Chance Jr. would only participate with his grin, looking like the Cheshire cat, in a Chance in the Winter Wonderland. Alice in wonderland fell down the rabbit hole, and a fantastic voyage was in front of her. For Noelle, he who has ignored entire Christmas seasons, oh what a night that he did grin through and bear. He is the Watchman, watching the citizens of North Star Village enjoy the Community Center Christmas Gala. He watched his sister- and Brother-in-law Nickolas and wife, and Price Waterhouse and wife dance also. Noelle watched his employees dance in the man-made mountains and the lifelike clouds brought to life with pretty lights.

The gift of remembrance returns in spirit, and deja vu ministers to Noelle very well. While he is walking toward the valet area of the parking lot, at the end of the Christmas gala, the sleeper awakens when a voice inside his head says that it seems we've been here before.

Noelle, seeing sister, brother-in-law, Price and Elizabeth Waterhouse says, "This is just like the Masquerade Ball, except I didn't dance tonight."

Price Waterhouse states, "Noelle, I'm glad your cruise control button worked tonight. You did a fantastic job of helping me and the Staff. I hope you found some time to enjoy the night, because everyone had fun and you worked all night. I'm tired now and want to get home and get as much rest as I can before going to Church. Thank you again," and as Mrs. Waterhouse waves goodbye, Price Waterhouse says, "Goodnight my friend, Merry Christmas."

Holly waves goodbye to Price and Elizabeth as a valet attendant drives their car to them, then turns to her brother and says, "El, you were on point tonight. A perfect host, you look great and you spoke well, it seems that you caught the Christmas Spirit."

Noelle responds dryly, "No way"

Jacob Sr. says, "El old man, I agree whole heartedly with my wife, all jokes aside. You did a good job tonight. I believe when North Star Village talks about this party, the R&B, S&G Gala will become a legend."

Holly jumps in to say, “We have some great pictures of this wonderland, and just so you know, Christmas steppin around the stage with DJ Casanova calling out dance moves, was spectacular.”

Jacob Sr. states, “I saw all of your employees step dancing, and everyone took turns on the lights of the checkerboard dancefloor. This party will be remembered as an instant classic, given by Mr. Waterhouse, who has had some great parties, but this takes the cake.”

Holly replies, “He’s a great Mentor to you, brother dearest. You should find someone to mentor, since you say Mr. Waterhouse is important to you.”

Noelle replies, “What’s come over me I cannot say, but it’s over now. This event was important to Mr. Waterhouse, and he is important to me. The theme of Red & Blue, Silver & Gold was quite a sight. The towns people had a great setup tonight, but I say it was far too much money spent on the day. Oh man I must be tired, that sounded like a rhyme.”

The sound of a smooth-running powerful engine approaches the valet parking pickup lane with their car, and Holly laughs while saying, “I’m not trying to preach to you, I’m going home and get some rest before we go to Church tomorrow. I’ll get my praise on and let the preacher preach.”

Noelle replies, “Holly, I will not be joining you at your Church tomorrow. I have a date with some work I brought home, my couch, and the television,” says Noelle as he hugs his sister and shakes hands with Jacob Sr., then says get home safely Jake, thank you for everything.

Noelle sees the car approaching is his. The attendant holds the door open for Noelle to get in who says sarcastically, “Well, you said you would take care of my car, Mr. Cole Bucks, and you did.”

“Thank you, sir, but my name is Vellman. I met you at the Masquerade Ball. Cole Bucks didn’t work here today.”

“Well, I received this valet ticket from him,” Noelle says sharply.

Vellman replies, “Sir, all of our attendants are courteous. I’m glad you’re happy with our service. Let me look at your ticket and I will commend the attendant who serviced you, his ID number is in the time stamp. Vellman looks at the ticket with curiosity, then says, well sir, this ticket doesn't have an ID number on it, there's no way for me to tell who you spoke to.

Noelle tips the attendant and says, "This is my car, somebody parked it, and you have brought it back to me as I gave it to you. That is good enough," said motioning to close the car door.

"Thank you, sir, have a safe and pleasant drive home," Vellman says as he stands at attention.

~

DEACON ALLEN PEOPLES greets the Congregation, "Good morning again!" There's cheer in the atmosphere of North Star Baptist Church after an inspired Call to Worship from the deacons. The fired-up Congregation powerfully sings the song Emmanuel. You can hear the church is excited on this Sunday, and ready to see the children perform in the Christmas story play.

"The children are ready!" Deacon Peoples says. "First, we will have a display of praise dance, from the Ladies of Praise. 9-ladies dancing enter the sanctuary as the choir begins to sing, Hallelujah, salvation and glory, honor, and power to the Lord our God, for the Lord our God is almighty. For the Lord our God is omnipotent, for the Lord our God He is wonderful Hallelujah, hallelujah, hallelujah, Ha lle lu jah!

Pastor Avery Mann watches from the pulpit, as the Praise Dancers stir up their gifts to show praise of the Holy Spirit through synchronized moves, moving in waves for each Hallelujah sung, each kneeling in prayer, as the Choir sings. He is wonderful, to end the song.

The deacons and congregation stand clapping their hands as the Holy Spirit pours out in this place. Amen is heard front to back, and Hallelujah from side to side. Pastor Mann gets out of the way, knowing when the Lord shows up in spirit, a joy surpassing all understanding flows. There are no strangers under the function of the Lord. Pastor Mann reminds all that Hallelujah, Salvation and Glory is the song called Revelation 19, written by minister of music A. Jeffrey Levalley, and brought to the churches by Gospel singer Steven Hurd.

Pastor Mann receives the fruit of the Holy Spirit and begins to preach. "He is wonderful, the Lord our God is omnipotent. He is everywhere at the same time, on Earth as it is in Heaven. He is in all things, suffering our doubts, our denials, and our betrayal. Honor and Power to the Lord our God, who loves us so much that He sends us His only begotten son, Jesus Christ of Nazareth, to Redeem us back to His Grace and Mercy."

Pastor Mann continues, "Jesus leaves His Royal Birthright in Heaven to put on the flesh of our human desires and take on the sins of the world. God has chosen us, we have not chosen Him. Oh, give thanks, for no man can come to God but by Jesus Christ. He is our wonderful Savior, let the Church say Amen! He knows when you are sleeping, He knows when you're awake, He knows when you've been good or bad, be good, for goodness sakes, He is not Santa Claus, He is Jesus Christ of Nazareth."

Pastor Mann says, "The Angel heralds His coming, He is asking you Do You Remember Me, my Sermon is titled, Do You Remember Me, based on Matthew chapter 2, verses 7 through 12. Matthew is the first book of the New Testament in the Holy Bible, it begins with a chronological lineage of Jesus, from Abraham to King David, to Joseph and His birth. Jesus moves Heaven and Earth for you and for me. There was agreement in Heaven for the Lord to come to Earth as our Messiah. A Star in the Heavens swings down, like it says in the chorus of the Gospel Hymn, swing low, sweet chariot, coming forth to carry me home."

The Church says Amen...

Pastor Mann continues, "The North Star, is a sign in the sky given to the wise men from the East, three Kings that give way to an

Angel that says unto them, follow the Star and it will lead you to the Messiah, promised by God. Christ thy Savior is Born."

The congregation shouts, "Yes Lord, thank you Lord," and Hallelujah's ring out in the Church with waves of Amen that move side to side, back to front, through the windows, the walls and above the ceiling.

Pastor Mann wipes his face and continues, "This is the greatest story ever told. You might find it unbelievable but that's alright, He knows when we sleep and He awakes us too. He also knows we have dreams that fade away, But God, somebody say But God, He will bring remembrance to your dreams and your dreams become real, but still you may not believe. Consider Mary, the mother to be of Jesus, visited by an Angel of the Lord while she was awake. Angel Gabriel tells Mary she is anointed by the Holy Spirit of God, to literally be pregnant with the Word of God, and give birth to a baby you will name Jesus. Mother Mary did say unto the Angel behold, the handmaid of the Lord, be it unto me, according to thy word."

"Hallelujah!" shouts the Church.

"Joseph, who is to be the father of Jesus on Earth, had his fit of unbelief in the story of his soon to be wife, who was now pregnant," Pastor Mann states. "But Joseph, in his righteousness, did not want to harm her, or see any harm come to her, Joseph planned to let Mary go away without a scandal on her or her family, he was protecting her, though confused by her pregnancy. But God, sent the Angel Gabriel to visit his dream, and tell him the Holy Child to be born of Mary was conceived by the Holy Spirit. By faith, Joseph believed the Spirit of God, and was instructed what to do and when to do it, listening to God, knowing his voice. We've got to stay with God, and see the light of His Salvation shine over the issues in our lives, and see the daily bread. Lead us, not into temptation but deliver us from Evil. Church, are we ready to believe by faith?"

The Church says, "Yes!"

"It's good that you say yes," replies Pastor Mann. "Because our faith is announced to the Evil King on Earth. Don't worry, by faith we see that Jesus is the Star light over the world."

Pastor Mann says, "By faith, you will have faith through life's tribulations. By faith you will see that Jesus has kept you, and given you sweet dreams to help you walk through the valley of the shadow of death. Matthew 2 verse 10 reads, When they saw the star, they rejoiced with exceeding great joy." Pastor Mann continues, "Oh come ye, oh come ye to Bethlehem, Glory to the newborn King, Christ thy Savior is born!" Pastor Mann looks at the Deacons, who are standing saying Amen, then says, "Jesus was intentional. He came to Earth under the threat of death from King Herod, who ordered all male babies born during this time, be killed. The Evil King was intent on stopping our Salvation on Earth, to prevent us from getting to Heaven. But God, by Jesus, Mary, and Joseph, blocked his plan. Jesus Christ is our branch from Heaven on the tree of life, that reaches to me and you. Jesus Christ is our Evergreen Christmas tree! Thank you Deacons, for putting spiritual wood on the fire. Let's have a Christmas morning church service this year," he said looking around the Sanctuary: Then continues to say, "Let's praise Him, our praise is treasure, oh come ye all faithful, joyful and triumphant, won't you come."

Pastor Mann turns and looks at the choir, who rise to their feet, then turns back to the Sanctuary and says, "Don't worry if you can't remember your dreams, The Holy Spirit of Jesus will bring your memory back, like treasure that you stored in Heaven, where no Evil can touch it, no thief can steal it, and its value will remain forever.

"Jesus was to be dead on arrival to Earth, but by dreams, He tells you where he will be, and by dreams, He ordered your steps through the Valley. Matthew 2 verse 12 reads, And being warned of God in a dream that they should not return to Herod, they departed another way." Pastor Mann continues, "Jesus made true the scriptures that said the Messiah will be called a Nazarene. These things were made known by The Holy Spirit." Pastor Mann lifts his arm to the congregation, and the choir director lifts his arm to the Choir. Pastor says,

"In closing Church, Jesus Christ will come to you and say, do you remember me."

The Choir echoes Pastor in the style of a Jill Scott poem, singing, "Do... you, re... mem, ber... me. "

The Sunday before Christmas Day is always filled with hope and a belief that joy will come on Christmas morning. This Christmas, Pastor Mann wants a Christmas morning Worship Service. The Deacons, Officers, Staff and North Star Baptist Church Congregation agree it's time to open. The Church is usually closed on Christmas Day, except the ministry outreach groups. Clergy and Staff are encouraged to enjoy a day with their families, without the preparation for a service, unless Christmas falls on a Sunday.

The people are not in a hurry to leave the Church today. One is Andy Fergusson, a guest of Nickolas Kingsly. Nickolas invited Mr. Fergusson, a Business Engineer, to visit the Church during last night's community center Christmas party. He won The Star in the Village Award, presented for excellent volunteer charity work.

Andy Fergusson says to Nickolas, "Thank you for your invitation to visit, and for taking time out to introduce me to your pastor. I feel welcome, and I enjoyed the service."

"You are welcomed Mr. Fergusson. I'm glad we talked last night. Congratulations again on your award," Nickolas says while waving to his wife and in-laws who are talking to Deacon Peoples.

Andy Fergusson says, "That's fine Mr. Kingsly, it gives me time to tell you something that crossed my mind during the sermon."

"Do tell," Nickolas quickly replies.

Andy Fergusson continues, "Pastor Mann mentioned that the church will have service on Christmas Day, and me loving numbers, I 've come across a mathematical equation that figures out the occasions Christmas falls on a Sunday."

Nickolas states, "Christmas on a Sunday? I've never really thought about that."

Andy Fergusson says, "Christmas on a Sunday can be seen on the calendar when it is based on a 28-year cycle and broken down into a

11, 6, 5, 6-year pattern. In this case, I've based it on 1994. The mathematics used are fascinating. If you and the Pastor would like, I'll make sure you get the article."

"Please do Mr. Fergusson, I'm interested, and I think Pastor Mann would be also."

The receiving line is filled with families, friends and out of town guests that are waiting patiently for Pastor Mann to emerge from his office, after cooling down from the Service. Pastor Mann greeted each person that waited, many stating they will return on Christmas, including Mr. Andy Fergusson.

Marie Davis was happy to be pressed into duty, and drive Mary and the children home, giving husband Matthew Sr. time to discuss becoming a deacon, Nickolas will drive him home.

Nickolas says to his wife, "Mary, I should be home about an hour after you get there. You guys go ahead and eat dinner, I will eat soon as I get home.

Mary replies, "This is great news for Matt, he is ready for elevation in the Church."

Christmas time is here, we'll be drawing near, oh that we, could always see, such spirit though out the year.

North Star Village is a picture-perfect Christmas town, waiting for snowflakes to fall, and like memories they do come down. The scene is something you would see within a snow globe after shaking it. Look again and see the hopes and dreams of New Adam and Christmas Eve.

Nickolas Kingsly is a man with a plan, happy that he setup a new Holiday work schedule, and even though it means his day begins an hour earlier, it's a cool perk on a cold Monday morning.

The Winter air makes your feet move quickly, as Mr. and Mrs. set out to conquer the day.

Mary is the driver, but she still found time to make her husband a sausage sandwich before taking him to work. His mid-morning break will be tasty for the co-workers too, who will all get to share three bags of bagels.

Nickolas gets to enjoy hot coffee from his to go cup, as the wife steers the van merrily on down the stream. The drive into work meets with the break of dawns early light, and it all causes him to say, "I love that smile on your face honey. Thanks for the bagels and my sandwich. I feel sorry that the weekend went by so fast, but I did get to take you out on the town.

Mary blushes and her dimples pop right on out of her cheeks when she says, "Mr. Kingsly, I love the way you love me, but the party ain't over yet. We've got New Year's Eve, plus my job is having our first after Christmas, Christmas party on MLK weekend."

Nickolas takes in a deep breath and states to his wife, "So this is how the early birds look. It is different than my normal morning rush, and I could get used to this light traffic. It's not heavy like it will be in an hour."

Nickolas, looking at his wife says, "Mary, I just got a flash back of you at the community center Christmas party wearing your red dress, and now seeing you in the light of the sunrise is beautiful. You are a daydream, but I have got to wake up and put my mind on work. We are almost there, and this is Christmas week.

"Thank you baebee, you know I love you," Mary says with a smile. "This will help you focus on work, after I come back to pick you up, we will go and pick Marion up from her job."

Mother Mary Kingsly continues, "Don't worry about the boys, Simon has a plan to keep himself and Chris busy. He says they are going sledding on Crestview Hill, he will boil hot dogs and have some hot chocolate for their lunch, then watch the College Football Bowl games.

There are just a few moments left in this happiness, togetherness, peacefulness ride into town. They simultaneously choose to listen to the sound of silence.

Mary pulls up to the N. O. Chance Financial Agency, then with a kiss says, "Have a great day."

"You have a great day also," Nickolas says bouncing into the cold with a smile. "See you later."

And the Melody still lingers on...

NOELLE OSCAR CHANCE JR. is well-rested when he hears the alarm on his clock, even though it was set an hour earlier than usual, but there's something wrong because the bedroom is pitch black. It seems to be a power outage. He begins to feel better when the darkness gives way to a light from the digital display, on the clock radio that reads 5:30am. Noelle awakes with a clear head, but he is not in his right mind, again failing to give thanks for a brand-new day. It's an old habit, and he will not change his ways but a change for a Chance gonna come.

Noelle fails to count his blessings, and he has developed another bad habit of challenging those who pray for his turn around. He continually says, "Don't worry about me, look at my financial success. I'm not worried because God knows my heart." But a change for a Chance gonna come.

Noelle walks over to the bedroom window, opening the blinds to see what he can see but all is dark. "That's damn strange," he says out loud, then looking back at the clock light, it disappears. Noelle's heart is beating fast now, and adrenaline pumps his muscles up but there's no use for the fight or flight reflex, he can't see anything to fight and there's nowhere to run.

"Calm down El," Noelle encourages himself, "There must be a power outage," said breathing heavy. Then he sees brightness outside of the bedroom door and walks towards the light.

"I don't know what light that is," Noelle says, moving slowly to the bedroom door. Then he follows the light through the house, to the front door that's lit all the way around the frame, and slowly opens the door to see a bright light down the hall.

"That's damn strange" Noelle says again, and suddenly fear tingles his spine, then he feels something is pushing him into the lobby. The spirit of the night is giving him something he can feel.

Noelle is now scared for his life. Things have changed in the blink of an eye and he panics, screaming out hello, and somebody help me. Then the light forms a Star shape and hangs in the air. The Star shaped light floats until it appears to sit on the top of a Christmas tree. There it twinkles for a moment before falling to the ground and rolling around as a ball of light that mesmerizes Noelle, as it changes to a light sitting on top of a lighthouse.

Noelle knows the Lighthouse light is a warning to him, like it is to ships passing by in the night, signaling danger is near. The lighthouse light falls to the floor, then begins rolling towards him, bouncing as it gets closer. It aims to hit his face but stops at the edge of his nose. Noelle has closed his eyes, prepared to get hit, but it doesn't happen. When he reopens his eyes there are pretty brown eyes, staring back at him. Noelle jumps back, but quickly realizes the eyes belong to a beautiful face of a woman, and mesmerized again he begins to stare. Then just as he was about to speak, the pretty brown eyes turn golden. The golden light fades until the time on the clock comes into focus, and the time moves from 5:30 to 5:31am, "All that in a minute?" he says.

Noelle should get the clue that he's going through life with his eyes shut, but he can't see past the end of his nose and forgets what has just happened, saying, "Let me get out of this bed. That was just my imagination, running away with me. "Bah humbug" he says as he jumps out of the bed, walks over to the window and opens the blinds to see it's still dark. But the Christmas lights shine in the courtyard in a way he hadn't noticed before, they seem to twinkle like little stars.

Noelle says, "The power of a hot shower is just the ticket for me to start the day. Then 10-hours of work and a few more days, before this commercial Christmas madness ends.

# Chapter 12

## *New Adam And Christmas Eve*

### Abraham, Isaac

> And the spirit of the LORD shall rest upon him, the spirit of wisdom and understanding, the spirit of counsel and might, the spirit of knowledge and of the fear of the LORD;
>
> —ISAIAH 11:2

The Pied piper shows the way to a brand-new day, blowing a horn that says redemption is one day away and everybody the whole world over is ready to play. The child within us all comes out to find 100 ways, for eleven pipers to be piping on Christmas Eve.

Mama may have, Papa may have, but God bless the child that's got his own. And a child shall lead them. Christopher Timothy Kingsly, in dress rehearsal for Christmas morning, woke up at 5:55am ready to open gifts, but he knows he must wait until 6, it is a Kingsly family rule.

Christopher gets out of his bed and runs to the Christmas tree to see if any more gifts are there to see, but there are the same number as before, none fewer and no more. He sits still in the dark room with thoughts of Christmas past. Maybe for the older ones, the year went fast, but for the young, 364 days have taken a long time to pass, and there's just one more day.

The Christmas tree is a beautiful sight, tonight the tree lights will stay on until the late day. Christopher takes another look back in time, only seeing the good things that Christmas Eve brings to him. Memories of past Christmas mornings, when Mom and Dad would still be asleep, and he runs to the tree in stocking feet, but not today. Today, Christmas Present is hours away and Dad is up early, and he sees his youngest child by the Christmas tree.

Turning on the living room lights Nickolas says, "Good morning son, welcome to a new day." His voice brings calm to Christopher, not startled by the surprise, he just opens his eyes.

"Good morning to you Daddy, Merry Christmas Eve," says Christopher.

"Merry Christmas Eve to you," but it sounds like angels singing because Mommy and Daddy say it together, their voices echoing through the room.

"That was cool" Christopher says. "You guys make a good team. I can't wait for tomorrow but I'm going back to bed. See you after you get off work Daddy," that said and practice being done, the youngest son runs back to his bedroom.

Simon Kingsly thinks he is too old for that kind of fun. He's done it before but seeing his brother all excited, reminds him of the joy of Christmas once more.

"Hey Chris," Simon says with one eye open, "I remember I used to practice on Christmas Eve. I still love Christmas. Did I hear you talking to Dad?"

"Mom and Dad are in the living room Sy man. I think I'm going to love Christmas forever," Pausing for a moment, Christopher says, "I'll be ready for tomorrow morning, but right now I'm going back to sleep. I bet you after we open one gift tonight, you will be ready for Christmas too."

"You're probably right, Chris, Simon says, closing his eyes. "Tomorrow you might beat me to the Christmas tree, but today I will be first to get back to sleep."

Nickolas says,"Honey you can tell Marion that I will pick her up from work tonight? It should work out fine because afterwork, I'm going to do my Christmas Eve shopping for bargains thing."

Mary replies, "I love you for keeping traditions alive. With Simon graduating from High School, and Marion one year older, this Christmas our children aren't so young anymore."

Nickolas says, "But they all look forward to hot chocolate and opening a gift on Christmas Eve."

Mary does not have to work today and plans to get right back into her warm bed. She's awake to see her husband off to work, but sitting together on the couch, they hug in the quiet moment. Husband and wife take advantage of the peace that Christmas Eve brings before daylight moves darkness from their living room. It's an early Christmas gift, sealed with a kiss.

Mary says, "I will tell Marion you're going to pick her up tonight and remember Nick, her store closes at 6, then she will be out of there by 6:30. Marion is a worker, let's keep praying and work together to get her a car. "You know her she won't let just anyone bring her home. She does not have a steady boyfriend but I don't think that's going to last much longer. There's a nice young man paying attention to her, I won't be surprised to see him at our Christmas church service."

"Our Christmas Eve tradition to open a gift will have two additions, Simon was asked to wait until tonight to open the envelope from his friend Ameenah, and Marion received an envelope from a male friend, who also asked her not to open it until tonight."

Anyways, Mary continues, "Auntie Marie is off today and so is Matt. They offered to take Marion to work, we'll pile into their truck, drop Marion off, then go to Market City Plaza, so me and my sister can keep our own Christmas Eve tradition alive. It will be fun, for us to be together, and we get to show Stephanie, Matt Jr., Simon, and Chris how we do it.

"Sounds like fun beautiful one. Oh look, I've got one mistletoe left to hang"says Nickolas as he stands up from the couch and says, "Mrs. Mary Kingsly, I want us to hang all the mistletoe", holding Mistletoe over his head, he continues, "I'll have my coffee to go, breakfast can wait."

~

Barry Bridgeman made haste from his hometown, driving through Holiday traffic to be with Jalisa and his children, who are in North Star Village with the In-Laws. Everyone was smiles and laughter when he arrived safely. Barry catches up quickly to the joy of family being together. It's easy to see the Grandparents are overjoyed to be spending Christmas with their Grandchildren. Jalisa is thankful that all are together. After the children go to bed, Barry, and Jacob Sr., find their way into the study to enjoy some Eggnog, while the ladies make their way into Jalisa's bedroom for a mother, daughter chat. Eventually they all meet in the kitchen. The kitchen table holds up under every conversation, but time waits for no one, this day ends, so Christmas Eve can begin.

The Eve of Christmas Eve marches like a toy soldier to its midnight demise, when one second past midnight Christmas Eve Day arrives. Jacob Sr., says, "Hey guys, you can stay up if you want to but I'm getting up a little early, and the clock is telling me to go to bed. Barry the stores will be open by 8 in the morning, let's get out there early, find some Christmas Eve bargains and any last-minute things we'll need."

Barry looks at the clock on the wall and says, "I had no idea it was after midnight G-Daddy," his nickname for his father-in-law. "I have got to go to bed now, so I can be ready to go with you."

Holly replies quickly, "Barry sleep in, I know you are tired from such a long day of work and driving here. You guys should be alright, if you get to whatever store you're going to by 10. Jalisa, I'm making pancakes for my grandbabies, so I will be up early with them."

"Thanks mom," Jalisa says while getting up from the table. "I will help you cook our Christmas dinner. Dad, you and Barry can bring back some Pizza's for our Christmas Eve party."

Barry, getting up with his wife says,thank you Mama G," his nickname for his mother-in-law, and G-Daddy" he says reaching out to shake his father-in-law's hand. "Goodnight to you both and see you in the morning."

~

NOELLE JR. HAS FOUND a complacency with being alone, a forced loneliness he seems to enjoy by constantly alienating people with his crude attitude, and a sarcastic wit that's nearly unbearable. Noelle cannot hear himself and believes his wit is useful in all conversations, but this state of mind only shows how little he cares, because he doesn't have a hearing problem.

Noelle does have a problem listening, and he doesn't listen to the groans of his soul whimpering, tortured by misdeeds of greed, yet rarely does he lose any sleep. Another day, another dollar dominates his thoughts that drain through his brain, perking like coffee in a money-making pot.

The smell of more money keeps him pouring hot new schemes, and when told a rich man cannot buy his way into Heaven, it's something he can't hear. Noelle says, "God knows my heart, more money until death do us part, Christmas Eve is just another day with an early start," This is said as a strange dream ends and his eyelid's part. Noelle awakens to a new day with that same old feeling, but today, he rises out of his bed with the joy of a child who will run to see what's for him under the Christmas tree. It's a shame that no one will see this momentary joy even misplaced, because he thinks he's won the race, and this is the last day of his Christmas wait.

Noelle only wants Christmas out of the way. He gets no satisfaction, missing the true present the gift of the new day is, and he gets sad, then gets mad, it's only Christmas Eve. Christmas is still a day away; the new day provides another smooth sleigh ride to work and life has a lot to say but Noelle is not listening. He does notice the morning traffic and realizes the business world has just a few hours left in it before everything stops for Christmas. Time is running out. Soon everyone will go home, even if going home is only in your dreams. Noelle is first in the office again, it's a home away from home, a welcome sight to replace being home alone. His cold heart has few hot spots, but this place is one. This place is where he got his start, if all good times must come to an end, this place is where it began. In this place it happened, then he lost his best friend. Thinking back is not a remedy to cure the past, or a means to deal with the present, it can blind you and give you future shock, but this doesn't stop Noelle from looking into the past.

Many years ago, the business was named Cashe and Chance Financial Agency. Khole Cashe and Noelle Oscar Chance Jr., have put work into their dreams, calling that work faith but can't find the reasons, or see God's Blessings in their success, gaining the world, but losing their souls. Cashe and Chance didn't check themselves, they wrecked themselves in the ways they got rich, and instead of joy and happiness, they have hearts of no repentance. When you get it wrong, it won't last long. They built tax shelters that rub pennies together and makes them shine like dimes.

Noelle doesn't remember well, his partner getting sick, Khole Cashe worked himself thin until the bitter end. Noelle didn't understand why his business partner kept saying he had wasted time and had nothing to show for his life. He couldn't understand why Khole Cashe began to call him church boy, or why he kept asking him about church. Khole Cashe began to talk about church a lot and he began to say, "No Chance you know the way to church? You can take me there," but he died before he would see that day. These thoughts are echoes in the hallway, as Noelle says to the wind, "I'm still working hard, like we always did my friend," said still standing in the doorway. He closes the office door, turns on the lights and heads to his office chair, then silence brings an uneasy peace, once he sits there.

A joyful noise can be heard in the hallway approaching the office door and Noelle Chance won't be alone anymore, as Kristen and Nickolas enter the room. If doom was there, it leaves fast. Kristen is filled with joy and happiness that will follow her through the day, and the world will suffer the children who are excited to say, Santa Claus is coming to town in just one day. Santa is a myth that delivers good things from his sleigh to children of all ages. There's always something to be found for grownups who have lost their joy along the way, and their frowns are turned upside down, now smiles take their place.

"Good morning Mr. Chance, it's Christmas Eve," says a smiling Kristen Flowers, standing at the office door of the boss. She continues to say "The heat feels really good. Jack frost is nipping at noses and toes, I'm going to turn the music on and get this business day party started."

Noelle looks at his secretary with amazement. She lights up the room with energy and causes the boss to snap out of his gaze, and he says, "Miss Flowers, I almost forgot it's Christmas Eve, but merry or not, this thing is almost over, and as for me and my house, not a moment too soon," then Noelle laughs and laughs at his own joke.

"Mr. Chance," Kristen says without hesitation, "this is the best Christmas ever. I'm going to turn on some Christmas music and get the breakroom setup for our staff meeting. Please don't sit in here all morning alone, we have bagels, pastries and of course coffee," said as she turns to leave the room, passing by Nickolas, who is standing in the doorway waiting to join their conversation.

"Good morning Mr. Chance," Nickolas says, like he's addressing the church before the deacons' devotional. "I had a spectacular drive into work, this mornings' sunshine was a hidden perk of starting our new Holiday schedule," said as co-workers enter the office.

"Good day Kingsly," is Noelle's emotionless reply. "I missed the big event of the sunrise, maybe later on this week I will catch it, or not. I thank you and Miss Flowers for making sure we have coffee and cakes. Enjoy your morning meeting, I will be in here working."

"Mr. Chance do come over to the breakroom for our breakfast and let me remind you now that we will be meeting after lunch, to discuss our best clients." Nickolas pauses, then says, "Please join us and share your ideas, it will be our windup session."

"Alright Kingsly, Noelle barks his reply. "I will join that meeting, but now I have some work to do, please close my door." he said as Christmas music begins to play on the office sound system. "No way!" says Noelle. "No Christmas music for me today, changing his personal music to Jazz."

Working like a beaver, is the clever deal weaver, in his unassuming role as the Holiday Season deceiver, who sits in his office alone, quiet as a Monk, until he hears the reminiscent sounds of Alvin and the Chipmunks. Christmas past, knocks on the doors in his mind, with thoughts that are riders in the storm for a man who would forget the bad, if he could.

Joy flourishes outside of Noelle's office, but there's something about Christmas Eve that he blocks out of his mind. Something from the past, yet he can feel it in the air. Noelle, looking at his Gucci gold pocket watch, says it's about lunch time.

Noelle calls his secretary at the front desk and says, "Miss Flowers, I'm going to leave the office shortly for lunch, I will be gone for about an hour."

"Very well Mr. Chance." Kristen replies, and she continues to say, "I just want to remind you that the staff is staying in the office for lunch today. We have a deli platter, pasta salad, meatballs, and for dessert there's Lemon poundcake and Neapolitan ice cream."

"That sounds good Miss Flowers, but I will be eating out. I'm leaving shortly, so goodbye for now." says Noelle, then as he puts his coat on the phone intercom buzzes, "Yes Miss Flowers,". he says

"Mr. Chance, Jacob Jr. is on line 3."

"Thank you. I will be leaving after I get off the phone." is Noelle's sharp reply.

"Hello JJ, is everything alright?" says Noelle with a concerned voice.

"Uncle El," Jacob Jr. excitedly states, "I was calling to speak to Kristen, but first I had to talk to you. I'm looking forward to seeing you and the rest of the family tomorrow. I love Christmas time, and this Christmas will be a special Christmas for me."

"JJ," Noelle says elevating his voice, "I am glad that you are happy, I'm glad that the family will get together too, but I have been reminded constantly and it is getting on my nerves. I understand the fuss, everybody loves to get gifts and stuff, but I'm not caught up in the fantasy anymore and with a little luck, you will get as old as me, then Christmas will become old hat."

"I pray Christmas will never become old hat for me;" Jacob Jr. says, "It just keeps on getting better and I pray for you to find the Christmas spirit and someone to share your life with like I have found with Kristen. Thank you for accepting our relationship Uncle El, I have said it before, but it means a lot to us. We have come a long way since meeting at Sylvia's Coffee and Cakes, I'm glad you told me to go there when you did, that's the day I saw her there and that's the day we began to talk. I don't believe in luck, I call it spiritual coincidence, because the timing was perfect." There's a long pause when Jacob stops talking, Noelle doesn't know what to say.

Jacob laughs and says, "Actually meeting Kristen was no chance."

Noelle finally replies, "Okay, nephew, you had me going for a minute. I'm just a little worn out by the Holiday Season. It seems to me that it began way back in October."

Jacob replies, "No problem, Uncle El, everything will work out, because you've got soul power. I know you're on your way to lunch, so let me get out of your way, see you tomorrow."

"Thanks for calling me JJ, you know how to cheer an old man up. I'm going to eat lunch at Sylvia's Coffee and Cakes, in honor of your relationship," Noelle says sincerely. "Goodbye for now."

Lunch time is over when Noelle returns to the office. The staff is preparing to end their workday and since he did not want a secret Santa giveaway, food will serve as a gift to the whole staff. Nickolas, "Saint Nick" Kingsly has made working on Christmas Eve an enjoyable task through the years, even with a disagreeable boss. There are now 10-hours until midnight, the Christmas countdown has begun.

Noelle stops at the front desk and says, "Miss Flowers have I received any phone calls?" said while looking around at his happy employees.

"No sir, actually the call from your nephew was the last call we've had today" Kristen says

"It was great to hear from him," Noelle replies. "He called me right on time and cheered me up, he does seem to be a happy camper. He speaks highly of you, it seems you're a good couple and have passed the honeymoon stage," then Noelle says sarcastically, "Let's keep hope alive, shall we?"

Kristen, knowing her boss well, quickly states, "Mr. Chance, Jacob Jr. is a good man, this will be our first Christmas Eve celebration together, and we are excited."

Noelle shakes his head no and sighs heavily.

Kristen continues to say, "Well, even if you've lost that loving feeling, you didn't take it away from your nephew today."

Nickolas works his way over to the front desk to speak to the boss and says, "Mr. Chance we are preparing for our end of the day meeting, are you going to join in?"

"I think I will Kingsly, let me go to my office, and I will join you in a few minutes." says Noelle.

Kristen looks at Nickolas and says, "Thank you Mr. Kingsly, your timing is impeccable."

"I know dealing with Mr. Chance is a challenge, Miss Flowers, and more so now that you date his nephew. Let me tell you my first Christmas with my girlfriend, who is my wife now, was great!" Nickolas states with joy. "I pray with you and for you to have wonderful Christmas moments."

The meeting goes well after a gruff start by the boss. Noelle's story telling centered on his client acquisition strategy with North Star Cadillac, and receiving the Businessman of the Year Award, but he does commend the staff before retreating to his personal office sanctuary.

Nickolas leads the staff in applauding the boss, then picks the next one to speak, saying he will close the meeting. Great stories were told about Food Truck Friday, Black Friday, the 7$^{th}$ day of Christmas office party and step dancing at the community center party. The highlight of the meeting was provided by Kristen speaking about Nickolas. She made it plain about how much he helps each employee accomplish their goals, and proudly proclaimed that their Office Manager is now a deacon.

Speech, speech... speech, everyone says in unison like a Chic Cheer.

In the blink of an eye, the sweet Spirit of Christmas makes its final turn toward the finish line and brings with it more of everything the season stands for. The Spirit falls on the happy and the sad, the joyful or the mad, it also falls on believers and nonbelievers. The Christmas moment is a gift that comes within the spirit of the wind. Where it comes from no one knows, where it goes nobody can follow, but when it comes it is always on time, giving a feeling that lasts a lifetime.

The world will come to know the truth at the discretion of the giver of all things, each person receiving, according to the talents given, measured onto them by the Lord. Kristen Flowers feels it in this place, and it exceeds anticipation, yet there are still 9-hours until midnight, it is time to go home, but first a word from the man, of the moment.

Nickolas Kingsly, the man of the moment states, "Although it's been said many times many ways, Merry Christmas to you." smiling as everyone gently laughs with him. Thanks again for making our holiday work schedule a success. I remind you that our workday will begin at 11am on the day after Christmas. Let's get out of here now and enjoy what's left of the daylight on this Christmas Eve. May you all be blessed with a double portion this Christmas, let's go home.

Noelle Oscar Chance Jr., stands in his office doorway watching his employees gather their belongings and head out the front door with no pomp and circumstance to their exit, except smiling faces and hands that wave goodbye.

Last but not least, Nikolas adds a sonic tonic to the goodbyes and his voice echoes when he says, "Good night Mr. Chance, Happy Holiday," closing the door behind him.

The next sound heard are shoes tapping their happy beat down the hallway, then immediately a strange peace falls on Noelle, who exhales and slowly walks around the quiet office. He begins to focus on the soft sounds of Jazz playing out of his office, again there's no rush to go home. Noelle sits down at his desk to work on new business schemes, working like it's a new day, pulling out the files of potential clients he can call, but not to say Merry Christmas, it is to remind them to make an appointment to see him in the New Year.

Time waits for no one, now 8-hours until the midnight hour when the myth of Santa Claus comes tumbling down the chimneys of the world to meet the truth of Christmas Day.

Noelle picks up his phone but instead of a dial tone, it is the voice of the Security guard,

"Hello Mr. Chance, this is Coleman at the front desk. It's quite a coincidence that you picked up the phone soon as I called. I called to find out how long you plan on staying in the office tonight."

Noelle replies, "Coleman, you startled me, your voice reminds me of a friend from long ago. He always asked me how long I planned on staying in the office. I'm sure you want to close up and be on your merry way, I plan to leave by 6pm".

"Fine Mr. Chance." Coleman replies quickly in a reassuring voice, "I want you to know that snow is beginning to fall, and I will be escorting you to your car."

"That's very good of you Coleman. I will alert you when I'm ready to leave, goodbye for now." Noelle says, walking to his office window to see the snow fall, which is always a Christmas Eve dream come true for young and old, who want to see snow on Christmas morning.

Shake a Christmas snow globe and you will see what captivates Noelle's eyes, as snowflakes are falling majestically on North Star Village. Look and see big feathery flakes of snow, each with its own purpose, fall into perfect place. Noelle watches a beautiful moment that could melt the heart of frosty the snowman, but for him it reveals loneliness, and what the lonely do at Christmas.

Noelle waits patiently for the radio to play another song, and instead of taking it as a clue to go home, he sits in his chair staring into the air. Silence sounds like the wind blowing softly, then there is a whisper in the air that clearly says;

*Hello my old friend,*
*I've come to talk with you again,*
*because a vision softly creeping*
*left its seeds while I was sleeping,*
*and the vision that was planted in my brain,*
*still remains.*
*Within the sound, of silence.*

Noelle thinks he hears the whisper as a familiar classic song from Simon & Garfunkel, but the sound of silence returns, and he waits for music. And time marches on, as a neon purple haze lights the room, but these tidings are not meant for comfort and joy. They accent the absence of noise. Noelle stops breathing and listens to the sound of silence, as the room becomes black and so dark, he cannot tell if his eyes are open or shut.

"Are you ready to give in?" says the whisper in the wind.

Noelle can't breathe, and the sound of silence grows.

The silence is broken, the whisper tickling Noelle's ear speaks clearly, Oscar, Oscar, Oscar, you have no fear of death that is so near, you walk through the valley of death, as we all must do, but the road you are on my friend is the road to Hell. I had good intentions Mr. No Chance. The road to Hell is paved with good intentions. Now you must breathe again, don't be like me, I died in this office on Christmas Eve. Please my friend, wake up and breathe.

Noelle unaware, breathes again and says, "Why is it so dark, and why do you whisper in my ear? Let me turn on some light, so I can see who I hear."

"Noelle, Noelle," the voice in the dark did say, "you walk in the dark with your eyes open wide, but you cannot tell the difference between the dark and the light. The light you see is false and based in darkness, it could only carry you this far."

Noelle demands, "Who are you? you sound familiar, but I can't see you, we have no light."

"It is me Mr. No Chance, it is Khole Cashe, I who gave you that nickname, and now you are determined to follow in my footsteps, even into death on Christmas Eve."

"Alright that's it, Noelle exclaims loudly, reaching out to touch his desk phone, he calls for the Security Guard, who answers saying, "Hello Mr. Chance," but he cannot hear Noelle's frantic reply.

"Come to my office right now. I have an intruder. Hello, Coleman can you hear me?."

"Oscar, Oscar, Oscar, calm down. No one can hear you but me. It's my job to get you off of this path you are on." Darkness fades away, becoming purple neon light that strikes the image of Mr. Khole Cashe. The light illuminates his unique head and shoulders, that he always held high. It looks like Max Headroom and the image sings.

*"Mama may have,*
*Popa may have,*
*but God bless the child*
*who's got his own...*
*faith."*

No longer singing, the image of Khole Cashe says, "I am here to tell you that, by the grace of other people's prayers."

He laughs. So does Noelle remembering how they would laugh together when they made money. Khole Cashe called it their Mo Money laugh.

Noelle states, "Why am I laughing with a dead man who scares the crap out of me in the dark?"

The image of Khole Cashe states, "You always had a smart mouth. So witty. So check this out. You are being saved by other people's prayers. So I'm saying, 'Are you down with O.P.P?'

"You get it? Other people's prayers," said laughing harder. But Noelle has stopped laughing and silence returns.

The image of Khole Cashe says, "You down with O.P.P?, Yeah you better be," said laughing again, until the laugh echoes into silence, and his face becomes a bright light.

The voice of Khole Cashe comes forth from the flashlight face to say, "Do I have your attention Noelle Oscar Chance Jr.? You have ignored my warnings by signs and wonders, at the Casino and the Masquerade Ball. On each occasion you explained the close encounter as a coincidence, but now by other people's prayers," Khole Cashe sings, *"I know a place, let me take you there."*

Noelle sees the Casino valet parking attendant and shouts, "I know you man."

"Sir, my name is Cole Bucks, you said I look like your long-lost friend, let me get closer to you."

Noelle is whisked back to his car in the blink of an eye, and he lets down the power window to reach out towards the light, which gets so bright he has to cover his eyes.

Silence returns and the light goes away and once again it gets pitch black. "Khole," Noelle says in a frightened voice, "I want this to stop, I have had enough."

"Open your eyes," says the familiar voice of his former business partner. Look out the window at the beauty of North Star Village at

Christmas time. I ran away from Christmas back then, but oh... how I love Christmas now."

Noelle, standing in the light of his office, looks into the snow falling outside his window, and notices his reflection in the window. It's the first time he sees that he looks sad.

"Khole Cashe, why did you have to leave me," Noelle says. "I gave up so much for this business. You were the only one that understood." He looks around to find that he is alone.

The booming voice of Khole Cashe jumps out of the radio speakers, sounding like a game booth attendant at an amusement park saying, "I tried to get away, but I couldn't get far. The man with repossession papers took my heart. He said, 'time's up'.

"It was on Christmas Eve, Mr. No Chance and other people's prayers could get me a reprieve my Brother. You got to get your own.

A Sparrow flies up to the office window and hovers in front of Noelle. He takes his eye off of the bird, breaking the vision, ending the truth or consequences trial from his unseen accuser. Everything fades to black. Noelle has to swallow this bitter pill.

The voice of Khole Cashe breaks through the black silence saying, "Mr. No Chance, this is not where you want to be. This is absolute zero."

A bright light appears over Noelle's head, but it is like nothing he has seen before. He hears machine gunfire, and a new voice yells out.

"Buffalo soldiers... incoming, take cover."

Noelle, is now looking through another man's eyes and he sees a black man say, If I don't make it back, you make it back home and live your best life."

He sees the faces of bravery and hears the faith of war heroes. Then comes the sound of another rocket, but adrenaline takes away all fear. Through these eyes, with these ears, he sees a hand pull dog tags out that read Avery O. Chance. The hand kisses the dog tags and waits for an explosion that hits sending shrapnel through the air. A purple rain on Black Forrest.

Noelle says, "My Grandad received a Purple Heart for an injury in a different attack. My God war is hell." Then all goes black. Noelle Jr., has walked a mile in his Granddaddy's shoes.

The next voice he hears sounds just like his daddy, but it's granddaddy Avery. Noelle Jr., shakes with fear when he hears him say, "Oh father, I pray to make it back to the States and have a child. It can be a son or daughter, that doesn't matter... in the name of Jesus Christ, I pray."

Granddaddy Avery's face is lit in soft sunlight. He is facing the sun and stands face to face to his grandson in the mist of the Black Forrest of Germany, during WWII. The sound of silence now contains war memories of a loved one. The quiet is broken when granddad Avery says, "What you gonna' do?"

Darkness returns, it looks like another love TKO, but there's a light that appears at the end of a tunnel.

It's the light of a pleasant memory. Noelle kept his promise to attend a family Christmas tradition, to eat dinner together on December 7th Pearl Harbor Day. The day of Infamy. Noelle joins his mother and father, sister and brother-in-law Jacob Evergreen Sr., to honor Daddy Chance. A Vietnam veteran and granddad Avery Oscar Chance. A World War II Veteran.

No longer in darkness, out of the tunnel and into the light of his office, the voice of Khole Cashe says, "Welcome back from heartache Mr. No. But it's time for you to let go of the past. You asked me why did I leave you? I will tell you this, I thought just like you think, that I could control my life, but I was wrong. And you are wrong too.

"It was my time to go, and I had neglected the truth of life. You were the only one who could stand being around me."

Khole Cashe comes into clear view sitting across the desk from Noelle. He looks great in a two-piece grey suit, white shirt, and charcoal color tie.

Noelle says, "I don't know what's happening, but grey suits were our business uniforms back in the day. We wore grey suits almost every day. Tell me cash money; a nickname for his former partner, why you doing this to me man? I thought we were friends."

Khole Cashe begins to get visibly tired. He folds his arms and lays his head on the desk. With a weary voice says, "I regret dying here on Christmas Eve, and that you had to find me like that on Christmas morning.

"I am here to save myself by telling you to save yourself. Put Mr. No behind you. He is a monster consuming your soul. I woke you out of a dead sleep because I want you to live again! You have got to fight the power, and don't ever give up."

"This is not real. It's happening because of the pressure Christmas time puts on everything. People everywhere are going around making themselves crazy over a fairytale. I never talk about you dying in this office on Christmas Eve.

"No one has been able to explain it to me. I mean you were a relatively healthy man; it was just bad luck that your heart stopped." Noelle continues to say in a huff, "I don't believe in Christmas, and I don't believe in all that baby Jesus in a manger stuff or the ho... ho... ho... Santa Claus story either. I'm smart enough to know it's all foolery."

Noelle Oscar Chance Jr., "It's new Adam and Christmas Eve for you," says Khole Cashe raising his voice but his head lays on his folded arms. In a whisper he says, "Now I lay me down to sleep, I pray the Lord my soul to keep."

The room returns to purple neon lights and the image of Khole Cashe, framed in dark purple neon light, is now standing in front of Noelle. He sounds like a classic Army Drill Sergeant when he says, "Mr. No, tonight is your night. For after midnight three spirits will come to test your heart, soul and strength.

"As I have tested your mind, there will be nowhere for you to run, and there will be nowhere for you to hide."

The neon lights frame the walls and begin to move in unison with the lights on Khole Cashe, pulsating with his voice. "The Spirits will be in the wind. What time they come to you and when they go, of that you will have no control." He laughs in loud echoes, that turn into thunder and lightning flashes as the purple rain falls. The voice of Khole Cashe returns, singing in a downbeat. "Noelle, Noelle the Angels did say, you could dance underwater, and not get wet today."

"Mr. No. Do I have your attention?" comes the voice of Khole Cashe.

Noelle shouts out, "Yes... you have my attention."

"The Angels will visit you just as I have, whether they are good or bad depends on you. I have done all that I can do. In 7-hours it will be midnight. Take my advice, to get out of the dark you got to walk in the light." His voice fades away into the sound of silence.

A sound of feet tapping a quick beat can be heard in the hallway. They sound like they are approaching the office. Noelle walks towards the front door, then runs as fast as he can, gasping for air as he gets there, saying, "This must be the way out of a bad daydream." He swings the door open, sees a big man that scares him, so he yells out, "Hey!"

Coleman emerges in the doorway having turned the doorknob at the same time it swung open. "Thank goodness it's you," Noelle says running out of breath. "I should have known it was you with those loud shoes on. Did the lights go out in the whole building?"

Coleman replies, "No sir. No problem with the lights at all. We've had smooth sailing since all the employees left at three. I apologize for giving you a fright, but I prepared myself to be here late with you, then you called and said you would be ready to leave at five. Here I am."

"I called you alright," Noelle says, "but I did not get through. I must have fallen asleep and the sound of your shoes tapping in the hallway woke me up."

"My shoes are the same as the last time you said you heard something in the hallway. I always wear soft sole shoes. Maybe it was something you heard on your radio Mr. Chance. It was pretty loud when you called me," Coleman says pausing before he continues, "Sir, Merry Christmas. I'm here to walk you to your car. It's just me and you left in the building."

Noelle replies, "Yes of course. Merry Christmas so says you. I don't remember much, although I do recall trying to call for a Security Guard. I must have fallen asleep at my desk waiting for you to answer the phone. That little nap was a daytime nightmare. Let me get my coat and turn off the lights so we both can go home."

Coleman, who knows to leave well enough alone states, "Don't rush Mr. Chance, it's now time to relax and enjoy the peace that is on the way."

Noelle and Coleman are the picture of opposite emotions for Christmas, and it is easy to see as they walk through the snow flurries to their cars. Coleman is excited and filled with cheer, while Noelle has a bothered look on his face and downgrades what he calls, the commercial holiday.

The Christmas story is the greatest story ever told. Some have to wait longer than others, but all will see that the North Star, which shined so bright on that silent night in the little town called Bethlehem, is the light of the world.

God Bless all the families in the world that struggle through the Christmas Season, not everyone is joyful on Christmas Eve, but the miracle of Christmas has its own way of making believers out of non-believers. It is a gift. North, East, South, West, it's a wonder, who does Christmas Best.

~

ALL IS WELL and getting better by the minute for Jacob Evergreen Jr., and around the world. The Island of Kiribati, called Christmas Island, is first in the world to celebrate Christmas. Christmas Island is located in the South Pacific Ocean, the inhabitants are the first to celebrate the new day, New Year's Eve and New Year's Day. It's the 11th day of Christmas and true love is in the company of Kristen Flowers, as Jacob Jr. prepares to serve dinner at his place.

The air is filled with an excitement only Christmas Eve can bring, made better by a song Jacob Jr. has in his heart.

The "Christmas Love" CD is playing on the stereo, as he sits across the kitchen table from the woman who inspires him to believe in love. This Christmas love flows in a breeze, which blows by and tickles Kristen's ears with sweet whispers, then begins to sing,

*"I walk into the Mall and saw ya doing your Christmas shopping... I caught you in the toy department... We met under the mistletoe, and I kissed you... and... whoa we fell in love... and it's our first Christmas."*

The Alexander O'Neil song plays along with the easy conversation of a power couple in the making. Dinner for two is chicken alfredo with spinach and hot buttered biscuits. Chocolate strawberry mousse cup will be served for dessert. Le Crema Pinot Noir Red Wine is chilling to enhance the aftertaste.

Kristen is blushing when she says, "JJ, did you make this meal, or did you order it? I ask because it is really good."

Jacob Jr., smiles confidently when he says, "I prepared the menu for our evening together. I wanted you to know that your man can handle pots and pans. I hope you like what I chose for dessert. I know you like chocolate and strawberries, so I got the dessert from the supermarket."

"That sounds delicious. You make our first Christmas together feel like a fairytale," says Kristen.

Jacob has the look of love in his eyes and a smooth tongue, "Thank you babe. I love Christmas and want you to enjoy yourself. After dinner we can have dessert in the living room by the tree."

Dinner comes out better than Jacob could have dreamed. Everything was done right and as they move into the living room, Kristen takes a look at the developing snowstorm."

"I want to introduce you to an Evergreen family tradition of opening one gift on Christmas Eve," Jacob says, barely containing his excitement.

"Aww... that is really sweet of you JJ. Your gifts are under the tree at my place. I'm glad I brought your Christmas card with me; I didn't know what to expect," says Kristen, "but I like it."

Snowflakes float through the air, weaving distinctive patterns as

Kristen watches them from the living room window. One after the other they dash through the snow, putting on a snow show.

One large snowflake looks like a heart, as it twirls like an ice skater in the sky. The snow dance momentarily catches Kristen's eye and she says, "JJ, this is a magical night. Snow is perfect for Christmas Eve. I remember when I was a kid, I always hoped for snow on this day.

"I am thrilled. Thank you for a delicious dinner and dessert. They were perfect. I'm already beginning to miss the time we have already shared tonight, but tomorrow will be even better, right?"

Jacob gets up from the couch and heads toward the Christmas tree, but Kristen is stuck in the moment, forgetting that he wants her to open a gift. She notices him standing by the tree.

"Jacob Jr.," says Kristy, "I want you to open a gift."

"I love opening Christmas gifts," is Kristen's excited reply.

Jacob hands her a beautifully wrapped gift about the size of a box of chocolates that she quickly begins tearing the wrapping paper off. She sees an elegant silver and gold box tied in a red bow.

"What is this"? she says with a big smile. Opening the box there are twelve Hershey's chocolate kisses sitting on the top of a red envelope, covered in red Rose petals.

Kristen puzzled by an empty box, reads the card that says, *Just look over your shoulders honey*.

She looks but doesn't see Jacob and thinks he is hiding behind the couch. She turns again to find Jacob Evergreen Jr. on bended knee, arms stretched forward. An open box in hand that reveals a fine... golden... ring.

Blushing as a would-be bride, she inhales deeply. The pause adds dramatic effect to the moment, when she says, "Is this what I think it is?"

Her eyes filled with tears of joy, sparkle brighter than the pear shape diamond engagement ring that twinkles in the lights.

"Kristen Precious Flowers, I love you," says Jacob. "Let's talk about our lives together as one. Let's plan our future. I want to get to know you better this Christmas, and for the rest of our life."

Kristen, shaking her head yes says, "Baby, you had me at hello!"

Jacob laughing with joy says, "Wait let me finish. I talked to your mother and father, who gave me their blessings and said, just be sure. Babe, I'm sure. Will you Marry me?"

Snowflakes of love are dancing in the air, putting on a Christmas Eve show for the citizens of North Star Village. The show enliven hopes, dreams and wishes on their way towards Christmas Day, which is now just a few hours away.

Chocolate kisses under the mistletoe is the celebration of love, as the stereo matches the lovefest with the song 'Snowbound,' by Fourplay. And the nearly-weds talk about a New Year September to remember, and their big Christmas Day announcement.

CHRISTMAS IS the crown jewel of the Winter Solstice festival in the Northern Hemisphere, and it is celebrated in all seasons and climates around the world. North Star Village beckons the heart to dance like it's the first time you fell in love.

The first-time love dance for Nickolas Kingsly, is now his wife Mary and their children young and old. They have made it once again to Christmas Eve, and they celebrate by singing Christmas songs before opening one gift. It's a family tradition.

Christopher wants everyone to sing 'Santa Claus is Coming to Town.'

Marion gets the family to sing, 'Jingle Bells'.

Simon says, "Feliz Navidad. Let me teach you the words to a Christmas song by Jose Feliciano called 'Feliz Navidad', which is Spanish for Merry Christmas.

"The song goes, *Feliz Navidad, Prospero Ano ye Felicidad*, which means Merry Christmas, a prosperous year and happiness. Then we sing, I want to wish you a Merry Christmas from the bottom of my heart," then Simon leads the family through the song.

Mother and father get the family to sing their favorite song, 'We wish you a Merry Christmas.'

Nickolas and Mary watch and pray, putting up the good fight for everyone's health, wellness, and continued success. I'll be home for Christmas is always a loving thought, there's no place like home to click your heels on Christmas Eve and traditional celebrations help families thrive.

This Christmas is very special, Christopher will soon be a teenager, Simon is sharing his first Christmas with a girlfriend and Marion believes God will send her the right man, in time.

"It's time to open one gift before it gets too late," Nickolas says. "Tomorrow the Church will have a Christmas service that begins at 10am. I will have breakfast ready by 7:30."

Christopher excitedly says, "Mommy, will you open your gift first," pulling her hand as they walk over to the Christmas tree. He then hands her a small beautifully wrapped gift box.

Mother Mary Kingsly recognizes the penmanship of her daughter on the note card placed on top of the gift. "Merry Christmas from all of us, we love you like a rock Mom," Mary says in a huff.

"What's this you guys," tearing off the wrapping paper to reveal a beautiful box case. She thinks it's a watch but it's a Mother's ring and she gasps covering her mouth.

"This is beautiful. It has all of your birthstones together. I love you all," she says. "I couldn't ask for a better gift," as the children get a group hug, but dad gets a kiss, mistletoe not necessary.

Nickolas, regaining his composure after a great kiss, says, "Merry Christmas to the Mommy. Okay gang who is next?"

"You Daddy," everyone says in chorus.

Marion pulls a gift out from under the Christmas tree and says, "Dad, this gift is from us all. We love you and appreciate all you do for the family."

Nickolas shakes the box and laughs saying, "I don't know why I still shake gift boxes. I have a little kid inside of me at Christmas time." said while ripping off the wrapping paper. It reveals a note card on the box that reads, 'this white dress shirt, gold African Kente necktie, matching handkerchief and tie clip will Jazz you up. Merry Christmas to our Jazzy Dad'.

Nickolas marvels at his gift and says, "African Kente. My goodness, I'm going to sound corny, but this is just what I wanted. You guys really are something else. Thank you."

The family finds themselves in another group hug. Then Nickolas says, "I give the next gift to Simon."

"Thank you, Daddy," Simon replies, The gift is the same size as the one just opened by his dad. It's beautifully wrapped and Simon wastes no time tearing the paper off and finds a note card on top of the box. Simon says, "I want to read this note card out loud."

Then he says, "To Simon from Mom and Dad. Merry Christmas son. You make us proud parents. Enjoy your senior year in High School. Don't worry about your future. The Lord will provide. He is a Way maker."

Simon pauses struck by emotion and says, "Wow, I just saw memories of so many Christmases flash by. Let me open my gift."

Simon pulls out a black dress shirt and an orange necktie with a matching bowtie. These are my school colors. Thank you, Mom, Dad. I'm going to sound just like you, but this is what I wanted," said with the same little boy smile from Christmas's past.

Simon is ready for Christmas; he can't wait to open the envelope he received after his date with Ameenah Mauritius. He promised not to open it until Christmas Eve, but family first. Simon says "Mom... it's just you and I left to choose a gift for Marion and for Chris."

Mary says, "Well I will go first," selecting a gift for her daughter. It's the same size of box she opened to start the festivities, but it's wrapped in elegant red and silver snowflake themed paper, tied with a red bow on top and a name card that reads, Marion.

"Thanks Mom, I probably would have picked this one to open

tonight," Marion says, gently pulling the bow off and reading the card. "It says, to our first child, a beautiful baby girl from Heaven. Marion, we love you. Merry Christmas. Mom and Dad."

Marion hugs her mother and father before she opens the gift, then says, "I don't know what this is. The card is great," said opening her gift neatly. She sees a pretty silver gift box and imagines it to be a watch.

She's surprised to see a Heart and Rose Locket necklace, that sparkles as she pulls it out of the case.

"Mom. Dad, this is beautiful. It really is just what I wanted. Mom, help me put it on. I've gotta' see it in my mirror. I will be right back, to see Chris open his gift."

Christopher Kingsly, the youngest of the crew and still everyone's sweetheart uses up the last bit of patience he has, waiting to open his gift. Then Marion comes running back to the room.

Chris looks to his brother and says, "Sy man, you can pick out my present now."

Simon gets the feeling this Christmas captures the last of their childhood innocence, as he pulls a gift from under the Christmas tree and hands it over to his little Brother.

Christopher tears the wrapping paper off of his gift and seamlessly opens it in one motion. The note card inside the box reads, *Merry Christmas Chris, from all of us. We love you.*

Christopher cheers when he sees a cell phone and says, "Sy man, you helped me get my own house key and now my first cell phone. You are too cool," said as they do their handshake.

Simon says, "Chris, Mom and Dad agreed that it is time for you to have your own phone, so Marion helped. We picked this one for you. We will help you with it, but I want you to read the instructions and learn the features for yourself."

"I will," Christopher says. He runs to hug Marion, Mom and Dad, and says, "I can't wait to show cousin Stephanie, Aunt Marie, Uncle Matt, and Matt Jr. my phone tomorrow. I can't wait to open more presents."

Mary says. "Alright Chris, we've all had a long day and need to get as much sleep as we can. We know you will be up early in the morning."

"Wait a minute. Before everyone goes to their rooms, I want you to know this Christmas is a special one for me," Nickolas states. "It's my first Christmas as a Deacon and looking at you all, it is easy to see that you are growing up. Remember the love we share and these times.

"Marion, I feel this Christmas and the coming New Year will be great for every part of your life.

"Simon, don't worry about college after you graduate, just finish strong and recognize your blessings when they come forth.

"Christopher, your patience, and hard work will get you into a new school. I don't know how but it will work out.

"Mary thank you for being a great mother and wife to me. I love you forever and ever. You have made each Christmas Eve together wonderful."

The last group hug is tighter than it has ever been.

Marion checks in by text with her friends.

Simon keeps reading a Christmas card from his new girlfriend, again and again.

Christopher says he's too excited to sleep, but Christmas Eve wins again. A promise to stay awake until midnight, is a promise he will not be able to keep. Way before the clock strikes twelve, the youngest Kingsly falls fast asleep.

"I'm going to bed old man," Mary says getting up from the couch. "Aren't you glad that this year there will be no staying up way too late to put together someone's present?"

Nikolas chuckles and says, "Yes dear. "We've both done plenty of that over the years. Now we can just look at the pictures." He pauses then says, "I will go to bed soon. I'm going to relax for a moment and stare at our beautiful Christmas tree," said turning the volume up on the stereo just a bit to hear the James Brown classic Christmas song, 'Santa Claus, Go Straight To The Ghetto.'

CHRISTMAS EVE GOES FAST and slow like the year it has taken to reappear, and life changes fast and slow. You can see that in the eyes of children.

Time makes you wait until the midnight hour in high anticipation of a great celebration, as the greatest day of the year goes around the world.

Minutes make up hours and the hours make up days, which make up the twelve months that take a year to come back.

We watch time take its time to get back to this moment. Then we hurry around just to wait for this moment where we stand at the Christmas Eve gate, for a Christmas Day that's got to crawl before it can walk, and walk before it finally runs to the end.

Christmas is a celebration that never gets old. It finds new believers each year that learn the truth of God's gift of love to the world. It's a season you yearn to return, that leaves too soon.

Christmas is the season for hope. It is undeniably in the air everywhere you go, and there's a real sense that peace on earth is imminent. If you stop, look, and listen, you will hear what your heart is saying,

There is another side to the greatest story ever told. Many people miss the ride on this Good Will Express and find themselves on the pain train of low self-esteem from a lack of money, the loss of a loved one or the loss of Spiritual Love.

The love theme of Christmas flows within the sands of these bad times. If you could put time in a bottle, it would flow like grains of sand, falling through an hourglass and there's no countdown until Christmas in this poor condition.

But when you look for Jesus; the Father of our time, there is always hope.

# Chapter 13

## *MAGGIEDOCIOUS WORDETTE*

### Naphtali

> For unto us a child is born, unto us a son is given, and the government shall be upon his shoulder, and his name shall be called Wonderful, Counsellor, The mighty God, The everlasting father, The Prince of Peace.
>
> — ISAIAH 9: 6

Noelle Oscar Chance Jr. has no good will toward men. It's gone with the wind, ashes to ashes, dust to dust, and he refuses to celebrate the Holy Spirit of Christmas. The holiday season cannot be stopped. People all over the world will get onboard the love train and ride the Polar Express non-stop, until the stroke of midnight on Christmas Eve.

Noelle Jr. has lost his cool since his encounter with the Spirit of his former business partner. He regains his composure by driving through North Star Village, listening to jazz on the radio. Noelle is trying to convince himself that his close encounter with a ghost was a daydream, but it's not working, due to the surreal dreamscape of the Christmas Eve snowstorm, putting real dreams in front of the windshield. A tangled web we weave, when at first, we practice to deceive, and the first most tragic victim to deceive, is yourself, when you lie to yourself.

Noelle accomplishes self-deception again, aided by a cold heart he refuses to refresh. He ignores warnings with the help of mirrors, now it's the rear-view mirror in his car. "Mirror, mirror tell me something good," says the well-dressed man. Noelle can't see the blessings of health and wellness in his life, only his financial success, believing that to be luck, or solely the work by man's hands. The mirror of his mind wants him to believe the close encounter was an illusion, a daydream and the ayes have it. He convinces himself the warning received from the spirit of Khole Cashe, was a mind trick, caused by grief from the loss of a friend during a Christmas past.

The drive does kill some time, but in the winter scene of North Star Village California, Christmas the present won't be denied, as the snowflakes hit the windshield, melt, and slide. Then the voice of the DJ stops the escapism ride.

DJ Brother Jazzy says, "You're listening to KNSV, in 5-hours the greatest day of the year takes flight. I'm Brother Jazzy and I'll be your host for a Christmas Eve jazzy breeze right down memory lane until 10pm, then Lola the DJ Angel will entertain your ear until 2am. Don't worry about late night gift wrapping or do it yourself assembly, we will play better music nonstop throughout your Christmas morning." The voice of the DJ pulls Noelle out of the vanity mirror, and he lends an ear, that may save his life.

DJ Brother Jazzy continues, "The rest of my radio show will feature some great Christmas songs, but right now hear this. As the world turns, Christmas will be celebrated around the world. The first people to see the new day, live on the islands in the South Pacific

Ocean and Australia, and onto the Malacca Strait, where the Indian Ocean meets the Pacific.

"We have a 20-hour difference in the Pacific Standard time zone from the first people to see Christmas day, but our time is coming like a high-speed train. Get ready for more, when Les Givings comes in at 6. This is DJ Brother Jazz on KNSV 100 FM, although it's been said many times many ways, Merry Christmas to you. Do you remember September, Earth Wind and Fire sings, remember the 25th day of December," and the song begins to play.

"Do you remember, the 25th night of December,
love was changing the minds of pretenders while chasing the clouds away.
Our hearts were singing,
in the key that our souls were singing,
as we danced in the night remember,
how the stars stole the night away,
ba de ya say do you remember ba de ya dancing in December ba de ya never was a cloudy day."

The music brings Noelle out the mirror trip and off the tracks of despair. He declares, "No way! It's time for me to go home!"

Noelle shakes his head no and his heart says no, while it beats a mix of ice and blood. He does not want to remember dancing in December and replaces those thoughts with thoughts of a soup for one dinner. Noelle will eat alone but he eats well, and he has a late date with the television.

There are no signs of Christmas in Noelle's luxurious home. Once he closes the door, he shuts off most concerns. A man's castle is his home, but no man is Tonga Island. Noelle lives alone, he not only leaves the world outside but has lost that loving feeling for life and for love. The world should be left outside, we all need to recharge in the sanctity of our home. Noelle has become an iceberg of empathy, devoid of funk, R&B, soul, Gospel, Jazz, Rock & Roll, Country, House, or dancing in the key of life.

Noelle loves good music in his house, but it's not good house music that plays. All that you can hear are the blues, because a house is not a home. He says he's not tired of living alone, but his tongue writes a check his heart can't cash. Noelle has lots of money but finds money can't buy you love, and there's no one else in his house, sitting in any of his comfortable chairs. Once upon a time, there was a beautiful girl and talk of marriage, which now is a distant memory, buried by the owner of a lonely heart. Love is a battlefield of casualties, where thoughts of cash rules everything around him, along with a materialistic logic, that fights off anyone that gets too close.

Noelle Oscar Chance Jr. listens well to the mirror that says not to feel sorry for me, home cooking and eating for one is not a humdrum affair, not for breakfast, lunch or tonight's dinner that consists of a Prime Rib and Broccolini main course, with Figgie pudding for dessert.

Noelle is not celebrating the Holiday, but you can't tell by his menu. "I'm ready to toast the end of Christmas." he says aloud, as he pours a glass of Brandy and continues, "I will not miss you when you end, and every time you come back, I shall be as glad to see you leave again. I do not consider you my friend, is the toast he drinks to, before walking to his favorite comfortable chair.

"No radio for me tonight, I don't want to hear Christmas songs at all. I will watch some TV or let the TV watch me." Noelle says resting his head, before he goes to bed.

It's 11pm, time moves towards midnight without fanfare, lest you consider the fine pajama set and smoking jacket Noelle wears. With a big yawn Noelle says, "Time for me to go to bed," He turns off the Living room TV, then the peace that comes before Christmas rushes in, surpassing all understanding, and all through the house it takes over, of that there is no doubt.

"I'll watch a movie from my bed and put all bad thoughts out of my head, if I didn't have to go to Christmas dinner, I'd stay in all day and have breakfast and lunch in bed. I would rather miss the whole Christmas Day." says Noelle pulling the covers up to his head and falling asleep to a movie scene of people boarding a train. He imagines them to be a group of black men of a certain age, all dressed in black suits and sunshine yellow shirts, with sky blue neckties that sparkle as they begin singing in harmony.

*"People get ready... there's a train coming... you don't need no ticket, you just get on board..."*

Noelle falls into a peaceful sleep, and a smile replaces his perpetual frown. Then it's the midnight ride that the whole world reveres, hate it or love it, Christmas time is here. Christmas is an Alpha and Omega experience for all to see. The one-day in which time seems to stand still, and run from its midnight beginning, until its midnight ending 24 hours later.

Noelle could not stay awake to see time move effortlessly into the new day, which starts as all others do, in the dark of night. But on this night, it is the Christmas lights that brighten the way for hopes, dreams and miracles, seen and unseen, like no other can or ever will. Parents suffer the children to stay up late so they will sleep all night, then they can turn into Christmas workers and work into the night, putting together new toys for the children's delight, wrapping gifts and we call it wrappers delight. Mommy and Daddy's Christmas rap is different from house to house. To each his own if it's not mine to have, it's not mine to own. Say a prayer for the children, God Bless the Child and God Bless the grown, for someday at Christmas each one will come to the meaning of the holiday, on their own.

Noelle has been asleep for three hours, and not one dream to disturb him has come. It is so quiet you can hear the planet softly moving through the air, a safe and restful sleep into nowhere land.

Noelle hears a horn blowing softly in the jasmine of his mind, it's the sound of a train horn in the distance that begins to disturb his subconscious, but he doesn't wakeup. The horn blows again, this time it is close. Noelle is awakened by the sound of loud thunder, followed by the sound of horns blowing in rhythm, with bass and drums. To him it sounds like a neighbor is having a party.

Noelle snaps off his covers, sits on the side of the bed, saying to himself, "Is someone having a Christmas party? They have lost their daggone mind. I'm going to kick someone right in their Christmas behind." says Noelle in a heated rush, as he storms out of bed, puts on his housecoat, and heads out of the bedroom to the front door and out into the hallway, looking to bang on the door of any neighbor that dares to be so rude.

"Who has the audacity to play music so loudly?" Noelle says. But now he hears no evil, sees no evil and can speak no evil, for it's a silent night, a holy night and he just stands in his townhouse hallway listening, but there's no music playing, and no one is stirring about. In his mind, there is a doubt fire of burning questions? Noelle can't believe he heard nothing at all and continues to walk down the hall, inspecting it for clues, like a child that's looking for proof of reindeers, Santa's helpers, or Santa Claus. However, Noelle only finds Christmas decorations and twinkling Christmas lights.

I was sleeping well; it must have been a dream. I know my neighbors would not play their music like that, I'm going back to bed. Then as he turns, he sees a man standing behind him and it scares him so much he jumps and punches the air. Then Noelle screams, "Who the hell are you!!"

"You don't need no ticket, just get on board, says a man sounding like the Godfather of soul James Brown, dressed in a blue Conductor suit, shirt, and tie with a blue Dress hat, styled like a Conductors hat.

Noelle, who is ready to run through the man to get back to his front door, says, "Man you scared me good, sneaking up on me like that.

The Conductor says, "Sir, whatever you do, don't step on these Blue Suede Boots.

Noelle turns away and finds his bed is in the middle of the hallway. He is stunned in dis-belief.

The Conductor says, "Look it here, I've got something up my

sleeve," then pulls out a rolled-up piece of paper, unrolls it and begins to proclaim, "Hear ye, hear ye, a poem, Spoken Word by MAGGIEDOCIOUS WORDETTE she calls it IF," and then he reads what was up his sleeve.

"IF WE COULD BE *free and tranquil;*
*to really know right from wrong;*
*to open up our hearts to each other, instead of our fists;*
*to look at a smile and not through it;*
*to look not at color, but just the people we are;*
*to realize that we are not here to defeat,*
*but rather to accomplish;*
*to fall, but keep going;*
*to know joy and not sadness;*
*to know love without the pain;*
*to be satisfied and content;*
*to see the beauties of God around us;*
*to let the living live;*
*to show the evil, good.*
*if we could do all these things,*
*"IF" would be none."*

The Conductor says again, "Hear ye, hear ye, are you ready for the Night Train?"

"Yeah!" comes forth a reply sounding like a crowd, and a train horn blows, and Noelle jumps again, as many men appear in the hallway at the other end.

"Are you ready for the Night Train!!" The Conductor screams again. The Many Men say "Yeah!"

The Conductor says, "Night... The Many Men say... Train... Night... Train... Night... Train...," moving in step to the beat their shoes tap clackity clack, sounding like a train rolling on the track.

The Conductor yells out, "All aboard the night train, and the saints come marching in," then he continues to say, "She is the Queen of yesterday's dreams, say ouch if she steps on your toes. She is so pretty, her skin glows and her Afro flows, don't tell no lies cause she already knows, shaped like Africa, her body goes, and when she speaks, it's always in prose.

The drummers drum, and the horns blow as The Conductor says, "Introducing to some but presenting to you, it's the hardest working woman in past Christmas stuff, sho-nuff it's MAGGIEDOCIOUS.

"That's the music I heard in my hallway, that's the music that woke me up!" Noelle says. Then she appears, it's MAGGIEDOCIOUS.

All Noelle can do is stare at the beautiful woman dressed in red wool slacks, black turtleneck sweater, green suede sport coat, big hoop earrings, red, black, and green big bead necklace, with matching wristlets and African bangle bracelets from wrist to hands, she's right on the scene.

MAGGIEDOCIOUS has a hip down for the cause attitude and a sweet Jackson 5 Afro. "Just to see her takes Noelle from a scared place to a sacred place.

"I know that beat your band is playing." Noelle says.

MAGGIEDOCIUS speaks like she's teaching a class on poetry slam. She performs with the fire of a warrior princess, inspired by Coffey Brown and she says, "Look it here, you are an L7 square," and she raises her right hand in the air, then the music stops, and everyone turns toward her to listen. She points at Noelle and speaks, "You have forgotten about Christmas past you dig, and I'll take you there, said with a smile on her face. She continues, "You have already met The Conductor, he gave you a Cameo. Hush your fuss 'bout the beat, it's Cameosis, a song that used to move your feet, but now baebee, it's a song 'bout me."

Noelle backs up and sits on his bed, closing his eyes, shaking his head, then he remembers what Khole Cashe said. It is at that moment, MAGGIEDOCIOUS taps his forehead and speaks, "On the twelfth day of Christmas, true love gave to me, twelve drummers drumming, eleven pipers piping, lords a-leaping, ladies dancing and MAGGIEDOCIOUS WORDETTE.

Noelle Chance Jr., takes a deep breath and pulls courage into his chest saying, "I was told today that there would be a test, but I don't believe all of this mess."

MAGGIEDOCIOUS speaks, "Ready or not, believe it or not, I'm the Ghost of Christmas Past and this train is non-stop. Now dig this look back and don't you cry, those crocodile tears are living a lie, and away we go. One if by land, two if by sea, 1776 running a Boston in Spades party with me. Let's look into your Crispus Attucks, to find Mr. No on your brain, it's your soul we must re-train, drop squad you back in the everlasting game. To the rear, march, back into Christmas of past times, bout the time when you were nine."

Noelle boldly says, "I was a kid then and I'm a man now, a grown man. I don't believe in Santa Claus or a Savior, no more poetry Maggie, for me it's wakeup time. If you were real and you're not, you should know that Christmas is a Pagan ritual and God knows my heart.

"Band!" MAGGIEDOCIOUS speaks raising her right hand, "This ole man don't know who I am, tell him."

The drums and the horns play together and the beat drops, as The Many Men march toward Noelle and circle his bed to the beat. The Conductor reappears and moves his feet. The Many Men begin to leap, and land in front of Noelle in his bed, this is what they said in Cameosis harmony.

MAGGIEDOCIOUS... MAGGIEDOCIOUS... MAGGIEDOCIOUS... MAGGIEDOCIOUS... The bed starts to spin, Noelle gets scared again, as he pleads MAGGIEDOCIOUS what do I do.

MAGGIECOCIOUS speaks, "Hold my hand, touch my ring, and listen close to what they sing...

"If when you feel it... then you'll know it... it won't be long... you will all be strong with... dig the sound, dig the sound... dig it with me... you can't believe it... if you try... you will do it... Everything goes black, then light comes back to reveal Noelle and his sister waiting at the top of the stairs, early on a Christmas morning in the past, and MAGGIEDOCIOUS lets Noelle see."

MAGGIEDOCIOUS speaks, "You grew up in a beautiful home, I see that you were not alone."

Noelle says, "Is that me?" looking at himself back in time. He sees himself at 9-years old and he sees his beloved big sister.

"Holly, is it time to open the presents!" young Noelle asks excitedly. Holly is excited too, but she says, "Mom and Dad said we can't go downstairs until 6."

"Well, look at the clock again," young Noelle says. Then the downstairs radio clock alarm, set for 6, comes on playing the Alvin and the Chipmunks Christmas song. "It's time!" young Noelle says, racing to the Christmas tree to open the first present he sees with his name on it, with his sister right behind. The kitchen table has a platter full of fruits and nuts, a must for every Chance Christmas.

Standing on the outside looking at this joyful memory, Noelle laughs as he sees himself opening presents and expressing happiness, realizing he got his wish for a toy. He sees little big Sister joyful too, when her wish for a Sewing machine came true.

MAGGIEDOCIOUS speaks, "The look in your eyes tell a story of love for your family. I can see your sister's love for you too. There's a whole lotta love coming through, but what's love got to do with it, you might ask. Your mother introduced love to your heart, a love she received from her mother and father, and Our father who art in Heaven, the warmth should melt your icy ways."

The view from this Christmas past changes. MAGGIEDOUCIOUS rearranges things, so the view comes straight at Noelle, and she speaks, "See your mother coming down the stairs? She is on her way to Christmas Sunday Sunrise Service, pressed in all white, she's an angel in flight."

Noelle hears his mother say, "Be quick but don't hurry, that's what my Mama used to say, pray about everything, and don't worry about the day. Mother Isabella Chance is ready to go, and her children run to hug her, then they say, "Thank you Mom. This is the best Christmas ever!"

Mother Chance says, "I got to warm up the car, I'm glad it didn't snow."

MAGGIEDOCIOUS speaks, "Look at your Mama and what do you see? I see a God-fearing woman who taught you right from wrong. She is beautiful, ain't she fine? Well you think you're rich today Mr. No, but look at a mother's love, it didn't cost you a dime. Cool boy, golden rule boy, Mama and Daddy sent you to Sunday school boy, take a good look at this scene, it won't last, say yes to the future, don't get stuck in the past."

MAGGIEDOCIOUS speaks, "Noelle run to the house, run real fast, get one last look at your mother, Father and Sister my brother, in the past," MAGGIEDOCIOUS laughs then speaks "on second thought, checking the list twice shows you to be naughty and not nice." Then as Noelle gets to the front door, MAGGIEDOCIOUS moves the years to a different old scene. Noelle sees pictures of his past life moving fast forward, like a video and thinks of the power it takes to connect distinctive moments over the years. He was happy the snapshots stop moving at last.

Noelle now stands before a 100-inch TV screen, which shows a luscious green garden scene.

The voice of The Conductor returns to say, "Follow the flight of the butterfly from flower to flower. Out of its cocoon, it finds the way to power, giving, taking, and making more flowers that find more butterflies, and more flower power, while teaching you to keep your eye on the prize. Hear ye, a spoken word from MAGGIEDOUCIOUS WORDETTE titled The Butterfly Effect."

The voice of MAGGIEDOUCIOUS speaks, "The double gift of perception and understanding are a reality mercifully given in small sips. Floodgates are momentarily opened, for a sip stuns, like a deer can't run, stunned, looking at oncoming headlights, stuck in a moment that would run it over. But the moment passes over, the hit is missed, and you are made aware how unaware you are of an angels' intervention. In a fight for your soul, the prayers of the righteous avails much for the unaware, but God bless the child who has his own prayers. Praying for others as they pray for you, within this duality, you can perceive the mercy and grace of your daily flight through this life. To be the butterfly is the desired effect, and as a butterfly takes a reality sip, and the vanity of your beauty gives way to your spiritual duty to honor the flowers in the garden with your prayer power. Doing this with respect, the butterfly effect impacts all flowers, within the power given to you by the lily in the valley. The power of the butterfly is sufficient in its subtleties to effect all."

Everything goes black again, then The Conductor's voice whispers, "LET THERE BE LIGHT." And there was light, and with the light came a new Christmas day from the past, and there's a new outfit for MAGGADOCIOUS WORDETTE.

The Grand Diva wears money green patent leather ankle boots, matching leather gloves with Jade earrings to complement her Lemon Grass color double breasted white pinstripe suit. She walks the walk and talks the talk like Kathleen Clever, looking like a cool cat, smooth as a black Panther.

Noelle looks at MAGGIEDOCIOUS and says, "I've seen enough of Christmas past, why are we still at my childhood home?" Please leave me alone and let all this trickery stop.

A Christmas song plays on the radio. "We wish you a Merry Christmas, we wish you a Merry Christmas, we wish you a Merry Christmas and a happy New Year, good tidings we bring to you and your kin, we wish you a Merry Christmas and a happy New Year. Oh, bring us a figgy pudding; oh, bring us a figgy pudding; oh, bring us a figgy pudding; and a cup of good cheer."

It could be the times, it could be the wine, it could be lost threads that connect a million synapsis of a mind, or Noelle as Sleeping Beauty can see hindsight is 20/20, now awakened by a sweet MAGGIEDOCIOUS kiss. Noelle knows Christmas past he can't redo, and knowledge should be wisdom, from the view of the past but now arriving fast, new memories seen on track number 2.

Noelle now believes the warning he got from Khole Cashe. The rewind on his mind was unkind to truths he wanted to leave behind. Now he stands in front of the living room window from his childhood home. It's a few years after the first view of Christmas Past. Noelle is temporarily lost in space, and everybody knows a mind is a terrible thing to waste. The "We Wish You A Merry Christmas" song, is part of a TV commercial, and part of a sweet memory.

Noelle remembers the time, because the whole Chance family watched the premier broadcast of the popular all black cast TV show Good Times, and their Christmas show. The show was one of a kind, as the entire Cast was featured singing and performing in a Christmas musical.

Noelle gets a sip of reality, looking at this Christmas view through the window. Like he dreamed he would window shop at Macy's New York, then he says, "Watching that show with the family was fun, but I outgrew Christmas by then. I was already 18-years old, I just watched that show with everybody because I was on my way to a party."

MAGGIEDOCIOUS switches the scene, to a time when Noelle Jr.'s mouth got mean, and she speaks, "GROWING, I met you again years later, we greeted each other with joy and surprise. We spoke, I did not know this person, I thought, I looked into his eyes, and knew, I saw that person years later."

Noelle, in a Christmas Past, sits alone with his mother in the living room and has something to say. This scene makes him shake his head no, and he begs MAGGIEDOCIUS, take the view away.

MAGGIEDOCIOUS speaks, "No way!"

Mother Chance says, "Alright Noelle Oscar Chance Jr., what's on your mind?"

Noelle replies, "Mom thanks for not making me go to church anymore. I appreciate that you and Dad are standing by what you said, that after I was 16 years old, I had to go once a month, then after I turned 18, that I could go or not as I want. Please don't be hurt by this, I'm going to be okay. I thought it was causing tension between us. I believe in God, but not all that Church stuff and the commercial Christmas stuff of buy this or buy that. And that baby in a manger stuff? Mom, that is for kids."

Mother Chance says, "I have done the best I can for you and your sister, I hope you appreciate that. As for the Lord and church, He will call you to Him when he chooses. Me and your father pray that you and Holly hear the Lord when He calls you. He has done great things for me."

Noelle interrupts to say, "Yes mom He is God. I will say God made everything and he knows me too. The greatest story ever told stuff. I don't believe that. And Dad hardly ever goes to church."

"Stop right there, young man," Mother Chance says. "Don't make a habit out of interrupting me when I'm talking to you. Your father is a War Veteran, a great husband and Dad. He was baptized before I met him. He believes Jesus is the only begotten Son of God.

Noelle retorts, "But Mom, I'm Baptized."

"El, you were Christened as a baby, but you are not baptized of your own free will. Your father and I agreed that you would have to choose the time, if and when you are ready."

Noelle Jr. had much more to say but MAGGIEDOCIUS speaks, "Not toodae. We're leaving this scene, your 18-year-old self was getting mean, and I snatched the words out yo mouth, snatched you right on out, because mean people are a drag on the ones that love them and that ain't cool at any age. I got one more stop for you to see, going back to love and broken hearts for a business you wanted to start, we're leaving on the Midnight Train, boarding on track number 3.

Noelle begins to pull at the threads of his man-made logic to conceive the infinite possibilities that would explain Khole Cashe and MAGGIEDOCIOUS WORDETTE. Each thread he follows gets lost in the butterfly effect of one action creating a reaction he calls coincidences. This mind set does not explain and can't connect the moment-to-moment purposes of each event, or their cause and effect. The butterfly effect is life flowing minute-to-minute, with the mystery of a cliff hanger. And Noelle hangs off the cliff of time itself, which is over an ocean, that he will fall into. Falling into the water, is the birth of your ripples through time, which we call the butterfly effect, because each ripple becomes the moments of who and where we are in our lives.

These waves are uncontrollable by mans' hands. God works in mysterious ways, His wonders to perform. It is a blessing to see the Hand of God as his divine plan, and not as serendipity.

Noelle cannot plead ignorant on judgement day. He cannot plead ignorant to the teachings received through Ministers of the Gospel and home teaching that showed him Bible chapters and verses, so he could learn it for himself. He has moved on from what he once believed, and turns a blind eye to his neighbor, boasting of his good life. He lives, not by faith, he lives by his works on earth.

But faith without the works of faith, bury your talents that are to shine for the Lord. It is then by your acts, you begin to shine for the Evil One, it is then that your works are dead, being alone. Noelle Jr. knows the Bible verse stating, train up a child in the way he should go, and when he is old, he would not depart from it. A man finds a good thing when he becomes a child of God, understanding what it means to say... when I was a child, I spoke as a child, I thought as a child, I understood as a child but when I became a man, I put away childish things, which is not to confuse the real celebration of baby Jesus born in a manger, with the movie story of Santa Claus.

MAGGIEDOCIOUS speaks, "Dig on this Mr. No, you are mean, hold my hand and touch my ring." They travel forward fast through the times of Noelle's past on a cloud they go until arriving at Graham Central Station in a puff of steam.

MAGGIEDOCIOUS speaks, "The Conductor is here with something to say so let me step right on out the way, I'll be back Mr. No to take you to a place deep in your dreams, let's call it a bachelor's retreat." Noelle is left alone in the empty waiting area of the train station, as he sits down The Conductor reappears standing on a small stage.

The Conductor says, "This is a man's world, but it wouldn't be nothing, without a woman or a girl." The Many Men reappear and The Conductor states! "Fellahs I'm ready to get up and do my thing."

The Many Men reply, "Go head!"

The Conductor says to Noelle, "Hey man, catch this drift cause it's kind of heavy. Think about outer space and how we are able to live in the Universe. Now if you can? Expand your Mind to the outer limits and see that we are astronauts riding on the third rock from the Sun, part of 8 in the Solar system. The rock is called Earth, it's home away from home but we cannot get back to our home, called Heaven, without the permission of the mission chief."

"Who is the mission chief? I'm glad you asked.

"Jesus is the mission chief. He is the connector for us to get back home. He is the apple of God's eye, who created all things and the mission. He is the Eternal Fire that gave Moses our original instructions, called Commandants. He is the flood that carried the Living Waters of Faith down to Noah, who by faith carried the Covenant and the seed of Father Abraham, his son Isaac and the son of Isaac named Jacob, called Israel, as a bridge to the New Covenant."

The Conductor steps off the small stage. The Many Men say, "Go head"

The Conductor says to Noelle, "Get up!" and The Many Men say, "Get on up," and Noelle gets up.

The Conductor says, "Get on the good foot, and listen to me, EVIL will ask you to prove your translation of the Bible, then state you don't know what you're reading or saying. Next question will be, how can you believe in something you can't see? The Holy Ghost does not exist."

The Conductor says, "Christmas has a written history, searchable through 42 Generations!" then says, "Hit me!" and the horns blow, he continues, "Love, let me count the ways, 14 generations, plus 14, plus 14, equals 42 generations found within the first four books of the New Testament in the Holy Bible, person to person, faith to faith. Love, let me count the ways and tell you of the speed of earth as it moves through the Universe is 66 thousand, 6 hundred miles per hour. Earth spins at 1 thousand miles per hour, while tilted perfectly on its axis. Let that enter the sanctum of your mind," and the room becomes quiet. Silence is golden, Noelle's sarcastic wit, in retaliation to any point made is cut off, his indifference too, is gone with the wind.

The wind is Divine intervention, from where it came cannot be perceived, where it goes it cannot be pursued. The effect of the spirit behind the wind is cut out of perfection, then polished by the perfecter to perform a surgery, and cut down to the bone of truth with a double edge sword.

Noelle has forgotten that life is a miracle, perfectly placed within an oxygen rich, perpetuating eco-system, created by the perfect Hand of God. God in all His perfect purposes would not allow the world to be ruled by chance. Noelle is speechless after this sip of reality, he looks like the statue of the Thinking Man, as he attempts to quantify his theory on life. Then he begins believing the truth of what's been said, although he buried the truth under his conscious mind. Now the thinking man wrestles with the facts of the exactness of life on Earth, because the planet could only exist at a perfect distance it is from the Sun, another miracle of life as a Universe traveler.

Noelle has created a false reality of success that allows him to bury thoughts of troubles over the years. Building a false security, gives him a fragile ability to escape anything unpleasant, but denial will give way to the trials of life. What you going to do when they come for you? Troubles of life, and the trials of reality that remove your sense of control. The mystery about the creation of life no longer allows you to think you are in control of anything, because you're not.

Noelle would not believe it to be so, but the prayers of the righteous avails much, and the Chance family prayers stand in the gap for Noelle. To stand in the gap, is to stand by faith and prayer for someone who does not pray, even for themselves, let us pray one for another. The Chastisement of Noelle is the oil of the anointing from the prayers of the righteous, who stand not only for a beloved son, brother, and uncle, but a poor friend. Noelle begins to remember being taught to rejoice in hope, be patient in tribulation and pray consistently. For we need the protection of Angels from the North, South, East, and West to endure the trials and tribulations of life.

The silence is broken, art does imitate life. When MAGGIEDOCIUS WORDETTE re-enters the waiting room in the thinking Woman pose, her dramatic entrance on the stage is framed within a spotlight, directed on her Butterfly loc Afro. The African mother lode is wearing a gold, green, red, black tribal print round neck, sleeveless Maxi Dress, accented by a gold African choker, matching earrings, and bangles.

The Many Men begin snapping their fingers in rhythm. Then MAGGIEDOCIUS speaks, "This ain't reality TV, love is real to me. Let me count the ways sweetheart, of which you broke an angel's heart. On track number three we can see, you back in love again with Milli from the Villi. The waiting room in Graham Central Station, turns into a seat with MAGGIEDOCIOUS on board the lounge car on the midnight train to Eboni Manor.

Noelle replies, "Are you talking about Millicent? Don't show me that, it was a hard decision. I had to leave her, and I would break up with her again to get where I am."

The Conductor appears at the other end of the lounge car, tips his hat and leans out of the door saying, "All aboard the midnight train! Last call, last stop... all aboard!"

"Miss Maggiedocious Wordette," Noelle says with a stern voice, "I believe you've made your point. Right now I am praying for you to leave, and I'll will stay in the real world. Thanks for coming, but by the power of my prayer, I'm not going with you anywhere." Then Noelle begins praying to wake up from a nightmare.

MAGGIEDOCIOUS speaks, "It's good that you remember how to pray, but you are still bound to O.P.P, because the heart to your prayer cannot be found. Even with you on your knees saying please, please, please, please. Open your eyes, look to the hills from whence comes your help."

Noelle opens his eyes to find himself in a train tunnel on the tracks. All that he can see is a big headlight that appears to be standing still until a train horn blows, and it's moving toward him.

MAGGIEDOCIOUS speaks, "Don't look long into the past, or it will catch up to you very fast. The moving light begins to sound like tap dancers, tapping clackity tap, tap, and the closer it gets the better it sounds. Noelle can't get out of the way, not to the left or to the right. Then he sees himself in the headlight talking to Millicent. She looks sad, this Christmas past catches up fast.

MAGGIEDOCIOUS speaks, "You choose to face the past now, which is wise, but realize when you broke Milli's heart, you broke yours too, the light on this train is the truth coming through. In the spirit of Christmas past, I'm here to help you find what you left behind, especially a young lady that had love on her mind. But don't you mistake my kindness for a weakness, you're not the first one to say MAGGIEDOCIOUS, I pray."

Noelle says, "MAGGIEDOCIOUS, I'd rather be with you, sitting on the train of truth, instead of without you standing on the tracks in front of it. Please take me with you to Eboni Manor."

The clackity tap, tap, that sounds like a train on the tracks, turns into The Many Men marching into the lounge car, led by The Conductor with a flashlight pointed towards Noelle's face. He is relieved to see The Conductor and The Many Men. The big light The Conductor carries turns into a silver chain that shines, as he reveals the night sky over the midnight train to Milli Ville.

MAGGIEDOCIOUS and Noelle sit on the right side of the lounge car. She is one seat ahead of him. The Conductor leads everyone in a parade to pass their inspection, stopping and smiling at MAGGIEDOCIOUS WORDETTE, in her African royal splendor. Then he tells a tale.

The Conductor, using a James Brown tone in Spoken Word style, says, "Oh... when you kiss me... when you mess me... hold... my hand... make me understand... I break out... in a cold sweat... then looks at Noelle and says, Mr. No, it's time for you to say yes."

Noelle replies, "Yes! By any means necessary yes, let's be done with the past, I will pass this test."

The Conductor says, "Can I hit it and quit it?" The Many Men say, "Yeah!"

The Conductor spins and goes down to one knee, saying, "Welcome to Eboni Manor, this is all you will see of the night train and me, watch your step on your exit." Then everything fades to black.

Out of darkness, into the light, in which we see young Noelle Jr. in a hug with Millicent Eboni Manor, his love bug, as he is hanging a piece of mistletoe over their heads.

MAGGIEDOCIOUS WORDETTE and Noelle are floating on a white cloud made up of dreams. The cloud floats in front of a Drive-In Movie Theater screen that shows young Noelle Jr. hugging Millicent Manor in the lounge of her Parent's home. He is holding mistletoe over his head and says... hey Milli, I'm sorry I'm late, I wanted to work a little bit longer to impress the boss but it's never too late for a kiss.

Millicent answers her boyfriend with a kiss, then says, "I see you brought your own mistletoe El. It's okay that you are a little late. I told my Parents that you would work overtime, even on Christmas Eve. We are all happy to be together, and your dinner was kept warm."

"Oh, that's good, people get so uptight at this time of the year" Noelle says, "It's not that serious."

"Noelle Chance Jr.!" Millicent quickly replies, "It seems the only thing you take seriously is work. I would like to think you take our relationship seriously. I love you and I want to believe there is a future for us to build together, maybe even buy a house someday."

"Sweetheart, you are beautiful inside and out," says the smooth-talking, Noelle. "I just want to have enough money to take care of us. I don't want to be poor; I just couldn't handle it. I see those guys always behind, oh my, I just don't want to live like that Milli. I love you too much for that." and they kiss again, as Noelle drops the mistletoe on the floor.

"She looks like me!" speaks MAGGIEDOCIOUS WORDETTE. Looking like Milli she says, "Noelle, from here you can go anywhere on the Earth. From here you can be anything you want to be. The past is built into the present, and from here we can build the future, but you can't see the beauty of this loving relationship is to be desired, and you crush it before it starts. Love is nipped in the bud. Your passion fruit withers away like petals on a dying flower, and this is a reason your heart is cold and you would deny Christmas."

MAGGADOCIOUS speaks, "Noel, Noel, Noel, Noel, gone is the tear of regret that just fell. Oh well, in the next blink of your eyes, our cloud will arrive to that priceless place where you and Milli first met. I bet you remember that time." Then Noelle sees Millicent's face when she enters the room for the Price Waterhouse Economics Mentorship Business program.

MAGGIEDOCIOUS and Noelle stand facing the class. Noelle says, "This is damn weird, I have forgotten how pretty Millicent was." Then young Noelle moves in the direction of young Millicent and says, "Hi, how are you doing? My name is Noelle. I had to introduce myself to you so I can focus on this class, and not on you."

Young Millicent replies, "Hello Noelle. My name is Millicent. It is possible that I would have introduced myself to you out of all of these handsome men, so that I could focus on my work and not you?" said with a beautiful smile.

Price Waterhouse walks up to the chatty pair and addressing both says, "Welcome to my Business Mentorship program. I was hoping that you two would meet. I am happy that I don't have to introduce you. I want you both to know I respect your High School and College work. I think you will find that everyone I've selected is talented and focused, please take your seats."

MAGGIEDOCIOUS speaks, "Life can change in the blink of an eye. The help you received from Mr. Waterhouse was not by chance, he engineered an inside track for you to get the top prize, which wasn't top honors in his class. Price Waterhouse is a successful businessman, his wife helps him be great but for you, help from Millicent would not do. Mr. No, I thought you were ready to say yes, but you ran Millicent off before she could pick a Wedding Dress. Parting is such a sweet sorrow, in a wink of the eye tomorrow is just a day away, and you can borrow something blue, they say breaking up is hard to do." MAGGIEDOCIOUS WORDETTE speaks, "Watch this sad goodbye scene, then take it from me, stop being mean."

Noelle is standing alone in the dark with his cell phone in his hand. The screen lights up the dark, to show Noelle and Millicent in a Christmas past, it is their last together.

Millicent and Noelle have their own apartments, they had been a happy couple for two years but that all ended on a Friday night in September. Friday night is date night, but Millicent, seated by the Island Counter in the kitchen, wants to spend part of the night planning a Christmas party for a few couples, and wants to know what days she can plan for, but Noelle has other plans.

Noelle, seated on the couch studying paperwork, doesn't notice Millicent has sat down beside him to ask him for his input. Noelle without emotion says, "Milli, I'm too busy now to consider anything about Christmas, and you should know it's not important enough for me to give up an opportunity to work overtime."

"El, we've been a couple for some time now, and I want to know where I stand with you. I want to believe there is a future for us as a loving couple that works together," says Millicent in a soft tone of voice. Then as she looks at Noelle, her brown eyes fill up with tears, which begin to drop at the sound of his voice.

"Milli we are not in College anymore," Noelle replies. "The Mentor program has given me a chance to make a good living and secure a great lifestyle, but I can't stop now, no way! It seems we want different things out of life, I just can't give up. I thought you would understand because you are a gifted businessperson, and I would never want to hold you back."

"Do you think I'm holding you back Noelle Chance Jr.?" Millicent says, wiping her tears away?

Noelle says, "Milli, I love you. It will work out for us in time. There is no other woman, just give us a few more years." Noelle says, as if negotiating a contract. "I have to dedicate myself if I'm truly going to be a success. I can't worry about social graces and I..."

Millicent Eboni Manor stops Noelle mid-statement and says, "You can't be the man I want, is that what you were going to say? Then she gets up from the couch, reaching her hand out to Noelle, who gets up and they hug and kiss until Millicent says, "What you want I can't give you, and what I want you won't give to me, let's just kiss and say goodbye."

Total darkness returns, as the scene with Millicent fades, and Noelle feels a teardrop fall into oblivion. Then MAGGIEDOCIOUS speaks in a spotlight. "Christmas just ain't Christmas... without the one you love... Christmas just ain't Christmas... without the one you love"

Noelle says, "MAGGIEDOCIOUS what will happen next, I haven't cried in many years. These tears may as well be blood, for all it's doing is making me weak, I feel so tired...

MAGGIEDOCIOUS speaks,

"Shh. Listen. Hear the delicateness, of that tiny tulip whispering in the wind.

Shh. Listen. Hear the quickness of those cars passing by.

Shh Listen. Hear those words of wisdom. Shh. Listen. Hear the baby cry.

Shh. Listen. Hear the sound of silence."

MAGGIEDOCIOUS speaks, "Take my hand, touch my ring, listen to what my band sings,"

They parade by like a dream team, twelve drummers drumming, eleven pipers piping, followed by ladies dancing, lords a-leaping, then once again singing in funky harmony. The band sang,

"MAGGIEDOCIOUS... MAGGIEDOCIOUS... MAGGIEDOCIOUS... MAGGIEDOCIOUS...

If when you feel it... then you'll know it... it won't be long... you will all be strong with... dig the sound, dig the sound... dig it with me... you can't believe it... if you try... you will do it..."

Noelle finds himself in bed, he is desperately trying to wake up from what he thinks is a bad dream, but this intervention comes without a guarantee of awakening. Noelle has a bad habit of holding his breath when he concentrates, then waiting to exhale forgets to breathe again and a breeze tickles his nose, causing him to inhale, then exhale.

Noelle has placed his daily bread into the hands of the Evil One, forgetting that each day is not promised unto the next, but the renewal of his mind must begin down in his soul. The Evil One has taken Noelle's soul down, enticing him to combine the best qualities from multiple religions, like ordering on a spirituality menu from a Faith café, that doesn't serve the Birth of Jesus Christ.

Noelle is hungry for other things than the truth, and multi-spiritual pragmatism destroys his faith, without it you cannot come to Jesus. He must be reminded that sufficient for one day are the tribulations of that day. Tomorrow brings its own troubles that will be sufficient for the new day.

Sleepless in North Star Village, Noelle tosses and turns because of the ghost of Christmas past, but our internal struggles are unnoticed by all but the one who knows when you've been sleeping and knows when you've been awakened to a new day, even when you turn Him away. Salvation cannot be purchased, and Faith is not for sale, but it can be received as a precious gift.

Christmas present is here. The transition onto the truth, like the transfer of guards at the tomb of the Unknown Soldier, is like a test of the Emergency Broadcast System. Had this been an actual emergency, Noelle's pragmatic beliefs would have him stuck in a lie of the deceiver, whose job it is to catch non-believers. Hark the Herald Angel sings, glory to the newborn King, and before his ice-cold heart can melt, Noelle is returned to his previous beliefs, unaware of a test, but more aware of himself.

Now woke, Noelle jumps out of the bed and seeing he is no

longer in the hallway gives a big sigh of relief, then standing in the light from his TV, he sees the movie called The Wiz. It's the movie he fell asleep on, and now blames for his bad dream, seeing that it's playing back-to-back all night. Noelle shuts the TV off and looks at the clock on the wall to see it's 2:55am. Then states, "What a dream that was. I'm going to sit up for a while and keep my eyes open and listen to the radio. I need some Jazz to calm my nerves. "Let me get out of this bedroom and sit in my chair in the Living room, so I can stay woke.

And not one minute too soon for Noelle, Gospel Jazz music takes over the sub-conscious state, providing cover for a weary mind and sweet denial of sleep. This time when he hears horns, they are the trumpet sounds of a Rod McGaha song titled, "I know The Lord Will Make A Way."

"I don't want to believe that Khole Cashe vision, or the dream I just had, if I do that means I'm in for another visitor." Noelle says shaking his head as he listens to inspirationally gentle music, but he can feel it in the air.

# Chapter 14

## *KING DASHIKI CHIC*

### Joseph

When they had heard the king, they departed; and, lo, the star, which they saw in the east, went before them, till it came and stood over where the young child was. 10 When they saw the star, they rejoiced with exceeding great joy. 11 And when they were come into the house, they saw the young child with Mary his mother, and worshipped him: and when they had opened their treasures, they presented unto him gifts; gold, and frankincense, and myrrh.

— MATTHEW 2: 9

Hang All The Mistletoe, I'm going to get to know you better... this Christmas and as we trim the tree... how much fun it's going to be... together... this Christmas... fireside is blazing bright... we're caroling through the night and this Christmas will be a very special Christmas... for me...

These undeniable words can turn Black Ebenezer Scrooge into Black Santa Claus, while stirring some lips to innocent kisses and others towards romance. Noelle Jr. loves to hate this soul song. This Christmas, (Hang All The Mistletoe) is a song that knocks on a heart's door, asking men and woman to search their feelings on Christmas and love, refreshing the listener yearly with the Spirit of Christmas Present.

Noelle usually remembers nothing from his dreams but remembers the Spirit of Christmas Past and all that was done to correct his thought path. He was getting too comfortable with his choices to go against the flow, like the Nile River, in Africa does. The Nile is the longest river in the world. It goes against pragmatic logic and flows South to the North, most every other river in the world flows North to South.

Noelle wants to flow against MAGGIEDOCIOUS WORDETTE, the Spirit of Christmas past. It was all a dream, but the ghost of Khole Cashe said there would be three Spirits to visit on this night, and one Spirit was enough. Christmas means more money and nothing else to Noelle Jr.. There are no dreams of a White Christmas, just a money green X-mas, where Christ; knowingly or unknowingly, is X-ed out, but Jesus is the only reason for the Season.

Noelle moves from his bed to the living room chair, he thinks it will keep him from falling asleep. Then he hears the radio play the song titled The First Noel. Not knowing that Noel is a French translation, meaning Christmas Season, Noel, noel, noel, noel, born is the king of Israel. The reason for the Christmas Season is the birth of Jesus Christ, as it is written is the Holy Bible, a belief that's buried in the heart, by Parents or Guardians who adhere to the Proverbs 22:6 verse stating; train a child in the way they should go, that when older they will not depart from it.

Noelle has no joy for Christmas and finds it easy to X-Christ out of everything: But he only sees the X as an abbreviation, ignoring the chastisement of the still small voice from the Holy Spirit, and not even recognizing Christ being moved out of Christmas. Noelle was given the Word of God as a child, now, whenever he writes X-mas it feels wrong. Christ is planted in the heart of mankind as fruit from God, fruit being a seed-bearing product from a flowering plant. Jesus is the fruit of Love, Mercy and Grace, a gift given to the world. Mother Isabella Chance and Father Noelle Chance Sr. prayed that the heart of their son would not reject Jesus, and as a result he gets a bitter aftertaste when Christ is X-ed out of his life. Their faith is the substance of things hoped for, the evidence of things not seen.

Noelle ignores the Christmas music playing and picks up a note pad off the table next to his chair, to look at some ideas he has written down under the title, extra X-mas money. He is becoming naked in the world, similar to the story of the King who had no clothes on. A story of a man so vain, he looks at himself in a mirror and does not see that he is naked. The King only wears his Royal Robe, but his loyal subjects lie to him, telling him he looks great in fear of losing their jobs, although he looks like a naked fool. The people the King has around him will not tell him that he is indeed naked, instead they feed his vanity with mirrors and tell him only what he wants to hear. Anyone that tells him the truth is immediately dismissed. This act went on and on until one day the King and his group walked by a certain little boy, who when asked by the King to tell him how he looked, tells him he is naked. The truth makes the King free, now he knows he was a fool who could not see the truth.

Noelle Jr. cannot see his faults, looking at his reflection in a mirror emboldens his mind. He is above all things and believes he is the innocent boy in the story of the naked King, the difference being that he tells the truth about Christmas. Noelle ignores the truth and needs a spoonful of sugar to help the medicine go down. Ignorance only helps him to count down the days until Christmas ends. The innocent child that is baby Jesus exposes the truth of Noelle's nakedness, but he sees himself as covered by fate, not by faith, like the naked King believed he was covered.

The truth must re-tell Noelle the story, that faith in the Lord is his only clothing against the cold ways of the world. But not so fast, he can't stay awake, or stop the Spirit of Christmas Present. Noelle falls asleep in his chair and once again the silent night returns. He hopes to escape all concerns on the night before Christmas, and sleep. Noelle did achieve that sleep, with nothing on his mind, nothing he believes but while the clock moves towards darkest before light, the second Spirit promised to appear, visits tonight;

Boom, boom, boom is the sound made by a pounding on the door, it's the loudest sound Noelle has ever heard, and it shatters his peaceful sleep, making him sit straight up in his chair. It is dark again and he thinks that the electricity has been interrupted. "Who is knocking on my door?" Could be someone from the power company, he thinks.

Boom, boom, boom, again comes the pounding sounds on the door but without light, Noelle does not move. Boom, boom, boom again, this time fear raises the hair on the back of his neck and the body's muscle milk, called adrenaline, shoots out of his heart making every nerve come alive.

The pounding on the door stops, replaced by a gentle knock, knock. "Who's there?" says Noelle.

"King!" comes the response in a deep male voice. "King who?" says Noelle standing by his chair.

"Thy Kingdom come, thy Will be done, on Earth as it is in Heaven" says the deep male voice, that is the Spirit of Christmas Present.

"If you are here to help with the electricity, tell me how long it will take, because it's starting to get cold in here," Noelle says.

Pink neon and flashes of white lights brighten the front door. "Do you have another flashlight? It's pitch dark in here." Noelle says. Then the light shining around the door highlights the ceiling and begins to drip white light to the floor. It forms a bright dancefloor that pulsates on and off, making the room go dark three times, before the door squeaks, as it opens slow.

The door opens, then the sight of a man standing 6-foot 8 inches tall frightens Noelle. The man's skin is caramel chocolate, he has black eyes, a handsome face and a perfectly round small Afro that pops out of a red Dashiki hat, which matches his red full-length Dashiki suit and robe.

"I am King Dashiki Chic. Are you struggling to find the Spirit of Christmas? Well I have the perfect remedy for you. Just vision Christmas as a close friend, who is back in town after a year to visit you, because you are the one that understands him" he says.

The King moves to the center of the lit dancefloor, drawing Noelle to him with a long candy cane, then says, "Mr. No, it's time for you to say yes to Christmas, once again misunderstood by many people. Christmas needs a friend on whom he can depend, he believes it is you that will defend him, and lift him up again.

"Me defend Christmas?" That children's story needs to end, Noelle says. "I am too old to start believing that again," said looking up at this giant man.

King Dashiki Chic replies, "Oh, that Khole was a merry old soul and a merry old soul he was, when he told you that after midnight there would be three Spirits coming to visit you. I am the Spirit of Christmas Present, after me one more will visit you, but now we have work to do."

King Dashiki Chic pulls a doll out of a red sack that is dressed like him. It stands on a mini stage and lights up the wall. Then the King says, "Meet my non-attorney spokesman. Call him Minnie KDC. We will show you this Christmas through his eyes. What you see is a projection, not a prediction of the real things people say about you on Christmas Day. Now, on with the show!"

"No!" protests Noelle. "I don't care what people say about me, stop this silliness, I can feel anyway I want. Who are you to tell me how to feel? Go back to Toyland you giant man. Leave the figment of my imagination alone. There is nothing you can show me, let my will be done."

King Dashiki Chic replies, "You are right Mr. No, and I will make you a deal. I will leave you alone because of your free will. But if you come with me, you are sure to see today's lottery numbers, and

I give you my word, if you go with me of your free will, when you come back to this moment, you can keep everything you see from today, is that a deal?"

Noelle says, "Yes King. I take that deal of my free will. Show me what you got."

King Dashiki Chic says, "Don't feel bad by how I say what I say, I talk like a commercial in everything I say. Just like in the movies, you have Free Willy today. Minnie KDC put it on the wall. Lights, camera, action! Let's dance underwater and not get wet." Then Noelle's sister Holly and the Chance family appear on the wall, sitting at the Dining room table for Christmas dinner. Noelle can see his mother and father talking, but he cannot hear them.

Noelle says, "King I can see them, but I can't hear them."

King Dashiki Chic says, "You can see the show, but if you want to go, you got to say so, and touch my robe, then hold on tight. I will walk through the wall and take us to the site." Then the King opens his arms across the room and when he closes them, they're in Holly's Dining room.

Noelle hears his mother say to Holly, "Please call your brother and tell him we are about to eat. Tell him not to worry about being late, just get here when he can. Knowing him, he fell asleep.

Noelle Jr. does protest, saying, "I thought you said this sight is from Christmas Present but that can't be right, I had every intention of being on time tonight."

King Dashiki Chic says, "This is not a prediction, it is a projection." then he says, "Next!"

King Dashiki Chic and Noelle Jr. stand next to Kiddie land. It's the kids table and it's where Noelle's Grandniece Lisa, and Grandnephew little Barry Bridgeman Jr., are sitting, waiting for their dinner plates. Lisa leans over to whisper in her brother's ear, something that no one else can hear. She says, "Let's make Grandma and Granddad happy, and tell them we are glad because Uncle Noelle has made them sad."

Little Barry Jr. says, "Okay, but I wonder why our Uncle doesn't like Christmas. I love it! I heard Granddad say Uncle Noelle used to love it too. If he comes over, I will give him a big hug!" Then everyone's attention goes to the front door.

Lisa says to her little brother, "Uncle Jacob is here!" then all the grownups gather around Jacob and Kristen and give a big cheer! Then suddenly Noelle Jr. can't hear.

Noelle Jr. does protest saying, "I can't hear what anyone is saying now, and I can't see what the fuss is about with my Nephew and my secretary, let's go over there so I can see and hear."

King Dashiki Chic says, "This is not a prediction, it is a projection, and I don't have the power to show you the future, but Christmas Present you can see.," then he says "Next!"

The King and Noelle stand by the back door, where Holly has called her husband over to speak in private, and she says to him, "Jake, something ain't right, I haven't heard from El all day."

"King, why all the mystery? You are Christmas Present, but this feels like history." says Noelle.

King Dashiki Chic says, "Noelle Oscar Chance Jr., you are a puzzle of many pieces that must be put back together in an exact fit. I have heard the cry of your loved ones, and you're going to need a lawyer for your crimes against the Creator of Christmas. This intervention is a gift to you, presented by other people's prayers."

"Minnie KDC, show what is next for us to see!" The scene changes to the Masquerade Ball on Halloween night. The King and Noelle watch from atop the see-through section of the ballroom ceiling and see Noelle walking a woman in a purple dress to the dance floor.

Noelle says, "King, I remember that scene. It was not long ago. I guess there is something you want me to see and to hear, so let's go, I want to be done with your commercial Christmas show."

The King turns to face Noelle and his demeaner gets meaner as he says, "Mr. No, you're protected by other people's prayers, but if you dare get smart with me one more time, you will find a fall from this height will not be kind. I am not your employee that you feel you can treat bad, it is best that you learn to have some respect." What Noelle sees next, gets the response the King expects, as they hover over the ceiling of the Palisades Hotel and the Masquerade Ball.

Noelle says, "King sometimes I say the wrong thing. From up here I can see the error of my ways, please accept my apology."

King Dashiki Chic says, "Mr. No, you are a blustery show of hot air. I fear that soon as you think this dream is over, you will return to the man who does not care. But before you wake up, let me take you to someone else who's got your respect, what you hear is what you get."

The King takes Noelle inside the Ballroom to zoom in on him walking to the dancefloor with the lady in the purple dress, Noelle says, "I remember this entire weekend. "Her name was Neveah, but I thought it was my former girlfriend Millicent Manor."

King Dashiki Chic says, "Mr. No, you said yes to the dress, the Stars in the sky lined up for you, your sister encouraged you to dance, Price Waterhouse too, and the dance had sparks of romance but at the stroke of midnight you lost that chance, when Neveah disappeared just as she gave your cold heart a reason to re-start. Halloween is on the scene, and you opened your heart's door for a mystery date, the last dance was your last chance, but it was too late. This is your life, things that you have said, things people have said about you, things you've done and things you continue to do, this is not a prediction, this is a projection." Then he says, "Next!

King Dashiki Chic plays visions of Christmas Present through the eyes of the tall doll named Minnie KDC. They light up the wall to look like a movie screen that shows Noelle at the midnight reveal of the Masquerade Ball. The memory stings when dance partner Nevaeh pulls her mask off, but runs away before he could see her face.

Minnie KDC replays the sequence of this encounter with a Black Cinderella, the scent of a woman is still a thrill for Noelle, then his lust for money kills the deal. Neither lips that are sweet as honey, or love just as sweet, can lay in-between Noelle Jr. and the smell of money.

King Dashiki Chic speaks to the emptiness of this vision and says, "Noelle, the hardest person to forgive is yourself. Everyone makes mistakes, but we all must remember there is only one perfect man who walked on Earth, only He can give you true peace and make your heart love again. Millicent Eboni Manor was your first love, and you broke her heart, but Milli has gone on with her life, as you must also do. Don't turn your next love away. I know that you felt like you were dancing with your lost love, but you don't know who ran from you at midnight. The prayers for your protection, keep you safe as you sleep, Evil disappeared without your soul to keep. An Archangel protected you, but come morning and you would give no thanks.

Noelle sees the secrets he has kept in his sleep on the movie screen and begins to wonder about all the things he has seen. Now hearing the Spirit of Christmas Present in a new way he says, "King, how do you know these things?" Looking up at King Dashiki Chic, who doesn't reply.

Noelle says, "I've done good, and I've done bad, take me out of this vision before I go mad."

King Dashiki Chic says, "I pray to know what's going on in your life, I'm here for a purpose. I want you to be happy, and so do the people who love you, but you have got to realize the best part of waking up, is not Folgers's coffee in your cup. Then he says "Next!"

Minnie KDC changes the scene to the office of N. O. Chance Financial Agency on Halloween. It's a pleasant memory of Christmas in the present time, and Noelle remembers it well because he received a business proposal from Nickolas Kingsly that was very good.

King Dashiki Chic and Noelle watch the meeting taking place. They can see Nickolas is excited about his proposal, and they hear that he is anxious to get home and help the family with their plans. Nickolas is a moral compass of faith that Noelle tries to ignore, but he does not ignore his business ability, and is ready to see his proposal for a new client, North Star Village Cadillac. Noelle's smile goes away, when the on-screen scene changes to a conversation the men had just before leaving for the day, remembering his cold remarks, that won't play back well.

Noelle hears his voice in this not-too-distant memory say, "Kingsly, you Holy folks are all a big commercial. You can fool many people, but not me. You talk holy enough, but tell me why do you celebrate evil and not fight against it? Why pretend Santa Claus is real? Kingsly, don't you know that Halloween and Christmas are Pagan Holidays?"

Nickolas Kingsly calmly replies, "Mr. Chance, the last day of October is now called Halloween. During the middle years of the 700's it started as All Hallows Eve, a day of fasting and prayer in preparation for All Hallows day. All Hallows commemorates all saints known and unknown on the first day of November. In the year 837 the world recognized November first as All Saint's Day."

"Then in the mid-900's the Holy festival got mixed up with an evil festival called Samhain that begun about the same time, (pronounced Sow-in). It focuses on fire, divination and the dead."

Nickolas Kingsly continues to say, "America took on the European tradition called trick or treat in the mid-1600's, calling it Halloween. The tradition has children and adults dress in costumes going house to house in their community stating trick or treat."

"The phrase would be met by the house owners giving out candy or money, but it can also include mischievous tricks. All Saint's Day is on the calendar. Churches honor it as a day of prayer for the Saint's and Christian unity."

"All souls Day follows on November 2nd and commemorates all loved ones who have died. The Holy festival and the Evil festival get mixed up by folks that don't know, but my house knows the truth Mr. Chance."

Noelle fires back, "Kingsly, all of that doesn't change the fact that it's a Pagan Holiday, just like the Christmas tree is a symbol of evil."

Noelle turns away from the scene on the screen as it begins to show snarling men yelling." It's the face of King Herod, who has ordered all babies born during the time of a Messiah's possible birth, be killed."

Noelle turns his face away again from the next scene, he doesn't want to see the face of Pharaoh Ramses ordering the first born of the Israelites killed, prompting Passover.

King Dashiki Chic spreads his arms, and the images take up both sides of the room, making Noelle look at the faces of evil.

Nickolas says, "Pagan is defined as having other beliefs than what is taught in the Holy Bible about Abraham," said while THE KING becomes a giant Christmas tree with gold speakers at the top.

Nickolas continues louder, "Pagan rituals celebrate evil and death, but paganism was called out of the Winter Solstice celebration in the mid-800's."

"The Winter festival or the festival of lights, celebrates the coming of the Messiah, but it had become a drunken affair of immoral and evil behavior, that forced the Christians to celebrate in the safety of their homes."

"Christmas is the recognition of Jesus Christ born on earth, recognized in AD. 270. 237 years after His crucifixion and resurrection in AD 33."

King Dashiki Chic returns to form and sits in Noelle's chair, which is now fit for a King and continues to say, "Noelle, AD stand for Anno Domini, which translated from Latin means the year of our Lord. The traditional date to celebrate Christmas on December 25$^{th}$ began in the year AD 336."

"No one knows the exact birth date of Christ, but it is the religious majority's choice. January and February were added to the 10-month; March to December, Roman calendar by Julius Caesar in 46 BC, making up a twelve-month calendar."

"The twelve month 365 days in a year calendar that's currently used; called Gregorian, was developed by Pope Gregory the Eighth and switched to in the year AD 1582."

"Noelle Oscar Chance Jr., the tradition decorating evergreen trees with ornaments and beautiful lights, was brought to America around 1530 by immigrants from France and Germany. It is true that trees were used as poles to show off the deaths of those killed by Evil Kings but mixing half-truths into recorded history is a means to confuse the truth and deny Jesus Christ."

"Christian families began to bring evergreen trees into their homes to celebrate the birth of Christ. The evergreen tree represents His everlasting love around the world."

Noelle receives correction and guidance from the spirit of Christmas Present, who is not done teaching and says, "Noelle you only spout what you have heard other people shout out."

"But you do so not knowing the truth about Christmas for yourself. I lift up my cup of champagne to toast Nickolas Kingsly, who spoke well to a man who spoke badly to him."

The King drinks then says, "Champagne came from France, around AD 1536."

Noelle interrupts and says, "King, I have to research what you have said, although I have no doubt that what you say is true. You have enlightened me."

King Dashiki Chic replies, "Evil is a fact of life that hides in plain sight to confuse the masses and make everything that is good seem bad, and you still don't believe."

"What we're going to do right here is watch your crimes in Christmas Present times."

King Dashiki Chic raises his right hand and says, "Stop this midnight madness. This annual clash of the Titans; evil and good, God will forever win."

"Christ more, Christmas and the Christmas tree... next!"

The scene showing on the wall changes back to the midnight mask reveal at the Masquerade Ball but this time Noelle is an Evil King chasing Black Cinderella. She hears the first strike of the clock, turns and runs away from Prince-not-so-Charming, heading to the light of the exit door.

Noelle has to fight his way to get to her. He has to go through the fires burning from Hell night, and the glowing embers sprinkle, to imitate Stars twinkling in the celestial heavens.

The demons of Hell night hold in contempt the Light of life, that arrives with the fanfare of Mother Nature, to help those tormented by evil. Darkness has had its time. The demons did the monster mash. It was a graveyard smash, smashed at midnight by a horn blowing sweet words of redemption. For them the new day must be recognized with praise.

"Next," yells King Dashiki Chic .

King Dashiki Chic takes Noelle to the top of North Star Village Mountain. From there he can see all the people of the village and the beautiful Christmas lights.

The King points to the North Star in the sky and says, "The North Star led the three Kings to the Messiah. You may think all the stories about Christmas are to amuse the children, but you must always consider yourself a child of God."

"The Santa Claus story that you talk about, is based on the legend of a Christian Bishop named Saint Nicholas, from Myra Turkey. He gave to the poor and the needy. Legend states Saint Nicholas would drop coins down the chimney of these homes, if the back door was closed and locked. The gifts were given and received anonymously.

"Saint Nicholas died on December 6$^{th}$ in the year AD 343. It wasn't until many years later in the 1700's, that stories of the generosity of Saint Nickolas became the Santa Claus, as you thought you knew it."

"Jesus is not to be confused with Santa Claus; Bishop Saint Nickolas, was inspired by The Lord."

King Dashiki Chic says, "I got one more trip up my baggie sleeves,"

He pulls Minnie KDC out of his red bag and the tall doll flashes a scene on a nearby cloud. It's Holly talking to herself after getting no answer from the 3rd phone call she has made to Noelle.

Noelle hasn't answered or called anyone in the family on

Christmas day. She is beginning to worry, as she looks at her phone and says, "Come on El, pickup your phone."

The King says, "Next!"

The scene changes to Pastor Avery Mann at North Star Baptist Church Christmas day service, and the Choir sings,

*"... Do... you... re... mem... ber... me."*

Pastor Mann, preaching, "He will move Heaven and earth for you and me. Remember there was agreement in Heaven to herald the coming of King Jesus. A star gave the sign to the wisemen from the East.

"Remember always that the faithful sun rises from the east. Are we ready to believe by faith that our faith has been justified by Christmas?"

Noelle replies, "King Dashiki Chic, this is a neat trick. How you have us suspended in air over North Star Village?

"Is this reverse psychology temptation from the ghost of Christmas Present... If I remember my Bible right, if I give my soul to you, I will have adulation from the people.

"Dear Sir, you offer me what I already have. I feel no different this Christmas, then I have in all of my adult years," Noelle says crying, "see my tears for fears and take me back to my home."

King Dashiki Chic returns Noelle to his comfortable chair and states, "Now has come the time to say goodbye. I hope you appreciate all that you did see. A staycation of Christmas Day.

"All we did was look at Christmas present. This is your life we did see. Just one day Noelle Jr., told the story of your life. We came to show you the errors of your ways and point you in the right direction.

"Minnie KDC showed me some things good, and not so good. The rest is up to you. This is the most wonderful time of the year, and there will never be another quite like it. Your time is running out. My gift to you is the present day, and this business card.

"You're going to need the best lawyers in the world. King, King and King, Defense Lawyers."

Noelle takes the business card and states, "I already have access to the best lawyers in the land, and the card you gave has no address or contact number. How do I even call them?"

King Dashiki Chic says, "Other people's prayers have afforded you this card. Keep it close to your heart. When it's time for you to contact them, you will know how to call. The answer is in your heart.

"Although it is Christmas day you still have one more visitor on the way. Who it is I cannot say, but have you played your number today?"

Noelle replies, "You said I would get todays lottery numbers, but I didn't see today's number."

King Dashiki Chic says, "All I have shown to you was true. The scenes were not a prediction, but a projection of your present Christmas day. I have one more gift to give to you, then your visit by King Dashiki Chic will be through.

"Minnie KDC show him what he has won."

Minnie KDC puts the vision on Noelle's TV that shows the lottery number for Christmas day is twelve twenty-five, zero, one, then we see Nickolas Kingsly and family preparing for dessert. Husband and wife are in the living room, sitting in front of the Christmas tree.

Mary Kingsly says, "Nick, I love you for all the things that you do, but you have shown me new things about my prayer life by the way you pray for your boss, Noelle Chance.

"I like the gift idea you have for him. I made one just like it for my co-worker, who said she would stop by tonight. Tell me if I missed anything in the bag. I put mistletoe, a Christmas coffee cup, chocolates, candy canes, a notepad, pen set and a personal Bible verses booklet."

Minnie KDC shows Nickolas Kingsly in slow motion answering his wife, but his voice can be heard in regular speed when he says, "Mary, that's everything I have in my bag. It has been a tough year but prayer changes things.

"I will give Mr. Chance his gift when we go back to work. We will keep on praying, being anxious for nothing," said as he looks around his house full of love and good cheer. "I'm thankful for what we got, and honey Christmas is not over yet!"

King Dashiki Chic says, "Next for you is something I can't do, a look into the future to view. I can't see past Christmas present day, but every time I celebrate, it's feels brand new and maybe you will fall in love with Christmas too. It's the best thing I have ever done.

"I have got to go, and when I'm gone, you will feel a great sorrow. You don't know it now, but time waits for no one, and my time is through. Like grains of sand, that have fallen through the hourglass, I'm done with you Mr. No.

"Merry Christmas to the happy and the sad, the glad and the mad, the broken hearted and those whose hearts were made brand new because they know what Jesus came to do... next!"

"No one knows the future. Make the most of the present-day. It's a gift. Remember when trouble comes your way, call your lawyer with all of your heart. He is all that you got. All you will need. He will defend you, when you stand accused."

King Dashiki Chic seems larger when he turns for the door. His royal splendor shows even more. He appears to float but each footstep he takes shakes the entire house. As he walks into the hallway he says, "Our new reality is born. Walk by faith, not by sight. The power is within us. Break free from the chains of sins that so easily besets us. Find your supernatural power. Leave darkness in your past."

The noise stops and peace rushes into Noelle's home. It feels like heat to a body that has come inside from out of the cold. He hears the sweetest voice saying, "You leave my Lion alone."

She throws water on the wicked witch who screams, "Water, the only thing I'm powerless against."

Noelle opens his eyes to see the voice he hears is coming from his TV. It's a scene from The WIZ movie, and there's no place like home.

Noelle survives another close encounter but before he can rejoice, he says, "There will be one more visitor. Maybe I can sleep the rest of the night and that ghost will just go away."

# Chapter 15

# *THE GHOST OF CHRISTMAS FUTURE*

## Benjamin

But seek ye first the kingdom of God, and his righteousness; and all these things shall be added unto you. 34 Take therefore not thought for the morrow: for the morrow shall take thought for the things of itself. Sufficient unto the day is the evil thereof.

—MATTHEW 6: 33

A dance of spiritual awareness tickles through the nerves reminding Noelle of his human condition. He has survived the spiritual visitors of Christmas past and Christmas present and is tired and frightened. But he waits for the bad dreams about MAGGIEDOCIOUS WORDETTE King Dashiki Chic and whosoever is next to end, not convinced the experience is real.

Vanity is a gift wrapped as a Christmas present for Noelle Oscar Chance Jr., given to him by the Evil One as a practical stumbling block. This gift of vanity says I can do all things. I can break all of the rules, then be forgiven by God.

The Evil One knows you cannot but tells you that surely you can. Now that you are isolated and depend on the shadow of doubt, a stumbling block waits for the right time to trip you. Now falling, needing him most, is when your fake friend leaves you lonely; lost in your troubles, losing your mind, and going to Hell.

A mind is a terrible thing to waste.

Noelle is sure that tomorrow will come, but time presses on by the commands of the Creator of time itself and he is ignorant of the stumbling blocks placed in his path. Ignorance is not a suitable replacement, neither is religious indifference, that has Noelle rejecting the God of Love.

The father of lies can be found in principalities, powers and seen through wickedness in high places. But The Lord is our protector in daydreams or nightmares. He is our NUTCRACKER; sweet is Jesus, and our Christian soldier is always there.

"Go and search for the young child," a voice says. The unfamiliar voice doesn't wake Noelle, who is half sleep, half-awake and still trying to hide from the world in his comfortable chair.

"When you have found him bring me word again, that I may come and worship him also," the voice of an Evil King wakes Noelle, but there's no picture on the TV. Just a white screen and more noise comes from the wall behind it.

Noelle slowly sits up in his chair and hears a Christmas song in the air, "Hark the Harold angel sings, glory to the newborn King. Peace on earth and mercy mild, God and sinner reconciled..."

Noelle says, "No way! That stupid song woke me up. Oh well I might as well go to work early."

He is not in his right mind. Another voice fills the room saying, "Man go and get your life back. Find out when you began to listen to voices that only tell lies. They don't tell the truth. What time is it? Find the truth and don't you look back no more. See that you are a new man."

"That sounds like The Conductor," says Noelle.

Noelle, looking at his TV screen remembers there is one more spirit to visit him. Then the room goes black. Noelle can only hear himself breathing. Then a golden light comes out of the TV and forms a door size hourglass, that moves slowly toward him. Golden crystals begin falling to the bottom of the hourglass. Then a golden neon sign flashes a message that scrolls across the glass saying, "When all the golden sands fall, there is no more time left for you."

The hourglass stops in front of Noelle's chair and suddenly a man steps through the glass. He is lit by a stage spotlight that follows him as he walks around the room. He is a well-dressed man in a three-piece walking suit and a black walking stick. He walks in tune to the spotlight and looks like Johnnie Walker Black in a dark gold suit with black vest, when he walks to the right... and looks like Johnnie Walker Red in a black suit with red vest, when he walks to the left. There's a perfect grey beard framing his face, he covers by holding the brim of his black Fedora hat down. His skin is the color of brass.

Stunned, Noelle says, "I've seen Christmas past and present. You must be Christmas future."

THE GHOST OF CHRISTMAS FUTURE doesn't speak but points to the hourglass and pulls out his gold pocket watch on a gold chain. It has a second hand that lights up like the golden crystals, and when he pulls the watch out, it stops time. He shows the watch to Noelle, turns, and points his walking stick at the hourglass. Holding out his elbow, waits for him to join arms.

Noelle says, "Like those before you, I must walk with you to see what there is to see. Seeing the future and what is supposed to happen to me. Before you showed up, I didn't think much about the future, just how to keep making money.

"I will make the best of what is to come like I have done with time that has passed me by. Let's get it over with Sir," and they step into the hourglass.

THE GHOST OF CHRISTMAS FUTURE takes Noelle to

the office of N. O. Chance Financial Agency in a distant future. He puts his watch into his vest pocket and time begins to move as the scene comes to life with them watching from the hallway door.

"This looks like my office, but no one is here... and my name is not on the door. If this is the future, when is this?" says Noelle.

He hears footsteps in the hallway walking towards them. It's Coleman the Security guard along with Price Waterhouse and his wife Elizabeth.

Noelle states, "My goodness man. Mr. Waterhouse and his wife look great, but they have put on a few years, why are they here?"

Coleman says, "We keep the area dusted and cleaned Sir. All the furniture is covered. I will turn the lights on, and you can take a look around the office. We were beginning to wonder if anyone would do anything with the office space."

Price Waterhouse states, "Well Coleman, time moves fast. I just thought that someone would have taken the furniture by now, but there was nobody to take care of the business. What made you think to call me after all of this time?"

Coleman replies, "I saw Mr. Kingsly at his Church not long ago, and we started chatting about the good ole' days at the end of the service. I told him how glad I was to see him and how it was a shame to let good furniture go to waste. It was then that he mentioned your name and told me how to contact you."

"Well, I am glad that you did. Me and my wife will take a look around and see what we can use."

Johnny Walker Red takes the gold pocket watch out of his vest and time stops. Pointing his walking stick to the left, holds out his arm. Noelle touches him and finds himself in another room.

"Where are we now? Oh my, where could this be?" Noelle says with a worried voice.

A young man runs by Noelle, but he can't figure out who's house it is and doesn't recognize who he's looking at as he looks fondly at a picture on a corner table in the living room.

"Come on let's go Barry. Mom and Dad are waiting. What are you looking at?" says a female voice impatiently.

Noelle cannot imagine who the young man is, or whose voice it is that he hears. He looks at Barry's face, and waits for the female to enter the room.

"Lisa, I love Christmas time. I am so glad Grandma Holly loves Christmas too. We always have so much fun with her and Granddad," Barry Jr. says.

"Lisa Bridgeman," says Brother, "I think you have a new tradition to go with hanging the mistletoe every year on Christmas Eve. I see you hug that picture we have of Uncle Noelle."

Barry replies to Lisa, "I want to hug him on Christmas Eve. He seemed like he didn't like Christmas."

Noelle then says to Johnny Walker Red, "I almost don't recognize them two at all. They look like teenagers. Are they my grandnephew and grandniece?"

THE GHOST OF CHRISTMAS FUTURE just pulls down the front brim on his Fedora, as Noelle tries to look into his face.

Johnny Walker Black pulls his pocket watch out and time stops. Before Noelle can ask another question, Johnny Walker Black points his walking stick towards the right and off they go towards another vision from the future.

The destination is a confounding mystery to Noelle, who now sits in the front row isle seat at the Symphony Hall watching dancers that are in the midst of a routine to the song 'Holly Jolly Christmas.'

"What possible reason could you have to bring me here? I certainly wasn't going to make ballet a part of any of my activities. Mr. Christmas Future please show me why I am here," says Noelle.

"Hello everyone. Thank you for being such a kind audience tonight. My name is Charity Land, and it is my job to award our top patron for this year's show. Would you all give your applause to our Golden Giver, Mrs. Holly Evergreen. The audience stands to applaud and Holly hurries to the center of the stage to receive her plaque. Noelle is overcome with joy.

Holly says, "Thank you North Star Ballet for recognizing me with this year's Award. On behalf of my husband and the Chance family, I dedicate this plaque to my brother Noelle O. Chance Jr.

"He was the first to tell me about your fine dance company."

Noelle jumps out his seat shouting, "Bravo! Bravo darling a job well done," waving his arms but getting no attention he shout's, "Holly it's me! Can't you see me?" forgetting he is with THE GHOST OF CHRISTMAS FUTURE.

Holly is joined on stage by her husband Jacob, and they begin waving to a group behind Noelle. When he turns to see who is there, all he sees is Johnny Walker Black pointing his walking stick toward the hourglass, which is now half filled with gold crystals.

*My time is running out,* Noelle thinks, as Johnny Walker Black holds out his arm to touch. When he does, they move like a flag waving in the wind, into the hourglass. The trip is different this time. It is bumpy and filled with flashing gold lights showing people say 'Merry Christmas to Noelle', until they arrive in front a slot machine lounge at the Bella Bella Casino.

Noelle watches a slot machine show three rows with the same picture of gold bars, then a bell rings and quarters begin falling into the money tray.

Johnny Walker Red shows Noelle his pocket watch and time stops as they leave the hourglass. At that moment a beautiful young lady appears and begins to rake the coins out the money tray.

"I just played one time," she says, "I am thankful that I followed my intuition, but I can't play any more right now JJ. We can come-back after I pick up my award."

Her back is turned away from Noelle, but he knows the profile of the one she called JJ. That is his beloved nephew Jacob Evergreen Jr. Noelle tries again to look at the face of Johnny Walker Red, but he pulls the front brim of his Fedora hat down to cover his face.

Noelle says, "I know the Bella Bella Casino and I know that was my nephew, but who is he with? Why are we here?"

Johnny Walker Red and Noelle move through the casino like a

flag waving in the wind, then stop in the same Ballroom Noelle received the Businessman of the Year Award. It's De Ja Vu to the future view. When the waitresses enter the ballroom singing 'Christmas Wrapping' and back to the future for Noelle in this scene, which doesn't seem like a dream.

The waitresses sing their song. Noelle continues to look at the man he thinks is nephew Jacob Jr. and continues wondering who's that lady sitting with him and Nickolas Kingsly. The table centerpiece says, 'Reserved for Employees of North Star Cadillac'.

Johnny Walker Red sits at their table looking smooth and cold as ice. Noelle glances at him and says, "It's beginning to look a lot like the future doesn't include me."

A waitress serves THE GHOST OF CHRISTMAS FUTURE a drink from a golden glass that shines as the scene changes. Noelle recognizes his secretary Kristen Flowers at the podium, and she says, "Thank you for awarding me Businessperson of the Year."

"Miss Flowers is the woman I saw in the casino."

The waitress comes over to Noelle to take his order but she says, "You've been served."

Then the scene changes without warning.

Noelle finds himself in a church standing beside his nephew Jacob Jr., and Amir Landison. Jacob's Best Man is close by. They are standing in front of the middle isle and a beautiful bride appears at the other end. She is escorted by an obviously proud man. The church is full of love and happy faces that all turn towards the bride. Pastor Avery Mann's voice comes out of Noelle's mouth, saying, "Here comes the Bride."

The bride is spectacularly dressed in a cream white wedding gown by Jewell. Her beads sparkle and catch every piece of light in the room. As she moves towards the bridegroom, the gowns train is attended to by her bridesmaids, wearing cream colored chiffon gowns.

A ring bearer and two beautiful young ladies dressed in white, spread yellow and red rose petals on the white carpet, rolled out by two of the Groomsmen, dressed in navy blue tuxedos.

Jacob Jr. whispers, "I wish my Uncle was here," to Pastor Mann, who is officiating the marriage ceremony. But it's Noelle he's talking to. Noelle closes his eyes in disbelief, but when he opens them he has taken the place of his nephew.

He hears, "Do you Jacob Evergreen Jr. take this woman to be your lawfully wedded wife?" Jacob's voice comes booming out of Noelle's mouth and says, "I Do"

Noelle hears the voice of Kristen Flowers say, "I Do."

Pastor Mann says, "What God has brought together let no man put asunder. I now pronounce you man and wife. You may kiss the bride.

Noelle, still looking through the eyes of Jacob Jr. leans in for a kiss, but sees Johnny Walker Black pointing his walking stick to the right. They move like a flag waving in the wind back to the chair in the living room, where it all started.

"That wasn't so bad," says Noelle, "I learned a lot about Christmas, and I will be kinder to the people who believe that stuff."

THE GHOST OF CHRISTMAS FUTURE shakes his head no.

Noelle says, "Why are you shaking your head no? I'm back home. This thing should be over. I'm sorry I hurt some people's feelings, but what about my feelings? I don't want to go through this harassment every Christmas in the future.

THE GHOST OF CHRISTMAS FUTURE points at the hourglass, which is behind Noelle's chair, sticking halfway out of the wall. Noelle looks at it and sees the last crystals fall, then a neon message crawls across the top saying, "One more trip. Then I will be through. You will be the last chance, if you don't make it through."

"Wait," Noelle says in a panic, "are you telling me I could have no future. I don't want to see that. Please don't take me. Give me a break."

Johnny Walker Black points to the hourglass again, and the neon message says, "No way." He holds out his arm for Noelle to touch. When he does, they leave in a rush.

Noelle is covered in a full-length black wool coat; a cold wind blows across his chin and through the pours of his skin. He has no idea where he is under a tent with Johnny Walker Black. Noelle sees a crowd of people walking towards him, then notices rows of tombstones in the distance unable to focus his eyes on things that are nearby.

Looking afar, he begins to understand that a funeral burial is taking place where he stands. Noelle wants to run away but he can't move. It's then that he understands who the ghost of Christmas Future is. He is the timekeeper with a pocket watch. The Grim Reaper, a universal man of action, not talk.

Noelle never attends funerals. He did intend to be at the funeral of his friend Khole Cashe, but he ran away at the last minute and now his nerves leave him again. He recognizes some faces from afar, and as the crowd gets closer, he knows who they are and says, "That looks like some of my family members, but who are they here to see?"

Life can change fast. A fact Noelle understands at last. Everyone is seated, their faces are covered by handkerchiefs, wiping away tears, for they lost someone who is dear.

Noelle turns to Johnny Walker Black and says, "No don't let it be my mother or my father. Don't let it be my sister. Who could it be? Not Jacob, or Jacob Jr., or Jalisa. Don't let it be anyone. Oh why are we here?"

Johnny Walker Black points his walking stick at Noelle in a way that he hasn't done before, and Noelle shouts out, "It's not me. No sir, I don't want to die."

Deacon Allen Peoples, the head Deacon of North Star Baptist Church has been given the task of speaking the last words to the family. He steps to the front of the casket and seems to look at Noelle when he says, "We believe this man accepted the Lord into his heart. Let us leave this place knowing that we have done right by him. Let us touch and agree by saying amen."

Johnny Walker Black changes the scene and takes Noelle under a ceremonial tent in a cemetery, but there is only one tombstone that can be seen. It looks like a large piece of coal.

"Why are you showing me this," Noelle says. Johnny Walker Black points to the large piece of coal and taps it. When he does it reveals an inscription that shines like diamonds saying, "Here lays a man more precious than diamonds, with a heart of coal... Noelle O. Chance Jr., Mr. No."

Storm clouds form above the tent, but it's not a wind and rain event. It is an unescapable reaction to the actions Noelle has taken in his life. An infinity of circumstances lines up like dominoes. It is time for them to fall. Life's incidences, chance meetings, butterfly effect and coincidences. Johnny Walker Black, THE GHOST OF CHRISTMAS FUTURE says, "It's Noelle's last Chance."

Johnny Walker Black waves goodbye to Noelle leaving him to face this Hell. It begins with images of his life flashing across the clouds, showing past and present times. Noelle can see his lifetime zoom by, then stop when a baby is born.

"Is that me," Noelle asks.

THE GHOST OF CHRISTMAS FUTURE walks away from Noelle, fading into the foreground, leaving him alone to face the Evil One. The Evil One uses the truth of our actions to convict us, ruling over the people with half-truths and lies, in a trial for your soul.

Noelle will need the best lawyer he can get to help him win this trial. But he must stand on his own beliefs and accept the consequences of his choices.

The storm clouds swing low and roll toward the tent covering the tombstone of coal and reveal a message that shows on the clouds, "Noelle Oscar Chance Jr., you are standing on the verge of falling into damnation, or into the light of life. Which way will you fall?"

The fiery darts of truth keep landing closer and closer to Noelle, pushing him towards the hole dug for the owner of the black heart. The accuser, who cannot be seen, states Noelle, "You hate Christmas as much as I do."

Two more hateful accusations form on the storm cloud, each one followed by a fiery dart. Noelle tries to run away but fiery darts shoot out from the cloud to keep him in front of the tombstone. It is clear that one more step back and he falls into the hole.

Noelle gets scared when he looks back and sees the hole appears to be a bottomless pit. He panics when lightning reveals another message that crawls across the clouds saying, "This is a trial for your life. There is no one to defend you," as a fiery dart fly's out of the cloud and lands right in front of him in a big ball of flames. This one makes him fall into the hole, but Noelle grabs the base of the tombstone and holds on.

A voice comes through in an echo. "El, we are praying for you, but you have to pray for yourself," cries a voice that acts as an Angel. It's the voice of his mother, showing up in a time of need. Her voice of inspiration stands in the gap for Noelle's lack of faith. But it is by faith that her prayers change things, in the form of a light at the end of this tunnel.

"Mommy," Noelle cries out, "I feel like I'm on trial for my life and I'm about to fall into Hell."

Isabella Chance replies, "Your voice doesn't sound right. I am holding on to you, but soon I have to let go. Your unseen accuser is powerful. He wants you in Hell and will charge and convict you with your bad behavior.

"All of his accusations are true and only one lawyer can free you from a certain sentence of hell fire and death. He is known as wonderful counselor. He is the baby born on a holy night, and He will stand up for you against the fiery darts of Hell, and your hateful truths. Jesus Christ is the wonderful counselor. He never leaves or forsakes you. He will defend you in your time of need, even when you have turned your back on Him."

Noelle looks up and sees his mother's face looking like a beautiful star twinkling in the dark that surrounds him.

"Believe in yourself. Oh yes believe in yourself," she sings. "Believe in yourself. Oh yes believe in yourself... Believe in yourself, as I believe in you!" Her wonderful voice is a beacon of light, which appearing at the end of a dark tunnel, shows the way out.

Noelle moves forward using all of his might to pull himself out of the hole, but his hands lose their grip, and he falls backwards, looking up into the darkness of the future.

It is then that he sees an image of himself dancing with a beautiful woman in a purple dress, but her face is buried into his chest and shoulder. That image is quickly followed by Noelle looking into a mirror and seeing himself as a King sitting on his throne, but his face is contorted in evil.

"Oh God, help me! Noelle shouts out." Then he hears, "10-9-8-7-6-5-4-3-2-1."

It's someone on a microphone doing a countdown you would hear just before midnight at a New Year's Eve Party. The champagne bottles popping, sound like a 21-gun salute to the dead, accompanied by a cheering crowd shouting Happy New Year. The song Auld Lang Syne can be heard as Noelle begins to feel the heat of Hell on his back, and he braces himself to hit something and die.

"Where did I go wrong? I will find it, and fix it, if I get another chance," said with the faith of a little mustard seed.

Far away Noelle sees his dad Noelle Oscar Chance Sr. talking to someone who he cannot see. A light begins to shine, and gets brighter the closer it gets, until he clearly hears his dad say, "Please tell me you ain't too proud to praise and pray."

Noelle pleads with all his heart, soul, mind, and strength. "Jesus! Jesus! Jesus!" crying and shouting, sure that he is about to die in Hell. "Please help me!"

Noelle's lawyer, wonderful, counselor, the saving light of mercy, grace and love reaches into the darkness and pulls him from the jaws of fiery Hell. The baby born on Christmas Day pulls the world out of the same, our savior is the light of the world.

Noelle returns to his bedroom to find the TV on and the clock flashing 9:33am and for the first time in a long time says I got to go to Church.

"Let me get dressed, get out of here and get there. I will be fine, as long as I get there before the service ends."

It's a glorious sunshine that lights up Christmas morning in North Star Village. Cold but the Sun warms everything it shines on, and brightens the fresh powdery snow that fell overnight. It is a perfect snow for children of all ages and easy for the staff of North Star Baptist Church to plow away in the parking lot or sweep away from the sidewalks.

Church Service starts on time with the congregation passing the peace, followed by prayer in a moment of silence, for the arrival of Jesus Christ.

Pastor Avery Mann looks at the congregation and is pleased to see new faces in the house of The Lord along with current members. He greets all warmly, thanking the deacons, ushers, trustees and church mothers for their work in putting together a Christmas Day Service, although regular Sunday Service will take place in three days.

"I won't keep you long," Pastor Mann says, "but let us all say a prayer for those who are thinking about us right now, whether they're out of town or at home. Wherever they are, Merry Christmas."

Pastor Mann continues saying, "Deny me in front of mankind, and I will deny you in front of my Father, who is God. For God so loved the world that He gave His only begotten son, so that whosoever believes in Him, would have eternal life. Praise the Lord! Today and forever more.

"Today we announce, like the three Kings did, that the Messiah is faithfully here. The Messiah has done what the prophesy of the word of God, said he would do. The Savior has come to earth to walk in the flesh of our sins. He has come as the son of man, and the son of God. Christ has come not to condemn the world, but to save the world," pausing as the church says, "Amen."

"We who are called according to His purpose, we who believe in the Holy Trinity, Father, Son, and Holy Spirit celebrate this day as your born day. Christmas is the day Father God gave us our most precious gift, His only begotten son. We thank you Lord Jesus. Although some may want to immediately take you to the cross for crucifixion, resurrection, and your glorious ascension to Heaven, we will no longer obfuscate the word of God. Neither will we dim the light of Life. That is the celebration of your birth on earth. Merry Christmas, Alleluia!"

Pastor Mann walks across the pulpit to encourage the congregation and he continues his sermon saying, "The Lord said let us make man in our own image. Jesus, the word of God, is with His father... so He is God of all creation. Yes, He did Rise after death. He said He must do so... that we may live with Him in eternal life."

North Star Baptist Church is a house of praises going up. Amens and hallelujah's move in the sanctuary from front to back and side to side. Pastor Mann has to take a praise break.

"Amen. Amen," Pastor Mann says with excitement. "Some call Him a prophet only, but we call Him the son of God. No one can come to God but those whom God has called to Him, and all who are called must go through Jesus. There is no other way.

"Jesus is intentional and personal. He came to us under the threat of death by the evil King Herod, who tries to stop our salvation. But Jesus is the extension of an agreement made in Heaven, that whosoever believes in Him shall live and not die... but live in Heaven. He is our savior. Christmas day is the day the Lord has made. Let us rejoice and be glad in it."

Amens and Hallelujahs rain down on the sanctuary. There is joy. There is hope. There is love, and there is the Holy Spirit of God.

"With great power comes great responsibility," Pastor Mann continues to preach. "The evolution of man, who was given dominion over all things on earth, must include submission to Jesus. This knowledge leads to wisdom, leads to understanding. We must seek first the kingdom of the Lord and His righteousness, because power is a great and addictive drug.

"Love the Lord, and know He is the beginning and the end of all things. Use the power He has given you, to return back to Him in Heaven. Oh, come all ye faithful... joyful and triumphant."

He alerts the ushers and states, "The doors of the church are open. Make today your day. Won't you come. Open your treasures to Him. Oh come ye, oh come ye... to the bread of life. Will there be one?"

No one comes forth to join the church, be baptized or ask for prayer.

Pastor Mann says, "No one has come forth today. I have done what the Lord has given me to do."

He motions for the congregation to be seated. "Our choir has prepared a song especially for us titled, 'Don't Stop, Ever Loving Me.' I say to you all... rejoice in the Lord, all who are righteous. Praise is beautiful, sing to Him a new song. The word of the Lord is righteousness, and all of His works are done in truth.

"Praise God in His Sanctuary. Praise Him according to His excellent greatness. Praise Him with dance, stringed instruments, and organs. Let everything that has breath praise the Lord."

Turning to the Choir the Pastor says, "Sing choir."

The choir director begins the song and the choir starts to sway reaching towards the sky. They sing in a soulful harmony.

"Don't stop. Ever... loving... Me... Don't stop. Ever... loving... mee... Jesus..."

~

Noelle Jr. pulls his car into the church parking lot, and a parking lot Angel has a space available for him in front. Walking into church he hears the choir singing, which quickens his steps. He is greeted by the ushers who are ready to seat him, but Noelle asks, "Can I stand and wait?"

The ushers reply, "Merry Christmas Sir. You are welcomed to stand."

The music thrills his soul. It resonates with all he's gone through overnight, dealing with the ghosts of Christmas, past, present and future. Noelle feels the spiritual weight of the song and thinks of Jesus defending him against the accusations of the Evil One.

Jesus is the lawyer prayer and faith brought forth to save his soul. In that moment of realization, unmistakable joy takes over.

Noelle looks at the cross in the pulpit and knows beyond the shadow of doubt what it means. He can't hear the singing anymore but hears a Heavenly voice speak, "You turned your back on me. Come back to me. I will come back to you."

Noelle Jr., steps into the sanctuary and stands with the congregation at the first open seat. He sees everyone is thrilled, moved by the Spirit of Deacon Allen Peoples who is a soloist that sings, "Jesus, don't stop ever loving me... no, no. Don't stop." His voice is reminiscent of Al Hudson.

Noelle, now focused on the choir, steps into the center of the isle, and slowly begins to walk to the front of the church, as Deacon Peoples ends the song singing, "*Oh Lord, you are the most-high, forever more. Oh Lord, how long shall the wicked. How long shall they speak hard things. Surely, you will deliver me, with your love.*"

North Star Baptist Church erupts into a sea of applause that tingles the spine. Through the expression of praise Deacon Peoples recognizes Noelle Jr., who has made it to the front of the church.

Deacon Peoples reaches out his right hand, then says, "Well Sir, I'm glad you are here. Merry Christmas."

Noelle shakes his hand joyfully. His family members see him and are shocked, wondering what's going on. He turns and waves to his mom and dad.

Deacon Peoples says, "Mr. Noelle Chance Jr., you have the look of someone coming forth out of the darkness and into His marvelous light."

"Deacon," Noelle says with a sincerity, "I have had quite a night. I thought I overslept and missed Christmas day. When I found out I didn't, I came running here. My family invited me. You and the Pastor invited me, but I couldn't hear you then, but now I know better. I just got here when you were singing and your song touched my heart. Then my feet moved to where I'm at now. I think I'm going to come back and join your church on Sunday."

Deacon Peoples motions to Nickolas Kingsly and Pastor Mann to join him, and says, "Mr. Chance, let today be your day. We would love to have you as a new member."

Nickolas Kingsly comes over in a joyous rush to greet his work boss. "Hello Mr. Chance," said proudly. It is great to see you this morning. Merry Christmas."

Noelle Oscar Chance Jr. smiles at Nickolas, and for the first time in the many years of knowing him as an employee says, "Merry Christmas to you Mr. Kingsly. Oh pardon me, Deacon Kingsly."

The Pastor says, "Mr. Noelle Oscar Chance Jr. the doors of the church are open. Won't you come."

Noelle Jr. continues smiling and says, "Yes, I want to join the church and I want to be baptized."

Pastor Mann makes an announcement to the church, "Amen, Lord have your way. Thank you choir, for your soul stirring song. You have truly blessed us today.

"Deacon Peoples, thank you for your awesome singing. Brother Minister you make your mother and father proud, and speaking of that, we have a man that stands before us ready to join the church. He is the son of our dear members Isabella and Noelle Chance Sr. Please welcome him as he comes forward." Again, applause rings out in the sanctuary.

Pastor Mann shakes Noelle's hand and says on the microphone, "God Bless you. We believe there is a mighty celebration going on in Heaven for you, for God is pleased to find one sheep that was lost in the world and bring him home.

"Noelle Jr., I do not have a Heaven to throw you out of, or a Hell to cast you into. This being said, let it be known by all in attendance your answers to a few short questions.

"Do you come forward today of your own free will?"

Noelle Jr. says, "Yes, I do."

Paster Mann says, "Do you accept that Jesus Christ of Nazareth is the only begotten son of God?"

"Yes, I do," says Noelle Jr.

"Do you believe that Jesus walked on earth as the perfect man without sin, and gave His life for you, dying on the cross, that His water and blood wash all your sins away?" Pastor Mann asks.

"Yes, I do," says Noelle Jr.

"Confessing His love for you, will you work as a Christian for Jesus, and feed His sheep?" asks Pastor Mann.

Noelle Jr. cheerfully responds, "Yes, I will Pastor."

"Let the Church say amen."

The church replies, "Amen."

Pastor Mann says, "Noelle Jr., this is the beginning of your walk with Christ. Salvation is yours by confessing with your mouth and believing in your heart that Jesus is the son Of God. God raised Him up from the dead, so you could be saved and have eternal life with Him.

"Welcome to North Star Baptist Church. Please give us a few words," said passing him the microphone.

Noelle Jr. turns to the congregation and is immediately struck with a double portion of blessings that takes his breath away. He looks into the eyes of his mom and dad, and about to sink into tears when he hears a joyful noise.

The voice of his sister lifts his heart when she shouts, "Hallelujah! Mr. No said yes," and the entire church laughs and smiles, giving Noelle Jr. the strength to speak.

Noelle Jr. laughs and smiles when he says, "Thank you Pastor Mann, Deacon Peoples, and my sister Holly who you just heard. I thank God that I woke up this morning in my right mind. Merry Christmas to you all and especially to my mom and dad, who I know have prayed for me to come to the Lord. Today is that day.

"I want you all to know that my family is a blessing to me, all the way down to the youngest, who are here today with my niece Jalisa and her husband. You all need to know your love, patience and prayers were needed to pull me through. I was down and didn't know it, or care to change. Seeing you all together makes today unforgettable.

"I am so proud of Deacon Nickolas Kingsly and his family. They all have worked on me for years. Some of you-well who am I kidding, all that know me are shocked that I would come forward to the Lord today or any day. But I come forward in the name of Jesus."

The Church erupts into applause and praises of the Lord. Holly shouts, "Won't He do it!"

Noelle replies, "Yes, He will Holly. He continues to say, "I have said many mean things about Christmas, all of them were lies. I don't blame any of you who may think my action is a business ploy of mine. I apologize to anyone I have hurt or offended with my actions or remarks. I had forgotten that Jesus is real, and Christmas day is the day we celebrate His birth on earth."

Noelle Jr. continues, "I literally just fell in love with Jesus after midnight. He saved my life and stood up for me upon my judgement when there was no defense for what I have said about Him, or my actions towards my neighbors.

"I am not worthy but yes Jesus loves me, and He love you too. This I know the bible told me so. I can tell you right now, the thought of losing His love scares me more than anything the Evil One can do to me.

"The Love of Jesus is more precious than anything the world could offer me. I'm blessed to be led to this church and here I am."

Noelle pauses briefly then says, "If you think you see him coming like the light on a night train, pray for that train to stop and if it does, get on board. Thank you for listening. Merry Christmas."

Pastor Mann and the entire congregation are taken aback by this testimony and before he can move on to close the service, three people present themselves to become new members.

Christmas Morning Service ended on a high note, as the choir sang Joy to World. Noelle Jr. was greeted by the family, who gather to take pictures in the sanctuary before anyone leaves.

Holly says, "El, we are going to take more pictures at our Christmas dinner. I know your nephew will be disappointed that he wasn't here."

Noelle replies with a sly smile, "I look forward to seeing him and Kristen at dinner. I know they have an important announcement to make."

"How do you know that?" Holly and Jacob Sr., sing in unison.

"Hey!" Noelle says laughing, "you should form a duet... like Marilyn McCoo and Billy Davis Jr.. I'll let you know at dinner, which of their songs I'm talking about."

Nickolas Kingsly stops by the Chance family group with his wife, greeting all and congratulating Noelle Jr.

"Mr. Chance that was a great testimony. I know your family is proud of you. This is my first time in the company of you and your parents. I have to learn how to address your dad."

"Deacon Kingsly," Noelle Sr. says. Family calls me Big Daddy. I'd be pleased if you call me that."

"Consider it done Big Daddy," says Nickolas who continues, "Mr. Chance, thank you for your kind words to my family. My wife and I appreciate that you would take the time to encourage our children. I do have some official business to take care of though. Pastor Mann asked me to take you to Deacon Peoples, who is waiting for you at the front of the Church. They want to take a few minutes to meet with you in the Pastor's office."

"Thank you, Mr. Kingsly," Noelle replies. "I will be glad to meet with them. Just give me a few more minutes with my family and I will be right with you."

Noelle takes a few more pictures and tells mom, Daddy Chance, Holly, Jacob Sr., Jalisa, Barry Sr., Lisa, and Barry Jr., he will see them at the family dinner.

Noelle Chance Jr. is happy to walk with Nickolas, Mary, Marion, Simon, and Christopher to meet Deacon Peoples. Once there, the family waves goodbye. Nickolas shakes Noelle's hand and says, "You've done a great thing. See you at work tomorrow."

THE EARLY START to church didn't stop Christopher Kingsly, who was first to the Christmas tree. Simon has passed the age of not being able to sleep on the night before Christmas, but little brother says he doesn't want to open gifts by himself and waits for big brother to get up. Nickolas begins cooking breakfast at 7am. Normally he would join Mary to watch everyone open gifts, then open theirs. But today there is a special Christmas Day church service.

Marion has begun sleeping as long as she can on Christmas mornings, which usually last until the smell of breakfast cooking wakes her up. Today she knows will be full of family activities.

This Christmas, Simon and Marion sense will be the last of its kind for them. Not how they feel about the celebration, just the part where everyone wakes up under the same roof. There's no time for thoughts of tomorrow. Today's trials are sufficient for the day.

First cousins Marion and Stephanie won't be staying at home to prepare the family holiday dinner, like they did for Thanksgiving. Everyone will be in that number when the saints march into North Star Baptist to celebrate the first Christmas with Nickolas Kingsly, as a Deacon of the church.

Stephanie, Matthew Jr., Matthew Sr., and Marie Davis spend their early Christmas morning in the same fashion as the Kingsly family. They plan to be at church before the Service begins at ten. Sister's Mary and Marie are happy with their plans to be together on Christmas day and make memories to cherish. But it's hard for Matthew Jr. to leave new toys and unopened gifts behind.

Marie says to her son, "Who is a year younger than Christopher Kingsly... MJ. You can open the rest of your gifts when we get back home after dinner with Aunt Mary, Uncle Nickolas, and your cousins. You know there will be some gifts for you at their house. I want you to eat some breakfast after you open three gifts, then get dressed so we will be on time for church.

It has been a few years since North Star Baptist has had a

Christmas Day service. The members are encouraged to enjoy time with their family. Any Ministry work is to be carried out by those without children at home.

Time goes by fast with children. They grow up even faster and just like everything else in life, the celebration of Christmas day will have to adapt. We all remember the wonder of Christmas and Christmas day. It cannot be duplicated. The Holy Spirit is refreshed each year of your life.

The church has commemorative Christmas tree ornaments as a gift for all who enter the sanctuary. Marion and Stephanie have volunteered to handle that duty. Simon has taken on the task to pass out the programs and assist the ushers. The pastor, deacons, ushers, choir, trustees and mothers of the church can feel there is something in the atmosphere as the pews fill up, and they were right. The opening prayer by the newest Deacon, Nickolas Kingsly was holy spirit fire.

Mary, Marie, and their husbands leave church together; followed by their children. Everywhere you look you see the people who attended saying goodbye with hugs, handshakes, wishing one another good tidings for Christmas and a Happy New Year.

Matthew follows Nickolas out of the parking lot. They are driving to the Kingsly home to finish their Christmas day celebration. Both turn on their car stereos to listen to radio station KNSV. A female announcer says, "You're just in time for a midday ride through the Christmas soul music classic by Donny Hathaway titled, This Christmas. It was released in December of 1970 and now is considered the holiday anthem for black people. Even the Black Ebenezer Scrooge.

"Hey all of you scrooges out there, enjoy this great Christmas song and as a bonus, I will play a half hour of some of the best renditions of the song by other singers. Now shake a hand, make a friend, and guess who the other artists are. Come on. Sing-along with me."

All hearts and minds in both cars take in the soul music classic. No one talks all the way to the house, taking in the wonder of what they seen and heard on Christmas day. The church was touched by the kind words from Noelle Chance Jr. Amazed that he of all people, would call out the Kingsly family as part of his inspiration to join the church and get baptized. Shock and awe, gives way to aw-shucks, as the Kingsly and Davis cars pull into the driveway. Each singing to the best rendition of the original song, which is done by "The Whispers," says the DJ.

Gift sharing takes place as soon as the families get settled in the Kingsly home. Matthew Jr. is not disappointed as the Kingsly's make sure each of their visiting relatives find a gift under the Christmas tree. Aunt Marie and Uncle Matthew have brought their gifts in a giant red sack and pass out their gifts while dinner; already prepared, is made ready to be served.

Simon and Marion team up. Simon gives a prayer of thanks and asks for a blessing on the food. Marion presents their father with a commemorative plaque, which has his name and the date of his ordination as a deacon engraved on a gold plate. A laminated replica of the prayer Nickolas wrote for the Sunday Christmas service is also included.

Nickolas says, "I'm blessed to have you all in my life." The moment truly leaves him speechless.

Simon sez, "Let's eat." Effortlessly said, relieving his dad.

Meanwhile at the home of the Chance family Christmas dinner...

Barry Jr., and Lisa are together with their parents at the home of Holly and Jacob Evergreen Sr; and their Grandparents, who are hosting the Chance family Christmas dinner. It is getting close to eating time. The family is still waiting for Noelle Jr., who said he would pick up a few things to bring to the festivities, after meeting with the church officers.

Mother Chance says to her daughter, "Holly, please call El and tell him not to rush. We will keep his dinner hot. But it's getting to time to eat."

Daddy Chance says, "That son of ours shocked the house today. He surprised me. Did he really join the church today and say I want to be baptized? I hope he didn't get home and fall asleep."

Barry Jr., says to his sister, "Lisa we're getting ready to eat. I'm glad because I'm hungry. I heard Grandma say they're going to call Uncle Noelle and tell him we're about to eat."

Lisa replies, "I have never heard Uncle El talk about church. I was surprised to see him join today. What a Christmas present to Grandma and Granddad. They were so happy.

"I'm going to give him a big hug," says Barry Jr., because last year we didn't see him on Christmas. Mommy and dad said he don't like Christmas, but that changed today."

Holly picks up her cellphone to call her brother and says to her husband, "Jake, I'm going to call El and tell him what Mom said. Would you please get everyone to the table?"

At that moment the doorbell rings. Holly goes to open the door and is pleased to see her son and Kristen Flowers at the door.

"Merry Christmas," she says. "Come in." Kristen is holding a bag full of gifts. Jacob Jr. has an open box with a cake in it, champagne and sparkling juice, greeting all in the house.

Jacob Jr., states, "Please everyone can I have your attention? I know you're ready to eat, but if you all would gather together in the living room. I have a short announcement to make."

The living room fills up. Jacob Jr., standing in front of the family with Kristen by his side says, "Merry Christmas everyone. You guys look great. I am glad that Kristen's first Christmas with us shows us to be a loving family. I only wish Uncle El was here to hear what I have to say!"

Noelle arrives at his sister's door with a bag of gift cards, an open box filled with champagne, sparkling water, and a salted caramel chocolate cake. He rings the doorbell and shouts, "Ho, Ho, Ho Merry Christmas."

Jacob Jr., says, "That sounds like Uncle El at the door. I've never heard him say Merry Christmas."

Barry Jr., runs to his grandfather Jacob Sr., and says, "granddad can I open the door?"

"Go right ahead Big Bear," says Jacob Sr., using the nickname he calls his grandson.

Barry Jr., swings open the door and says, "Hi Uncle Noelle," hugging him as soon as he walks in the door. I thought we were going to eat without you, but you like Christmas again."

"I sure do Big Bear, and I am ready to eat," says Noelle Jr.

"Uncle El... is that really you," says an exasperated Jacob Jr. Kristen is equally surprised.

Noelle Jr. says hello to his mom and dad and shakes hands with all the men. Grandniece Lisa is next to hug him, followed by his sister.

"I'm glad everyone is in the living room," said as he hugs Kristen Flowers for the first time in their relationship. Then his beloved nephew Jacob Jr.

Noelle Jr. asks his sister, "Do they know?"

She shakes her head no. Then he says, "JJ, Kristen, let me be the first to tell you that I woke up this morning a new man. I gave thanks to the Lord and went to North Star Baptist Church. Seeing mom, dad and the family together touched my heart in such a way, that I joined the church and asked to be baptized."

Jacob Jr. and Kristen light up like a Christmas tree. Jacob Jr. says, "Uncle El, that is incredible. Oh, my goodness." Looking at his mother and father he says, "Mom... prayer changes things.

Kristen Flowers, with a big smile on her face says, "Congratulations Uncle Noelle."

Noelle Jr. pulls the couple together and hugs both of their shoulders and quietly says, "You guys are good for each other. I love you both. Don't let me steal your announcement. I will support your marriage in every way I can.

JJ and Kristen gasp in amazement and before they can ask Noelle how he knows, he replies, "The lord works in mysterious ways. His wonders never cease."

Noelle smoothly switches the focus back on Jacob Jr. and Kristen, who step into the spotlight with the style and confidence of a power couple. Jacob Jr. recreates the moment he asks Kristen Flowers to be his wife, taking a knee in front of all. "Kristen, will you Marry me?"

Kristen Flowers excitedly says, "Yes," then pulls Jacob Jr. up off of his knees for a kiss and hug that lasts as they spin around the room. She shows everyone her engagement ring.

The Chance family did eat, drink and be merry on Christmas day, but time; as Noelle Jr., knows all too well, waits for no one. He wants to see Nickolas Kingsly and family before it gets too late to visit his home. Noelle feels the need to explain to the family that he is compelled to visit the Kingsly family because they have been so nice to him over the years. This would be the first time that he wished them a Merry Christmas.

All is well, as Noelle promises to come back after work on return day, known as the day after Christmas.

Away he goes looking like a Dapper Dan snowman. He's not frosty but he is chilly cool, dressed in a royal purple three-piece, three-button suit with a royal purple leather vest over a dark purple turtleneck pullover. Noelle tops his head with a black all weather crushable dress hat, and his suit with a full-length black wool topcoat. Purple and grey wool knit scarf, black leather gloves and black leather ankle boots. Over the river and through the city, to the Kingsly house he goes.

~

SUNRISE, sunset. Sunrise, sunset, quickly goes the time on Christmas day. A day that begins like it will last forever, begins to countdown to its end. What a friend we have in Christmas. All of our sins and non-belief it bears.

Nickolas Kingsly and family have enjoyed a Christmas day of gift sharing and merriment. Dinner is great, and all things work together for the good of these loving families, sharing the day together.

The grownups, older children and the young boys find themselves together doing what they do. Christopher and Matthew Jr. are in his bedroom playing video games on their mobile units.

Stephanie, Simon, and Marion talk about their lives as they clean the kitchen table and prepare it for dessert. Stephanie says, "I'm not interested in boys yet. Not seriously," said laughing.

Simon replies, "Take your time cuz. I waited until my senior year, and I just started talking to my girlfriend. My dad brought us on our first date. I took her to lunch at the mall."

"Sounds nice... Si man," Stephanie says. "I want to meet her. She must be cute if she stopped you."

Marion states, "I'm the oldest and I am still waiting. I will just keep achieving as much as I can. Any relationship for me has to be real and there is nothing real going on for me with men right now. Although I did get a nice Christmas card from a nice guy."

Simon leaves to check in on the young ones, then Marion says, "Steff, I was invited to a New Year's Eve party by a friend. He's the one who gave me a Christmas card, but he says we would just go and enjoy the celebration. I might go... I'll let him know tomorrow.

The grownups have been talking for a while, enjoying each other when Marie says, "B-law, let me ask you a question before we go. How in the world did your boss join church today? Maybe you haven't complained about him, but he was the Black Ebenezer Scrooge."

Mary answers her sister before Nickolas can say anything and says, "Marie, I got chills when that man walked up to the front of the church during that song. If I wasn't a member, I would have joined today. That was powerful, but Mr. Noelle Chance Jr. is the recipient of prayer power."

Nickolas replies, "Mr. Chance is a complex dude. He had some issues, but I could tell he was fighting something. Many times he would say things to get a reaction out of me."

Matthew Sr. jumps right in to say, "You mean he was messing with you on purpose?"

"That's a great way to put it Matt," says Nickolas, "but he was only messing with himself. I just prayed that I wouldn't respond to his wicked wit in a way to get fired. He did give me a job."

Mary says, "Nick, you are a humble and kind man. That's cool, but some of our prayer time concerning that man and your job was very intense."

"Intense sweetheart, we have had some Smokey Norful type prayer sessions to keep our minds right."

Nickolas says, "God is good all the time."

Everyone else says, "All the time. God is good."

Nickolas continues to say, "Whatever happened to Mr. Chance last night? At the very least, he had the good sense to go running to the church. I'm glad we were there for him, because we have all been where he was, and God pulled us out."

Mary says, "Well, God bless him. Like his sister said, Mr. No finally said yes, and now it's time to say yes to dessert, ya'll."

Marie says, "Yes, sister dear, but we will take ours with us, and get home so MJ can finish opening his presents. Stephanie too, even though she's right on the verge of thinking Christmas is for the younger kids."

"I can help you with that," says Mary as she gets up to go to the kitchen. "Matt, come with me, let me cut the cakes and pies for you, and give you containers to put it in," then the doorbell rings.

Mary states, "I'll get it," and walks to the door with Matt close behind. Mary looks out the window on the door and gasps. Looking at Matthew Sr. with surprise on her face says, "Matt, Mr. Chance is at the door."

Matthew Sr. replies, "That's wonderful. Open the door."

Nickolas moves towards the door and says, "Did I hear you right? Mr. Chance is at the door?"

Mary nods her head yes, then opens the door to the regal splendor that is Noelle Chance Jr., on Christmas evening.

"Good evening Mrs. Kingsly," Noelle says. "Please excuse me for stopping by unannounced, but I wanted to surprise your husband with a visit. May I come in?"

"Oh of course, Mr. Chance. Come right in." Mary says. "This is my brother-in-law, Matthew."

"How do you do Sir," Matthew states in a warm welcome.

"Merry Christmas to all," says Mr. Chance, as the living room fills quickly. Nickolas makes his way to the front door to shake hands with Noelle, who has removed his gloves and coat.

"This is quite a surprise Mr. Chance," says Nickolas. Please sit down. Tell me what brings you here."

Mary says, "Let me take your coat. I will put it on the back of your chair."

"Thank you. I won't take long. I see I'm interrupting you," says Noelle with all his charm.

Mary states, "No, your timing is uncanny. We were just getting ready for dessert... and now that you are here, you can meet my sister Marie Evergreen again. You've already met her husband."

Next in line is Stephanie, who comes over to greet Noelle after he shakes her mother's hand. Then Holly states, "I understand you have already met this young man; Matthew Jr.," who already has his coat on. Excited to get to his unopened gifts at his home.

Marie says, "It is great to see you again, Sir. I want to thank you for what you said about these Kingsly's today. It was really nice of you." Turning to her sister, she states, "Mary, we are going to take our dessert home. Let the kids open the rest of their presents and drink hot cocoa."

Marie, Matthew, and their children gather their things and desserts before saying goodbye. Nickolas sees them leaving and excuses himself from the conversation. Noelle had just begun telling him that Jacob Jr. and Kristen had just announced they will be getting married.

"Sir, please hold that thought. Let me see my family off," Nickolas gets to the door to hug his niece and nephew, give Matthew their special handshake and high five Marie—who was giving him the eye. "Call to let us know you got home safely," he says.

Nickolas returns to the living room and says to Noelle, "Mr. Chance, Kristen and Jacob Jr. are getting married. I think that is wonderful. They make a good couple."

"Well Mr. Kingsly, I wholeheartedly agree with you. They want you to know they have given me their blessing to tell you tonight. But that's not why I'm here," Noelle states emphatically.

Looking Nickolas in his eyes says, "Mr. Kingsly, something happened to me last night, and it has changed my life. I would like to tell you more sometime soon. But a long story short, God showed me that Jesus is the reason we celebrate Christmas. I am sure the Lord saved me for a reason, and I'm going to work towards that purpose, whatever it is, for the rest of my life." He stops talking suddenly, like he had done before. But at that time, he was lost in evil.

Now, as it was back then, Nickolas effortlessly picks up the conversation, saying, "Mr. Chance, the best thing about all of what you have said is you found God through Jesus Christ. I'm happy for you and I could see how happy your entire family was for you today."

Noelle's voice is sincere when he states, "Mr. Kingsly, you live up to your nickname Saint Nick. Thank you for pulling me out of my own dropped conversation. You did it so well, I almost forgot what I was trying to say. Thank God for my right mind today. If you would, Sir gather your family together and allow me to give you all some gifts."

Noelle kindly interjects, "No Sir, that won't be necessary!"

"I've come a long way, literally, figuratively, and spiritually," Noelle says with charm and grace. "You are a humble man, Nickolas Kingsly. Now be gracious in receipt of your just due."

"I stand corrected Mr. Chance," Nickolas replies, "give me a moment to gather my family."

The Kingsly family gathers together to hear what the man formerly known as Mr. No has to say. Nickolas states, "Mr. Chance, the floor is all yours."

"Merry Christmas everyone," Noelle says with cheer. "Let me get rid of any negativity that you may have about this moment on what I have to say. I don't blame you for being apprehensive. I was a cold man, and even so, you all have shown me great kindness.

"I know that you all have prayed for me. Mrs. Mary Kingsly, thank you for keeping your husband strong through the years he's been an employee of N. O. Chance Financial Agency. He has been solid and has made my company a constant success. Please accept this gift from me as a thank you," said handing Mary an envelope. The Christmas card contained a check for $500.00.

"This Christmas has shown me the errors of my ways, but one thing I did right was to hire you Mr. Kingsly. I want to begin a mentor program, and I want you to be my protégé. I will teach you like Mr. Price Waterhouse mentored me. Then we will build The Give a Chance Mentorship Program. I want you to lead this program and help others find success. We will begin tomorrow when you come in to work."

"Thank you, Mr. Chance," Mary and Nickolas say in unison as they hug in celebration.

"I'm not done," Noelle says, calling out Marion's name as he continues. "Young lady, I know you are a remarkable retail manager. I will recommend you to Mrs. Waterhouse, who has a business program for women. I am sure they will contact you right after the New Year."

Marion stands still, almost speechless. She says, "Thank you Mr. Chance. Mrs. Waterhouse has the top program for woman in North Star Village. This is great."

"I'm not done," Noelle says. "Not done by a long shot, am I Simon Kingsly. You are the smart one. You told me you're the boy who was going to make the breaks he needs to help his family. Anyone can see you are a man of character, like your father. I want you to keep your grades up and you will be the first recipient of the Avery Noelle Chance College Scholarship, which will pay your tuition to any State College or University."

Simon says, "Mr. Chance, I remember our talk in your office. College is a dream. I had no idea how I was going to make it and I was losing hope. This is a great Christmas gift," said reaching out to shake Noelle's hand. Then he says, "This is our special handshake," as he shakes hands again. This time after touching thumbs, they fist bump."

"I like that handshake, Mr. Simon Kingsly. Now we have our own. That's a first for me, but I'm not done," Noelle says.

"Christopher T.T. Kingsly," and the youngest one has a look of surprise on his face. Noelle continues, "T. T. was your family nickname. It stands for Tiny Tim. I know that you are not a little boy anymore. You got your own house key. You rode the city bus, and you got your own cell phone, but what impresses me most is your faith. I want you to promise me one thing before I give you a gift."

Christopher looks at his father, who gently nods his head yes. Christopher replies, "Yes Sir."

Noelle continues, "Don't ever give up on Christmas. Keep your excitement for as long as you can. I used to love it just like you do. I forgot how good it feels to give presents, and I forgot how good it feels when you receive a gift that lets you know someone is thinking about you. I also forgot that the reason for the season is to celebrate the birthday of Jesus Christ. Christopher, promise not to forget these things," Noelle says with a smile.

Christopher says, "I can promise you those things, Mr. Chance."

"Every child should receive a toy for Christmas," Noelle says, "so here is a $50.00 gift card good at any store you go to. I will also pay for your additional studies at the Bella Learning Center."

"Wow! that's great Mr. Chance. Thank you for not being mean no more." Everyone laughs, then Christopher shakes Noelle's hand and says, "I have a best friend handshake. We touch hands, do spirit fingers and double fist bump. Do you want to try it?"

Noelle does the best friend handshake and says, "Christopher, I will remember our handshake."

Christopher asks, "Mr. Chance, how do you know all those things about me growing up?"

"It's the spirit of Christmas. My prayers helped me to see things and hear things I was missing."

"I see," Christopher replies. "God helped your hearing and your talking, like a Christmas present."

Noelle replies, "That's the best way to put it young man. Very well said." Turning back towards the family he says, "Thank you all for being so gracious to me, but I must be going now."

Mary says, "Mr. Chance, will you stay for dessert?" said at the same time the doorbell rings. "I'll get the door," Mary says. "Nick, see if you can talk Mr. Chance into staying with us for dessert. We have apple pie, lemon pound cake and a salted caramel chocolate cake."

Nickolas, looking at Christopher and smiling, says, "Mr. Chance, would you spend a little more time with us?" then Christopher gently touches Noelle's hand.

"How can I resist?" Noelle says.

Marion, Simon, and Christopher head Noelle to the dessert table, as Nickolas looks to the door.

Mary opens the door and says, "Girl... Merry Christmas. I'm so glad you could make it." Hugging her friend who is a co-worker, Mary says, "How was your day?"

"Everything went great," she replies.

Mary says, "Let me take your coat, and you make yourself comfortable. Nick... look who made their way to our house."

"Hey, Merry Christmas to you. It is so good to see you outside of work. Mary told me you wanted to stop by, and I'm so glad you did," Nickolas says in a warm greeting.

"Your timing is great. We were just about to have dessert. I will let you two catch up. Please have a seat in the living room. Mary just signaled me to wait here with you. I'm sure she is checking on my boss who came by to visit. We are trying to get him to stay for dessert. Here she comes now. She's got our kids in tow to meet you. After you guys talk, I want to introduce you to my boss."

It's a joyous parade that leaves Noelle at the dessert table, following Mother Mary marching to the living room to meet her co-worker, who is also a friend. Nickolas effortlessly transfers from one guess to another. A man and a woman that represent ships about to cross paths on a dark night, that otherwise would be unaware of each other.

This Christmas, serendipity sinks under the infinite waves of possibilities, and without divine intervention; in which God we trust, all hopes, and dreams would have no chance. But Mr. Noelle Chance Jr. slows down and listens to a still small voice that says, don't run away from your blessings, allow the Kingsly's hospitality to increase your territory.

Christmas night will reveal itself to be anointed, just as Christmas morning and daytime are. The two ships meet, their paths enlightened. Their masquerade reveals two hearts that were once in the dark, have now to find light that resides in one another. This too was seen in a vision from THE GHOST OF CHRISTMAS PRESENT.

"I know your voice," Noelle says upon being introduced to Mary's friend. "What did you say your name is?"

"My name is Nevaeh."

"That's the name of an elusive lady I danced with," says Noelle. I had on a mask, so did she. I thought it was someone from my past. Could it be that it was you?"

Neveah is wearing a royal purple pleated sweater dress, which matches what Noelle is wearing.

She looks at him and says, "I danced at the Masquerade Ball around midnight. My name is Nevaeh. Your voice is familiar, but the tone is different. Was that you I danced with?"

"For a moment, it was like we were on a cloud," Neveah says. "I remember the stars in the sky winked at us. But you, Noelle was dancing with a ghost named Millie. I was dancing with a man whose heart had grown cold. A conflicted and dark soul he had... and yes, I did run away."

Nickolas and Mary are a humble power couple, but this Christmas, they have clearly witnessed the Holy Spirit working in their family. Everyone has gotten to know each other better, and they moved as one when they saw the sparks of a new relationship start to fly in their living room.

Noelle Jr. meets Nevaeh again. The new couple didn't notice they were left alone. The Kingsly's left quietly to the dining room and set up two more places at the table. The family then talks about their day and night, sharing stories of what they loved about this Christmas day.

~

"I THINK you are a black Cinderella, and I would like to be a King. I was that conflicted dark soul you ran away from, but if you left a piece of your heart, Neveah, I did pick it up as if it were a glass slipper. The piece I found in a careless whisper, can only fit she who left it. If that was you sweet lady, then please give me another chance?" Noelle says with a romantic voice.

He continues, "I will leave the Prince of that dark heart in the past, to begin anew with you."

"You do sound different Noelle. What happened to you?" Neveah says.

Noelle, standing by the Kingsly Christmas tree, looks up, sees mistletoe hanging, then says, "I hung all the mistletoe... and I got to know God better!"

"Here's my phone number Noelle, let's talk more." Neveah says.

Noelle replies, "What are you doing New Year's Eve?"

"We apologize," Noelle and Neveah say in unison as they hurry into the dining room.

"No need for apologies. We are glad you two have found each other. It is a great Christmas present for us to see," replies Mary.

Nickolas says, "We have set places for you at the table. Please tell us which dessert you want, and yes we have ice cream."

Nickolas states, "Please join me in prayer as we ask the Lord to bless our food. Lord, we thank you for this food we are about to receive. Let it nourish our bodies in Jesus' name. Amen."

"Oh, what a night. Late December to keep in our memories. The conversations flowed around the dining room. Everyone reflected on the past, cherished today, and has high hopes for tomorrow.

It was getting to the time to say goodnight; it was like everyone looked at the clock on the wall at the same time and saw their best friend, named Christmas Day, getting ready to leave.

The day has been such a joy. No one took account of the sands of time that were running out.

New love has a bright future to look forward to. Three hours and this Christmas Day is through.

Noelle says, "I will walk Miss Neveah to her car," as they get their coats and prepare to leave. Then he states, "Nickolas Kingsly and family, although it's been said many times, many ways, Merry Christmas to you."

Neveah says, "Mary, thank you for encouraging me this Christmas. I will see you soon."

Christopher Kingsly stands in front of the door and does his best Diana Ross impression when he says, "Stop! — in the name of love. Everyone, shake a hand, shake a hand."

All form a circle.

Christopher says, "I want you to remember the feelings only Christmas can bring. We will have to wait a whole year for this great day to come back again. We're going to miss Christmas as soon as it is over, but let's take care of each other and pray every day. "

God Bless us, everyone.

The End

# Epilogue

I met Charles Dickens, A Christmas Carol, in my Grade School years and began to pay attention to Ebenezer Scrooge after I played the part of Jacob Marley in my 5th grade play. It is amazing how a year can go by and your feelings for Christmas—good or bad—have a certain place that they rest until being unlocked at an unknown time, before the greatest day of the year appears.

The gift of fatherhood is as indescribable as is the change in basic assumptions of all things created on earth lining up to praise the Lord, triggering a change in the body. The body of the human race is one with the Universe. The spirit of Christmas comes in like the wind, from where we don't know and where it goes, we cannot follow.

"This Christmas" (Hang All The Mistletoe), by the late great Donny Hathaway, written by Nadine McKinnon and Donny Hathaway, makes me feel a certain way about the whole experience. Past, present, and future Christmas is a friend to have faith in.

The son of a black man that worked hard for all he had is who I am. My Dad gave me an appreciation for work, a roof over my head, cleanliness, a kitchen table, chairs, and a heart to care about things that are important. He also showed me how to lead in all situations, when to follow and how to love a woman, as he did love my mother.

*I'm going to get to know you better*, is a way of life I witnessed through the 1960s and saw come to life between two people that I loved with all my heart, in a song during Christmas time, 1970.

This Christmas we give thanks for all that we have. Some people would say they have more, and some people would say they have less, but we will not complain or compare. Just give and receive. Give a gift from your heart or receive a gift given with the heart, is how Christmas grew in my heart. Remember the moment when the spirit of Christmas said hello to you, even when you didn't want it to. Peace on Earth and mercy mild, God and sinner reconciled.

# Afterword

Thank you for reading "Hang All the Mistletoe." It is the product of three years of work, which is hard to process for me until I see written. I had tough moments of doubt along the way, but in spite of every struggle, I loved finishing the journey.

Authoring this book was supposed to take months. But a funny thing happened to me. After creating the character of Noelle O. Chance Jr. I began to remember that first flush of the giving spirit, and how the holiday season changed the atmosphere. It was a great feeling, but it came with the stress of memories of money woes, and self-inflicted trouble I had created by spending too much money.

I began writing from my memory of the original Charles Dickens's 'A Christmas Carol' and how it made me feel. My storytelling became poignantly sharp, when I saw the time I didn't get the spirit until late one Christmas Eve. I'm thankful that the real reason for the season would always shine through. I had gotten lost in childhood memories of going to Sunday School, Nativity plays and all the wonderful gifts I have received over the years.

These memories came fresh with emotions, good and bad, I had kept locked away. The old feelings added words and chapters to this story, making me put away the calendar and go with the flow. It was then that I began to wonder if I was saying what was on my mind for the Black Ebenezer character.

I had built a city, a Church, and people around. I added a Bible verse to begin each chapter as a guide, knowing in my heart that there would be obvious connections to story points. There were some unknown tangents of places and spaces to cherish, since we all walk our own paths. The names of the 12 Tribes of Israel are there to remind us of our short comings, our greatness, and the Christmas miracle.

I thank my brother Stanley E. Dewberry Sr. for stating to me, "Plant the seed, and it is the Lord who adds a blessing of understanding."

Christmas is not about skin color, but it can become about the color of money and the games people play to get money out of your pockets. Commercialism is a commodity. Keeping up with the perception of Christmas can be seen as a material pursuit and the only way to be happy, making the buildup to the day seem like a sales event.

It is my hope that you got the magic of a shift in the atmosphere from this story. Let Hang All The Mistletoe refresh every year, as Christmas time always does. Christmas will never get old. The more love you put into the season, the more love you get out of the season. I look forward with faith that one day at Christmas, the Birthday of Jesus Christ of Nazareth, will be judged by the content of its character, not by any other means.

# Biography

## Author, John Gary Dewberry

It rhymes, it's in sync and it sits in Block.

John Gary Dewberry laid out in print set, that's what he learned about his name on paper.

The name would be first seen in a professional setting on flyers and posters as a Disc Jockey on College radio, in dance parties, fashion shows and concert promotions. He was the camp coordinator as a kid, always putting together fun activities for family and friends.

It is here where writing things out on paper developed. Drawing inside the lines at first with colors of distinction. His parents said he had the 'Rich' eyes and touch of someone else in the family, because if he touched it, not only was it expensive, but it was the best quality.

John Gary, as the South and North Carolina family called him was an inclusive leader. Skin color, girls, cool boys and the not so cool were in the hang out circuit for the 1960 baby. Then things changed after Mankind went to the Moon. The Space program put John Gary in the library, reading all he could on rockets and astronauts. But that excitement would not hide the fact that books done in black and white had no black representation, only white.

That didn't stop the interest from soaring but did make a point about inclusion in all things that are American life.

The biggest thing for John Gary was Reverend Dr. Martin Luther King Jr.

John Gary the Author was and is still fascinated with the way he formed spiritual chants to water the seeds of word craftsmanship by storytelling.

Nichelle Nichols is an influencer because the fiction storyboard of the TV show Star Trek showed her, as Lieutenant Uhura, she is the bridge over the racial gap of inclusion for Black People into the future.

White and Black school teachers in Springfield Massachusetts, home of many scholars and Authors, including Theodore Geisel; Dr. Seuss, (Theodore Geisel is the creator of the Dr. Seuss character, born in my hometown. He is known as Dr. Seuss, 1904 - 1991) would feed all curiosities and open every book, encouraging the inquiring mind to read, research and write down their thoughts.

This adventure into writing is not new. There are business proposals for production and creative entertainment projects for direction on the shelf and within file cabinet drawers. Hang All The Mistletoe is a culmination of these experiences.

www.ingramcontent.com/pod-product-compliance
Lightning Source LLC
Chambersburg PA
CBHW010535170726
48285CB00008B/2625
* 9 7 8 1 9 4 1 9 0 7 4 9 8 *